THE TUNNELS

Ian Watson

This book is a work of fiction. Names, characters, places and incidents are either products of the author's imagination or are used fictitiously. Any resemblance to actual events or locales or persons, living or dead, is entirely coincidental.

First published by Secret Name Books in 2026
Front cover painting by Billy Reeves
Cover design by Sarah Christie

ISBN 9780993014925

Printed and bound in Great Britain by Clays Ltd, Elcograf S.p.A.

For Adrienne

1

Sam Samuel didn't have a middle name. He was only Sam Samuel. Not Sam Arthur Samuel or Sam Horace Samuel or Sam Kennedy Samuel or even Sam Alonso Samuel. He was Sam, given name, and Samuel, surname, and nothing in between. Which meant that all he could be was himself, no one else. This was unfortunate.

On the night he left his house to go to the supermarket, the moon shone out of focus, distant in the early evening sky. Spots of rain dotted in the puddles on the hill down to the railway and every so often, maybe every twenty-five steps or so, Sam had to wipe the spots of rain from his glasses, to be sure of where he was going and what lay ahead.

As he walked, there was a time, from the fifth step to the twentieth step, when he enjoyed his vision being disjointed, the raindrops and the streetlights conspiring to scatter reality before him. Look at this unfinished world, implored his senses, drift on through it. Face these blurred shapes and smudged lights and press on. Nothing will go wrong.

In the first house on the left after the footbridge, a dog lay waiting. It had nothing to do, no list of chores to attend to, no foes to watch out for. Nothing but the autumn train timetable and the way the house shook intensely for just a very short time. Like someone was digging for gold and then giving up, digging for gold and then giving up. Ten minutes gap in the morning, thirty minutes in the afternoon.

The dog loved the passers-by. Oh, what fun. He couldn't see them, but he could sense them – not just their smell, or the sound of their footsteps, or their breathless energy as they clomped down the footbridge stairs, gravity steering them to the solid ground below. It was something more. A nervous thrum, a shift in the air currents. When a new victim approached unawares, nature sang.

What would a barking dog say if you could understand it? A torrent of abuse? A wrrahhh-wrrahhh-wrrahhh-wrrahhh of get-out-of-its and who-do-you-think-you-ares, a savage bombardment of insults, outrage, and a hint of aiming at the furthest brick wall, playing at full volume to the gallery? Or would you discover that what a dog barks and what a dog means are one and the same, that there is no better language for the job?

Sam considered his options as he crossed the bridge and made his way down the stairs, approaching the house. He could speed up or slow down. He could make his shadow a blur, a blink of an eye, or he could freeze it, no movement to disturb the calm. He could walk on air or walk underground, no noise, nothing to echo. He could zip or creep, like a sudden breeze or a ghost.

The dog made no noise. The house made no noise. The rain patted so softly that whatever noise it did make was lost in the general background clatter of the neighbourhood. Because a place like that was never truly silent. There was always something going on. Whether it was your business or not really your business didn't seem to make any difference. Whether you chose to hear it or not, there was always something there, like breathing in and out, a ribcage moving.

Sam got past the house, past the church, past the garden centre, past the Chinese takeaway, past all the clues that you could follow to find the treasure, if you really wanted to. Have you been paying attention? Read back over everything if you need to. Can you see where the X is? All of these places exist, I'm not making anything up. Once you find the spot, you can start digging. Down, down, down into the darkness below, you'll find everything there.

Sam reached the end of the street and turned right into the supermarket on the corner. He'd made it.

2

The lights from the passing buses shone through the rain-splattered windows of the supermarket, a gentle reminder that the world outside still existed. On the bus stop, the LED sign delivered the bad news: next bus due, second bus due, third bus twenty-nine minutes. There was nothing there and no sign of anything approaching. The system had gone wrong again.

Sam walked down the first aisle, negotiating the colours. The vivid reds and oranges of the yoghurt section, the blacks and purples and reds of the fizzy drinks shelf, the whites and greens and reds and blues of the milk cages, all offset by the not-quite-white packaging of everything, everything. It was dizzying and beguiling all at the same time – like drifting through a kaleidoscope.

At the far end of the aisle lay the bakery.

If the supermarket was a siren's call of sensation, then the bakery was the sweet temptation at its core. Shoppers were drawn by a magnetic proposition – the dream of perfect pastry. To walk into that first aisle was to surrender yourself to the inevitable. Your feet would glide over the polished floor, your mind focussed only on what lay ahead. The delights, the rewards. Who cares if you'd just had breakfast or lunch or a nibble to see you through. Your card had been marked.

The bakery was a castle, its battlements wicker baskets of cinnamon swirls and chocolate croissants. Most adventurers would end their quest here. For this was true salvation. A tenderness on the tongue, bliss melting into your mouth, and a comfort that reached deep inside. If there was a wound in your soul that you didn't know existed, then the pastry would find it and heal it. Heaven wasn't far away.

But a few hardy souls knew the truth. There was no Shangri-La. There would be no melting. These things had sat in the wicker baskets since mid-afternoon and they'd long gone stale. The real prize lay beyond. Within the castle walls.

Sam peered into the bakery. The coast was clear.

This made Sam nervous. Something wasn't quite right. Sam's experience of visiting the bakery, and his experience was extensive, was that there would be someone in a little white hat and what looked like a lab coat either manning the battlements or tinkering around in the background, usually placing a tray of wonderment on the side to cool. They were comforting figures, these angels, something you could rely on. You weren't going to walk into the abyss on your own. They were there to hold your hand.

This time, there was no one there.

The world, usually so constant, flickered for a second, like vintage film suddenly stuck in the projector. Here was a frame, overexposed. Here was a frame, unexpected, unbidden. Sam's head flickered too, although no one could see it. He blinked, taking his time, pressing reset on what was before him. All you needed to do with perception was try and try again, that much was obvious.

Still no one.

But there was evidence, an aroma, an atmosphere. It wasn't just a nice smell and a biological reaction, the essence of sweetness heading straight for the saliva glands. There was a sense of being at home. Even though Sam had walked out of his house to come here – an impersonal, corporate shell packed with branding and barcodes – what he wanted most was something that reminded him of home. Or at least something that reminded him of the idea of home.

What was he to do?

He could smell it, but he couldn't see it.

He was close enough to touch it, but he wasn't allowed to cross the line.

Then he noticed the coat.

Lying on a worktop, just visible through the slats of the battlements, was a white baker's coat. You could put this on to conjure up the crown jewels of pastry, to finally find the cure for everything that was wrong with everything. It was armour. It was a gateway. And as long as you had this draped over your shoulders, it was like you were invisible. You could make all the missteps and all the mistakes and no one would ever notice.

Sam did a quick check of his immediate surroundings. No staff anywhere. At the far end of the store, the beep beep beep of the self-service checkouts, the colours flashing under the bright lights of the scanner. But no one of authority down this end. Just the bakery and a closed door.

Sam's mind grew hazy, as it usually did in this kind of situation. The distractions of the real world melted away and he was left with a perfect sense of clarity.

And he was inside.

He froze, trying to assess the damage. He waited, suddenly paused, senses heightened, ready for calamity. Any minute now there would be an outcry. Sirens wailing, people shouting, the sound of shutters slamming down. But everything carried on as usual. People walked around the supermarket, picking things off the shelves, depositing them in their baskets, bickering and laughing and changing their minds and just getting on with it all, and no one made any comment. Maybe they thought it was best if nothing was said. If you don't acknowledge something, then it can't be something. And if it isn't anything, then there's nothing to be seen.

How long did he have?

He couldn't know for sure, it was impossible, there was no way on earth of knowing, no way at all, apart from the digital clock on the wall above the oven, counting down.

Five minutes, fifty-five seconds.

Five minutes, fifty-four seconds.

Five minutes, fifty-three seconds.

The clock didn't give him a moment to catch his breath, to take in where he was and what was happening.

It had a job to do and it was going to get on with it, in big, bold red numbers.

Five minutes, fifty-two.

Five minutes, fifty-one.

Five minutes, fifty.

Sam walked calmly over to the white coat and slipped it on. Now he was a superhero, part of the machinery. Once the coat landed on his shoulders, he felt like he could do anything, like he could alter space. He glanced at the clock and felt time slow.

Five minutes, forty-six.

Five minutes, forty-six.

He moved his hand through the air and felt the air move through his hand at the same time.

He had forever.

3

Just as he'd hoped, a tray sat on the worktop, laden with treasure. Freshly baked, glistening with promise. Crumbly, flaky, charged with enough sugar to send tidal waves racing through the blood.

Sam reached his hand towards the tray and was just about to make contact when he heard what might have been a cough. This wasn't a regular cough – a cough to clear the throat or to draw attention or to make a point or to do all three in a grand flourish. It was a cough that sounded like a typewriter reaching the right-hand side of a page, a noise that suggested – ding! – that that bit was finished and – hough! – this bit was ready now.

Standing by the oven was a man in a sharply cut white suit and white trilby, like a professional dandy who couldn't bear to put on anything as distressingly nondescript as a baker's coat. He sported a white cravat and a silk white handkerchief poked out of his top pocket, a pointless detail that he'd clearly spent hours perfecting with a set square and micrometer. He had a circular compact mirror in his hand and was checking his own reflection with pursed lips.

"Finally," he said, still gazing into the mirror. "What time do you call this?"

He took out a cosmetic brush and applied some foundation to his cheeks, frowning slightly. Traces of electric purple light ran along the straight lines of his outfit, outlining the hat and the cravat and the handkerchief and the hemlines of his jacket. He looked like an unholy collaboration between haute couture and the national grid.

Sam went to ask the man a question, only for him to raise his hand quickly, palm outwards. The man didn't make a sound, but as he moved his hand, a stream of ancient runes followed in its wake, glowing in the air for a moment before fizzing away. If Sam had been able to read the archaic language that had been conjured before him, he would have instantly frozen. But it was all lights and dust, lost in the moment.

The man frowned once more.

"Well? It's twenty past and you were told to get here for ten minutes to. That's you docked half an hour straight away."

Sam blinked, not quite sure if he could trust what he'd just heard.

"Now, before you attempt any sort of explanation, can I just tell you that, as much as I enjoy unlikely stories and unfathomable excuses, and have been known to be an enthusiastic participant in both from time to time, today is not the day. We really can't keep everyone waiting for any longer."

Sam's face must have communicated his confusion, the lines in his forehead rippling with disbelief.

The man sighed, as if he didn't expect this all to take so long.

"Where's your chit?"

Without thinking, Sam patted his pockets, nervously checking for a chit that he obviously didn't have. Nothing in the left pocket, just his wallet and a loose five pound note. Nothing in his right pocket, just his keys and some matches, left over from before.

Where was it?

Sam opened his mouth and was just about to stumble his way towards an excuse when the man spat what looked like raspberry treacle on the floor of the bakery.

"Because I'm in a good mood, I'll give you five minutes to go and bring me another. Because I'm in a good mood."

He motioned over to the corner of the room, where a ladder stretched down into a hole in the ground.

"I'll count you in," said the man.

"Five, four, three, two…"

The endless, opaque everything that flowed from corner to corner and point to point and joined up every dot in every dimension throbbed for a moment in technicolour, like the greatest dancefloor ever invented.

Then, nothing.

Sam scrambled down the ladder, not thinking what might be waiting for him.

If he'd been a broader, stockier man, the type of action hero that blusters through locked doors and barrels into unnecessary obstacles, then this could have been a difficult endeavour, as the space around the ladder was a tight squeeze at the very best. But as it was, he seemed almost tailor-made for the occasion, as if he'd sweated and trained and pounded the endless streets night after night, just to ensure that he'd be ready, ready for this moment, when he abandoned all reason and followed his instincts downwards.

There wasn't an instant where he lost his footing or stumbled over the rungs in the dim light, no flailing limbs or awkward elbows. He had his purpose now, so he knew what he was doing.

The ladder ran out before there was any hint of solid ground, so Sam completed the final stretch of his journey with the help of gravity, ending up in a tumble in the corner of a stone chamber.

The chamber had a solemn, ceremonial feel, like something you'd find at the heart of a pyramid. A row of wooden torches flickered on the walls, sending washes of orange and red light rippling across slabs of terracotta marble. A disused furnace lay open, waiting to be fed, and on the far side of the room, two groups of four people and one group of three turned from a figure standing on a small box and transferred their attention to this new, rather undignified, arrival.

A few heartbeats of silence passed and then the figure on the box tapped his clipboard with an air of self-assurance.

"Ah, welcome! You're very, very welcome. So pleased you could join us." He smiled the broad, ravenous smile of a seasoned salesman. "If you could make your way over to your group, then we will continue. Don't worry, you haven't missed too much. Once you're settled, we'll do a quick recap."

He motioned towards the group of three and visibly waited. He was poised, paused, eyebrow meticulously raised, emanating steady vibrations which clearly said: I would like to continue.

Sam made his way over to the group of three. He wondered if he ought to introduce himself and also wondered if this perhaps wasn't the right time. He had a sense that the figure on the box wouldn't take kindly to any more interruptions.

He came to a halt on the periphery of the group of three and then let the moment drift.

The right thing would happen soon enough.

4

There was something slightly irregular about the figure on the box. He was five foot eight but with the air of someone who, until very recently, had been a few inches taller. He was of a slim to medium build and wore a dark blue suit which didn't quite fit – a little too snug around the waist, an inch or so missing from the cuff – as if he'd dressed in a rush and picked out the wrong outfit. He had short dark brown hair and a neatly trimmed moustache, functional and personal, not really for show. And his eyes glowed with an eerie blue light, a few shades brighter than his suit, part neon party trick, part distant memory.

He tapped on his clipboard once again and began his recap.

"It's all very straightforward," he said, with a nod of satisfaction. "You're divided into three teams, which is this team here and this team here and this team here."

"You," he continued, gesturing to Sam, "are part of this team. I don't know if this is what you asked for, but the others are now full and this is the only team left with a vacancy, so I'm afraid you're going to have to accept it. I'm sure your teammates are as delighted as you are."

Sam didn't feel that proceedings were getting off to the best of starts, but didn't think it would be wise to glance around and see if anyone agreed with him. He suspected that everyone did agree with him, which somehow made it all worse.

"You need, in whichever order you feel suits, to find the following items: four small golden goblets decorated with an engraving of a slumbering lion; a black velvet blindfold; a hero's headdress; a music box which plays a pertinent tune (you will need to check you have the correct music box, as there are many scattered throughout the course); a handful of grave dust; a red fountain pen (I'm tempted to give you a further clue here, but my instructions expressly forbid it); two hundred pounds in polished two pound coins; a pocketful of posies; The Book Of The Dead; and an emerald key. Once you have all the items, turn to page 422 of The Book Of The Dead, where you will find a map showing you the location of The Door. You will then proceed to The Door and unlock it with the emerald key. The first team to collect all of the items and unlock The Door will be declared the winners."

The figure straightened his dark blue tie and looked even more satisfied than before. Everything had been relayed perfectly. The pieces were all in place. The scene had been set. He'd done a job to be proud of.

"If you have any questions, now is the time, although I cannot guarantee that my answers will be helpful."

There was a flurry of chatter, as the teams reacted to the figure and his instructions.

From the team huddled by the disused furnace, dressed head to toe in sky blue and all sporting red caps, the chatter had an indistinct soapy feel to it, as if the language being spoken slipped a bit too easily off the tongue. Sam had travelled here and there in his time and he recognised the sense of the language – a hint of Portuguese, a dash of Galician, an aftertaste of sea salt and winter sunshine – but he couldn't pick out any individual words. Whatever they were saying, it rushed by in a blur.

The team directly opposite said nothing. They were identical in dress – black trousers, black shoes, black roll neck jumpers, white gloves – and seemed of indeterminate gender. They stared at the figure with one collective look, each brow minutely furrowed, any shared conversation happening in a realm far beyond this one – a realm where question marks were bobbing above their heads. Black and white question marks, moving slowly but urgently.

Sam's team weren't having any of it.

"That's ridiculous!"

The words erupted from what seemed to be their team leader like steam escaping from a pressure cooker. Sam would later learn that her name was Pat and that she liked to be clear with her opinions. If her dyed red hair hadn't been cropped closely to her skull, then the individual hairs would have pinged skywards in disgust, all static electricity and indignation. Pat wore a vibrant yellow hiking jacket and carried a walking stick cum totem pole that was almost as tall as she was, and she brandished it with gusto.

"She's right!" Gerald wasn't carrying a walking stick of any description, but if he had been, he'd have joined in with comradely enthusiasm. Instead, he gripped his yellow hiking jacket – bought to match Pat's – and stuck out his lower jaw. "How in heaven's name are you supposed to know if a tune's pertinent or not? Pertinent to what exactly?"

"Perhaps it'll be obvious at the time?" said the third team member – this was Jonno – while not brandishing a stick or grasping at a bright yellow jacket, mostly because he didn't possess either. He favoured the kind of dark green coat usually found in army surplus stores, and had paired it with a light green shoulder bag, also ex-forces, big enough to carry a compass, some string, and perhaps a notebook for jotting down important information, such as train registration numbers. "Maybe it'll be all about…" – he infused his final word with a weary, withering significance – "*…context.*"

"Don't give me context!" cried Pat. "I want facts! I declare this round null and void before it's even begun. The objects are too vague and that word pertinent is too open to interpretation."

"Quite so," smirked the figure. He tapped his clipboard with contentment. "You're entirely correct – it is open to interpretation and it is all too vague, and it's deliberately so. There are trapdoors within trapdoors and you have been set up to lose. Congratulations on noticing."

"Well, we won't stand for that!" declared Pat.

The silent team started filing their way out of the room.

The chatterers intensified their chatter and then quickly followed them.

Pat, Gerald, Jonno, Sam and the figure all stood looking at each other in the suddenly uncrowded room.

The figure tilted his head and smirked once more.

"Well, that's bloody marvellous," huffed Pat, before turning to Gerald. Gerald thought about turning to Jonno but the look on Pat's face – storm clouds gathering, thunder imminent – put a spring in his step. Jonno turned to Sam and stuck out his hand.

"Welcome to the team. You have just completed your entrance exam."

He shook Sam's hand with mock ceremony.

"You failed, but we're taking you anyway."

5

No one could quite remember exactly how long the game had been going on for or which number round this was, but what they did know was that they needed to win this round or there'd be trouble.

Pat and Gerald were from the coast and Jonno was from the city. Or was it the other way around? Sam had sworn he'd been keeping up but he couldn't shake the notion of trapdoors within trapdoors from his mind. How did that work exactly? And why couldn't he keep hold of anything they were saying? Every time he thought he'd grasped onto something, a mental trapdoor of his own would open and it would tumble out of view, hurtling towards his already befuddled subconscious.

There'd been someone else before Jonno but he'd dropped out or had been disqualified or had gotten lost along the way or something, and so Jonno had been drafted in from another slightly more successful team. Jonno gave the impression that he was far too good to be on this team, thank you very much, and he was going to prove that by not really trying as hard as he might have done. If he wasn't going to be on a team of winners, then what was the point?

Pat and Gerald were annoyed with Jonno for not trying very hard and also for not being the old team member (who was never named, even when Sam asked clearly and directly), but then Pat was also annoyed with Gerald for something (which seemed to be related to the resignation/disqualification/misplacement of the old team member), and Gerald was annoyed with Pat because he didn't think it had really been his fault and he was also annoyed with the old team member for the same reason.

With team spirit already at a worrying low, they filed out of the exit into a tunnel. On first glance, it looked like an old tube train tunnel, part of an abandoned network of channels that ran beneath the city like forgotten friends – but the more Sam gazed at the space around him, the more something seemed wrong.

The perspective was too sharp and the walls carried a lingering threat, as if they could close in on you at any moment, should the notion strike. But then as the tunnel stretched off into the distance, the perspective suddenly felt too soft, the picture too indistinct, as if it thought it could get away with being partially formed now that hardly anyone was looking.

A metal pipe ran at arm's length above head height along the length of the tunnel, stretching off into the distance in both directions. There were marks in the dust and earth that covered the floor that appeared to suggest that train tracks had once lain there, but there'd been too much traffic of all sorts in the interim, and the outlines had been mostly scattered.

There were no torches, but a dim orange phosphorescent glow emanated from the brickwork, giving off just enough light for the team to make out what lay ahead. Sam thought about nipping back into the room and grabbing one of the torches from the walls, but the others were pressing forward with confidence and he really didn't want to be left behind.

"It'll either be the goblets or the pens first," Pat was saying, as they strode down the tunnel. "You always find the first item quickly, that's the way it works. Get you hooked straight away. And I can't see it being any of the fancy stuff to begin with. That's for later on."

"Sounds like there's at least one set piece," Gerald nodded in agreement. "If not more than one. The pen and the music box. The grave dust and the posies. Not to mention The Book Of The Dead."

"Always The Book Of The Dead," groaned Jonno.

"Well, it's a rollover, isn't it?" said Gerald. "None of us found it the first time or the second or the third time, so now they're just mocking us."

One of those question marks was about to form above Sam's head when a distant cheer rang through the tunnel.

Everyone stopped dead, frozen.

Pat went first. "Damnation!"

Then Gerald. "What? Already??"

Jonno managed a kind of mini shrug.

The other two teams had headed without hesitation in the other direction, as if they knew something that Pat and Gerald didn't. So it had made perfect sense to not follow them and see if they'd have better luck the other way.

Pat made one of those "tchaww" sounds that only appear at moments of utter frustration and continued the forward stride. It didn't matter if this was the wrong way – it was their wrong way, and they were sticking with it.

The others hurried after Pat with Sam hurrying after the others, but it wasn't long before they came to a sudden halt once again. There were two small open doorways opposite each other in the tunnel walls, one on the left-hand side and one on the right, and beyond them two small passages - about wide enough to take a group of explorers in single file - led off into the gloom. But what had really caught the team's attention was an aluminium box on the right-hand side of the tunnel, about the size of a coffin. It was battered and discoloured and a little misshapen and looked like it had seen active service for quite some time.

Pat stood back while Gerald leapt forward.

6

Gerald grabbed the lid of the aluminium box and yanked hard, expecting it to fly upwards dramatically, but it didn't budge. He gave it another yank, with the same result. A third yank saw him really put his all into it, calves and biceps straining and a vein in his forehead bulging to an alarming degree, but to no avail.

"Wrench!"

His hand shot backwards, outstretched in expectation. Within seconds Pat had slapped a grimy, indistinct hunk of metal into his palm, and he got straight to work, pulling and twisting like he was opening a giant tin of ravioli.

Sam was impressed. Without any fuss, the power dynamic in the team had spun on its axis. One moment Pat was the undisputed leader and Gerald the put upon right hand man; the next the roles had swapped, in line with the need and circumstance. Now Gerald was the head surgeon and Pat the expert assistant. Jonno didn't seem to have a role, or if he did – the anaesthetist perhaps? – then he was sleeping on the job, oblivious to the screams and sobs of the helpless patient.

Within moments, the box was open, its treasure exposed for all to see. There was a collective gasp, four pairs of eyes widening at once, and then a scrabble of hands as they rifled through the contents.

There was a pen! There was a goblet! There was a bunch of keys! There was a music box! There was a second music box! And a lumpy, jangly brown bag, tied with cord at the top, like an artefact from a Disney movie come to life.

"Now this is more like it," purred Pat.

She picked up the goblet first, turning it over in examination. Pat couldn't be sure of what it was made of, but it gave off an encouraging golden gleam in the phosphorescent light. On one side there was an engraving of an animal, a mighty four-legged beast, clearly jungle royalty, taking a moment's rest.

"What *is* that?" blinked Gerald, leaning forward.

"Well, it's a lion, isn't it?" said Pat. "That's what it's meant to be anyway."

"It looks a bit chunky for a lion," frowned Gerald. "Lions are powerful but, I dunno, like...sleek. This thing is powerful but solid. It doesn't look like it's going to tear you limb from limb. It looks like it's going to sit on you."

"Maybe it's a just a bad engraving?" said Sam, trying to be helpful. "Just because it doesn't look like a lion, that doesn't mean it's not a lion. Does it?" He was losing confidence with his argument as every syllable made it out into the open air.

"And what is *that*?" said Gerald.

They all leaned forward again. The lion looked like it had recently suffered a severe blow to the head and was sporting a handsome bump as a result.

Jonno let out a heavy sigh.

"It's a horn," he said, his habitual deadpan stepping up into the spotlight, ready for its time to shine.

"That's not a lion. It's a rhino."

He was right. On further inspection, the bump obviously curved, horn-like, from the creature's head, and suddenly – in the time it takes for a bubble to burst – the lion didn't look like a lion at all any more. It was definitely and incontrovertibly a rhino.

"Oh, for heaven's sake!" The axis had shifted once more. The surgeon was now off duty, the team leader was back to crack some heads.

"That's no good, is it? We're after – and I quote – 'a small golden goblet decorated with an engraving of a slumbering lion'. This is obviously a dud."

"A red herring?" asked Sam.

"Yes, you get them every so often. More so often if the games master is feeling smug."

They all thought back to the figure. That was one smug games master, no doubt about it.

"What about the rest of this stuff?" said Pat, already moving on, grabbing at the nearest item in reach.

The cartoon money bag felt promising, like it was brimming with doubloons. Pat pulled at the cord at the neck and plunged her hand into the bag, bringing out a handful of golden coins. Smart, shiny, gleaming, golden, beautiful pound coins, about twenty of them.

"Those are pound coins," observed Jonno, gloomily.

Sam groaned – the figure had specifically stated two pound coins.

The pen wrote beautifully, its green ink gleaming.

The set of keys had rusted many years before, maybe decades.

The first music box played the unmistakable melody of 'Rasputin' by Boney M, which immediately inspired an argument about whether or not the tune was pertinent.

The debate – a lively one, even by this group's standards – grappled with a clutch of weighty topics:

(a) Whether the song's depiction of the socio-economic privilege of the St Petersburg elite in the wake of the 1905 revolution was "little more than pantomime stuff and nonsense" (Pat) or "clearly intended as a deconstructionist satire of the bourgeoisie" (Jonno).

(b) If the folkloric traditions of Baba Yaga and Koshchei The Deathless were a direct influence on the song's hyper-sexualised portrayal of Rasputin and whether this could be read as a comment on the institutionalised inequality of the 1970s (mostly Jonno, with some surprising contributions from Gerald).

(c) If the use of the phrase "a shame" in the chorus was still the greatest understatement in pop.

After much passionate discourse and philosophical back and forth, it was decided that, while the tune was broadly pertinent to society as a whole, it didn't feel pertinent enough to their current predicament to be the one they were looking for. And something about the music box being part of the crate of junk didn't fill anyone with any confidence that this was actually it. But even so, they decided to keep it. Hell, they were keeping all of it. As Jonno wryly observed, even if the unthinkable happened and they were to lose the contest – a wild, crazy concept, he was the first to admit – then at least they'd be twenty quid up.

Pat stood with the second box in her hand, pausing for a moment, aware of the ceremony of the final item.

She pressed open the top, just as she'd done with the first music box.

But rather than begin playing another potentially pertinent tune, the box violently disgorged a coiled spring and a clownish nightmare of a figure, a decapitated head smeared with white and red face powder and what looked like fresh splatters of blood. And accompanying the head came a gleeful, spiteful cackle – like an evil child celebrating a perfectly executed practical joke – which echoed off into the depths of the tunnels.

"A-ha-ha-ha-ha-ha-ha-ha-ha-ha!" went the cackle, travelling into the distance. And then after a few moments, another cackle came back in return: "A-ha-ha-ha-ha-ha-ha-ha-ha-ha!"

Sam thought he heard another distant cheer, but no one remarked upon it.

7

The decision had been made for the team to split into two groups of two – Pat presiding naturally – the motion passed unanimously without consultation. Gerald always trusted Pat to lead the team to certain glory so there was no resistance from him. Jonno was convinced that they all held a one-way ticket to abject disaster so the route they took to get there wasn't worth arguing about, as far as he was concerned. And Sam, through a mixture of terror and canny survival instinct, had decided that the only way he was going to get out of this hullabaloo alive was to keep his mouth firmly shut.

Pat and Gerald took the left-hand passageway and strode off with a purpose.

"I always feel better about everything when you have a plan, Pat," Gerald's voice could be heard saying as they disappeared into the passage.

"Well, no one else was going to come up with one, were they?" the voice of Pat replied, on the edge of earshot. "Certainly not that Jonno, who has been a waste of oxygen ever since the day we were lumbered with him. And not that…that…what is his name, the new guy?"

"Jimmy?"

"No, I don't think so."

"Al?"

"No, definitely not."

"Then…ah…"

"Says it all, doesn't it? We don't even know what he's called, that's how assertive a team member he's been. We might as well call him Jonno 2, for all the good he's worth. First chance we get, we'll get rid of him."

"Really? Already?"

"Yes, nip it in the bud. We didn't do it quick enough last time."

And then they were gone.

Jonno also didn't complain about the plan because the new dynamic of just him and Sam meant that he was in charge. Finally, things as they should be.

The right-hand passageway stretched ahead in a straight line for ten minutes, one person wide. Jonno plodded onwards, Sam ambling behind him.

"Why do you bother?" Sam asked, after a while.

"Bother?" said Jonno.

"Yes. With this team. With Pat and Gerald. You obviously don't like either of them. Why bother being part of it?"

"I'm not sure I like that word bother."

"You don't?"

"No, it suggests I'm doing this half-heartedly somehow. And let me assure you that's a considerable distance from the truth."

"I don't see how."

"Look," Jonno would have turned round to face Sam at this point, but the passage was too narrow and the light too dim for them being face to face to have any real emotional impact, so he carried on walking as he spoke. "If you want to succeed at this…this…" He struggled to find the right word for a moment. "…game…then you have to put in the hours. Get to know the scenarios. Get to know your enemy. Get to know the people you're up against. Find out how they think. Familiarise yourself with their triumphs and their mistakes."

"So you're like a spy?"

"I suppose so. But not for anyone. I'm strictly a sole agent. Just here for myself."

Jonno was about to continue when the passageway widened and an open doorway could be seen at the far end. Sam drew up beside Jonno and the pair silently exchanged a nod. They could discuss the whys and wherefores at a later date.

They crept up to the opening and peered out.

There was a tunnel, much like the one they'd left behind. It stretched off to the left and right and a metal pipe accompanied it at much the same arm length's height as before. There was another open doorway opposite them, and an aluminium box beside the doorway, its lid thrown open.

Sam opened his mouth to say something, when Jonno brought a finger to his own lips, motioning silence. He held up his other hand, as if to say "wait", his eyes darting to the left. And then Sam heard it. A faint shuffling and what sounded like the rattle of a chain. And then something else. Yes, definitely something else. A shuffle, a rattle, and, there it was…the sound of someone grumbling.

Jonno and Sam slinked back into the shadow of the passageway, hoping to be hidden by the gloom.

In the tunnel, a figure slowly came into view.

It was tall, maybe eight foot tall, and wide, muscled, powerful. It looked like it would have no trouble ripping your head clean from your body, should it choose, and yet around its ankles and wrists were short lengths of chain, the ends jagged and frayed.

It grasped a cardboard rectangle, perforated with a neat line of dots in the upper third.

Its feet were bare yet leathered.

Its legs and arms and torso were black with dirt, and it carried a threadbare backpack so filthy it could have been part of its body.

Its tail hung limply behind it.

And its head was bowed, its mighty horns and solid animalistic features heavy with fatigue.

Sam couldn't believe what he was seeing.

"My god. That thing…that creature…that monster…"

"It's a minotaur," whispered Jonno. "The body of a man and the head of a bull."

"It can't be. That's impossible."

"Nothing's impossible down here, chum."

The minotaur shuffled towards them, grumbling as it went. If it had heard them, then it didn't seem to care one jot that they were there, but this wasn't an entity that was looking outwards. It was gazing inwards, battered by routine.

"Oh Hecate, oh Cratos, oh spirits of the underworld. Give me the strength I need to go on."

It shuffled onwards, staring blankly ahead.

"You have to get up in the morning, early in the morning, just in case, but there's no promise of anything, is there? Do we need you today? We don't know. Is your day going to be worthwhile today? We don't know. Are you going to earn anything today? We don't know. But do you have to be there when we tell you that there's nothing for you? Oh yes you do. And the heavens help you if you're not there. For your punishment will be long and hard and unmerciful."

The minotaur glanced at the cardboard rectangle in its hand.

"And if there is any work for you, is it really worth doing?" it continued, exasperation seeping slowly from its pores. "Does it give you any satisfaction? Any joy? Pick this up, take it here, put it down, don't stop, pick it up, pick it up, quicker now, take it here, put it down, don't stop, quicker, quicker, pick it up, put it down, why have you put it down, don't put it down, pick it up, quicker, quicker, oh Theseus come for me."

It reached the aluminium box and then bent down to rummage inside. It was slow and uncaring at first, as if it was operating on autopilot, but then it got quicker and more frantic, its pace picking up as panic took hold. It sifted and sorted and stuck its head as far into the box as its horns would allow, but all to no avail, and then it leapt back and thrust its arms to the sky in torment, howling in anguish.

"No! No no no no no!"

Sam moved cautiously backwards. He didn't like the way this was going. Here was a powerful, formidable, mythical beast, that was perfectly capable – even at its lowest ebb – of reducing both him and Jonno to a bloody mess in a matter of seconds, and it was angry. It was very angry. And once it had exhausted yelling at the ceiling as a way of venting its anger, then it was going to look for something else to take it out on. And Sam and Jonno were in growling distance and the obvious candidates. This was not going to end well at all.

"God! Damn! It!"

The minotaur tore its backpack from its body and started rooting around.

"Of all the things to happen to me today! Why would they? What use are those keys to anyone else apart from me?"

It fished out another bunch of keys, as rusted and misshapen as the ones that currently lay in Pat's rucksack.

"Well, you're not going to defeat me that easily!" it snorted with satisfaction. "I'll get what I came here for, just you see!"

The minotaur strode over to the inside of the opposite doorway and ran its hand over an area around waist height. Or minotaur waist height, I should say. Almost chin level for Sam. A metal box corrugated with slits appeared and the minotaur inserted the cardboard rectangle into it head first. There was a clamping sound and a bell rang faintly overhead, on what must have been another floor. A pinprick of light appeared in the wall and the minotaur inserted the key into the light.

A doorway opened in the side of the passageway.

The minotaur drew itself up to its full height and stepped inside.

8

There was darkness, just darkness.

Darkness in all directions, darkness in all dimensions, darkness in all units of measurement. Darkness in miles, in years, in fathoms, in echoes, in memories, in seconds, in heartbeats. Imagine a hall of mirrors but filled with darkness, an infinite amount of reflections showing an infinite amount of darkness, stretching on and on and on and on, as far as the eye can't see.

How long had the darkness been like this? It was impossible to tell. But if anyone had been there earlier, they would have seen a flash of technicolour zip through the endless black pixels, like electricity rippling through the void towards life. But no one had been there then, so they'd missed it.

There was a clomp and a gasp of surprise.

"Pat, is that you?"

9

Jonno stood staring at the aluminium box.

They'd waited for a minute or two or ten to make sure that the minotaur was gone for good and wasn't about to dash back to collect something it had forgotten in its rage, and then crept out of the gloom of the passageway into the tunnel.

Jonno now seemed a little unnerved by what they'd just witnessed. For Sam, the whole experience of being in the tunnels was so unlikely and so unattached to reality that his brain had given up trying to question what was unfolding before him. And being around people like Jonno who, until this moment, had faced reality being diced, flipped and overturned – like a Rubik's cube being repeatedly shuffled by an impatient ghostly force – with little more than a world-weary "not again", made it all easier to accept.

But as Jonno stood staring at the aluminium box, mumbling something under his breath, Sam began to feel properly nervous.

"What is it, Jonno?"

Jonno kept staring at the box.

"What is it?" Jonno repeated, a sing-song, out-of-body, not-quite-here tone to his voice, as if he was suddenly distracted by something. "Well, it's the box, isn't it?"

"It's a box," said Sam.

"Yes, a box. But also the box."

"You mean the same box we went through before? But it can't be. That box was in the tunnel behind us. This is in the tunnel right here."

"Yes. Right here."

"There's probably boxes like this scattered all through the tunnels."

Jonno turned to face Sam.

"Take a look and see what you think."

Sam peered cautiously into the aluminium box.

It was mostly empty, although the expectation of what might have been there seemed to fill it to the brim. There wasn't a pen, a goblet, a bunch of keys, a lumpy brown bag, or a music box. Their absence floated spectrally within, sending goose bumps rippling across Sam's skin. But there was a second box, which had been opened, its demonic clown-like contents plain for all to see.

There was also a pack of sandwiches and a flask.

Sam stared at them with horror.

The minotaur had forgotten its lunch.

"We've got to get out of here! Quick!"

Sam grabbed Jonno's hand and ran forward to the passageway, letting go as soon as he got to the entrance. He ran full pelt down the narrow corridor, scraping his elbows on the walls as he went, ignoring the pain and the discomfort as fear surged through his bloodstream. He didn't worry about looking ahead, just sprinted blindly forwards, running, running, running, doing everything he could to get away from what was bound to be a very angry and very hungry minotaur.

He reached the end of the passageway and emerged into another tunnel.

Jonno was standing next to the aluminium box, looking confused.

"What *are* you doing?" Jonno said.

Sam felt dazed.

He'd run forwards and ended back where he'd begun. Either someone had drastically shrunk the Earth to a radius of about 100 metres or something truly extraordinary was happening. Something several leagues stranger than the odd stuff he'd already accepted.

"I ran through the passageway and ended up back here."

"Yes, I know."

"It's the same box as before."

"I told you that."

"This shouldn't be happening."

"Yes. That's what worries me." Jonno frowned. "But that still doesn't answer my question – why were you running?"

The blood drained from Sam's face.

"Look in the box."

Jonno was familiar with the box by now. He'd had some time to spend with it while Sam was sprinting through the passageway. It still made him feel nervous, but he wasn't scared of it any more.

"It's the same box we looked in before. I know it's impossible but it's true," said Jonno. "Look, here's the jack-in-the-box from hell, and here's my lunch."

Sam stared at the sandwiches, stunned.

"That's your lunch?"

"Yes, mozzarella and tomato sandwiches with a dash of basil pesto," said Jonno with relish. "I always stash my supplies somewhere safe at the beginning of the game. You never know what's going to happen down here. You have to prepare for the worst."

Once Sam had accepted that the minotaur wasn't about to burst back in on them at any moment, he and Jonno started to consider their options.

One, they could go back along the main tunnel towards the cheering they'd heard earlier. Perhaps they'd find an artefact too, and finally make some progress in the game?

Two, they could keep on going along the main tunnel to whatever lay ahead. If it had been the discovery of an artefact that had prompted the cheering, then it was long gone by now. They were best to press on.

Three, they could follow Pat and Gerald into the left-hand passageway. They knew it couldn't be a looping passageway like the right-hand one, because Pat and Gerald had disappeared, quite pointedly, swallowed by the gloom. The darkness looked darker in the left-hand passageway somehow. Like it had an appetite.

Four, just Sam could go into the left-hand passageway, while Jonno waited in the tunnel to see what happened. If it did turn out to be a different kind of looping passage, then it was important to have someone stationed in the tunnel to maintain observation.

Five, Sam thought there should have been another option, but Jonno said it wasn't necessary.

Jonno closed the lid of the aluminium box and reached for his sandwiches.

"See you in a bit then."

10

As Sam edged tentatively into the gloom of the left-hand passageway, he thought back to how he'd felt when he'd been running for his life, only a short time earlier.

When he was a child, he'd been chased by a wolf through an alpine forest.

No, that couldn't be right.

When he was a child, he'd been chased through a forest. That bit he knew for sure. His memory was of a wolf and of snow and red eyes in the darkness, of hot breath and ravenous panting, of growling and drooling, of his heart pounding in time with his feet, of slipping for a moment on a patch of icy ground, of scrabbling and panicking, of pulling ahead and getting away. The details were like echoes, all there at once and all around, surrounding him, surrounding him.

And yet.

Now that he stopped to consider it, he wasn't so certain.

He tried to think, tried to see through the fog of his memory.

When he was a child, he'd been chased through a forest.

Why did he think that?

As he'd been running through the passageway, the fear had felt familiar. He remembered it from that time in the forest. As he'd pushed himself forwards, elbows scraping, lungs screaming, his sight had clicked into tunnel vision, blinkers of darkness protecting him from the margins. If his elbows had passed through the walls of the passageway rather than scraping against them, he wouldn't have noticed. If ghost wolves had ran alongside him, weaving in and out of the living rock, leaping and darting, he wouldn't have seen them.

Sam walked slowly onwards.

The light began to dim, the phosphorescent glow gradually being swallowed by the shadows. At first Sam could make out the crumbling masonry of the passageway walls and the well-worn granite slabs under his feet, but before long they'd bled into the darkness, with only his memory of where they'd been guiding him onwards. The passageway had seemed straight and uniform – as it had been in the loop – so Sam followed the ghost of the passageway as it flickered in his subconscious.

In the forest, they'd made a fire in the clearing. Gathering the fallen branches of the trees - some dry and brittle, others mossy and sticky - they'd built a tiny pyre, ready to pay tribute to the gods. The early evening was surrendering to the night and the gloaming was almost upon them, but there'd still been light to see and no real need for a fire – it certainly hadn't felt cold enough for one. But it had seemed the right and necessary thing to do, and the branches had crackled and fizzed, popping sparks of fire into the air around them.

As Sam walked further into the passageway, the sparks from his memory went with him, dancing alongside him at head height, soaring and swooping around and about him. It was easier to see now, the shadows no match for the forest fireflies. Sam felt himself starting to laugh, and the sparks danced with glee. His pace quickened, his confidence rising, and the sparks were in raptures, drawing perfect arcs and parabola, tracing out mysteries and solving riddles, the solutions burning out before they could be noted down.

Sam stepped out of the passageway into a large octagonal room, dimly lit by five stained glass windows, and the sparks blinked out of existence, their purpose fulfilled.

In each of the eight walls, there was an open doorway, much like the one Sam had just stepped out of.

Eight walls, eight doorways, five stained glass windows.

The windows were a jumble of colours and imagery, as if five other stained glass windows had been smashed and then these windows assembled from the fragments. And yet there was nothing random about the way these windows were put together, nothing jarring. The symbols and depictions felt like they'd make sense all at once, if only you could see all five windows at once. But no matter how hard he tried or which perspective he stepped back to, Sam couldn't quite survey all five windows at the same time. He wasn't ready to see them all, so he couldn't see them all.

There were snatches of a cornfield scattered across the windows. Children playing. Children working, picking the corn. There was a church on fire. There were animals stampeding. There was an eagle. A group of men marching with banners held aloft. There was something in the sky. A waterfall giving away to a lagoon. People dancing. Many people dancing. A dagger dripping in blood. An old leather book thrown open. A cup of something hot.

Before each window, the shattered coloured fragments conspired to throw a circle of light on the ground, each circle a different colour before each window. Yellow, red, purple, brown, black.

A black circle of light.

Sam wished he had the fireflies to help guide the way. They would know what to do with a black circle of light. Or they would fly into it first, to see if it was going to consume them. But the fireflies had returned to the forest and Sam was left alone.

Sam had entered the room at six o'clock, he'd decided, and the stained glass windows were arranged evenly above the doorways.

Sam walked into the passageway at three o'clock and was only mildly surprised when he walked back into the room from nine o'clock. Nine o'clock going to six o'clock, he didn't see coming, but he could live it with it. The others ending up randomly amongst themselves seemed obvious. Sam didn't try walking back through six o'clock, because if that didn't lead him back to Jonno and the passageway, then he really was in trouble.

So all that was left were the windows and the circles of light.

Yellow, red, purple, brown, black.

Sam scanned his eyes over the windows, trying to piece together the fragments as he switched from window to window, turning back and forth.

And then he stepped onto the red circle of light.

11

Sam found himself in a small rectangular room which looked like it was part office, part storeroom, part kitchen. Stainless steel worktops and a vast industrial fridge fought for space with metal shelving units and an old mahogany desk that looked like it had fallen in from another room entirely. It was a complete mess, a complete and thorough mess, as if the whirlwind that had clearly ripped through the room had come back a second and third time, just to make sure it had done the job properly.

Sheets of paper were scattered everywhere, some crumpled, others stained with dark rings and splodges of brown. Plastic cutlery and wooden cutlery and paper napkins and coins and sugar sachets and paper clips and drawing pins and small tubs of milk lay around and about, on the surfaces and the floors. There were box files on the shelves that looked like they'd exploded from the pressure of the paperwork within, and others that looked like they'd imploded – that the numbers secluded inside had been so bleak they'd caused the surrounding reality to collapse and abandon all hope.

And there were cups, polystyrene cups, many with a chunk bitten out of them. All bearing the same, instantly recognisable logo.

The arrival of a Costa on the high street had caused much drama in the local area. There were some, perhaps those who'd wanted to move to the rather more buttoned-up and well-to-do area close by but had found that their budget couldn't quite stretch to it, who'd been delighted. No matter that this was a high street chain that could be found serving something in the way of a hot drink in every train station and pedestrianised precinct the land over, its opening to them signified the arrival of civilisation.

At last, at long, long last, their gamble was going to pay off, and the area would be magically transformed, terraformed in tone and class, barren rock made green and vibrant. The grubby old shops would suddenly vanish and in their place would appear gleaming visions, destinations, confirmation that all was finally well. A store selling homeware and furnishings and gifts. A boutique with things no one would ever buy or even look at, let alone afford. A bike shop that was also something other than a bike shop – it didn't matter what. A pet-grooming parlour. Please god, a pet-grooming parlour.

Was that really too much to ask?

Alas, it had not gone well for Costa on the high street.

There were others who'd said that the street had enough cafes of its own. The Italian cafes a few doors down from the RSPCA charity shop that did the cat neutering on the last Saturday of the month – the queue of owners and plastic pet boxes snaking along the pavement. The Portuguese cafes by the chemist that also sold fashion items of unknown origin. The greasy spoons that piled up the bubble so high you could use it to communicate with the stars. The one little family run place that was popular with the new crowd, which seemed fair enough actually. And the old wooden panelled cafe that dated back to the 1930s and had appeared in Hollywood blockbusters and small screen potboilers, a place where you could make history be whatever you wanted it to be.

That was enough cafes, they said. We don't need a Costa as well.

But Costa knew best, or at least thought they did. Their corporate style was to have a "Hello [insert name of local area]" message laminated onto the front door of the branch, but unfortunately they opened with the wrong area name inserted into the gap, and by the time they'd corrected the mistake, the damage had been done.

Sam glanced around the back room of the abandoned Costa, wondering what he was doing here. The branch had closed six months previously, as the foot soldiers of gentrification had resolutely failed to march into its premises and the locals had continued frequenting the existing cafes, as if the Costa didn't exist, which, after not very long at all, it didn't. But instead of being snapped up and instantly transformed into another exciting new venture, the cafe had remained shuttered and dormant, black paint on the windows, the lamination peeling from the front door.

Sam turned his attention to the mahogany desk. Amidst the industrial detritus of the cafe back room, it looked curiously out of place. Not just an item from another room, but from another distant century. It was riddled with tiny drawers adorned with tiny brass handles, so many packed so closely together it was hard not to wonder what the furniture maker had been thinking. Why so small, why so many, why and who and what for? And at the back of the desk, set as the centrepiece with the myriad of drawers forming a frame, were three arched alcoves. Too small and oddly shaped to really be of any use - too precise in their measurements to have been made as an afterthought.

Sam opened one of the drawers and found a cache of tiny golden ball bearings, like the leftover hundreds and thousands from a millionaire's birthday cake. In another, slightly larger silver ball bearings, this time the size of marbles. In other, dried rose petals, their colour almost lost to the passing of time, a grey, brittle decay creeping over what used to be red and pink and lavender.

He worked his way through the drawers, trying to think back to the list of items the teams were looking for. What could he possibly find here? A pen maybe? The goblets? Some of the coins? Oh yes, the coins! Sam scanned the rubbish-strewn floor and, yes, there they were – some coins! He scrabbled around on his hands and knees, picking up, examining and discarding in what felt like a professional blur, and after five minutes, he held in his hand one shiny two pound coin.

It was, he supposed, a start.

He went through the rest of the drawers, but there was nothing. In fact, most of them were full of dust and sand.

Sand. Why sand?

On the stainless steel worktop, there was an old metal tankard and a kettle. The sides of the tankard were mottled, the metal discoloured with age, and the glass bottom was covered in crayon and felt tip scrawlings. The tankard itself was full of straws.

A noise came from the front room. Someone was outside the cafe, struggling to open the door.

12

Next to the door between the front and back rooms, someone – a canny architect, a suspicious boss, some workshy workers – had installed a short row of glass bricks at around eye level. You wouldn't necessarily notice them in the main room of the cafe, but in the back room, you could peer through them and monitor goings on. Were there customers to be served? Workers slacking off? Bailiffs and monsters and gangsters demanding service? Hiding from the world while keeping well informed had never been easier.

Sam kept watch behind the glass bricks, as whoever was outside the cafe battled with the front door. Inserting the key into the lock had been easy, but turning the damn thing was proving to be a challenge. Much frame rattling and distant swearing led to what sounded like a blazing row, albeit a blazing row between two people who were trying to keep their voices down so they wouldn't draw attention to themselves.

Eventually, whoever was trying to turn the key gave way to whoever had been offering advice/encouragement/angry criticism, and a further bout of rattling and grunting led to the door suddenly flying open.

What could only be described as a large man squeezed himself through the doorway. He was somewhere between middle age and an age he didn't like talking about, his black hair receding with a grimace. He was wearing a tight black suit that was struggling to contain him over a tight black shirt that had long since given up.

After him, came what could only be described as an even larger man. He took some time getting through the doorway, using a method involving trigonometry, determination, and the bodily equivalent of a three-point turn. He was wearing a similarly tight black suit over a black t-shirt, a mass of gristle and bone.

"Close the door!" hissed the first of the two large men. He was the Big Heavy and he obviously thought he was in charge.

"Sure thing," replied the second but larger man, and he gently – surprisingly – clicked the door back into place and locked it, the lock offering no resistance from the inside. He was the Heavy Heavy and he knew how to get things done.

"Now, where is it?"

"Here you go."

The Heavy Heavy took a shoebox-sized package from under his coat and placed it on a nearby table.

The front room of the cafe was almost as big a mess as the back room. There were cups and napkins and tiny milk cartons everywhere, and spilt coffee on almost every surface. Most of the chairs were broken, the legs snapped off or the frame shattered, and the tables weren't much better, some lurching at a disturbing angle. The glass cabinet at the bar, which once held all manner of temptation, was smashed and empty, and the till behind the bar was open and relieved of cash, its final transaction – two pounds forty seven pence – still blinking in its display.

"If this is a repeat of last time, you are finished."

The Heavy Heavy looked offended.

"That's not fair," he protested, his expansive brow furrowing. "You knew what we were doing. You'd arranged it."

A further furrow of the brow.

"Actually hadn't it all been your idea?"

"No, no, and no. It was a terrible idea."

"No, it wasn't. It was a good idea that just didn't happen to work."

The Big Heavy stared balefully at the remains of a wooden crate in the centre of the room.

"Well, the rats have gone now. Probably down into the tunnels."

"I hope so," replied the Heavy Heavy. "They'll like it down there. That's what we want."

Sam glanced around the room, from plastic cup to paper napkin, from discoloured menu to unwashed cutlery. The chunks bitten out of the cups had looked like they'd been made by a ravenous toddler, but maybe, possibly, they were rat-sized.

"We'll have to get some more," said the Heavy Heavy.

"Only if this works."

With the Big Heavy watching intently, the Heavy Heavy opened the box and took out a small rain stick. Interwoven runes were etched along its length and they gleamed and sparkled in the dim light. The Big Heavy smiled and nodded in approval.

When Sam had first moved to this part of town, he'd gone to a party in an abandoned house up on the hill. The house had been an orphanage up until the end of the 19th century, but then it passed to private hands, only for it to fall into disrepair not long after the Second World War. It was a wild and rambling place, tall hedges keeping it hidden from the everyday world.

At the party, Sam had met a man with a rain stick. The man was very pleased with his rain stick and had insisted on introducing it to everyone present, to widespread irritation.

It was a terrible party. At least the ambulance arrived quickly.

"Where did you get this?" asked the Big Heavy, eyes shining. "From The Emporium?"

"No, not this time. I found this at the boot fair."

There was a moment's silence while the Big Heavy processed what he'd just heard.

"From the boot fair," he repeated slowly.

"Yes, that's right. It was pretty expensive, but I think you'll agree it was worth it."

Sam felt a crackle of electricity in the air, like a storm was approaching, the Big Heavy its epicentre.

Luckily for him, the Heavy Heavy felt it too.

"Not the regular boot fair at the dog track," he quickly clarified. "You won't be finding gear like this amongst the knick-knacks and the knock-offs. This was at the," he paused and glanced around for effect and then whispered pointedly: "*other* boot fair."

The Big Heavy looked at him like he was mad.

"You know, the one at the cemetery."

The local cemetery was a grand place, one of the notorious Magnificent Seven. It was a sprawling jumble of cracked gravestones and supersized mausoleums, of weeds and overgrown paths, with a spooky Greek Quarter tucked away in the upper right-hand corner. Sam had heard tell of midnight rituals in the temple in the Greek Quarter, and candlelight processions through the catacombs beneath the temple, but he'd never heard of there being a boot fair. It was a shame, as he was a fan of a bargain, and would definitely have wandered along.

The Big Heavy seemed placated by this explanation and the electricity storm subsided.

"Now, what went wrong last time is that the rats got into the tunnels, as we'd planned, but then nothing much happened after that," said the Heavy Heavy, holding the rain stick in his right hand. "We'd wanted disruption, but rats aren't really out of place underground. As I say, it was the right idea, but just done wrong."

The Heavy Heavy took a matchbox from his pocket and flicked it open with his left hand, allowing a cockroach to crawl onto the ground before him.

"We're big men, you and I," he said, looking at the Big Heavy. "Normal rats aren't going to do the job for us. We need something bigger."

At which point he shook the rain stick in the direction of the cockroach.

The runes on the side of the stick glowed, fire tracing through the curves and lines. There was a moment of tension and then a wash of bright light flooded over the cockroach, obscuring it for a second.

"Now you're talking," said the Big Heavy appreciatively.

A cockroach the size of a woodland boar stood glaring at the two men. Maybe all cockroaches glare all the time and they've simply been too small for anyone to notice, or maybe the enlarging process was the kind of thing that would leave a creature in a foul mood, nerves frayed and jangling. Whatever the reason, this was not a happy insect, and it began to advance menacingly towards the pair.

"Look at it!" said the Big Heavy with glee. "A pack of these roaming the tunnels and our troubles will be over. Excellent work!"

The antennae on the cockroach's head zapped to attention. It looked primed to attack.

"I love it!" laughed the Big Heavy. "OK, show's over," he said, glancing at the Heavy Heavy. "Shrink it back down again."

13

Sam had been thankful of his position hidden in the back room when the Big Heavy discovered that the Heavy Heavy didn't know how to shrink the cockroach.

The Big Heavy had assumed that the rain stick enlarged and shrank. That was the practical thing for it to do, after all. The Heavy Heavy, he admitted, had assumed the same. But as much as he waved the stick at the cockroach, trying in vain to make the enlarging motion in reverse, the cockroach stood firm. If anything, every time the Heavy Heavy waved the rain stick, the cockroach got bigger and bigger.

Sam felt a hand clasp slowly but firmly over his mouth.

"Don't make a sound," a voice whispered in his ear.

Sam froze, shocked.

He hadn't been planning to make a noise anyway, but he definitely wasn't going to now.

"These gentlemen are currently indisposed," continued the whisper. "But let me assure you, if they heard you, they would find you. And if they found you, they would kill you."

The Heavy Heavy kept waving the rain stick frantically at the cockroach.

"Our friend's problem," said the whisper, "is that he's bought a sonic enlarger thinking it would also be a sonic reducer. But that's the old DB02 model he has there. The combined enlarger and reducer doesn't come into play until the DB07."

Sam kept his eyes on the advancing mutant cockroach, his mind swimming with letters and numbers.

"I suppose it would be interesting to see who would come off best in a fight between a giant cockroach and two mini mountains. Entertaining even," continued the whisper. "We could take bets, if only you could talk, which you mustn't. I wonder who would come off best. I wonder which side you'd plump for?"

The Big Heavy snatched the rain stick out of the Heavy Heavy's fingers.

"But we haven't got time for that now," said the whisper. "Such a shame."

The hand moved from Sam's mouth and a figure drew alongside him. She put a tin whistle to her lips and blew a single soundless note.

The cockroach came to a sudden stop, paralysed.

The Big Heavy hadn't lasted as long as he had in the business without being able to recognise a good opportunity at a moment's notice. He spun round to the door, turned the key, opened the door and pulled the Heavy Heavy through with him, slamming the door shut and locking it in as much of a frenzy as he could muster, which was quite a lot under these particular circumstances. The door rattled in its frame for an instant and then came to a rest.

With the two men gone and the shop front now empty, the figure opened the door and walked towards the cockroach.

The first thing Sam noticed was the suit. It was the same dark blue as the figure who'd greeted the contestants back in the tunnel, but instead of being slightly ill-fitting, it was trim and tailored. The dark brown hair was short, but grown out a little, with more of a curve and a flourish, and there was no moustache.

The figure glanced at Sam, her eyes sparkling.

The figure walked over to the cockroach, took a smaller, slimmer, lighter and cheaper to produce rain stick from her pocket, and made a flicking motion towards the cockroach, which shrank back to its original size. The figure then took a transparent cube from her pocket, bent down towards the cockroach and then paused, seemingly changing her mind mid-task. Then a black leather brogue stamped down hard on the cockroach, twisting and grinding it into the ground for good measure.

"Can't be too careful with these things," the figure said, turning back to Sam. "The DB07 is a fine piece of kit, but even so, whatever's been zapped never quite gets over being enlarged to five or ten or twenty times its size. A cockroach may just be a household bug, but a delusion of grandeur is a powerful, dangerous force. You don't want too much of the stuff let loose in the atmosphere."

Sam stared at her.

"I'm Takara, in case you were wondering. And, yes, the other guy is my brother."

Sam took a moment to process what was meant by "the other guy".

"Oh," he said, finally connecting two and two. "So you're part of the game?"

"Hell no! I wouldn't waste my time getting people to scrabble around for these trinkets. I mean, a job's a job and all that, and I can't blame him, I hear the money's excellent, but really. I have far more important things to be getting on with."

Takara did a quick sweep of the shop front, just to make sure everything was as it should be, and when she'd confirmed that it was a mess and a disaster, she headed to the back room.

"These guys work for someone who isn't happy about the tunnels," she said, addressing the air in front of her and assuming that Sam was keeping up. "Apparently the tunnels interfere with their '*business plan*'. The cheek of it. So they're trying – ineptly and unsuccessfully, thank god – to mess the tunnels up. Which I really can't allow."

"The big one said something about a boot fair. Is that part of their plan?"

"What the booty? No! Never! They wish!"

"I didn't know there was a boot fair in the cemetery."

"Hardly anyone does, that's the beauty of it. You can't be shifting the stuff you find at that booty at a regular boot fair – people would get excited. You have to do it somewhere off-radar. Who would think there'd be a boot fair in a cemetery between two and four in the morning, every full moon? No one ever. Or at least, no one, in their right mind, ever."

"But how do people find out about it?"

"I dunno. How do people find out about the game?"

Sam had been wondering the same thing. It would be a while before circumstances slowed down enough for him to take stock and think things over, but the first question he was on the verge of asking was simple. Who were all these people? And where had they come from? That's two questions. Only a short while ago, he'd been under the impression there wasn't anything at all under the high street, apart from a crumbling drainage system and full fibre optic broadband cables. But now it seemed it was teeming with life.

"Do you want to go and see it?"

Sam tried to pull himself back into focus.

"The boot fair? We can go if you want. It's on tonight."

Takara undid her blue jacket and held it open.

Stitched into the lining were five rows of pocket watches. Some were high end and expensive looking, with white gold and diamond fittings. Others were retro-futurist, a quaint vision of modernity with an LCD screen and rows of minute buttons. The rest were old-fashioned, elegant golden circles with a neat chain.

But what really caught Sam's attention was the lining itself. It was deeper than it should be and fluid somehow, like looking up into the endless night sky. It felt like Takara could reach into her jacket and pull out anything.

She plucked out a watch decorated with moons instead of numbers.

"Look, see? Full moon tonight, almost two. We're in luck!"

"OK, then. I suppose I would like to go. Why not?"

"That's the spirit! I have a few chores to attend to first, though, if you don't mind."

Takara went over to the mahogany desk and opened the drawers full of golden hundreds and thousands and, using a miniature ladle, started to transfer them into a dark velvet bag. Once one drawer was empty, she stood back and watched, and in a flash the drawer filled up again. Takara grinned at Sam.

"I love it when it does that."

She carried on for ten minutes more and then closed the drawers for the final time. The velvet bag was full.

"Can you grab those papers off the worktop for me? Great, thanks. Yes, as many as you can manage. Oh, and bring the kettle too."

Takara pressed a button on the front of the industrial fridge and waited.

"Why do we need the kettle?" asked Sam, standing beside her.

"Because," said Takara, opening the top of the kettle, "you'll be wanting these."

And she pulled out a handful of beautiful red fountain pens.

14

Sam had tried his best to keep up, take track of every twist and turn and lay down mental breadcrumbs that he could follow upon their return, but Takara made it impossible.

The fridge turned out to be an elevator which took them to a spiral staircase which led to a mezzanine and then another staircase upwards and then a hexagonal room with a different set of stained glass windows and then a series of passageways that led to a second mezzanine and then a combination of staircases and then they were behind a bigger stained glass window and then they had to climb through a narrow notch in the wall and make a sharp left then right then right again…all with Takara barking: "Keep up! If you fall behind, I won't come back for you!"

They eventually emerged into a murky chamber that made Sam feel instantly claustrophobic, the thick smell of damp enveloping him, along with the sense that there was something that he couldn't quite see that was much closer than it should be.

At the end of the chamber, there were cast iron bars and a rusted gate that looked like it hadn't opened in living memory. As Sam's eyes slowly adjusted to the gloom, alcoves set into the walls became apparent, and shelves within the alcoves, and boxes upon the shelves. Long thin narrow boxes, all in various states of decay.

"Don't worry, no one's going to leap out and attack you," said Takara, wrinkling her nose with displeasure. "As you can smell, these guys have been here for quite some time."

Sam stared at the coffins with horror.

"Let's see who we've got here," said Takara, brushing the dust from the end of the nearest coffin. There was a serial number and a name. "Bartholomew Bloom. Now there's a good chewy name, very olden times. I like it." She brushed away a bit more dust. "Oh sorry, pardon me. Dr Bartholomew Bloom. Even better. But a doctor of what, I wonder? Of medicine? Of philosophy? Or the type of doctor that stitches together body parts and waits for the weather to turn? My favourite type of doctor."

"Where are we?"

"We're in the catacombs," said Takara, sounding surprised. "Haven't you been here before? I thought everyone round here had done the tour. Through the hidden wooden door, down into the darkness with candles and macabre stories, exploring the labyrinth, thrilling at the spookiness of it all. Such fun. They say there's over 3000 coffins down here, you know. The cemetery was getting overcrowded, so they opened a new wing."

"3000?" said Sam, sounding amazed.

"Yes. So many dead people. Best of all, we're in the part of the catacombs that's under the Dissenter's Chapel, so all this lot are bound to be the misfits and the ingrates and the wrong-believers. By which I mean the interesting people. The people who discover things."

"What kind of things?"

"Well, just…things!" replied Takara. "No one ever really has an original idea, you know. They follow what's been done before, decide to have a stab at it themselves, and some of them get it wrong and do something else, entirely by accident. That's when invention happens. When the lightning hits the pond scum. Or the body parts, thoughtfully provided by our dear friend Dr Bloom."

"That's not true," said Sam. "What about inventors. People like Da Vinci and Edison and…"

"Fakers! All fakers! Tried to copy, messed it up, fronted it out!"

Takara took a pair of glasses from deep within the lining of her jacket and slipped them on.

"Anyway, enough history lesson. Time for me to get scrubbed up."

She opened the gate at the end of the chamber and walked into a large, equally dank tunnel. Rusted gates leading into similar chambers were dotted along the sides of the tunnel, like a prison for the dead. It looked endless, the tunnel and the gates stretching off into the gloom in both directions.

"Now, I've got a couple of options and I'd like to know what you think. Which do you prefer? Do you like *this*?"

Takara tapped the right side of her glasses and everything changed.

The blue suit and black brogues were replaced by a vivid white wedding dress, so white it was practically fluorescent, like a Christmas tree made out of lightning, absorbing all colour and all hope. The fabric pulled and gathered and cascaded, seemingly in constant motion, an avalanche of elegance and imminent danger, all offset beautifully with lace that had buried centuries of unsuspecting bridegrooms. Across Takara's face was a veil fashioned to resemble barbed wire, the twists and knots obscuring her features, leaving only the eyes and mouth visible, while on the body of the dress there were rough red splotches of what had to be blood, as if she'd come straight from paintballing in an abattoir, as if whoever she'd just bludgeoned to death had tried to clamber up her body in their desperate final moments.

"Magnificent, isn't it?" Takara beamed. "I once had a dream that I attended a fashion show in a plague pit and this supernova of a supermodel wore this very dress, and as she glided along the catwalk, everyone she passed by dropped gracefully to the floor, giving up the ghost in an instant at the sight of such perfection. The evening began to rapturous, overwhelming applause, and ended in silence, with myself, the last woman standing, sighing with joy, my hands clasped together in supplication."

"When I woke up, I was wearing the dress. And I haven't wanted to take it off for even a second since that day."

Takara frowned, her bottom lip jutting out slightly.

"But it can be a bit much, I do have to concede that. So I have a second option. What do you make of *this*?"

She tapped the right side of her glasses once again.

The wedding dress blinked out of existence to be replaced by a black suit, cut for a matador. The jacket had high shoulder pads overlaid with panels of dense material covered in obsidian sequins while the arms and body were plastered in twisted black embroidery. The trousers were tight and tapered leading to dramatic pointed black shoes. Everything was covered in a layer of white dust, and the previous owner of the outfit had clearly attended the same paintballing party as the murderous bride, as dark red splodges of blood complimented the dust, the embroidery, the mirrors and the sequins perfectly.

Perched on Takara's head was a black collapsed top hat - like a normal top hat were it was being sat on by a huge invisible vulture. And just below the hat, a thin, fastidiously groomed moustache ran along the edges of Takara's top lip and then gave a theatrical, swashbuckling twist at either end.

"My god Takara," spluttered Sam. "You've turned into a man."

"I have?" Takara replied with a mildly surprised tone. "Oh yes, of course, that's right. It comes with the outfit. I'd forgotten all about that."

Takara had a twinkle in her eyes that suggested that she knew full well that a gender switch accompanied the outfit, and that seeing people react to it was a huge part of the appeal.

"I have to admit that this wasn't entirely what I was thinking of when I ordered this getup," Takara went on, brushing some of the white dust from her upper arm. "In my mind, it was going to be rather more voodoo megalomaniac - part Willy Wonka, part Papa Lazarou. You know the thing. Half wildly eccentric chocolatier trying to prove a grudgeful point to an uncaring world by leaving a trail of distended and distorted children in his wake…"

"Didn't one of them die?" interrupted Sam.

"One? All? Who's counting?" retorted Takara. "So, yes, half that and half disturbing voodoo bogey man, with lots of skulls and little white crosses, and the most dreadful teeth, like a shaman in desperate need of a makeover. Not my usual style when it comes to presenting myself to the world, I'll grant you, but I thought a change of pace might be fun. But then my subconscious got to work and this kind of shaman matador outfit arrived, and I am quite taken with all the sequins and the mirrors, not to mention the delightful cobweb embroidery. So I've decided to run with it."

"Do you feel different being a man?"

Takara frowned slightly.

"I'm not a man," she tutted, raising a hand as if to twiddle her moustache. "That's just how I present for this outfit."

"So what are you then?"

"Now, that is the question!" beamed Takara. "But it's not fair to answer your question before you've answered mine. Which is it to be – traumatic nightmare death bride or creepy nightmare circus demon?"

Takara looked at Sam expectantly.

"I'm starting to think that none of this is real and therefore nothing I say or do really matters."

"Yes?" Takara nodded, smiling in encouragement.

"So stay as you are – saves the bother of having to switch back."

Takara raised her hand to the right side of her glasses for a moment, hand poised, trembling, apparently ready to tap the glasses once more, and then she whipped them off her head and slipped them back into her jacket.

"Excellent!" she said, clapping in delight. "You really are getting into the swing of things."

15

The full moon - bright and ominously low in the sky - bathed the Greek Quarter of the cemetery in a spectral silver glow, making what was already a reliably atmospheric corner of the graveyard feel even more unearthly and not quite of this world.

Had they walked through the cemetery from the high street, like regular people do on regular days, Sam and Takara would have passed the usual Victorian sights. Moss covered gravestones, many at an angle, bearing the names of the long departed. Discoloured statues of forgotten dignitaries, lost children, defeated angels, broken-hearted widows, snarling hounds. Mausoleums erected to sugar barons and slavers and unrepentant Scrooges, the last defiant cry of "Look upon my works, ye mighty!" before the darkness took hold. And on a normal walk on a normal day, it would have been a quite cheery but also rather disquieting experience, as all walks in cemeteries generally are.

The Greek Quarter, though, was something different. Surrounded by a low metal fence, it was – as Takara took great glee in explaining – a necropolis. A city of the dead. And once within the environs of the city, the atmosphere shifted a notch. The wind dropped, the birds fell silent, and a chill crept into the air - along with the unshakable sense that someone had once witnessed something terrible here, and not so long ago.

"Fantastic, isn't it?" chirped Takara, raising her collapsed top hat to her surroundings, presumably dislodging the invisible beast that had been resting there.

The centrepiece of the Quarter was the Grand Temple, an imposing and rather pleased with itself mortuary chapel that was supposedly based on the Parthenon in Athens.

It stood surveying the necropolis like a disapproving parent, its Doric columns a brooding display of wealth and power, its walls and cornices adorned with carvings that depicted bloodshed and torture in a myriad of forms. Were the dark lords of publishing ever to produce an illustrated How To guide for Decapitation And Dismemberment, like a Kama Sutra for serial killers, then these panels would surely be their starting point. If it could be chopped off, lopped off, sliced off, slashed off or hacked off, then it was etched, lovingly, into the cold, hard stone of these temple walls.

Behold the common thief! Caught with his hand where it shouldn't be, he is relieved of his hand, via the pickaxe, the guillotine, the scimitar, and countless more. Witness the blasphemer! Daring to take the lord's name in vain, he's introduced to the tongue tearer, which ensures that he will keep his counsel forevermore. Regard the braggart! With knives and stakes and glowing pokers, he finds the humility that had previously escaped him.

Sam ran his eyes over the carvings, feeling strangely at home.

There was a simple, artistic beauty to the variety of ways these poor unfortunates were meeting their end, almost like it was ballet rather than bloodshed. As a young man, Sam had devoured mythical tales, following champions and rogues, misfits and unbelievers, as they'd hacked and slashed and won the day, but these images were more medieval, more untethered. He could appreciate why an important person would want them slathered over their eternal resting place – they were a boast and a warning, a final, flamboyant rattling of the stick.

"Here, let me show you my favourite!"

Takara stood gazing at a fresco that showed, in detail, the numerous steps in the process of cutting off someone's big toe and then pulling their organs, tissues and assorted bodily contents through the resulting wound.

"Oooh, ouch, right?" exclaimed Takara with delight.

Sam stood beside her, taking in the full, unlikely horror of it all. The intestines, the spleen, the ligaments, the kidneys, the pancreas, the heart, the veins, the eyes.

"Now, I am a woman who will try anything once, but even I have my limits," Takara said. "This one? Never again."

Of all the mythical tales he'd read in his youth, one had stayed with Sam - that of a leper sent to another realm. It had the shape and spirit of a classic fantasy, awash with Cavewights and Demondim and an evil adversary who revelled in the name of Lord Foul (and the audience did boo and the popcorn did fly and all was well with the world). But at its heart it carried a simple question: could any of this really be trusted?

"You know, I'm now starting to think that not only is all this not real, but also that not a word of what you say to me is the truth."

Takara span round to look at Sam, her moustache glinting in the moonlight.

"Well, that doesn't add up. If none of this is real, then nothing I say can be the truth, can it? The two cancel each other out!"

"What? No. That's not right at all."

"Anyway, you're wrong. This is all very real. And almost everything I tell you is true. And that's a guaranteed fact."

"Almost everything?" repeated Sam, slowly.

"That right. Now where's this boot fair? I can't see it anywhere."

16

The boot fair was, of course, all around them.

The Grand Temple stood on the central thoroughfare of the necropolis, what was probably supposed to be the High Street Of The Dead, alongside the largest and most ostentatious of the tombs. Those who felt that their passing should be marked by an extravagant edifice – an octagonal stone crypt or a domed granite sepulchre, festooned with crosses and carved lamentations – had reserved a spot here. Running off the high street were smaller side streets, these populated by the more modest but still striking memorials – the mosaic of a sobbing Jesus, clearly distraught at what had been lost to the world; statues of varying size and disposition, some having surrendered a hand, a limb, or in one unfortunate case, a head, to time and the elements; nativity scenes carved from marble, crammed with miniature figures, some celebrating a historic birth, others bewailing an uncalled-for death. And lining these streets and side streets, on every paving slab and every patch of greenery, there was a seller, their wares strewn hopefully on the ground before them.

Sam was a fan of boot fairs. There was something innately uplifting about the drudgery of it all, he always thought, something about the setting and the people and the things they'd misguidedly decided were worth selling that celebrated the everyday, that said that if you stripped away status and trappings and privilege, then underneath we were really all the same, fellow travellers, all stumbling towards hope on the level playing field of the boot fair.

A morning was never really wasted at the boot fair, even if

all you had to show for your time was a fried egg sandwich and an old football top for your nephew that turned out to be two sizes too small. There was something reviving about being in the open air, on the hunt for nebulous stuff, an unspecified, unwanted doodah that was going to fill a gap in your life that you didn't know existed until you saw whatever it was, laying there, battered and worn, yours for 50p, mate, an entirely jeopardy-free triumph. And there was something exhilarating about being on that hunt with everyone else, shoulder to shoulder, united in a needless, pointless quest, that made Sam feel like he was part of the human race after all.

The human race, however, had not been invited to this boot fair. The human race was tucked up in bed, wrapped in the armour of its bedclothes, protected from the nocturnal and the nefarious.

Sam had wondered if Takara was going to be the inevitable centre of attention in her voodoo ringmaster getup. But now he realised it was he – dressed plainly in a white baker's coat and clothes so unremarkable the words fall off the page every time a description is attempted – who stood out.

As the spotlight of the fulsome moon picked out the many inhabitants of the boot fair – the sellers, the buyers, the hustlers and the passers-by – there was only one person who had neglected to bring the extra along with their ordinary.

"I think we might need to find you something rather more suitable for the surroundings," said Takara, pointedly. "In the meantime, have some of this." She brushed a palmful of the white dust from her suit into the air before her and then, with the determined puff of an heir apparent on their birthday, blew as much of the dust as she could over Sam's face and clothing.

It was surprisingly effective. Now covered in a light dusting of light dust, Sam looked like he'd been scrabbling through the tombstones, looking for something he'd dropped the night before. He looked, for the first time in his life, the part.

"Now let's see what we can pick up for you," said Takara. "Is there anything you fancy? Anyone," she gestured in a sweeping circle around her, "you feel inspired by?"

Sam felt inspired to: run away, pass out, shake his head, blink repeatedly, shake his head once more, and pinch his nose and see if he could somehow neutralise normality.

It wasn't just the people dressed extravagantly, cosplaying history with no concern for anything adding up. The Roman centurions carrying emerald-tipped spears and whips made of braided copper. The Elizabethan courtiers with melodramatic wigs, part towering beehive, part alien octopus. The zombie flamenco dancers, their colossal golden hooped earrings glinting against putrid green skin. The peroxide Hollywood starlets, their Oscar gowns shredded and their white foundation stained with blood. The emperors from the Zhou, Tang and Qing dynasties, their robes trailing fireflies. The Victorian Dream Detectives, hunting their prey with butterfly nets and magnifying glasses. A mime in a striped top and black braces, an oversized black tear streaking down his face. The things that were just giant oblong faces, like huge Day Of The Dead masks that had become sentient, and able to travel without legs or any limbs of any sort. The Kraken. Someone who looked like they were on the trail of The Kraken. An undertaker, dressed for mourning, with an assistant carrying a silver bell. Ayesha, She-Who-Must-Be-Obeyed, resplendent in gold leaf and leather, a string of willing corpses laying in her wake. Druids with flowing black robes and flowing white beards, withered flower rings perched on their heads. The anthropologists with shrunken heads. The anthropologists with expanded heads. The Sacerdotal priests, bloodied Bibles clasped to their bosoms. The Aztec Blood Gods, bearing feathered headdresses and clubs swathed in spikes. The doomed opera singer, dressed for her final, triumphant performance, ready to hit that fatal high note one last time. The She-Wolf and the Romancers, the Beasts and the Super-Beasts. The deranged harlequins and manic jesters, running amok, darting through the crowd, laughing uproariously as they went. The clean-cut jock, the homecoming queen, the inquisitive nerd, the scrawny guy, the scrawnier hound. The scientists and the surgeons, the gangsters and the go-betweens, the dark suits and the red ballgowns, the steady stream of inhumanity going on and on and on and on and on and on.

No, those people were fine, mostly.

It was the people dressed as buildings that really got to Sam.

The people dressed as late 19th century New York brownstones. The people dressed as towers with princesses imprisoned at the top. The people dressed as the mausoleums and tombs that they were surrounded by.

Those people were freaky as.

Takara noticed the expression on Sam's face and smirked.

"Oh, don't worry, it's just the guys," she said, before waving indiscriminately at no one in particular. "Hi guys. How are we?"

The guys ignored Takara completely and continued their shuffling.

"Great!" said Takara, looking pleased. "We have blended. Even you. Now let's go grab your outfit."

17

Once again, Sam struggled to keep up. Takara weaved through the crowd with a confident fluidity, never dropping a beat as she side-stepped and shimmied between the costumes and body shapes. If there was even the slimmest of opportunities to skip past someone, she'd glide through without hesitation, and she seemed to have an uncanny ability to spot gaps in the crowd that no one else could see.

Sam, meanwhile, was all elbows and apologies, bumping hither and thither with the social grace of a pinball ricocheting down the table.

"Sorry! Oops, no, my fault, sorry! Ah, no, sorry! Yes, after you. No, you...oh dear. Really sorry!"

Sam was just beginning to think he was getting the hang of it all when he walked slap bang into the person in front of him. Takara had stopped dead suddenly.

There was a shout and a scuffle and three figures in hooded blue jerkins burst through the crowd, clearly hotfooting their way out of there. Another shout and a scramble of activity followed close on their heels, but the figures spotted the gap left by Takara's sudden stop and dived through it, disappearing into the mass of bodies.

"Stop! Thieves! Grab them someone!"

An overweight man with a string vest and a ruddy, verging on puce, complexion clambered through the crowd towards Sam and Takara, evidently in pursuit of the hooded figures even though he really wasn't quite up to it. He came to a rest in the same gap that the thieves had darted through and stood there, panting.

"Stop..." he rasped, gasping for breath. "Someone..."

Takara took hold of Sam's arm and steered him forwards, past the spluttering string vest.

"Just keep moving," she whispered in Sam's ear. "Nothing to see here."

"But shouldn't we do something? Try to help in some way?"

Takara pulled Sam deftly out of the way of an oncoming ballerina and her entourage of mammoth swans.

"Not at all. There's nothing out of the ordinary happening here."

"But the thieves..."

"Thieves? What thieves? We only have our well-fed chum's word that they were thieves, and why are you possibly going to put your trust in him?"

"Well, they were running away from something."

"Of course they were. We're all running away from something. But let me assure you that black and white concepts like ownership and theft, like possession and dispossession, don't carry much weight in a place like this. So, yes, the nimble-fingered hoodies might have lifted an item or two from some poor unfortunate's stall, but where do you think the items came from in the first place? The people selling at this boot fair aren't the types who've rummaged around the garage for some old bits and pieces to try and flog on a slow Sunday. There'll be artefacts here that have fallen off the back of a lorry onto the back of a chariot and then onto the back of a train of elephants picking their way through the Himalayas and then onto the back of a griffin mid-flight and then into the hands of a humble trader, who just happened to be standing there all innocent-like, as manna fell from heaven into their hands. So when you see a gang of hoodies like that enacting a daring hit and run in the middle of a crowded public place, who's to say they weren't the original owners of whatever it was, reclaiming what was theirs? Or employees of the original owners? It's not for us to judge or tamper with."

"So this place is lawless?"

"Oh no, not at all. There are rules and conventions and statutes, but there are also things of importance and things of unimportance. The former – you know, the big stuff – will be dealt with by the Council. And the other stuff…well, that kind of looks after itself."

Still doing his best to keep up with Takara's pace as she pressed ever onwards, Sam turned her words over in his mind.

As much as his time in the tunnels and at the boot fair had been categorised by chaos, by things seemingly happening at random and for no apparent reason, he hadn't been able to shake the notion that something was controlling it all, that it was somehow all happening for a reason. From the figure declaiming the rules of the game to the minotaur laid heavy with the weight of duty, there'd been another higher force at play, a hidden hand. Perhaps it was this Council that Takara had mentioned?

"The Council?" he asked simply, trying not to place too much significance on his question.

"Yes, yes," replied Takara. "The Council Of Fools."

As they moved onwards, Sam passed by a wooden cage, with a handful of despondent rogues sitting inside. Someone had obviously decreed that whatever they'd done had been of enough importance to warrant being turfed into a cage for a cooling-off period of no shorter than half an hour, but even so Sam couldn't help wonder if that was the Council right there.

"The Council Of Fools?"

Takara grinned.

"It's quite a good system actually, and one that I see your people have been experimenting with. Using a rigorous series of tests followed by something akin to an election, we select a crack squad of the biggest fools and idiots available. Folk for whom every utterance is a disaster, people who wouldn't dream of basing their opinions on any sort of facts, even if they knew how, numpties and dunderheads and imbeciles of the very highest, or should I say lowest, order. And then once we have the Council Of Fools assembled, we present them with our most pressing matters. Crimes that would shock the marrow out of your bones. Crises, both national and international, with the potential to change the course of history. Calamities and mishaps and acts of derring do and derring don't. We lay them at their feet, respectfully request that they consider, cogitate and conclude, and then once they deliver their verdict to us, their grateful waiting servants, we do exactly the opposite. It doesn't always work, but it's almost never wrong."

Takara's eyes gleamed, as something ahead caught her attention.

"Talking of fools," she said, with a grin. "Here's our old friends, the Big Heavy and the Heavy Heavy."

She gestured towards a stall about twenty yards away, where two familiar faces were engaged in an almighty bust-up with a stall holder. The Big Heavy from the Costa loomed over him, shaking the faulty rain stick with his right hand while jabbing his left forefinger in the seller's face, coming perilously close to taking one or potentially both eyes out. The Heavy Heavy loomed even larger beside his partner, feeling slightly left out as he didn't have anything to shake or an immediate reason to gesticulate, but that didn't prevent him from adding the required sense of threat and impending violence. Sometimes he thought, on those moments when he took time to reflect and consider his career choices, the best menace isn't the menace of deeds, but the menace of presence.

"I'm telling you this is a piece of junk," snarled the Big Heavy, beads of fury gathering on his ample brow. "I don't know if it's broken or if it never worked in the first place or if it's just a roll of cardboard with some random runes painted on it, but the fact remains that it's a dud. It's bust, it's done in, it's useless. It doesn't do what it says on the box, it doesn't have a box, it might as well be a piece of garbage that you peeled off the bottom of your shoe before you sold it to us, and I'm not sure that it actually isn't. It's dead, it's defunct, it's a total bloody disaster."

"No, it isn't."

The seller looked blankly at the Big Heavy, with the certainty of someone who has the truth on their side.

"Yes, it is!"

"No."

The seller reached over and plucked the rain stick from the Big Heavy's hand, not asking and not waiting for any permission. He took a moment to scan his eyes over the objects on his stall – not the glowing purple cubes, not the lizard-lion figurines, not the vortex spinners, not the reversible hydras – and then picked up a cockroach that looked suspiciously similar to the cockroach the Heavy Heavy had zapped in the Costa.

He pressed a button on the side of the rain stick and five tiny gold lights flashed up in sequence. He locked gaze with the Big Heavy.

"Still has its charge, I see."

Then he placed the cockroach on the ground beside his stall, took a step back, and then flicked the rain stick towards the cockroach.

Time looped.

The runes on the side of the stick glowed once again, fire tracing through the same curves and lines. Once more, there was a moment of tension and then a familiar wash of bright light flooded over the cockroach, obscuring it for a second.

"Boom – big cockroach," said the seller, nodding towards the now boar-sized creature. "The item's in perfect working order."

"Yes, but…"

"Cockroach is big, item works."

"Yes, but," the Big Heavy said more forcefully this time, leaving no space for interruption, "that's all this thing does. Try and shrink the cockroach back down again and it's a dead loss."

"That's because it's only a sonic enlarger. Look, it says so right here."

The seller turned around and rummaged through a pile of discarded boxes behind his stall. Box for echo catcher, box for memory squeezer, box for orgone accumulator, jumbo box of vortex spinners – ah, here it was. He pulled out a crumpled, opened box for the DB02 sonic enlarger, and pointed at the red sales flash on the side: "Vintage model! Enlarges only!" He then reached inside the box and took out a pristine instruction leaflet, with the same warning printed at the top.

"I did ask if your man here wanted the box, but he wouldn't hear of it. He was in a bit of a hurry, if I remember rightly."

The Big Heavy spun to glare at the Heavy Heavy, who had turned an intriguing shade of sheepish-meets-terrified.

Sensing her moment, Takara started inching forwards.

"We can have some fun here," she said.

"But you said they were dangerous, that we had to keep out of their way," Sam protested, grabbing her forearm. "I remember it very clearly – 'If they see you, they'll kill you'."

"Your memory really does need an overhaul. I said if they found you in the back room of the cafe, they'd kill you. And quite understandably so. What right do you have go poking around in their business, game or no game? But here in the common ground of the boot fair, everyone is equal. You can stand cheek by jowl with them and you won't even have to buy a ticket."

"A ticket?"

But it was too late. Takara was already halfway to the stall, moments later right beside the Big Heavy.

"Johnny Boy!" she said, greeting the stallholder like an old friend. "How's it going, my old china? Still fleet of foot? Swift of hand? Faster than the eye can trace, eh?"

The seller, who wasn't called anything like Johnny Boy, looked at Takara with fresh horror.

"I won't keep you long," continued Takara, "but I just wanted to check how you were getting on with that dodgy batch of sonic enlargers I dropped off last month. Managed to shift any yet? Run into anyone stupid enough to take one off your hands? Look, I don't expect you to have gone through them all, but an indication would be...oh, sorry," Takara broke off suddenly, "I didn't realise you were with customers. Sorry gentlemen, so rude of me to interrupt. Do forgive the intrusion, don't mind me. Johnny, me old mate, I will give you your day back. We can do this all later, yeah?"

And with that Takara grabbed Sam and marched them both off through the crowd.

Even above the hubbub of the boot fair, the sound of violence was inescapable.

"My god!" said Sam. "Why did you do that?"

"I told you! A bit of fun!"

"Fun? Look," said Sam, gesturing back to the dust cloud surrounding the stall. "They're beating heaven, hell and several dimensions yet undiscovered out of the poor guy. It doesn't look like it's much fun for him."

"Oh, I don't know," said Takara, wistfully.

"Well, I don't understand why on earth you did it."

"Unfortunately, I do," said a voice behind them.

Takara turned a slow one eighty.

"Ah, Inspector. How lovely to see you."

18

The Inspector pursed her lips, giving Takara a look that was part disbelief, part exasperation, part eye-rolling not-this-nonsense-again. It was the look that a farmer might give a fox that they've caught sneaking towards their chicken coop for the umpteenth time, a look that declared: "I repaired the hole in the fence, I set the extra traps, I buried land mines, employed snipers, and spent a fortune on an elaborate alarm system of pulleys, weights and eardrum-shattering sirens, and even after all that, you *still* got in?"

It said something that the Inspector's expression made an immediate impact, because her eye and face makeup and overall look really didn't allow for it.

She was a perfect study in black and red, a meticulously constructed depiction of power that wasn't meant to be disrupted or bent out of shape. Her bright red hair – literally bright red, not an extreme shade of ginger – was a short shock of backcombed spikes that surrounded her face like an aurora. Her face was white with face paint and a black stripe ran across her eyes like a blindfold. Her lipsticked lips matched her hair colour precisely, and red lightning bolt earrings hung from her ears. Her black suit had a sharp, sleek cut, much like the blue suit that Takara had worn when Sam had first encountered her, and the black shirt beneath the suit radiated displeasure, judgement. Her trousers were sharply cut to match and her pointed black brogues looked strangely familiar. On her lapel, a red lightning bolt broach sparkled with electricity.

"I understand all too well, don't I, Takara?"

Takara shrugged, trying her best to seem nonchalant, but actually looking, Sam was surprised to notice, a little nervous.

"If you say so."

The Inspector pursed her lips even more.

"Why don't I explain to your friend here what you're really like? Why don't I tell him who you are, what you've done, what you want to do, and then set aside an hour or two to list all the people who want to see you dead, decapitated, or worse?"

Sam cleared his throat. "My name's…"

"I know who you are," snapped the Inspector, cutting him off.

A vivid white light charged through the red lightning bolts

"Do you want to know Takara's biggest problem, Sam?," her dark eyes locking onto him like an infrared sight. "It's herself. Her stupid, vain, extravagant, troublesome, easily bored self. If I didn't have a million and one better things to be taking care of, I'd have her marched off to The Cage – or better still The Dungeon – quick smart. I do wonder if I shouldn't order that anyway. That's where she's going to end up in the long run, so I'd be saving everyone's time."

"On what charge?" asked Takara, still doing her best to keep up her nonchalant air.

"Well, let me see," said the Inspector. "There's incitement to violence for a start." She waved towards the still vigorous dust cloud surrounding the seller and his stall.

"That was nothing to do with me," Takara countered. "I can't be blamed for a disagreement at the boot fair. They happen all the time."

"Then there's deceit," the Inspector continued, looking once again at Sam.

"Not a crime. Also nothing that's relevant to me."

"There's larceny."

"What? You don't even know what that means!"

"We both know what it means, Takara."

"Speak for yourself."

"And then there's theft."

"See! I knew you didn't know. Larceny is theft!"

"Yes. And you're guilty of both."

"Never! That's..."

Takara paused for a moment, trying to grasp a word from thin air. The pause stretched into two moments and then three until Takara cut it short with a final flurry of panic.

"Balderdash!"

If he hadn't been surrounded by an endless cast of costumed outlandishness set in an environment that constantly nudged the outer reaches of what he'd previously thought was possible, Sam would have questioned the use of the word "balderdash".

"What have I stolen then?" demanded Takara.

"You know very well."

"Oh I see! Still going on about *that*!"

The Inspector took out a golden pocket watch and flipped it open.

"You're fortunate that I have to be elsewhere," she said, closing the watch. "Or perhaps unfortunate. You do know that The Duke is here, I assume?"

"What?" Now Takara looked properly nervous.

"Oh yes. And last I heard, he was very keen to catch up with you. Very keen."

"Now just wait a second."

"I'm afraid I can't wait for you or anyone. I have an appointment that cannot be unmet. Such a shame. While I'm here, no one would dare do anything to displease me. But once I'm gone, there's no telling what terrible deed could be carried out. It chills the blood, it really does. But, alas, once my back has turned, my back has turned."

"What if I confess?"

"To what? To stirring up trouble that was going to happen anyway?"

"I could."

"Or to the larceny you so rashly scoffed at just now?"

Takara paused for a second.

"This is a trick, isn't it? You're trying to trick me."

"Is that what you think?"

"I confess nothing!"

"Perfect."

The Inspector tapped the red lightning bolt on her lapel and was gone. No flash of smoke, no retina-melting dramatic effect, no dizzying aftershock – just gone, efficiently and undisputedly.

Takara's hair started to display flecks of grey.

"OK, I think you've seen enough."

"But we haven't *bought anything*."

Sam was surprised to hear himself sound positively indignant.

"What?" retorted Takara.

"You can't go to a boot fair and not buy anything," said Sam. "That's not how the universe works. It doesn't matter if there's nothing that you need or nothing that you want or nothing that catches even the tiniest part of your fancy. If you leave a boot fair with nothing, then you leave with a lot more than empty hands. You leave with an aching gap in your soul. You've been presented with a vast selection of stuff you never dreamed existed, a conveyor belt of delights and surprises, and you've come away with nothing? What does that say about you as a person? What does that say about your lust for life? What does that say about your ability to keep on keeping on?"

"I think it says that you've got good sense and fine judgement and haven't totally lost your mind in a sea of tat."

"No. It says you have nothing left to live for. If you can't buy a single thing just for the sake of it at a boot fair, then you might as well hang up your boots."

"I'm not wearing…"

"You know what I mean!"

Takara grasped at the air with exasperation for a moment and then turned on her heel.

"Come on then. Let's find something. Quickly!"

She marched along the stalls with a visible sense of purpose, dismissing the contents as she went.

"No. Nothing. God no. Oh my days. No. How could you? Really? Oh god. No. What is that? No. No. Definitely no."

She strode past a stall laden with ornate tomes and manuscripts, some still covered in sand from the Syrian Desert, others caked in dust from Angkor Wat, Borobudur and the Lost Pagodas Of Henan. The soapy-tongued blue and red team from the contest were rifling through the books and chattering in a state of high excitement, bubbles all but floating out from their mouths and off into the night sky. One of them grabbed a black book covered in crosses and held it aloft, to cries of delight and amazement from their teammates.

Takara shook her head and surged onwards.

"No, no, thrice no, no again, no once more."

Then she came to a halt before a stall which really didn't look that much different to the others.

She whistled softly under her breath.

"Now hang on a moment."

Takara glanced up at the stallholder who was busy dealing with another customer.

"Here, look!" she said to Sam, gesturing at a blue cloth bag covered in gold embroidery.

"The bag? Well, the design has some character I suppose, but it's not really anything special."

"That shows how much you know," said Takara, keeping her voice down. "Look at all the stuff on here. Low-level magical trinkets at the very best. A wand that fires iridescent stars into the sky. An orb of snooping. Glitching powder. Fake pixie ears. But this bag, now this is actually useful."

"What is it?"

"It's a bottomless bag," grinned Takara. "Put anything you like in it or as much of anything you like in it, and it will never fill up. Put yourself in it, if you like. Sometimes that's the best option. Throw in a library, the contents of several skips, and a lorryload of hundreds and thousands, and you won't even begin to touch the sides. These things are wonders."

Takara looked up at the seller.

"How much for the pixies ears?"

The seller broke off the conversation he was having with the other customer and gave a low grunt.

"Four a pair."

"Great! I'll take ten."

Takara began to scoop up the ears with gusto.

"Do you have a bag?"

The seller gave another grunt. These interruptions were annoying.

"No bag."

"No problem! Look, there's one here, I'll take that one." Takara piled the ears into the bottomless bag and tossed some purple and green bank notes onto the stall. "There's forty for the ears and a couple more for the bag. Be seeing you!"

If The Inspector had been around, things wouldn't have progressed any further.

"Come on! Let's go!"

Takara marched into the crowd before anyone could utter a word of protest. Sam stared at the bank notes fluttering on the stall for a second and then gave in, hurrying off in the same direction.

19

They were rushing, ignoring all possible distractions, back the way they came.

"Who's The Duke?" asked Sam, once he'd managed to catch up.

"Pray you never find out," came the grim reply.

"We're going to meet him, aren't we?"

"Why do you say that? Don't say that."

"It just feels inevitable."

Takara picked up the pace at these words.

"And why doesn't anyone have a name here, anyway?" continued Sam.

"What?"

"The Duke. The Inspector. The Big Heavy and the Heavy Heavy. The seller. Both sellers. Your brother."

Takara blew invisible steam of exasperation out of her ears.

"Brother? What brother?"

"You know, the guy in charge of the game. You said he was your brother."

"I did? Oh yes, so I did. Well, don't worry about that now."

Takara slowed suddenly, grabbing hold of Sam, so he didn't keep barrelling onwards. Up ahead, the Big Heavy and the Heavy Heavy had completed their altercation and the dust clouds were beginning to settle. Even a newbie like Sam could see that walking past them at this precise minute probably wasn't the best idea.

"Here, put these on."

Takara thrust a pair of pixie ears into Sam's hands.

Sam had never worn pixie ears before. He didn't know if he should hook them behind his ears or slide them over his ears or stick them on the side of his ears somehow. They'd come without packaging so there were no instructions to consult.

Takara grabbed the pixie ears out of Sam's hands and jammed them roughly over his ears.

She looked at Sam expectantly.

She looked at Sam expectantly again.

Nothing happened.

"Bloody hell! Duds!"

"Why, what was supposed to happen?"

"I don't know. Something!"

"Perhaps you could take them back for a refund?"

Sam didn't need telling who had made that last suggestion.

20

If The Inspector had looked at Takara like a farmer squaring up to a persistent fox, then The Duke looked at her like someone who was certain they'd ordered the eradication of all foxes and was intrigued to discover that their edict hadn't been administered to the letter.

He was a small, precise man, with a large dark overcoat thrown over his shoulders, as if he didn't plan on staying outdoors for any longer than strictly necessary.

He didn't appear to have any companions, but he had the air of a man who never travels alone. Sam glanced around instinctively, scanning for likely suspects. The man checking his watch under the statue of the fallen angel perhaps, or the guy queuing for whatever it was they were selling at the fast food stall, or the chap idly rifling through the trash and treasure on a nearby stall, his hat a jaunty, all-too-suspicious angle. It could be anyone, or no one, or everyone, every single last person there ready to leap to The Duke's defence.

Takara gave The Duke a smile that was pitched somewhere between "What a pleasant surprise!" and "Please don't kill me!"

"Oh, your grace," Takara stuttered, "What a…"

"Disastrous turn of events?"

"No, no."

"Catastrophic turn of events?"

"Not at all."

"Really?" said The Duke, raising an eyebrow. "Your optimism never ceases to surprise, Takara."

Takara took this as a green light to start making her excuses.

"Now, I know I'm a little late in returning the item to you, and I will of course pay any overdue fees that may have accrued in the really very short time that it's been in my possession, but there are just a few minor details that I need to clear up before I can confidently and successfully say that I'm ready to start the process of returning it to your rightful hands." Takara let out a short, nervous laugh. "Can hands be rightful? I suppose your hands can be anything they like. Rightful? Wrongful? It's all so hard to tell these days, isn't it?"

The Duke seemed to pay little attention to Takara's babbling.

"I see you've found another victim," he said, casting his eye over Sam. "Aren't you going to introduce me?"

"Yes! Yes!" Takara beamed, delighted by the welcome change of focus. "Your grace, this is, erm..." Takara looked at Sam as if she was seeing him for the very first time in her life. "Erm, it's ah...sorry, what was your name again?"

Sam felt quietly dumbstruck.

"It's Sam," he said, with the tone of someone unexpectedly having to explain what a banana was to a close relative.

"Well, I never!" Takara looked impressed.

Sam's sense of dumbstruckness began to grow in volume.

The Duke trained his eyes on Sam.

"Let me tell you something about your new friend, Sam," he said, echoing the tone The Inspector had used earlier. "Takara has enough room in her head for three or maybe four Important Things, and when those things have her attention and are aligned with what I've grown to understand is her readiness to face up to them, then she can tackle these things with some skill. There are tasks that I've given her in the past that she has executed perfectly. With the stars aligned, I would almost go as far to say I can trust in her, even though I would never trust her, not even for a second. But if you add another Important Thing, or two, or more dangerously, five or six Unimportant Things to her head, the initial Important Things simply fall out, never to be considered again."

"And this has been a concern for me as Takara is both an enthusiastic collector of Unimportant Things, and a keen borrower of Important Things. If something is new or unusual or novel or spectacular or unlikely or ridiculous or impossible or absurd, then she will be drawn to it, and will wish to claim it. She will take it and store it away and tell herself she's keeping it safe from all harm, but then a new thing will catch her eye, her head will overflow, and she'll forget all about the first thing she's collected. Or borrowed. And the more she claims, the more she forgets."

Takara's face had been a flashing array of emotions during this speech, the feelings passing by like the spinning reels of a fruit machine – indignation, pride, amusement, embarrassment, cherry, strawberry, cherry, strawberry, strawberry, golden coin. But as the reels slowed and the emotions lined up, an Important Thing reappeared in her head, or came back in view, after being lost to the darkness for quite some time.

"Actually, I have a system."

The Duke let out a long, low chuckle. He had heard this before.

"Yes, we're very familiar with Takara's claims of a system," he continued, still looking at Sam. "And we're all eagerly looking forward to evidence of its existence. It must be an organisational triumph. I, for one, am very keen to see it in action."

"And you will – sooner than you think!"

"Well, it can't be later, darling. You would have to rearrange the laws of time for it to be later."

The reels of the fruit machine shifted on an emotion. Takara really didn't like being called darling. And The Duke had said it with a casual fluidity that suggested that he'd called her darling many, many times.

"What has she borrowed?" asked Sam.

"From me or just in general?" replied The Duke. "Because I'm not sure I have enough space in my schedule if you mean the latter."

"From you."

"We'll get to that in a moment, but first I have a story for you. A story about something else she borrowed and forgot to return, and what happens to the things she forgets about."

21

The best storytellers walked while they talked, said The Duke, so they walked - Sam and The Duke side by side, Takara trailing close behind, the invisible companions calling ahead to clear the way.

The Duke had an old-fashioned belief in the power of walking, and always made his most important decisions and secured his most significant agreements while on the move. Be it a short, friendly stroll to a waiting car or a longer ramble across a golf course to a secluded patch of woodland, he found that the act of walking helped quicken the brain and bring priorities into sharper relief.

They walked for a short while in silence, The Duke building the mental pace he needed to begin. Sam found his heartbeat matching that pace in anticipation.

"When Takara was a young woman…"

"Was? I'm still young now!"

"When Takara was a young woman, she had one close companion, perhaps her only companion. She was named Satomi. They were bright like fireflies, but burned with a different coloured flame. Satomi was the most brilliant white, so pure and intense, while Takara was a fierce red, passionate and consuming. Their flames complimented each other, and their characters echoed their flames, but they also envied each other's flames. Satomi coveted Takara's passion and Takara coveted Satomi's purity."

"OK, well this is wrong already," butted in Takara. "For the record, I have always looked good in red or white. Some people can carry off those flag colours and I'm just one of them. I'm blessed, what can I say? Whereas she was fine in white, I suppose, but the red? What a disaster! It never worked. Never!"

The Duke strolled onwards.

"Takara and Satomi studied together. The usual subjects – philosophy, sociology, dance, textiles and design, electrical engineering, combat, disguise, guerrilla warfare, a smattering of law, a modern language I believe."

"She was better at that than me, I'll give her that. I could never be bothered with all the word lists. So many words."

"Satomi was, in fact, better at most subjects, but then her pure white flame helped her focus on her studies. Takara's flame left her open to distraction."

Takara smiled sheepishly.

"She was distracted by things. Distracted by people. Distracted by experiences. Distracted by what she felt was her nature leading her where she should go. Distracted by The Universe beckoning to her and pointing towards what it suggested was her true path. If she was to neglect her work and instead spend a week or three carousing and exploring and indulging, then this was actually her undertaking her proper education, Takara fulfilling her grand destiny. Because when you are young, you believe everything has to happen for a reason."

"What can I say? I had fun! But I did learn a few things too, you know."

"Satomi, meanwhile, flourished. She excelled at her studies. She grew as a person. And she met her true love, a fellow student, a kindred spirit."

"Oh god, that guy. What a jerk he was!"

"He was serious, focussed, driven, successful. He was born to be a leader. We all had the highest of hopes for him."

"He was pompous, arrogant, self-satisfied, smug, relentless, just bloody relentless, and oh so so very boring. He was annoying *and* boring – how can you be both of those things at once? And he treated her like dirt. I wouldn't have minded so much if Satomi had met her soul mate and they stood side-by-side, equal partners in pious tedium, but she was like an accessory to him, like a box to be ticked. If I could have zapped him out of existence, I would have done so in an instant."

"Takara was jealous."

"Absolutely no!"

"And when Satomi announced her intention to marry, Takara flew into a jealous rage."

"Not jealous! But damn right I was angry."

"And then things really took an awful turn for the worse when Satomi showed Takara her wedding dress."

The cemetery, already crisp and frosty under the full moon, took on a suitably dramatic extra chill. Sam waited for a bell to toll, but the tense silence remained intact.

"It was the morning of her wedding day. Satomi had called Takara to her lodgings to try and persuade her to attend the ceremony. She had asked her to be the Maid Of Honour only for Takara to refuse, but still Satomi held out hope. Perhaps if she showed her the wedding dress, Takara's heart would melt and they would prepare for the day together, companions once more."

"But Satomi had forgotten about Takara's flame red nature, about her ungovernable attraction to spectacular new things. And so when Takara saw the dress, she had to have the dress."

Sam looked back at Takara, his eyes widening.

"The dress truly was a wonder," continued The Duke. "I had never seen its like before and have never seen anything remotely comparable since. Sometimes during the wildest thunderstorms, the night sky raging with electricity, I fancy I can see its intricate beauty. Sometimes when the snow falls on the open graves and overgrown battlegrounds, I feel I can sense its power. It wasn't just a garment or a look or a statement – it was a moment of destiny made flesh. And Takara, who had been consumed with chasing destiny, had to make it her own."

"But simply stealing the dress and possessing it wasn't enough, it wasn't realising its innate destiny. So Takara did something truly unforgiveable."

"Come on, you're ladling it on a bit thick now, aren't you?"

"For the dress to fully fulfil its purpose, it needed to be worn on a wedding day. And Takara wanted to be the one who fulfilled its purpose. So instead of helping her friend on what was meant to be the happiest day of her life, she used the guerrilla warfare skills she had accumulated to incapacitate and tie up Satomi and her disguise skills to take on her appearance. And then she donned the wedding dress and attended the wedding disguised as her friend."

"No!"

"Fraid so, kid," said Takara with a shrug. "As the man says, I was a slave to my impulses back then."

"Everyone was at the chapel. I was there myself. It was to have been a moment of great pride for the community – everyone was willing this wedding to happen."

"Again, not true! The wedding might have been approved of by *your* community – by which I mean you and your dubious cronies – but there were plenty who weren't impressed by him, his family, his family's connections, his family's questionable activities, your even more questionable activities, the bonds you were trying to forge for your own gains, and the choice of starter and some of the more outré items on the wedding list. And by outré, I don't mean outré fun or outré weird or outré outrageous, but outré tacky and outré tasteless. So, yes, I was doing it partly because of the dress, but I was also doing it to protect my friend and to prevent a great wrong from being committed."

"I know that's what you tell yourself, but you can't really believe it."

"Of course I believe it! I believe it because it's the truth!"

They had reached a moment of stand-off. They stared at each other wordlessly for a minute or so, before The Duke resumed his tale.

"So Takara arrived at the chapel dressed as Satomi, and she was received as Satomi, as a goddess, as a queen-in-waiting. She walked slowly up the aisle, basking in the adoration, absorbing every last possible drop of appreciation from her surroundings, breathing it all in, like a vampire. You could see the dress moving with her heartbeat, a visible embodiment of the uncut joy coursing through her system. And when she reached the altar, she turned to the groom, her veil still lowered, letting the atmosphere hang in the air above her."

"And then she screamed."

"And she continued to scream as she began to verbally demolish the poor groom, listing his soul-destroying shortcomings, his intolerable habits and opinions, his horrific dress sense, her all-consuming hatred of him, the sheer impossibility of their marriage ever being completed, and something no one quite understood about the unsuitability of the starters."

Takara was mumbling happily away to herself, her eyes glazed in reverie. Sam wasn't sure but at one point he thought he caught the whispered phrase: "plum-faced, puss-brained, pimple-headed, port-stained, perfidious, parsimonious, pestiferous, piggish, over-privileged, pathetic, prancing little prince" – but he really couldn't be certain.

"Having delivered her speech, Takara swept out of the chapel, to shocked silence. I will never forget the look on that poor man's face. Here was a winner, an over-achiever, someone who was used to taking what he wanted, and to his utter astonishment something was looking him square in the eyes and saying no. He had stood at the altar in triumph and had clearly been relishing the moment, a moment he'd been trained for all of his life. Once Takara departed, he was left lost and wounded, his pride in ruins."

Takara smiled wistfully.

"The fallout from the wedding was immense. The upset, grief and fury of the day gave way to bedlam when Satomi was discovered trussed and gagged in her lodgings. Takara's shame was revealed to the world and the two lovers were reunited, but the trauma of the wedding had dealt a lasting blow. This was to have been his day, his moment of victory for all to see, and it had been ruined. He was hurt and the hurt quickly solidified into enmity, a blind-hearted rage against not just Takara, but Satomi as well. His future wife was meant to have been flawless, but Satomi had come hand in hand with this devil, this evil banshee. He couldn't bring himself to look at her in the same way ever again."

"See? I told you! What a scumbag. I could tell he was like this and I'm glad I forced him to show his true self to the world. I think Satomi should thank me. I think she does thank me, but she's too proud to admit it. It's just two little words, Satomi. Not much for a dear heart who's saved your life from catastrophe, is it?"

"Plus he called you an evil banshee," said Sam.

"Well, if the cap fits," said Takara with a smirk, giving a small curtsy. "I am your humble servant, Takara – harpy, harridan, evil banshee, and all-round bringer of good times."

Their walk had brought them, via a most circuitous route, back to the entrance to the catacombs.

The Duke stood looking at Takara with a mixture of resignation and mild exasperation, the kind of exasperation that's left after many years of having to put up with something that you really shouldn't have to put up with.

"Can you not just say sorry to her?" he said, his voice softening a little. "I know you believe you had her best interests at heart, but even you must see that your solution was a little extreme. Apologise for that, if nothing else."

"I don't do apologies, your grace. You know that."

"Well, then at least give the wedding dress back."

The Duke opened the door to the catacombs.

"My problem is that I am all heart," said The Duke to Sam, as the unseen figures made the necessary preparations to move on to the next destination. "It is true that I must sometimes dole out punishments, sometimes as retribution, sometimes as a deterrent, but I always try to give someone a second chance, if I can. And with a special case like Takara, I have given many second chances."

"You lent her something."

"Yes, against my better instincts, I did. But she promised that she would take the utmost care of it and would return it in a flash, so I agreed, more fool me."

The Duke looked at Takara for a final time.

"What did you want The Book Of The Dead for anyway?"

"The Book Of The Dead?" spluttered Sam. "That's…"

"A very, very valuable and important book," cut in Takara, "and one that will be delivered back to your honourable hands without delay. In fact, we will return to my little store of precious things now, and I will begin to set in motion the steps needed to prepare for its conclusive and safe dispatch."

"Bring it to me yourself, Takara," said The Duke, stoney-faced.

"Or I'll get her to come and take it from you."

22

"The Book Of The Dead!"

"Yes! The very same!"

"But that's one of the items we have to find for the game."

"I know! What a coincidence!"

Takara began moving as soon as the doors of the catacombs closed behind her. She dashed along the tunnel, counting under her breath.

"One hundred and twenty-two, one hundred and twenty-three…right here we are." She turned to Sam. "Hold open the bag, will you?"

She knelt down and scooped up a handful of dust and dropped it into the bottomless bag.

"I think that should qualify as grave dust. Catacombs are graves, aren't they? If they're going to pull you up on a question of semantics then the game really isn't worth wasting your brain cells on, in my opinion."

Takara peered at the gate to the chamber. It was closed.

"That's strange," she said. "I'm sure we left that gate open when we were here earlier. I'm not really a gate-closing kind of person, and quite frankly you're not paying enough attention to any of this, so I can't imagine that you closed it. I mean, we were in a graveyard and you didn't think to collect some grave dust? What kind of amateur hour behaviour is that?"

"I don't know," spluttered Sam. "I'm finding it hard to take everything in. There's so much of it and it just doesn't stop."

"Well, start taking it in, and hurry the whole process up!" said Takara, opening the gate. "What have you collected so far? A selection of red pens, one of which is hopefully the red pen they're after, and now a handful of grave dust. There's still a whole bunch of stuff to find, including…oh, damn, damn, damn, damnit!" Takara's face looked like an electric current had unexpectedly passed through it. "The bloody posies! We forgot to pick up a pocketful of posies to go along with the grave dust. Damnation!"

"We could always go back, it's not too far."

"No! We can't run the risk of running into his Dukeness or herself for that matter. We'll have to keep pressing on and pick some up later on."

At which, Takara grabbed Sam's hand and pulled him forwards with her as she ran into the chamber, past the shelves of coffins, and straight towards the back wall.

"Atishoo atishoo!" cried Takara, and leapt towards the brickwork.

The route back was even more tortuous and confusing than before. There were staircases and stained glass windows and more hexagonal rooms and doors that seemingly took you back to where you started and doors which apparently led you to rooms without walls or floors of ceilings, just infinite void – throughout which Takara screamed and waved her hands in the air, as if she was on the scariest and most exciting rollercoaster in the world – and more staircases and more and more and more.

"Bloody stairs!" panted Takara, at one point. "I knew it was a mistake to get Escher in to do the interior design."

"Escher?" asked Sam, rushing along beside Takara.

"You know, staircase guy. I met him when I was fitting carpets. Man, that job was annoying!"

Eventually, they reached the octagonal room with the circles of light on the floor.

"You know, we could have gone out of the front door of the Costa, walked up the high street past the fish and chip shop and the Tesco, and gone in the front gates of the cemetery. Would have taken all of five minutes. But where's the fun in that?"

Not for the first time, Sam stared at Takara in horror.

"Not really," she said, laughing. "We would have been in the same physical space, sure, but not in the same dimensional space. Many of the fabulous creatures you saw cavorting at the boot fair wouldn't be able to exist in the real world because their very essence doesn't follow the laws of physics. Or biology. Or any of the sciences. Nothing truly fun does."

"And what about the tunnels we're in now? What dimension are they in?"

"Hard to say really. This is all a kind of interdimensional hinterland, if you can forgive me for saying the words interdimensional hinterland. Like a big, convoluted waiting room. Or a needlessly confusing airport terminal – which, of course, is all airport terminals. You come here as the first stage of your journey before heading off into the great and unpredictable unknown. Here, look."

Takara nodded down at the circles of light on the chamber floor.

"Each of these is a fast track connection to somewhere either inside or outside of the tunnels. You would have stood on the red one to get to the Costa, which is only slightly quicker than taking the stairs. It was the first one I attempted so I only went for a short hop to begin with. The others go to other places. I haven't put one in for the catacombs yet, but only because I can't really decide which colour it should be. Black, I suppose, but black's already taken. Grey perhaps, but grey is so uninspiring, don't you think? And anyway grey isn't an option. Purple at a stretch, but that's gone too. You can see how upsetting it all must be for me."

Takara stopped talking suddenly and stared at the black circle. It was pulsing.

"Oh my gosh," she said, with the worried air of someone who's just remembered they set a bath running before nipping out to the shops. "I clean forgot about them. Oh dear."

She reached out for Sam's hand and then stepped onto the brown circle.

23

Once again, Takara was counting.

This time backwards.

"Two hundred and fifty-six, two hundred and fifty-five..."

And as she counted, parts of the room they were standing in slowly came into focus.

"Two hundred and fifty-two, two hundred and fifty-one..."

To begin with there were lights - distant, opaque, knowing, faintly in motion, as if twinkling behind frosted glass.

"Two hundred and forty-eight, two hundred and forty-seven..."

Then there were shadows, patches of darkness behind the lights, and lines stretching out from them.

"Two hundred and forty-three, two hundred and forty-two..."

And then windows of vagueness congealed into patches of reality. A collection of browns and blacks became a wooden crate. A blur of yellows and reds gave way to a stack of shelves. A wash of whites and blues sharpened into a glass cabinet.

"Two hundred and twenty-nine, two hundred and twenty-eight..."

Then as the numbers fell and the squares of colour melted into smaller squares of colour, there was something else.

A sense of space.

A sense of vastness.

"One hundred and eighty-six, one hundred and eighty-five..."

The room they were standing in couldn't really be called a room because rooms don't stretch on for ever and ever.

As he gazed forward, Sam had a sense of his line of sight disappearing into the void, like a balloon that's floated so high it's drifted off into space.

His brain tried to quantify what he was seeing in manageable, recognisable terms. One football pitch, two football pitches, three football pitches, four football pitches…

And then it gave up.

"One hundred and twelve, one hundred and eleven…"

It was the most beautiful thing Sam had ever seen.

Perfectly angular, a gigantic, majestic, triumphant, subterranean hangar, a warehouse on an operatic scale, a space that could only be conveyed with stirring strings and a tracking shot that went on for hours.

Everything was precise. The lines were correct, the angles just so. Everything connected together perfectly.

"Seven, six, five, four…"

The last piece of reality slotted into place, and Sam stood for a moment, scanning his eyes over everything that lay before him, searching for the cracks.

There weren't any.

"Can I cook or can I cook?" said Takara, her eyes dancing, waving her hand grandiosely towards the middle distance.

What looked like a small mechanical suitcase on wheels whizzed past their feet and headed straight down the middle of the room. Seemingly taking this as a cue, everything else sprang into action.

Automated baskets ran up and down and along countless rows of shelving, collecting trinkets and curios and assorted objets d'art and delivering them to the mechanical suitcases, which then whizzed off with them at high speed, only to return moments later with more of the same which were then delivered back to the baskets and filed away without a moment's notice. Bijou fork-lift trucks, no taller than the average human male – five foot nine inches, not a penny more, not a penny less – shifted crates several times their size in impossible moves that contravened at least two of the laws of motion, utilising an eight-point turn that could only work if you switched off the theory of relativity for a moment. Small sponge-like creatures glided across the surface of glass display cabinets, buffing and polishing and cleaning, singing a joyous sponge work song as they went, audible only to a select number of wildly fortunate individuals. The cabinets themselves, many of which floated in the air above the rows and rows of shelving, contained rotating tables, designed to show off their contents from every conceivable vantage point. And perched on the shelves at strategic intervals, CCTV cameras cast an ever-watchful, ever-suspicious eye over the proceedings, a red light blinking as they recorded everything, all-seeing, all-knowing.

In the centre of the room, there was a large circular table. It also floated in the air, a few feet above the floor, but unlike the cabinets which were still and serene and gave the impression of being bolted solidly into the atmosphere, the table was supported by an elaborate series of wires and cables, and visibly wobbled at the slightest provocation. The table was completely empty, and dotted with a series of inconvenient holes that allowed the cables to pass through from whatever they were connected to above to whatever they were connected to underneath. It was a true work of art, emitting uncertainty, asking the question that all great works are duty bound to ask – why?

Seated a few paces away from the table, at a small stand-alone workbench big enough to hold a computer and a pad of blotting paper, was a man wearing a long brown coat and a flat cap. He peered at the computer screen, frowned, and then tapped at the keyboard, using only his extended index fingers to type. He paused, peered at the screen once again, frowned once again, and then looked up.

"Hello boss," he said to Takara. "I'm glad you're here. There's a couple of things that I need you to take a look at."

"Yes, yes, Harrington, in a minute," replied Takara, airily. "But first I want you to meet Sam. Harrington, Sam.

Sam, Harrington. Sam is undertaking a very important quest and we are going to help him, as much as we are able."

"Yes boss, but..."

"Harrington, what have I told you before?" said Takara, pointing at a sign that had just appeared in the air before her saying in large, officious letters: 'Never Say Yes Boss But'.

"OK boss, but..."

"Now that's cheating, Harrington. Which, of course, I commend. However, I must insist that we do what I want to do first. Sam, hand me the bag."

Takara took the bottomless bag from Sam and started to root around inside it while walking forwards. Her hand emerged from the bag grasping the red pens that they'd picked up in the Costa and held them aloft for a moment, pausing for gasps and applause, before moving to scatter them on the surface in front of her.

"Not the table boss, no!"

But it was too late.

The pens arced through the air in graceful slow motion, like Exocet missiles tracing a dotted line towards their destiny, hitting the table in an instant that slowed almost to the point of freeze frame. They rolled forwards for a few turns, losing energy as they went, and then the table made a sudden, decisive noise – the noise of frozen ice suddenly cracking. It tilted towards Takara, the pens shaking in anticipation, Takara's eyebrows raised to the heavens.

Harrington exhaled dramatically. Takara turned to look at him, a victorious smile lighting up her face. The table wobbled slightly but moved no further.

"Oh, isn't it wonderful!" said Takara to Sam. "It's a Temporary Contemporary table, you know. I bought it from some ruffians from the northern wastes. It's a table for people who, well, don't really like tables. It's practically unusable!"

"Tell me about it," muttered Harrington.

"If, like me, you're the kind of person who can't stand being stuck in a meeting for more than five minutes," continued

Takara, "then this is an absolute gift from above. It wobbles, it lurches, it can barely take the weight of a single coffee cup, it threatens to collapse at any moment and makes the most spectacular sounds as it does so. Any meeting held around this table is bound to end in disaster."

Takara turned back towards the table.

"But observe, the pens remain," she continued, her voice hushed suddenly. "The table accepts their presence."

"Do you want me to open a new catalogue number for them, boss?" asked Harrington.

"Not yet. Sam needs one of these pens for his quest. We just need to work out which one."

There were six luxury fountain pens, all of them red.

"Your brother said he was tempted to give us a clue about the pens but his instructions didn't allow it."

"Which means the fact he wasn't allowed to give you a clue," said Takara slowly, "is the clue itself."

"You think?"

"Without a doubt. You've only spent a very short time in the tunnels and seen a mere fraction of what this place is capable of, but even you will be able to appreciate that reality is often fluid down here. Just because you can see six red pens that doesn't mean there are six red pens. Only when you grasp each one firmly and connect your sense of self to its sense of self will its true nature be revealed. And this is not an endeavour without danger, let me promise you that. One of these objects could turn out to be a gravity vortex and suck you and all of your surroundings into a very sticky spot indeed. One could be a historical flash bomb and explode back through time, leaving you, your parents, your grandparents and your many forebears blinded, or at the very least dazzled and a little shaken. One could be an expanding anaconda…"

"Harrington, do you have any paper?"

Harrington brought Sam his finest writing paper, embossed with a family shield depicting a chimera intertwined with a lotus flower. Sam placed the paper on the Temporary

Contemporary table, which gave the briefest creak before clearly thinking the better of it, and then he unscrewed the lid of the nearest pen and signed his name, Sam Samuel. In black ink. Then the next – green ink. Then blue ink. Then purple ink. Then green ink again. And then finally red ink.

Takara screwed her nose up in disgust.

"Standards really are slipping. That would never have passed quality control in my day."

Harrington gathered the black, green, blue, purple and green ink pens and took them over to his work station, where he index finger tapped at his computer, before a suitcase on wheels arrived to collect the pens and take them off to one of the baskets.

"And here," said Harrington, handing Sam the remaining red pen and a small square of paper, "is your receipt. Now boss, I really must…"

"Can you hear banging?" asked Takara, still frowning at the disappointment of the fountain pens.

"That's what I've been trying to tell you."

"I think it's coming from over there."

Takara pointed towards a row of wooden crates stretching off into infinity.

"Yes, it's…"

A red globe the size of a blood orange started to flash on Harrington's desk.

Takara's eyes widened with delight.

"I'm needed upstairs! What fun!" said Takara, giving three little claps of excitement. "I'm afraid the banging will have to wait, Harrington. Duty calls."

Takara reached out for Sam's hand once again.

"Come on. I have something incredible to show you."

24

There was no counting this time. Everything was immediately in focus, sharp and vivid like sunshine in the morning.

They were standing at the back of what looked like a very cramped hardware store. Before them stretched three aisles, barely wide enough for two people to pass each other by, packed with so many bits and bobs and thingummies that the narrow space was reduced even further, turned into a rat run of protrusions and protuberances.

The shelves appeared to contain everything.

Literally everything.

Everything imaginable and everything unimaginable too.

Some items so unlikely it took a major mental stretch to accept that someone had actually invented, designed and manufactured them rather than them suddenly popping into existence by a kind of cosmic accident. Like the Big Bang Theory if it was the Little Bang Theory and it created flotsam, jetsam and tat instead of a multitude of universes.

There were saucepans and cheese graters, chopsticks and plastic plates, thermos flasks and tubes of wrapping paper, baking trays and latex gloves, plastic sieves and pizza cutters, cafetieres and corkscrews, odour eaters and slotted spoons, rubber bones and egg slicers, carving knives and water bottles, napkins and rolling pins, orange and yellow tennis balls tethered for no discernible reason by short lengths of orange and yellow rope to other orange and yellow tennis balls, vases and door mats, draught excluders and wind chimes, clothes pegs and fire lighters, travel pillows and extension leads, umbrellas and curtain rails, tea lights and lunch boxes, bread bins and tea cosies, crumb catchers and dish racks, pressure cookers and vegetable steamers, glow sticks and ice fountains, candles and picture frames, table covers and doyleys, party poppers and bags of flame retardant confetti, felt tip pens and calculators, shatterproof rulers and set squares, light bulbs and bird feeders, raffle tickets and garlic crushers, and, at one point, a bunch of mini punch bags the size of a generous garlic sausage.

And that was just one aisle.

What, wondered Sam, was the thinking behind the mini punch bags? They were roughly 15 inches high and maybe five across and came packaged with boxing gloves that were almost as big as the bag itself. What type of aspirant pugilist would submit to such a pint-sized workout? Was this an executive toy? An anger management aid for toddlers? Or was this proof that the warped reality of the tunnels had made its way up onto the high street, that what lurked below had been in plain sight all along?

"Are these for goblins or halflings?" Sam asked Takara.

Takara leaned over and consulted the label.

"No. It says 'Recommended age from 3 years old' here."

"But they are mystical in some way, magical."

"No. They're just punch bags for kids. I guess it's better they whack these things rather than punch seven shades of hallelujah out of each other."

"But children that age aren't violent."

"What? Have you met any kids? One bit my skull once. My skull! I really did have to admire his dedication."

"But this shop is magical though, right?"

"No, not especially. You do know where we are, don't you?"

Its registered name was Pound Squeezer. Or if you wanted to give it its full, official title – presumably bestowed during the last Royal Jubilee – then it was Pound Squeezer: Many Discounted Hardware And Homeware Items Available Inside, the words proudly displayed in white on the red canopy outside the shop. But everyone in the local area called it the Pound Tardis. It was a tiny cluttered cut-price general store about the size of an average newsagents that somehow managed to stock absolutely everything there ever was in the world. In that respect, then, the word many on the canopy was either a touching display of humility or a winking mic drop – "yeah, we say many, but you know we mean every." Raised eyebrow, pivot to camera.

It was easy to see why Sam assumed the Pound Tardis was magical, because, really, that was the only sane explanation. No matter what you were looking for, they had it in stock, or could have it in stock, and would, on request. Even if you conducted a thorough search of the shelves, trawling through the polymers and plastics that made up the majority of the items on offer, and found that, this time, alas, what you wanted was nowhere to be found, all was not lost. The man at the front of the shop would call to the man at the back of the shop and he would lead you to your heart's desire, past the frying pans and plastic flowers and lava lamps, to a shelf that you could have sworn had, only moments previously, been crammed with air fresheners and nothing but air fresheners.

Where it all came from was a mystery.

Only now Sam was starting to piece it all together.

"You're something to do with this, aren't you?"

"Who me?" replied Takara, sweetly. "Whatever gave you that idea?"

"Well, the Pound Tardis has…"

"Oh, I do love it when people call the store that. Time and relative dimension in shopping. What a beautiful, perfect idea."

"Yes, well, it's always defied the laws of physics somehow, crammed an impossible amount of stuff into a space that was much too small for it, but we've been happy to go along with that, and turn a blind eye, I suppose. Because joking about it and calling the place the Pound Tardis is much easier than facing up to what exactly is going on here."

"And what is going on here?"

"Something fishy."

"Well, of course," nodded Takara. "There's something fishy going on everywhere. But, as you say, that's the problem – if you admit that something fishy is going on here, then you have to acknowledge all of the other fishy stuff too, and there's a myriad of debatable and dubious things going on all around. And if you have to face up to all the fishy stuff, then you're probably going to have to tackle all the fishy stuff. And that could be a very tricky undertaking. What happens if you clean up all the fishy stuff and everything else suddenly stops working?"

"No more discount egg slicers."

"Exactly. And nobody wants that."

Sam toyed with one of the orange and yellow tennis balls tethered for no discernible reason by a short length of orange and yellow rope to another orange and yellow tennis ball, wondering briefly what it was for.

"Anyway," he continued, "now I've seen your little store of precious things, by which I mean an infinite cave containing an infinite amount of everything, I feel a lot better about it all. I mean, it's all still impossible, but at least it's an impossible I understand."

"That's all anyone can ask for," said Takara, sagely. "At the end of the day, we're all just rubbing the impossible until it bursts."

Takara reached into her jacket and pulled out a pocket watch with tiny hourglasses instead of numbers. She consulted it and then nodded with satisfaction.

A commotion came from the front of the shop suddenly. The man at the front of the shop called to the man at the back of the shop. Only there was no man at the back of the shop, only Sam and Takara.

"Now, if you'll excuse me, it's time to go to work."

And she reached up and tapped the side of her glasses.

25

Takara made her way to the front of the Pound Tardis, sporting what was clearly the shop uniform of long brown coat and flat cap. Her hair was shorter, shaved close to the bone all the way up to the cap, and this time the gender switch had resulted in a thinner pencil moustache, the kind favoured by World War 2 Spitfire pilots in starched 1940s black and white dramas or wily spivs from class-busting capers made a decade later.

At the front of the shop, a shorter man with thick horn-rimmed glasses, also sporting a long brown coat and flat cap, was looking perturbed.

"Alright there, Balfour?" said Takara, a cocktail stick suddenly sticking from the side of her mouth. "Anything I can help with?"

"Yes, boss," replied Balfour. "It's these gentlemen. They're unhappy with their purchase."

Standing in a row at the shop counter were the four members of the black and white team. As before, they were identical in dress – unchanged in black trousers, black shoes, black roll neck jumpers, and white gloves – and, as before, they shared a collective look, this time of quizzical dissatisfaction, the look of someone trying to understand something they were incapable of being able to understand, a look that said simply: "Why did you do that?"

"Afternoon gents!" said Takara, cheerily. "What seems to be the problem?"

"We purchased this melodic receptacle here in an earlier time segment," said the third team member along. Their voice had a faint metallic echo, as if being broadcast from somewhere

where someone had forgotten to mute all the nearby devices. "We were assured by the Sales Operative that it would emit a 'pertinent' melody, but our research has called this judgement into question."

The third team member – we shall call them Number Three – proffered a brass music box for inspection.

"Oh yes, a magnificent piece, from our Travelling Companion range," said Takara, turning the music box over in her hands as she spoke. "A truly outstanding piece of craftsmanship at, may I say, a very reasonable price."

"We are not dissatisfied with the standard of manufacture of the receptacle."

"Then what's the beef, my good sir?"

"When functioning, the receptacle emits this melody…"

Number Three took the music box out of Takara's hands and set it in motion. The tinkling, unmistakable sounds of 'The Wheels On The Bus' began to play as a soothing lullaby.

"So beautiful, so pertinent!" cried Takara, overcome with performative emotion. "If, like me, you were born and bred on these very streets, you too would shed a tear at this rendition."

"These words are very similar to the ones used by the Sales Operative," said the second team member, henceforth Number Two.

Takara looked at Balfour, nodded, and gave him an approving thumbs up.

"And after consulting our local culture expert," continued Number Two, motioning along the line to the fourth team member, "we assigned these words as accurate."

If it was possible for a blank face to look sheepish, then Number Four was looking as sheepish as could be.

"My research indicated that the words of this composition would be of particular emotional resonance to the citizens of this locale," protested Number Four.

"How so?" replied Number Three.

"Due to a severe reduction in municipal transport services, some made by necessity as a cost cutting measure by local authorities dealing with ideological cuts made by a national government uninterested in a public transport system that itself does not use or require, and some as a result of staff shortages and petrol shortages due to an unfortunate combination of global upheaval and regional mismanagement, the concept of a bus in operation would naturally be a great cause of celebration, and indeed a poignant and pertinent sight in a time of ongoing uncertainty."

"Bravo!" cried Takara. "I couldn't have put it better myself!"

"Unfortunately, the men and women on the street did not share this assessment," said Number Two, their stoney face looking ever stonier. "We played the melody to a stratified sample of passers-by and their responses were far from positive."

"One informed me that I was 'a bleeding nutter'," said Number One.

"One said they were going to 'call the social' on me," added Number Three.

"Another opined that my future transport arrangements would involve an ambulance," said Number Four.

Takara rearranged her face into a sympathetic frown and pursed her lips in a show of solidarity.

"You're lucky if they even send an ambulance these days," she said.

Number Four nodded solemnly in agreement.

"Look," Takara continued, "I can see that you've had a difficult day and I don't want to contribute to your worries and woes, so why don't we swap this music box, which I think we all agree is perfectly serviceable and a fine example of affordable craftsmanship, for another which might better suit your particular needs. I believe this range features a selection of alternative tunes. Balfour, could you fetch a replacement for these fine people, please?"

"Yes boss."

Balfour disappeared into the bowels of the shop and reappeared moments later with three more brass music boxes.

Takara picked up the first and fiddled with the mechanism. The glorious sweeping melodrama of 'Wuthering Heights', rendered expertly in music box tinkles, floated up into the air.

Takara looked at the team, the team stared blankly back at her. She mouthed the opening line at them, with the first makings of expressive hand gestures.

The team looked at Number Four.

"I can detect no relevance to our quest in this composition," said Number Four, not wanting to make the same mistake twice.

Takara switched off the box.

"Yes, you're probably right. OK, then, how about this one?"

This time 'Let's Face The Music And Dance' drifted off into the ether.

Takara started to sing the first verse but then looked at Sam, who was standing beside Balfour, and abruptly turned the music box off.

"No, that one doesn't work!" she declared briskly. She picked up the box and passed it to Sam, who had learned enough about Takara's character in the time they'd spent together to know exactly what was expected of him. He slipped the box into the bottomless bag and then held the bag behind him, firmly out of sight.

"Third time lucky!" beamed Takara, setting the last music box in motion.

The mournful yet triumphant, heartbreaking but ecstatic, tear-sodden yet world-beating, all-time, first class, show-stopping, barn-storming melody of 'The Winner Takes It All' emerged from the box, somehow made to sound even more poetic and, dare one whisper the word, pertinent, by being gifted to the world via the medium of music box tinkles.

Takara's eyes widened with elation, well-honed by years of salesmanship.

"Listen!" she said, her voice hushed with excitement.

The team listened, blank faces rigid with concentration.

"I am not familiar with this composition," said Number Three. "Nor I," added Number Two, to metallic murmurs of agreement.

Takara saw her opportunity and pounced.

"This song, my friends, is called 'The Winner Takes It All'." She paused for emphasis. "The winner. Takes it all." She paused again, allowing the song title to be absorbed by the team. "I don't know what you're up to, but if you're taking part in some sort of competition, then I ask you – is there anything more pertinent in the world than being the winner? And not just the winner, dear friends, but the winner who takes it all!"

Four blank faces processed this latest piece of information.

Sam wondered at which point salesmanship pushed it too far. And how did you know when to stop?

Number Three came to a decision.

"This replacement is acceptable. Ready the cloth container."

Number Four brought out a bag that looked very similar to the bottomless bag, only it was emerald green instead of blue. The gold embroidery glistened under the fluorescent strip lighting of the Pound Tardis.

"It is ready."

Number Four opened the bag and placed the music box carefully inside.

Takara's eyes widened once again

"We will conduct further testing on the replacement timepiece," said Number Three, "and, if necessary, return once more."

"And should an ambulance be required, we will be sure to make an exact record of its response time," added Number Four, helpfully.

Takara nodded, keeping her mouth shut. Something about the way she held herself reminded Sam of her reaction to The Duke.

Balfour raised a solitary hand to the departing team.

"Cheerio then."

26

"Shut the shop!"

As soon as the team were out of sight, Takara gave in to a state of high agitation.

"Balfour! Shut the shop now!"

"No boss, we can't!"

Balfour's voice cracked with distress.

"Pull down the shutters! Shut off the till! Turn off the lights! And do it now!"

"No boss! It's not ten o'clock yet. We can't shut the shop! You know we can't!"

Takara stopped in her tracks and stared at Balfour.

"You know we can't shut before ten, boss. There's too much at risk. What if someone needs something? When darkness falls and the moon comes up. That's when it all starts to happen. We can't shut, we can't!"

Takara kept Balfour's gaze, breathing in and out heavily.

"Damn! Damn damn it!" said Takara, her cheeks flushed with frustration. "OK, don't shut the shop. But you're going to have to keep your eyes open. We're in trouble."

"What's the matter?" asked Sam

Takara took a few moments, her breathing slowly coming under control, a look of purpose and determination coalescing in her eyes.

"It's the bag," she said. "The green bag. I thought it had to be a bottomless bag like the one we have, but when that person opened it, I saw right into it. And I saw something I never thought I'd ever see in my life. I saw the bottom of the bag."

"You've flown into a blind panic because you saw the bottom of a bag?"

"Not just the bottom of any bag, you numbskull. The bottom of a bottomless bag. And that's impossible. Everyone knows you can't see the bottom of a bottomless bag, that's the entire point. And if I saw the bottom, then that can only mean one thing – they're winning!"

"What, the team? They're winning the competition?"

"No, not the stupid bloody competition! I mean, *them*! You know, *them*! The Big Heavy and the Heavy Heavy and the creep that they work for. *The bad men*! What other explanation is there?"

"Well, it could always be a dud."

"What?" said Takara, with the irritation of someone trying to bat away a particularly persistent fly.

"You bought the pixies ears from the same stall where we got the bottomless bag and you thought they were genuine. Turned out they were duds. Maybe the same thing happened with the green bag."

Takara stared at Sam with disbelief bordering on horror.

"My god, you're right! How is that possible? OK, Balfour don't shut the shop. But you still need to keep your eyes open. We still have a big problem."

"We do?"

"I didn't just see the bottom of the bag. I saw a jumble of things in there. A bunch of posies tied up with old thread. A great big handful of dust, maybe two handfuls worth. A strip of black velvet with a purple and yellow raffle ticket sellotaped to it. And one of our keys."

"No boss, that can't be right."

Now it was Balfour's turn to sound panicked.

"It was. You know what they're like. They're unmistakable."

Balfour made a small, strained sound, like air escaping from a high pressure environment.

"How did they get one of our keys?"

"I don't know, but they had one."

"Was it green as well?" asked Sam. "Maybe they thought it was the emerald key we have to find for the competition."

"No, I wish it was," said Takara, grimly. "Our keys aren't quite as straightforward. They are at once all the colours and no colours at all. Depending on which angle you look at one, or with which eyes you use to look at it, you will see either a beautiful, endless, rippling kaleidoscope of colour or no colour at all, not even black. This means they are both a spectacular work of art and also very discreet."

"I did what I could," said Balfour, bashfully.

"The keys are our little contribution to the high street," said Takara. "They give certain, select individuals, representatives of businesses that we feel contribute positively to the community, access to the tunnels. Which they are then free to use as they see fit."

"You know the old public toilets in the side street by the cemetery?" said Balfour. "The ones that have been shut up for ages. That's the entry point."

Sam knew the toilets well. Everyone did.

At one point in the last decade, a local entrepreneur decided it would be fun to convert them into a wine bar, a quirky bijou place where the newly arrived could marvel at the offbeat setting and raise a toast to the massed forces of gentrification. Intrigued by the prospect, Sam went along on the opening night, only to find that the entrepreneur had kept the original row of urinals and placed the tables and chairs beside them. Sam spent the rest of the evening in a state of mild shock.

The wine bar closed for good not long after the opening night.

"Each team leader of the competition gets a purple temporary key which allows them to use the entry point," continued Takara. "So there's no need for them to have one of our keys."

"They must have just found it," said Balfour.

"Yes. But whose key have they found? And how?"

Sam's mind flicked back to the contents of the green bag.

"You said there was a strip of black velvet in the bag as well. Could that have been the blindfold? That's on the list too."

"Ah, that's what it was! I'd totally forgotten about that. Yes, that would have been the black velvet blindfold alright. Our friends have been busy. That's three items they have already. The posies, the dust and the blindfold."

"Four," said Sam. "You forgot the music box."

Takara and Balfour burst out laughing. It was precisely what they both needed – the air pressure rushing out of Balfour, the last remnants of Takara's high agitation being swept away by the moment.

"But it played the song!" said Sam. "'The Winner Takes It All'. What could be more pertinent than that? You said so yourself."

Takara looked at her trusted right hand man.

"Balfour?"

"Written in the key of G-flat major, 'The Winner Takes It All' tells the heartbreaking story of a relationship breakdown from the perspective of the loser in love, the person who has been abandoned for someone else, the divorcee rather than the divorcer. The first line of the chorus is not, as some might assume, a triumphant declaration of victory, but there to serve as sharp relief to the subsequent line about the loser, and it's this contrast that gives the song its powerful bittersweet sting. Thus the song is not about winning at all, despite any indication given by the title, but in actual fact about losing. And so if the melody emitted by the music box were to carry any pertinence, it would only do so to someone who was facing defeat."

"So you sold them a dud," said Sam. "Another one to go along with the bag."

Takara shrugged.

"It's not my fault they don't know anything about music."

"But they knew enough, though, didn't they? Enough to come into possession of one of your precious keys. Enough to find the velvet blindfold."

"Yes," said Takara. "And not just a blindfold, but a blindfold with a raffle ticket taped to it. A very interesting looking raffle ticket. A very distinctive looking raffle ticket. The kind of raffle ticket that a raffle ticket expert would be able to identify immediately. And luckily for us, I can think of just the person to ask."

Takara started walking towards the back of the shop.

"Eyes peeled, Balfour!"

"Sure thing, boss."

27

"Forty-six, forty-five, forty-four…"

The cavern of precious things came into focus with less fuss this time around, as if the squares of colour remembered how to melt into each other from before.

Harrington opened his mouth to speak but Takara raised her hand to silence him and strode purposefully towards the row of wooden crates. They were vast and endless, piled high on the Y axis and stretched out to the horizon on the X, some branded with logos and heraldic designs, others plastered with bold, threatening lettering – EXPLOSIVES, FROGS, AVALANCHES.

Set slightly apart from the other crates stood an ominous pitch-black cube, shiny yet impenetrable, like a carrying case for the night sky. While the rest of the crates were piled on top and alongside each other with the kind of chaotic thoughtlessness that secretly rules all warehouses, the black cube touched nothing else and nothing else touched the black cube, the other crates quite rightly keeping their distance.

A banging sound emanated from the black cube.

Also shouting.

"I said let us out!" shouted the shouting. "This is an outrage! Let us out this instant! Do you hear me? Let us out!"

At least that's what it sounded like inside the black cube. Outside, muffled by the dense material that made up the cube, a material only found by those hardy adventurers who dug deep down into the periodic table to the murky underworld beneath recorded science, it sounded more like someone with woollen hiking socks stuffed in their mouth yelling into a slab of cotton wool.

"Brrrghhh bhhhhggg hrrrhhdddd," muffled the muffling.

It had been going on for some time.

Takara faced the cube and drew herself up to her full height.

"Exhale! Exhume! Ex..." She paused. "What was the third one again, Harrington?"

"Exhibitate, boss. But..."

"Exhibitate? Is that even a word?"

"Well, no, boss, but that was the point. First time we tried to set the password, it said it wasn't strong enough. The only way we could make the cube happy was to make a word up."

"Oh yes, so we did. OK then – exhale, exhume..."

"But it doesn't matter anyway, boss, because the password function's broken. It hasn't been working since that business with The Portal."

"Oh god, The Portal," groaned Takara. "Most of the time, I love throwing open unexpected, ominous doors. The enchanting things that emerge! Dragons and dinosaurs and beasts from the depths, oh my! I love nothing more than coming face to face with a prehistoric sea monster empowered by nuclear radiation or an eight-headed aberration from the fiery underworld! The drama, the spectacle, there really is nothing to beat it. But The Portal..."

Takara's shoulders dropped at the memory of it all.

"You were only young, boss. You really weren't to blame."

"That's kind of you to say," said Takara, smiling at Harrington for a moment. "We learnt a lot that day. And we lost a lot that day too. And now it seems some valuable property was damaged as well. Which is inconvenient. How am I meant to open the cube if the biometrics are buggered?"

"The old-fashioned way, boss," said Harrington, throwing a key fob over to Takara, who caught it deftly with her right hand.

"How quaint!" said Takara, looking at the key fob with delight. "I love this. Why did we ever give it up?"

She pressed a button on the key fob and a light at each

corner of the cube flashed twice, each flash accompanied by a profoundly electronic beep.

Takara beamed at the cube, overcome with retro futurist nostalgia.

The front face of the cube slowly swung forward, forming a drawbridge into the darkness within.

The darkness was absolute, pure, complete.

There were no chinks of light, no shades of grey. It was black as black could be. One hash tag, six zeroes.

The darkness was throbbing, as if it were occupied.

Throbbing as if the pressure within was building to bursting point.

And then, stumbling from the darkness, emerging into the light, came two pallid humanoid figures, their skin drained of vitality, their eyes dazzled by the brightness of the outside world. Two subterraneans set free at last, two troglodytes on the hunt for revenge.

"Finally! What in the blazes do you think you've been doing? Who is in charge here? I demand an explanation!"

Still brandishing her walking stick-cum-totem pole, still clad in her vibrant yellow hiking jacket, still deeply dissatisfied with everything and everyone and everywhere, Pat gazed around the room, half-blinded by the sudden rush of light. She looked like you'd imagine someone who'd been wrongfully detained for a very long time in a cube of pure darkness to look – shell-shocked and furious.

A few steps behind her, also still clad in his matching yellow hiking jacket, looking significantly more drained than his companion, Gerald sported an expression of simple relief – he wasn't entirely sure what had happened to him back there, but he did know one thing. That, inexplicably, unexpectedly, thankfully, praise be, it was over.

"I said who is in…" Pat's gaze managed to make sense of a small section of what was being presented to her. "What the devil? What are *you* doing here?"

Sam smiled nervously and raised a tentative hand of greeting.

"Oh, er, hi Pat, hi Gerald."

A broad grin spread across Takara's face.

"Oh dear," she said, with a mixture of glee and incredulity. "Are these friends of yours, Sam?"

"Certainly not!" thundered Pam.

"Not really, more colleagues I suppose," said Sam. "We're in a team together. Pat is the team leader."

Takara's grin grew broader.

"The team leader? Oh deary me. This gets better and better."

Pat looked like she was about to explode.

"If you're the team leader, then you will have been given one of the temporary keys," said Takara. "Chiefly for access in and out of the tunnels, but they also have some miscellaneous uses. Did they run through those with you, by any chance?"

"Temporary key?" asked Gerald, the overcast clouds of a frown starting to gather on his brow.

"Yes, small purple thing," beamed Takara. "Nice and brightly coloured. Meant to be easy to find and difficult to lose. That's the theory anyway, but you would not believe how often we have to replace them. That's why Pat here would have paid a deposit."

"Pat?" asked Gerald.

"A few pounds, it was nothing," she replied.

"Well, if you'd have taken the time to look around inside the cube, which I do appreciate is fairly difficult as the darkness really is immaculate, then, after an extended period of trial and error, you would have, well might have, found a small purple keyhole. We colour code these things to make them more user-friendly. And then you could have let yourself out."

"Hang on, I said I thought I saw something purple…"

"Do be quiet, Gerald!"

"That's what you said then, as well. You said my mind was

playing tricks on me. And then you went back to shouting and banging on the wall."

Pat wasn't standing for it.

"Your mind was playing tricks on you," she stated firmly. "And this person here is playing tricks on us as well. And as for Sam, he was clearly added to our team as a hostile agent. This has all been a monumental act of sabotage."

"What? That's not true!" protested Sam. "Whatever mess you've gotten yourself into is absolutely nothing to do with me. I've had plenty of problems of my own to contend with. The sights I've seen with Takara have been enough to..."

"*Takara??*" interrupted Pat.

Both Pat and Gerald looked as if a bolt of lightning had been rerouted through their spinal cord.

Takara gave a curtsy and a small wave, 20% gracious, 80% smug.

"At your eternal service," she smirked.

"Well, that explains everything!" stormed Pat. "I thought that ending up in the cube was simply a stroke of rotten luck, but I can see it now for what it really was. A trap! A dirty, malicious trap set by a dirty, malicious fiend!"

Sam turned to look at Takara.

"What are they talking about, Takara?"

Takara shrugged.

"Search me."

Sam turned back towards Pat and Gerald.

"I'm afraid we've heard the name Takara before," said Gerald, with a sigh. "Every game has a rogue element, what you might call an impish foe or a wayward adversary. They're included to make what would otherwise be a straightforward treasure hunt just that bit more demanding. Sometimes they're chaotic sprites, who take pleasure in upsetting apple carts and spooking livestock, while others are more mean-spirited, dedicating their lives to actively thwarting our plans and destroying our chances."

Sam looked at Takara, thinking about the dud music box that she'd given the black and white team.

"We're given the name of the adversary in advance and a danger rating, and in this game, its name is Takara."

"A rating?" leapt in Takara. "Out of how many? What did I get?"

"Nine out of ten."

"Nine! I've never been so insulted in my life! I don't get out of bed for anything less than a ten, and not even then sometimes."

Sam looked dumbfounded. "So you're a bad guy? Like some kind of villain?" he said slowly.

"No! Of course not!" cried Takara. "Yes, I'll admit I do enjoy a bit of chaos, and it's always amusing and exciting when things go wrong for other people, and I have always admired those Lords Of Misrule guys, because they really do seem like they're having the greatest time ever, and I do have a short attention span and I am easily bored, but I assure you, I am not a villain. I don't go out of my way to mess things up for anybody. I simply don't have the time. Sure, my actions may have certain consequences, but none of it is personal, I promise you. I like to think of myself as more of a hazard than a bad guy."

"Like a windmill on a crazy golf course."

"Exactly! I knew you'd get it. The windmill doesn't dart around trying to get in the way of the ball. It just gets on with what it's doing, turning its sails in the sea breeze, and if a ball whacks into it, then that's the ball's fault, not the windmill's."

"A likely story!" raged Pat.

"No, it's true. Listen, when they said they were going to hold this leg of the game in the tunnels, I was like 'OK, well if you must, but I'm warning you now that I'm not going to be changing my business practices for anyone or anything, so your competitors are going to have find a way to work around me, understand? I am running an important operation here, and we have various safety measures in place to protect our interests, and it's not going to be my lookout if anyone falls foul of those safety measures'. Did it mention any of that in your precious player's handbook?"

"No. Just Takara, 9 out of 10."

"Damn, that still hurts!" mugged Takara. "Look, I'm sorry you ended up in the cube, but it truly wasn't my fault. Let me guess what happened. You were in the octagonal room with the stained glass windows, right?"

"Yes, that's right," said Pat, cautiously.

"And one of you decided to stand on one of the brighter circles of light, yes? The yellow perhaps or the red?"

"That was me," nodded Pat. "I chose the yellow."

"Quite right too. Who in their right mind would stand on a black circle of light? You'd have to have a wobbly hinge. But then someone else noticed something in the stained glass window, didn't they?"

"The church was on fire," said Gerald, forlornly. "It's the House Of God. It needed to be saved."

"And the only way to do that was to grab your team leader's hand and step into the darkness, oui?"

Pat's face began to redden again.

"I don't know what came over me," said Gerald.

"Mind-control, simple as. We've got a very sophisticated surveillance system in place in that room and if it detects that your intentions aren't good or that your heart isn't pure, then it'll compel you to step on the black circle and lock you up in the cube for safe keeping. It's a very efficient system. Too efficient, in fact. I've been caught by it myself several times."

"But we're just here for the contest," said Pat. "Our intentions are pure."

"Gerald?"

Gerald chewed his lip for a moment.

"Well, I've always thought if I could pick up the odd trinket for myself along the way, well, you know, in the grand scheme of things, what's the harm?"

"Gahhhh!!!"

"So there you have it," said Takara. "It wasn't me, guv, it was the system. It's always the system."

"A system set up by you."

"It is, I agree, a fine line," nodded Takara. "But the point is that I am not actively trying to disrupt your efforts in this noble contest. In fact, if anything, I'm doing my best to help you. Ask Sam. Who picked up the red pens in the Costa? Who remembered to get the grave dust in the graveyard? Who stashed away the music box that plays the correct and only pertinent tune? As I said when we first locked eyes upon each other, I am Takara, your eternal servant."

"Is this true, Sam?"

Sam nodded. "All the stuff's in the blue bag."

"Well, that's something at least," said Pat reluctantly. "But this could all still be a devious trick. Why would you possibly want to help us?"

"Because of the book," said Sam.

"Yes, The Book Of The Dead," said Takara. "Once in my possession, then foolishly misplaced, now on your list of items to track down. I borrowed The Book Of The Dead from a very important and unforgiving person and need to return the book with some urgency, so Sam's right, there's my motive."

"I still don't trust you," said Pat.

"And so you shouldn't. But do we have a deal? I help you track down the bits and bobs for the contest and play an important part in you winning the cup or whatever it is you get given when you triumph, and I get to keep the book and return it to He Who Really Should Not Be Displeased For Any Longer Than Strictly Necessary. It's a win-win situation, right? Good for everybody!"

Everyone looked at Pat.

Pat ground her teeth for a minute or so and then looked at Gerald. Gerald nodded.

"OK then," she said.

"Great!" said Takara, giving a familiar little clap. "Now we have to go and see a man about a raffle ticket."

28

Before they went back into the octagonal room, Takara talked Sam and Pat and Gerald through the steps needed to get past the surveillance system.

"Ultimately, it's super simple," she said. "Just be pure of heart. Easy peasy, pudding and pie. I suspect Sam will be able to pull this off with no effort whatsoever. But just in case there's the tiniest shadow of a dark thought lurking in your subconscious, a smidgeon of temptation or a soupcon of self-indulgence, then you can beat the system with the password. This is a word hand-picked by our crack squad of experts – Harrington and Balfour working together, the dreamiest of teams! – which, when recited continuously in your mind, will ward off the unwanted attentions of the brain scanner or whatever it is that gives this contraption its powers."

"Don't you know how it works?" said Sam.

"Well, I paid for the thing and told the guys what I wanted it to do, and there was some sort of explanation, but you can't expect me to listen to that kind of stuff. All I need to know is that there's a new password every month that lets you sneak past undetected. And the word this month is…"

"Xylophones," said Harrington.

"Perfect!" beamed Takara. "Who doesn't love a xylophone?"

And so Takara and Sam and Pat and Gerald inched through the octagonal room, their brows furrowed in concentration.

"Xylophones xylophones xylophones," thought Takara.

"Xylophones xylophones xylophones," thought Gerald.

"I wonder if I really am pure of heart?" thought Sam

Pat scowled and followed the others with a look of stubborn defiance.

"Xylophones xylophones xylophones," she thought secretly.

Eventually, they found themselves back where the passage gave way to the tunnel.

Sitting on the now closed aluminium box, Jonno was resolutely mid-lunch, a half-eaten sandwich in his hand, the lid of his flask full of a murky brown liquid that in a hitherto undiscovered dimension might have passed for tea. He glanced up with a look of pursed consternation. He wasn't ready to be disturbed yet. Here was a man who was still on his break.

He ran his eyes slowly from Pat to Gerald to Sam.

"That was quick."

Then his eyes continued onto Takara.

"Oh no."

Takara flashed a broad, wicked grin.

"Oh yes, Jonno! Oh yes! Of all the aluminium boxes in all the dank tunnels of the world, you had to sit on mine."

"This can't be your box," shot back Jonno. "It isn't anywhere near slippery enough."

"Huh! Maybe it is slippery and you're fighting against it? Doing your best to stay on the box because you can't bear to tumble off? Perhaps it's time for you to admit just how obsessed with the box you really are."

"Go to hell, Takara."

"Been and gone already, thank you very much. Didn't you get my postcard? 'Boiling in eternal hellfire – wish you were here!'"

Jonno turned pointedly towards the tunnel wall and resumed eating his sandwich.

"Still got the flask you bought me, I see."

Sam looked at the flask. Its original design was cracked and faded, but he could still make out an intricate pattern made up of thick vines and startled faces, like a beanstalk weaving its way between figures caught frozen in a moment in time.

It reminded Sam of a sculpture park he'd visited once when he was younger, set on the outskirts of Oslo, a short walk through the rich browns and oranges of an autumn woodland.

He'd hummed "Norwegian Wood" to himself as he strolled through the woodland, enjoying the sensation of somehow living inside a song, but he soon fell silent when the forest gave way to a flat expanse of green dotted with statues depicting all forms and stages of the human experience.

He made his way around the park quietly and carefully, as if he didn't want to disturb the statues or upset the petrified scenes. Families embracing. Lovers quarrelling. A woman dancing. A man attacked by babies. Enemies wrestling (or were they dancing too?). A lone child set apart from the others, crying its eyes out. And in the centre of the park was a foreboding monolith, like a stone spoke in the middle of a verdant wheel, made of hundreds of sculpted bodies piled on top of each other, a mass of humanity compacted into a granite cylinder for all of eternity. It was supposed to make a statement about the journey of life, but Sam thought it looked like a vision of hell. Here is where you go to pay for your misdeeds – in a sausage of stone bodies, faces jammed against torsos, for as long as the elements would allow it.

"What is that?" frowned Sam, peering at the design on the flask.

"Isn't it great?" cried Takara. "So full of joy! So full of darkness! Like a beautiful forest at the end of the world! Jonno bought me that flask for Christmas once, but then he started using it and then it became his flask. Not my flask at all. What do you think of that? Is that any way to treat someone you..."

"Shut up, Takara!" growled Jonno. "You didn't deserve the flask anyway."

He resumed his pointed consumption of his tea-like beverage.

"I did deserve it, and you know it," said Takara. "But you took it from me. You swiped it. You spirited it away. And we both know why you took it. Because owning the flask is the only way you could possibly stay close to me."

"Ha! You didn't want the flask! You never used it. You said 'why do I need a flask when I own all of the beautiful things in the world, including a cathedral, a national park, a beanstalk, a clay army, and assorted monoliths, megaliths and ancient stone circles?'"

"Sorry? What?" Sam wasn't sure he was hearing things correctly. "You own a beanstalk?"

"Yes! Isn't it wonderful?" said Takara, with delight. "It's in the cave of precious things. I'll get Harrington to show it to you when we're next in there."

"But that's impossible."

"I know!"

Jonno poured the last trickle of the brown liquid onto the tunnel floor and then screwed the lid carefully back onto the flask.

"I saw that you were the assigned menace for this game, but I was hoping we'd be able to avoid you," he said. "More fool me."

"Avoid me? Avoid me? Why would you want to do that? If you really wanted to avoid me, you would have kept well away from the tunnels. Not sneaked onto a random team at the last minute in what could only be termed suspicious circumstances. I don't think you want to avoid me. I think you came in here looking for me."

"And why would I ever want to do that?"

"Because I'm so much fun! And you can't get enough. And because even now, after all the things you've been through, I'm still able to surprise you."

Takara took out a purple and yellow raffle ticket and waved it seductively in front of Jonno's face.

"Where did you get that?" Jonno asked, his interest piqued, despite everything.

"Yes," chimed in Sam. "Where did you get that?"

For a second, Takara seemed uncharacteristically stumped.

"Well, I…I…made it," she conceded, with a sigh. "Or rather I got Harrington to make it. To my precise specifications, based on my expert eyewitness account. But it's not where

I got it or how it came to be that's important. It's what it represents."

"Which is?" said Jonno.

"It's a doorway. It's a doorway to the next chapter in our fantastic journey. It's a doorway into another time and another dimension. And only one person can lead us through that doorway, Jonno, and that person is you. Because you're the only person who could be boring enough to be able to recognise the design of a raffle ticket and tell us where it came from. Others may fall asleep in your presence, others may slip into a coma as soon as an utterance tumbles from your lips, but not me. I kneel before the altar of your encyclopaedic knowledge of useless stuff and give thanks for the bounteous info we are about to receive."

"Really, I know you said you've just been, but go to hell, Takara, and once you get there, stay there."

"And miss out on all the excitement here? No fear!"

Sam turned the raffle ticket over in his hand.

"It's for the game," he said. "Takara managed to see which items the black and white team had gathered so far and she saw a ticket like this taped to the velvet blindfold. What I don't understand is how that helps us. If they've already got the blindfold, aren't we better off looking for something else?"

"No because…" started Gerald.

"I'll handle this, thank you Gerald," interrupted Pat, stepping forward a pace. "When you've taken part in as many contests as I have, you've heard all of the questions, and you do know all of the answers."

"But it's…"

"Now I can remember a time, young Sam, when I thought the same way as you did," continued Pat, puffing herself up as she spoke. "If this is a treasure hunt, then it must be a race to get to the treasure first. And yes it is. And no it isn't. Because even though the other team have the blindfold, that doesn't mean there won't be another one waiting for us exactly where they found it. Don't ask me how it works..."

"Or me," chipped in Takara.

"But a few seconds after you've picked up any item, another exact copy appears in its place, ready to be claimed by the next team that comes along. I believe the idea is to make the competition fair somehow, so that everyone has the same chance of finding each item. If they didn't reappear, every contest would descend into an awful chaotic mess where the teams would be trying to steal the items from each other, and it would inevitably end up in a huge fight, bloody and bitter and needless."

"Oooh, I like the sound of that!" said Takara. "I must speak to the powers that be about changing the rules."

"So knowing where a rival team found an item is in fact very useful," continued Pat. "It would give us a chance to go to the same location, pick up said item, and then hurry on to claim the next object on the list while the other teams are hopefully tangled up in an inconvenient and unexpected predicament."

"Like being trapped in a Stygian cube," said Takara, helpfully.

Pat glared at Takara for a moment.

"But then why didn't we do that when we heard the other team cheering at the start of the hunt?" asked Sam. "It sounded like they'd found something straight away."

"Professional pride," said Pat, in a tone which suggested that professional pride had a lot to answer for.

Takara nodded with approval.

"Beautifully put," she said, with a smirk. "Which just leaves the question – is Jonno really boring enough..."

"Hey!"

"...to know where this raffle ticket has come from?"

Everyone turned to look at Jonno.

Jonno sighed and got slowly to his feet.

"Come on then."

Takara clicked her heels with glee.

"I knew it!"

29

The ticket came from the theatre bar.

Jonno had recognised the distinctive purple and yellow design straight away, apparently, and as the party walked along the tunnel in the direction of the graveyard, he went on to give a detailed talk on the history of the raffle ticket, which no one particularly listened to.

This was a shame, because it really was very interesting. Did you know the origin of the humble raffle can be traced back to the ancient Babylonians? Jonno did, and he expounded on this subject for quite some time.

The theatre bar was a strange place, even by the standards of the local area.

The theatre itself was originally built as a fire station in the 19th century in the gothic revival style. It was grandiose and formidable, a sturdy four-storey building adorned with rows of windows topped with twisted pointed arches, like lines of disapproving eyes set in a sea of spikes.

At ground level, two giant red doors sat under their own imposing limestone arches, a once grand architectural feature which had cracked and grown discoloured over the years. The doors were tall but narrow and had originally been designed to accommodate the horse-drawn carriages that were in service in the Victorian era. The building as a whole had the air of a mill or a workhouse, a grave edifice built for industry, and rising high above it all was a watchtower that looked more like a chimney, ready to belch smog and dirt into the pea soupers of the day.

This was not a kind or a dutiful structure, and its forbidding air was amplified by the gnarled flourishes of the gothic architecture. If you were to discover that the fire station had somehow pushed its way up to the surface from the blazing depths below, then you wouldn't have been too surprised. If there was ever a place to believe in the unforgiving fury of the Old Testament, then this was it.

When progress brought the advent of the fire engine, the doors of the fire station proved too narrow, and so the station was abandoned. It lay empty for decades, through the turmoil of the Great War and the firestorms of the Second World War, which caused unfriendly bombs to rain down on the electronics factory a few hundred yards from the station. And during that time, the empty, untouched building, once a display of power and status in a bygone era, became shrouded in a brooding air, like it was sulking.

The fire station was converted into a theatre in the early 1970s, by a group of ragged evangelicals so caught up in the excitement of the liberal arts that they totally failed to notice that the building didn't want them there.

The rooms that once housed the horse-drawn carriages were converted into a performance area with a proscenium arch and a gently raked stage. The arch was decorated with gold gilt and surrounded by red drapes, giving the space a rather high and mighty tone, much to the displeasure of the gothic building that was hulking around it. If it had previously been sulking, now it felt queasy, as if it'd eaten something rich that was disagreeing with it.

It wasn't long before accidents started to happen. Pieces of scenery crashed unexpectedly to the ground during rehearsals. Light fittings shattered without warning, sending shards of glass flying in all directions. Actors found that the raked stage would sometimes be rather more raked than they remembered, causing them to lose their balance and tumble to the ground mid-soliloquy.

Unperturbed, the company soldiered on with the conversion, turning their attention to the all-important matter of the theatre bar. To begin with, this was to be set in the floor above the main hall, with small windows looking out over the auditorium, like spyholes or arrowslits. The players would be able to observe the audiences as they were taking their seats and determine whether they were truly worthy of that evening's entertainment – and their patrons could delight in what was sure to be yet another widely acclaimed triumph in the utmost of privacy.

Work was just about to begin on the transformation of the second floor when a stagehand opened a previously untouched door backstage and discovered a staircase leading downwards.

Judging by the deep crust of dirt on the stairs and the thick, mottled cobwebs that span across the width of the staircase, no one had ventured this way for quite some time – years, possibly decades. The air had a dank, stale feel to it, and even though the torches in the actors' hands were battery operated, they shone dimly, struggling to cut through the fog of accumulated gloom.

Eventually the company, with the brave stagehand pushed to the front, reached another door at the bottom of the staircase.

The door creaked open to reveal a large circular room.

A layer of faintly luminous silver dust lay over the tables and chairs arranged in the centre of the room. A few glasses were scattered across the tables - some wine glasses, some cocktail glasses, some tall thin glasses that looked almost medicinal in purpose – all empty, but with the sense that they'd once contained liquid of some sort, but it had long since evaporated. Around the curve of the back wall was a wooden bar, dotted with brass beer pumps that had turned green with age, and framed by shelves of glassware and bottles clouded by mould. To the left of the bar was a modest cloakroom area, and on the wall opposite the cloakroom lay a small stage, empty save for a single high-backed chair.

Daguerreotype photographs of dignitaries and performers circled the rest of the room, their faces peering out of the darkness like eternal witnesses, forever caught in time.

And under each photograph was a small brass plaque bearing a name, the list of names reading like the members of a secret society – The Nightstalker, Dame Rosina Vestris, Mortimer Mimms, Countess Brigida, Sir Augustus Henry, Flora Strange, The Masked Marksman, Hector Hugh Munro, Eleanor Lockhart, The Grey Clown, Matilda Cuvering, The Marchioness, The Illusioneer, E.F. Valentino, The Human Fly, and Horatio Egg, to name just a few.

The actors were dumbfounded at their discovery.

There was no record of a theatre standing on the site before the fire station. In fact, the old maps showed the area to be wasteland, a corner of the parish that had grown ragged with neglect. A convent and a church were the closest structures, but neither had any published affinity for the performing arts. And the fire station certainly wasn't the kind of place you'd have expected to secretly harbour exuberance and joy.

And yet here it was. A fully formed theatre bar, just as they were thinking of building one.

The moment the doors of the bar were thrown open, the accidents stopped. The pressure had been equalised, an equilibrium reached. The silver dust was brushed from every surface, the frames of the photographs were repaired and polished, and if anything unusual was noticed during the renovation – fingerprints appearing on the mahogany of the bar, the rattle of keys emanating from the solid walls – then they were not remarked upon.

The actors were slowly starting to understand how to live with the building they'd inherited.

A truce, of sorts, was called.

And so no one poked their noses into places they weren't welcome

And no one noticed the false panel at the back of the stage.

And no one found the second staircase leading downwards.

30

As Jonno led the party further along the tunnel, an air of disquiet fell upon Takara. She abandoned her usual penchant for chattering away about random nonsense, ridiculous notions, unlikely stories, herself, and the dizzying variety of Venn diagrams that encompassed all of the above in an unceasing manner of ways, and had adopted the manner of a teenager who'd been dragged to a particularly worthy museum against their will.

Sam fell into step alongside her.

"Is everything OK?", he whispered, taking care not to alert the others who were forging ever onwards.

Takara frowned.

"I thought this was going to be fun," she hissed under her breath. "But I didn't realise we were going to go *there.*"

A light flashed up ahead of them.

It kept steady at waist height and then wobbled a little before regaining its composure.

It started as a dot and then grew, slowly.

Steady, steady, wobble, steady, steady, steady.

"Stand aside everyone," commanded Pat, directing her teammates to the very edge of the tunnel.

A bicycle courier hove into view, with an outsized rectangular box strapped to their back, as if they were urgently transporting a fridge to a region of acute ice cream crisis.

The box was covered in a purple and black livery centred around a strident, triumphant capital K. It was a K of tree roots and lightning strikes, of sandstorms and sunspots, of flying clouds and infinite pleasure. Golden light crackled along its branches while the tips of the letter appeared to stretch out and then retract slightly, as if it were about to experience a sudden growth spurt or give birth to hundreds of tiny letter Ks, all as spectacular and unearthly as their parent.

In the wake of the box was a billowing purple and black cloud that had forks of golden electricity sparking through it. The cycle courier seemed to be trying as much to frantically outrun the cloud as make their destination in good time, although it was clear that the box and cloud were part of the same entity. Wherever the box was going, the cloud was going along with it.

Sam pressed himself against the side of the tunnel, hoping against hope that he could avoid being engulfed by the fumes and static. Pat had obviously encountered this hazard before and knew the best way to survive it. Sam tensed his body and held his breath hard.

The others, however, did precisely the opposite. After stepping politely out of the way of the courier, they puffed themselves out and appeared to present themselves to the cloud, their bodies stretching like the K itself, reaching out with as much surface area as humanly possible.

Wooosh!

The air turned purple and black.

The air inside their lungs turned purple and black.

Their hearts turned purple and black.

Their eyes turned purple and black.

Their minds turned purple and black.

Sam felt something immeasurable pass through him and pass through his system, through every cell and synapse, through every atom and membrane, through the levers and pulleys and arrays and indexes, through the in trays and out trays, through the arteries, veins and intestinal tubes, like he was a stretch of fibre optic glass wire transporting light and knowledge at maximum speed.

He felt exhilarated, illuminated, punch drunk and dizzy.

And it all smelt amazing.

Like, wow, what did you put in that?

As the courier reached level with Takara, they lifted their left hand from the handlebars and gave the briefest of salutes. Takara's eyes were too busy rolling back into the far reaches of her skull, her body too caught up in the overwhelming enormity of everything inside her going ping at the exact same time, to give any sort of meaningful response, but the courier didn't seem to mind. They had seen this happen many times before. They knew the score.

As the cloud dissipated, the golden sparks turning red in their final moments, the companions awoke from whatever individual coma they'd slipped into, and started to tidy themselves up and set everything back to how it had been only moments before. Pat patted down her yellow tunic and gathered up her walking stick. Gerald took out a handkerchief and dabbed his forehead, achieving very little in terms of personal grooming and hygiene, but his face radiated the serenity of a man who really did feel so much better. Jonno shook his head as if trying to dislodge some errant bees and then coughed three times. And Takara brushed some of the lingering grave dust from her suit and let out a low whistle.

"Phoo-wee. Gets you every time, huh?"

The smell lingered long after the cycle courier and the cloud had disappeared into the gloom of the tunnels. Sam's nose hairs tingled with ecstasy as the precious scent particles floated around him and he breathed in deeply through his nose as often as he could, almost as if he was trying to smell a memory.

"It's…it's…it's like smelling heaven," he stuttered in awe.

"Your first time?" asked Takara, smiling. "Lucky you. I'm jealous."

"What is it?"

"Paneer pasanda," replied Takara. "Cheese and cream joining forces for the good of the universe."

"Curry? That can't be right. I've had paneer before. It's never been anywhere near as mindblowing as that."

"That because it wasn't made using the illustrious K spice, a spice so swathed in mystery that no one knows where it originated, how it's made, or where to buy some from. Only Mr K knows, and he cut out his own tongue several years ago to prevent the secrets being beaten out of him by nefarious forces, and then just to be doubly sure, he underwent hypnosis to wipe the knowledge from his waking consciousness. He's only able to summon the spice if he goes into a particular type of trance, and he can only go into that trance if he's in a locked room by himself. Convenient, no? How much of this is the truth and how much of it is richly spun baloney, no one really knows, but then the wonders of the K spice are so overwhelmingly overwhelming that no one dares to question it all."

"I've never experienced anything like it," said Sam.

"Ah, but you have," smiled Takara. "Just for not as long as that. It's a common experience for most people, but it's generally over in a millionth of a microsecond. What the K spice does is magically stretch that millionth of a microsecond into a minute of ecstasy."

"If only we had a T spice that could magically shrink overblown speeches into pithy bullet points," huffed Jonno. He had been enjoying leading the party for once and didn't appreciate Takara snatching back the spotlight.

"Jonno's only grumpy because he's one of the few people for whom that common experience isn't common at all. In fact, it's barely an annual event."

Jonno smile-sneered at Takara and then turned to continue walking down the tunnel.

"The rumour is that even Mr K doesn't understand exactly how it works, but what the K spice does is infiltrate your entire system, from your lymph nodes and your bloodstream to your spine and your nervous system, and then once it's in complete control of everything, it sparks off a good idea in your brain. That feeling of wonderment you had when you were inside the cloud was actually the feeling of you having a good idea.

Normally it's over in a flash, but with the K spice at the helm, it's like sighing out paradise."

"But I didn't have an idea, good or bad. I don't remember anything like that. Just ooooo-eeeeee times a hundred."

"Yes, I know! Can you imagine how powerful the spice would be if you could remember the good idea? Can you picture the uses it would be put to? The wars it would cause, the bloodshed it would be responsible for, the greed that would chase it down? Oh yes, I'm sure everyone would cure cancer and all that in week one, but after all the good stuff has been taken care of, then what? 'Oooh, we could use it to make some money! That's a good idea!'"

"No, that's a bad idea."

"Depends on your perspective," said Takara. "Anyway, if you could somehow view the process from the outside, you'd see the moment the good idea flashes into existence inside your brain, it's accompanied by a spark of golden light. You probably saw some of the golden sparks as the cloud was approaching us. Then the K spice guides the golden spark out of your system into the open air where it crumbles in the face of reality, whereupon it turns red. Maybe you saw some of those guys too? And so the idea doesn't linger in your brain long enough for it to take hold. And – wooosh – the idea is gone!"

Takara gazed upwards along the tunnel at the slowly dwindling form of Jonno and sighed.

"And as the idea goes, so does the moment."

"Quite so," said Pat, rattling her walking stick. "Let's not get left behind."

31

Jonno came to a halt in front of a blank stretch of tunnel wall.

He slowly ran his eyes from the top left of the wall to the bottom right, moving in straight lines from left to right, mumbling sums as he went, and occasionally counting on his fingers. Eventually he seemed satisfied and rooted around in his canvas shoulder bag, finally pulling out a crimson pocketbook stuffed with folded sheets of yellowed parchment. He flicked through the book, still mumbling, before settling on what was obviously the right parchment for the job. He removed it from the book and unfolded it gingerly.

The parchment appeared to be both a blueprint and a star chart. There were lines and jagged dots forming a disjointed tessellated pattern, the gaps marked by archaic mechanical symbols and incomplete circles containing varying numbers of degrees. And in the background and yet also somehow overlaid on the pattern were scattered stars and planetary objects, the constellations and heavenly bodies positioned to flow through the blueprint like electricity.

It looked like the first draft of a new dawn. All it needed was someone to turn it on.

Jonno turned his gaze to Takara.

"Would you mind?"

Takara pursed her lips in disquiet.

"Must we? Really? Not for this."

"Come on, you know you enjoyed the hunting and gathering. Well, now it's time to put it all to use."

"Look, I love a heist as much as the next super villain." At the word "villain", Takara turned to look pointedly at Sam, Pat and Gerald. "And Syria is always a hoot. But using this precious, hard-won treasure to help us get into *there* seems like a bit of a waste."

"Just open the watch, Takara."

Takara pulled out a platinum pocket watch and flipped up the cover.

Like the watch decorated with moons and the watch decorated with hourglasses, this watch wasn't burdened by anything as commonplace as mere numbers. The centre of the face was consumed by a fluid, living image of an imploding star – a starburst of cosmic brilliance with the darkest of hearts - and the rim was a thick band of pulsing dots of energy. As the seconds flew by, dots of energy from the rim were pulled into the unforgiving core of the imploding star, and a single arm moved silently clockwise. It was the most beautiful and the most disturbing thing Sam had ever seen.

"We had to sneak past guards, shimmy down an ancient burial chimney, negotiate tripwires and poison darts and a silver scimitar that nearly sliced the top of your head clean off," said Takara, unblinkingly. "We had to cheat death, trip up death, run away from death, negotiate with death when he caught up with us, give death the slip, and lead death such a merry dance that he lost his bearings completely and fell into a dazed stupor. We had to vault crevasses, turn pirouettes on precipices, swim crocodile-infested rivers and dress up as package holiday tour guides, and you want us to use that priceless, irreplaceable, uncategorisable, unknowable, once-in-a-lifetime parchment on this?"

"It's multi-use, Takara. Stop being such a drama queen."

Jonno might as well have asked the universe, as represented by Takara's pocket watch, to stop collapsing in on itself.

Takara narrowed her eyes a pinch and pointed the watch towards the parchment. The clock hand continued its onward, endless journey, and the pulsing dots of energy continued to break off the rim and be pulled into the heart of the imploding star.

Jonno held out the parchment expectantly.

Takara's eyes narrowed a touch further.

"I told you this was..."

"Look!"

A dot of energy had broken from the rim but rather than being pulled towards the centre of the star, it had drifted out from the watch and was heading towards the parchment. Five pairs of eyes followed it as it voyaged through the empty space, a lone adventurer heading bravely into the cosmos. It reached the parchment and landed on one of the six stars that made up a central constellation, the moment of touchdown accompanied by an elegant burst of colour. The star switched on, glowing triumphantly.

The parchment began to thrum in anticipation, as another dot of energy began the pilgrimage from the watch.

Jonno maintained eye contact with Takara as the dots of energy slotted into the stars on the parchment.

"Get ready."

"I know!"

When the sixth dot of energy broke free from the watch, Takara snapped the cover shut, and she and Jonno breathed a heartfelt sigh of relief.

The sixth star burst into light and Jonno let go of the parchment, leaving it levitating in the air. He and Takara took a step backwards, and everyone else hurriedly took a step backwards a millisecond later.

There are moments in time that feel like destiny. Moments that feel like an ancient prophecy finally coming true, like thousands of years of narrative reaching the ultimate conclusion, like a giant, planet-sized tick being placed in a giant, planet-sized box. Moments of satisfaction and rightness, moments of everything being as they should be, seamlessly, perfectly.

Six beams of light shot from the six stars to six points on the tunnel wall. Four marked out the four corners of a door, one marked out a dot at waist level and one marked out a dot at eye level.

Under normal circumstances, Takara would have raised her hand like a magician unveiling a master trick, while Jonno would have shaken his head in exasperation. But Takara seemed too tense for her usual amateur dramatics. She stood stock still, eyeing the door warily.

"Do you want to do the honours?" said Jonno to Takara, with a smirk.

"Certainly not!"

Jonno turned to Sam, his smirk turning into a wider smile.

"Our new friend then."

Jonno stepped to one side, as if presenting the door to Sam.

"Welcome, Sam, to a very special doorway. Sought by many, found by…well, a surprisingly large amount actually. But only opened by a few choice souls. Some have the secret password. Others have…is there a key, Takara?"

"You bloody well know there's a key!"

"But brought to you today by the harmonious partnership of one of my favourites scrolls and a timepiece from Takara's uncustomary collection. All we have to do now is open it. As you can see, here are the four corners of the door. And here is the door handle and here is the door knocker. Now, what do you think we should do next?"

"What should we do? Or what would I do?"

Jonno nodded approvingly and glanced over at Takara.

"He understands more than he lets on, doesn't he?" Jonno turned his gaze back to Sam. "What would you do?"

"Well, I imagine the canny thing to do would be to try and open the door as quietly as possible, and sneak in without alerting our presence to whatever's in there waiting for us. There's clearly something unpleasant, as Takara seems to be having a nervous breakdown. But even though that's obviously the clever thing to do and the clever game-playing thing to do as well, I can't help think that it's better to be polite. So I would knock and see what happens."

"Be my guest."

Sam stepped up to the door and pulled back the circle of light representing the door knocker and rapped it on the door, three times, solemn and precise.

A bell tolled in the depths of hell.

A creature bellowed in the shadows.

An ill wind whipped through the tunnels, dispersing the last precious particles of the K spice.

And the door opened slowly inwards.

32

Pat stepped forward. She was still the team leader, despite all and any appearances to the contrary, so she was going to go first. Gerald went next. Where Pat goes, Gerald faithfully follows.

"After you," said Takara, generously ushering Sam and Jonno onwards.

"No chance," said Jonno. "I'm not having you absconding once my back is turned. You can be the sweetmeat in our adventuring feast. Nice and snug in the middle of the marching order. In you go."

Takara sucked her lips against her teeth and stepped in. Followed by Sam, and then Jonno, who closed the door carefully behind him.

Sam found himself at the foot of a staircase, although it was unlike any staircase he'd ever encountered or even imagined.

It was made of a vague blue-white light. At times, white with blue tinges, like the purity of all colours giving way to an icy halo. At others, blue with white tinges, like a perfect glassy sea slowly freezing over. It seemed indistinct yet vivid, both hard to take in and perfectly in focus. Right there, just out of reach. It curved gently upwards, hugging the stone of the tunnel on one side, a shimmering banister protecting the traveller on the other. It was a work of true beauty, and yet it felt to Sam like it was infecting the space rather than inhabiting it, like it really shouldn't be there.

Pat and Gerald were already a few steps above them and were progressing onwards. Takara had come to a halt before the first step.

"No. Sorry, but no."

Jonno placed the flat of his hand on Takara's back and pressed her forwards as he walked onto the staircase.

"Come on, Takara. You've faced far worse than this. Really, it's only a..."

"Don't say it!"

Sam gripped the banister and followed the others upwards. He could understand why Takara had been reluctant. Even though the treads of the staircase supported his weight easily, he couldn't feel them underfoot. There was no reassuring sense of solidity or stability, and the staircase's habit of phasing in and out of reality every so often made Sam feel empty inside. It was like walking on air, if walking on air was simply a confidence trick. Lose faith, his insecurities told him, and this will all come tumbling down.

"It's incredible," said Sam, in slightly terrified awe.

"It sure is," nodded Jonno, "This is the Spectral Staircase, and it's one of the wonders of the underworld."

"The Spectral Staircase! You mean it's a ghost?"

Takara flinched.

"Be careful with the g-word in front of our friend here, if you don't mind," smiled Jonno. "Takara has a complicated relationship with the not-fully-departed."

"Really? I thought she would have loved all of that stuff. Ghosts and rattling chains and hauntings and people being frightened out of their skin. She seemed to be perfectly happy with it in the catacombs, if I remember rightly."

Takara pursed her lips, sulkily.

"Oh, it's all showbiz in the catacombs," said Jonno. "And the graveyard. Especially the graveyard. You won't find any actual wraiths or phantoms there – just people dressed up as them. And, yes, I suppose she does love the theatre and the melodrama of people being scared of ghosts. It's just a bit ironic that she's scared of them as well."

"I am not scared of ghosts!" spat Takara.

"Takara is scared of ghosts."

"I am not!"

Jonno made a squidgy "yeah, right" face

"I don't think there's any shame in being scared of ghosts," said Sam, trying to calm the situation. "In fact, I think it's perfectly rational."

"For the last time, I am not scared of ghosts! I simply can't stand them, which is very different. They're stupid and annoying and I hate them. And I hate people who like ghosts as well. Bloody ghost people. They're the worst."

"You can't hate ghosts," said Sam. "What have they ever done to deserve that? After all, they don't want to be ghosts, do they? I'm sure they'd much rather be something else entirely. Like alive."

"They love it! And that's what drives me wild."

Takara was starting to work up a head of steam.

"It's always the same with ghosts. Boo-hoo, woe-is-me, life didn't turn out exactly how I expected, and now I'm going to embark upon a pity fest for all of eternity, sucking the sympathy out of anyone that comes anywhere near me. It's all me-me-me with ghosts. They're so needy. They've always got a ridiculous sob story about being pushed from a third storey window or falling into some sort of pit, and they expect you to listen and care and go 'oh dear, that is dreadful' and *emphasise*, again and again and again and again. And they don't care if you've heard their story before. And heard one ghost story, heard them all, frankly. They'll launch into their unbelievably tiresome saga at the slightest provocation, and will continue and continue and continue until you're looking for the stairs to the third storey as well. I like to live and enjoy my life, thank you very much, whereas ghosts are intent on draining that life from me. They're absolutely not for me. Thank you, but no."

"Takara's scared of ghosts."

"I'll turn you into a ghost in a second!"

Sam turned Takara's words over in his mind, in his usual slow, considered manner.

"OK, I think I understand where you're coming from," he said, as they trudged onwards. "But why be scared…I mean annoyed by a staircase? That's not going to tell you its life story, is it?"

"Yeah, but it's where it's taking us that worries me."

"Jonno said we're going to the Theatre Bar."

"And who do you find in the theatre?"

"Actors?"

"Huh! They're almost as insufferable!"

"Critics?"

"See? It's getting worse by the minute!"

"Ice-cream sellers?"

"Well, maybe I've been a bit too hasty."

They reached the top of the Spectral Staircase, the shimmering banister giving way to a sparkling balustrade surrounding a final stone platform. At long last, they were back on solid ground.

"Takara is quite right, of course," said Jonno, his hand still firmly on the small of her back.

"You can't have a theatre without some ghosts."

33

A luminous, celestial handprint glowed on the wall at the top of the Spectral Staircase.

The balustrade sparkled, crackling with stardust and cosmic energy, while the light of the staircase cascaded into the depths of the tunnels, like a beacon or a pathway.

"All very eye-catching, I'm sure," tutted Pat, who had no time for such frippery. With a brisk, efficient air, she placed her hand on the luminous handprint, and waited, impatiently.

The handprint seemed to think about it for a moment, and then went back to the business of celestial glowing.

"You do it," Pat barked at Gerald. "You usually deal with the admin anyway."

Once again, Sam saw the practical, hands-on side of Gerald come to the fore. He approached the handprint not as an irritation to be swiftly dealt with, but as an artefact to be treated with respect. He stood before it as a man of experience, ready for the experience. He drew himself up to his full height, pulled his shoulders back, and looked the handprint square in the eye (approximately), and nodded, with confidence.

Then he pressed his hand firmly against the handprint.

The handprint somehow put its glowing on hold.

There was a disconcerting silence, suggesting that rather than dutifully considering Gerald's request by itself, the handprint was actually taking a moment to check with its superior. The pause grew in its pregnancy, and then the wall before them swung forward.

The five companions stepped through the opening into the theatre bar.

The bar looked much as it had when the actors first discovered it, all those years ago.

The tables and chairs were still in roughly the same position. There was a similar scattering of glasses, all of which appeared to have been abandoned during active service. And the layer of faintly luminous silver dust had returned, covering the objects and surfaces like a preservative.

Oh, they'd had some nights in that theatre bar. Some legendary nights. Some massive nights. The bon mots, the anecdotes, the glittering repartee, were all still echoing through the ages, passing on the triumph of the perfect thing said at precisely the perfect moment to generations eager to learn. The brilliance, the flamboyance. They were untouchable then, they were inextinguishable now. These were not moments lost in time, but fires lit for all eternity, matter created out of nothingness, the big bang of the big night out.

At least that's what they told themselves.

The framed photographs stared out into the room, still bearing their eternal witness. For good or for bad, they'd seen it all. They'd seen the reality. They'd been the sober person at the table of drunken fools. They knew where the bodies were buried. They really did.

Three of the tables were occupied, each by a single figure.

"Steady as we go now," whispered Jonno, creeping carefully forward.

At the first table, a young woman sat staring forlornly into the middle distance, seemingly adrift in space and time. She was in her mid to late twenties, and dressed in work overalls and heavy boots, her hair tied in a headscarf. She was, head to toe, scarf to boots, completely grey – grey skin, grey eyes, grey scarf, grey overalls, grey boots, grey demeanour, as if the system had put her on temporary hold, waiting to be reanimated with life and colour when the time was right.

She gave no impression of being aware of the party's presence. She didn't glance up or shift in her seat or stir involuntarily. She didn't even seem to breathe. She was caught perfectly in stasis, locked in grey.

Pat waved her hand in front of her face, trying to get a reaction, but nothing happened. Gerald looked at Jonno who looked at Sam who tried to look at Takara, but Takara was keeping her distance, as far away from the woman and the table and the greyness as it was physically possible to be. She would have lurked in the shadows had she trusted the shadows, which she very clearly didn't.

At the second table, a slightly older man – say 31 or 32 – sat gazing into the same infinite nowhere. He was dressed rather more formally – in a black suit that seemed cut for performance rather than business, with a white shirt topped by a dark red bow tie, with a matching dark red carnation in his lapel. His jet black hair was slicked back, and a single silver dagger lay on the table before him, unsheathed. The colour of his clothing contrasted vividly with the greyness of the woman, but his skin and his eyes carried the same grey wash, an indication that here too was a person on pause.

Sam leant slowly forward, bringing his eyes level with the man's, their noses almost touching. The man remained transfixed by the great beyond.

At the third table, an even older man – mid 40s perhaps – sat in a similar state of grace. He was dressed for cold weather – a heavy overcoat, thick woollen scarf, and fingerless gloves, with a flat cap protecting his head from the elements. Running from under the hem of his overcoat, down past his shins to the tip of his ankles, hung a discoloured, once green apron, tied around his waist with fraying cotton ties. His boots were sturdy but battered, boots that had braved the working week, come rain or shine. A thick but neatly trimmed moustache spread across his face with military precision, and directly underneath, a white shirt and grey tie gave the impression of a man dressed for service.

His skin and eyes were also grey, but a whiter shade of grey. Permanent grey. Stage 4 grey. The kind of grey you don't return from.

"Well then, Jonno," said Pat, surveying the three figures before her. "You're our resident expert. Which one of these characters is likely to have the cloakroom ticket?"

Jonno's eyes flicked from table to table.

"Not the woman, I don't think," he replied, cautiously. "And not the chap in the flat cap either. They both look like they're still dressed for work. But the fellow in the middle looks more the part. I can imagine he placed his top hat and cane in the cloakroom before taking his seat."

"Yes, I agree," nodded Pat. "Go through his pockets. Let's get this done and dusted as quickly as we can."

"Hang on, you can't do that!" protested an alarmed Sam. "That's theft. And violation of personal space. I don't know if these…" - Sam struggled to find the right word – "…*people* still qualify for the notion of personal space, but even so it still seems wrong."

"They're ghosts," said Pat. "They gave up their rights the moment they shuffled from this realm to the next."

"Yes, but they haven't shuffled, have they?" said Sam. "They're right here, right in front of us, in glorious monochrome. I'd say that has to count for something. And anyway, aren't we more likely to find the cloakroom ticket in the, you know, cloakroom?"

As one, the party looked towards the open hatch of the cloakroom to the side of the stage.

And as one, they noticed another figure standing in the shadows by the cloakroom door.

Never trust the shadows.

The figure stepped forward into the light.

"Your young companion is right, of course," it said, with an air of supernatural satisfaction. "They do have rights. We all have rights, even here."

The figure seemed neither human nor inhuman, neither young nor middle-aged. It was its own category, in its own time. And its own category was so inarguable and so inescapable, it made any other definitions seem petty and unnecessary.

It was a clown. A grey clown. The Grey Clown.

"And your interference would indeed be a violation."

Its head, completely bald save for three dark tufts of hair that spiked up like horns, was vivid grey. Not wiped out, on hold grey or too white, too late grey, but deliberate, purposeful grey – grey with the consistency and shine of greasepaint.

Its eyes were two sunken pools of kohl, the blackest of black eyes filled in with charcoal – and peering from the dark centre of the eyes were quizzical pinpricks of light, like close circuit lasers beaming out of the abyss. Its lips were plastered in grey lipstick, tracing an eternal, menacing grin. Dabs of grey rouge gave its cheeks an unnerving blush, while an oversized ruff flared like a startled sea anemone.

Its costume was covered in dark polka dots and awash with folds and ruffles, an effect that would have once seemed chintzy and approachable, but now felt anything but. Striped stockings encased its arms and legs, and it sported sharp, pointed shoes that looked like they could do severe damage at close quarters.

It smiled at them.

But then it was always smiling.

34

Pat marched forward.

"Now see here," she said briskly to the clown. "You know why we're here. We're not the first to visit you today, we know that for a fact. So if you can pass over the cloakroom ticket, then you can fulfil your duty and we can be getting on our way."

The Grey Clown considered Pat with a cold, unwavering gaze, the two pinpricks of light peering blankly towards her.

"My duty?" it said, in a distinctly unimpressed tone. "I'll tell you about my duty. It isn't to you tourists and trespassers who come marching through here without the vaguest hint of an invitation. It's to these poor souls here, waiting for justice."

The Grey Clown walked over to the three seated figures and stood before them, like a prosecuting barrister standing by his clients.

It stared at Pat with icy disapproval.

"You think you can come here and see right through them, as if they don't exist. Or if they do exist, then they're mere footnotes, for you to disregard. But what gives you the right? The fact that you're living? Or the fact that they're not?"

The pin pricks of light grew more intense.

"Are they really ghosts?" asked Sam, his voice small with nerves.

"They are," replied The Grey Clown. "Although we don't like to use the term 'ghosts' these days. We prefer to call them The Unresolved."

The words hung in the air – defiant against even a hint of criticism.

"The Unresolved?" asked Sam.

"Yes," nodded The Grey Clown. "I'm sure you have a very romantic, rather human view of ghosts – that they are lost spirits with unfinished business, damned by circumstance to an eternity between this place and the next. And I suppose that is true for many of them. But that's their business, not ours. As far as the system is concerned, The Unresolved aren't able to move on because they haven't satisfactorily completed the paperwork."

The shadows at the edges of the room grew darker in sympathy.

"You're saying they're ghosts because they're bad at admin?" asked Sam, with disbelief.

"Not bad, especially," said The Grey Clown. "More unwilling. You have to cross your Ts and tick the boxes and write in block capitals if you want to make the eternal journey across the lake of tears, and many of The Unresolved just aren't ready to do that."

Sam met The Grey Clown's dispassionate stare.

"Whyever not?"

"Well, some of them want to stay put because they're scared of what might be waiting for them. Quite rightly as well, I can tell you. But there are others who have a more complicated relationship with being recently deceased, who simply can't let go of what they have become. To move on, you have to want to move on."

Sam nodded.

"A friend of mine was telling me recently that they think ghosts enjoy being ghosts," he said. "Almost a little bit too much."

The Grey Clown laughed out loud. An empty, hollow laugh that sounded like a skeleton rattling in a rusty metal cage.

"I suppose enjoy is one way of putting it," The Grey Clown said, its eyes devoid of mirth. "Like a praying mantis enjoys eating its young."

"My friend said they were needy."

"Oh they are, the piteous souls. Very much so."

"Needy for attention."

"Not quite. They don't want to move on because they are addicted to grief. Soul-shattering grief. The life force of the universe. At first, they are consumed by a tidal wave of the stuff – at the funeral or memorial service, their loved ones sobbing in pain, their sadness ablaze – and it hits them like a narcotic. You living creatures get what I believe they call a dopamine hit when something affirming happens to them, and it's the same with The Unresolved. Each broken heart and despairing wail lights them up like a Christmas tree. They are valued, they are loved, they are missed, they are worth something. But that initial rush of all-encompassing grief never lasts – that's not how grief works. It soon progresses into a slow burn, a shadow that's always with you, and that shadow offers less of a hit."

A look of resignation flitted across The Grey Clown's face.

"At this point, some spirits decide to move on. They know the party's over. But there are others that can't let that feeling go. Others that have been ensnared by that feeling. So they hang around, hoping to catch another grief high. On the first anniversary of their passing. When a significant song randomly comes on the radio. When someone else dies, and their loved ones can't help but be reminded. When a new family member is born or flourishes or breaks into the wider world, and they're not there to share it. They await the morsels, hungrily. But it's never enough, and so they try to seek out the next best thing from strangers – sympathy."

"Woe-is-me sob stories, my friend said."

"Yes. The desperation of the starving."

Sam looked towards the three seated figures.

"But these three aren't doing anything. They haven't retold their life stories. They haven't fished for sympathy. I don't know anything about them. They haven't said a word."

The Grey Clown sighed. A sigh that sounded like the last breath of a condemned criminal.

"Because these are the truly Unresolved. Fear does not touch them. Grief does not nourish them. They have unfinished business that supersedes all."

"And so they refuse to complete the paperwork."

"They can't let go."

"Look, this is all very interesting I'm sure," huffed Pat, sensing that this was the opportune time to chance an interruption, "but I fail to see what this has to do with us. You know why we're here. We're after the cloakroom ticket. Now if there's any reason why you can't pass one onto us immediately, now is the time to let us know."

"Right now? Are you really sure?"

"Yes!" said Pat. "I can't imagine you subjected the other team to this blasted lecture, did you?"

"No, I did not," said The Grey Clown, looking towards the back of the room. "But then they didn't have her with them, did they?"

35

Takara stepped forward into the room with a familiar look on her face, part sheepish, part proud.

She was dressed in her default outfit, the tailored blue suit and black brogues she'd been wearing when Sam first met her in the back room of the Costa. Her skin glistened in the dim light, drawing energy from the luminous silver dust, and her short brown hair had that same heroic flourish.

She looked like she should be standing in a spotlight. Sam gazed at her, wondering who she really was.

"I'm sorry," said Takara, giving what could only be described as an ironic curtsy. "Have we met before?"

The Grey Clown looked at her with an unrelenting contempt, like thousands of years of bad blood.

"You know I really do think you must be getting me mixed up with someone else, because your outfit is very distinctive, and may I say very stylish, and I'd definitely remember it, and you. I mean, look what you've done with those tufts of hair. So fiendish! So demonic! And those eyes…really those dark, dark eyes…"

The two bottomless plague pits that made up the craters of The Grey Clown's eyes emanated venomous ill-will, the kind of ill-will that could corrode arteries.

"Yes! Yes! That's it. I'm getting a tingle up my spine," beamed Takara. "You really must show me how you do that one sometime."

The laser pinpricks of The Grey Clown's irises flashed in anger.

"You haven't changed, I see," it growled. "Still the same stupid, self-absorbed, annoying Takara."

Takara gave another, deeper curtsy, all irony momentarily dispensed with.

"I suppose I shouldn't be surprised that you don't remember me," The Grey Clown continued. "Why would a cyclone remember the hedgerows and homesteads it destroys as it carves its catastrophic journey? Why would a deadly virus remember the faces of the trail of dead bodies that it leaves in its wake? Why would…"

"Yes, yes, OK. No need to be melodramatic," said Takara, letting her hand fly upwards in what could only be described as a melodramatic fashion. "And no need to take offence, for that matter. I'm just bad with names, alright? It's nothing personal."

"That's the problem," frowned The Grey Clown. "It may not mean anything to you. But it means the world to those poor unfortunates that happen to stray into your path. It's extremely personal."

Takara wobbled her head from side to side, like someone who didn't quite know how they were supposed to react, and was hoping that a vague, non-committal gesture would do the trick.

"Here," said the clown. "Let me see if I can jog your memory."

It walked towards the tables where the three members of The Unresolved were holding their silent vigil. As it moved, Takara felt herself drawn along behind it, as if caught in the tractor beam of its displeasure. The others also felt themselves drawn forwards, their physical forms no match for The Grey Clown's righteous fury.

They came to rest before the young woman in work overalls.

"You're sure these are definitely the non-talky types, right?" said Takara. "I don't mean to be rude, but you are quite the drainer yourself, and I'm not sure I could handle a ghost chipping in with more of the same."

"Silence!" commanded The Grey Clown.

And their mouths were firmly shut.

Takara nodded, impressed, like a magician appreciating a fellow professional at work.

The Grey Clown took out what looked like a snow globe from within the folds of its costume. Only it contained nothing that resembled snow, and it glowed the kind of phosphorescent green usually associated with ghost stories written for children – bogeymen with smelly socks, or ghosts who spewed ectoplasm at the slightest provocation.

Inside the snow globe was a miniature replica of a cemetery.

There were tiny gravestones and tiny bunches of flowers laid on those gravestones. There were tiny pathways between the gravestones, and tiny signposts to help along the way. There were tiny, tiny, tiny shards of green glass gathered inside tiny stone oblongs on the graves. There were tiny trees and tiny bushes, and tiny weeds and roots creeping across the graves that lay unvisited.

Sam recognised it straight away. It was the corner of the cemetery near the necropolis, just across from the tranquil rose garden. There were no imposing mausoleums and grand structures here. Just quiet ordinary graves tended by quiet ordinary people. A place of calm and reflection, wholly unsuited for a boot fair, a ritual, a hoedown, or any other nocturnal happening, clandestine or otherwise.

The Grey Clown placed the snow globe on the table before the young woman, and the straight lines and accepted dimensions of reality began to slowly melt. The trappings of the theatre bar faded into the background, and the gravestones and the flowers and the trees and bushes emerged from a phosphorescent green fog, growing in size and taking up positions, like a scenery change at an accomplished production.

Soon everything and everyone was in place. The woman was standing over the grave, with a bunch of purple flowers in her hand, and The Grey Clown, Sam and Takara and everyone else formed a semi-circle around her, an unnoticed audience observing from a close but respectful distance.

The engraving on the headstone read:

Marianne Kingsley
1858 – 1886
Bewitched And Beloved

The woman kneeled to place the flowers against the headstone and then stood gazing at the engraving.

"Oh Marianne, what am I going to do?"

It was late afternoon, perhaps four thirty. Judging by the russet leaves on the trees and the gathering chill in the air, autumn had settled in for the duration. The sky, though, was darker than you'd expect for that hour, and thicker, as if contaminated. Flashes of red and orange illuminated the sky beyond the surrounding buildings, and the woman had a thick overcoat thrown over her work overalls.

"I shouldn't really be here but he said I could nip out for half an hour," she said, talking to the gravestone. "He's ever so good to me really. Said he'd cover for me, although he's the foreman so I don't know who he's covering up from. The bosses never come down to the floor at this time of day. They're too busy up the stairs."

The woman glanced over past the high street to the church by the factory.

"I'm all in a flap, because he's asked me to marry him. Says he wants to make it official. Tell everyone. Tell her. He says they've been engaged for three years but nothing's ever happened and she doesn't really seem to care about it any more. You remember what I told you last time. I was a fool, but it was a flattery and I thought what's the harm, no one will ever find out, and it's here today and gone tomorrow, just something to keep us both warm until this horrible war is all over."

"But now he says he wants to do the right thing, but I don't know if it is the right thing. I know it's not the right thing for her, and I'm not sure if it's the right thing for me. I'm only 25.

Not much younger than you, and look at everything you did with your life, all those adventures and the excitement. All the stories. I wanted to be like you, do my best to follow in your footsteps, but then all this started, and we've been twisting wires and doing our bit for years and years now. And now he wants to marry. Make it right. And I'm scared that that's going to be it. That my life will be over before I've even had a chance to begin."

Sam turned to The Grey Clown and whispered.

"When is this?"

"October 24th, 1944."

The woman glanced over towards the factory once more.

"I should be getting back. We've got this big order and we've got to work late to get it all done. Important for the effort, they say. I just needed to tell you all this. Ask you. What am I going to do?"

A low rumble suddenly filled the air above them.

A grinding, industrial, malevolent rumble, like a headache or a bad mood in motion. It sounded unstoppable and unbeatable. Like destiny.

The woman jumped with fright.

And the rumble stopped.

And then there was silence.

And that sounded worse than the noise itself.

The explosion set the sky on fire and shook the earth and the trees and the foundations.

"Noooooooooooo!"

The woman screamed and started running towards the explosion, running towards the factory. And as she ran, the green phosphorescence rose to greet her, swallowing her, surrounding her. Leaving only the onlookers behind.

The gravestones and the trees and the benches and the signposts slowly faded, the scenery resetting to default.

All that remained was the bunch of purple flowers.

Sam picked up the flowers and gazed at them.

"Did she die in the fire?" Sam asked The Grey Clown.

"Oh no, she was lucky. Thanks to the kindness of her lover, the foreman, she was the only worker at the Tannoy factory not to perish in the bombing. A V1 rocket can make a terrible mess when it manages a direct hit. Everything and everyone went up in flame. The workers on the factory floor, the urgent order of radio parts, the bosses upstairs, the invoices and inventories, all gone. By the time she got to the factory, all she could do was stand and watch."

"But she died not long after? Of a broken heart perhaps."

"No, no. She lived to see the new millennium. Met another, settled down, had children, grew old, gave in. But if you could draw a line in the story of her life, pinpoint a moment where her options shattered and her ambitions crumbled away, then this was it. No one is ever the same throughout their time on your earth, but she was resolutely and comprehensively not the same after that night."

"But then why is she a ghost? I can't see any injustice in any of this. No more than usual. It was bad luck, that's all, surely. What remains unresolved here?"

"What indeed?" said The Grey Clown, picking up the snow globe from the table in front of the young woman. It peered into it for a second, as if trying to find something, and then walked over to the third table, before the older man in the overcoat and apron. It placed the snow globe on the table and then stepped back.

36

This time, a street scene materialised around them.

A row of tattered market stalls stood on an unkempt side street. All save one were empty, the torn remains of tarpaulin sheeting clinging to the weather-beaten frames. If these stalls had once had a time in the sun, then that time had long passed. Glory days of happy customers and non-stop trading had been replaced by a quiet air of defeat. Everyone had packed up and gone home. The dream was over.

The one open stall was laden with the leftover stock from all of the other stalls. There were books and bones and broken bottles, empty animal cages and rolls of threadbare fabric, tarnished spoons and what looked like the remains of a bird's nest. A pile of yellowing newspapers lay on the right-hand side of the stall, offering yesterday's news to a clearly indifferent world. In the centre of the stall, presumably in what was meant to be the pride of place, was a selection of children's toys – rags dolls and marbles and rusting cars. While the rest of the traders had looked reality in the face and walked away, the toy seller was carrying on, like a soldier who refused to accept that the war was finally over.

Unlike the young woman, who had sprung into life as soon as her surroundings had finished spawning around her, striding into the flow of her narrative without losing a beat, the man stood before his stall, rigid, unmoving. His grey, blank eyes stared straight ahead, looking through Sam, Takara and the others as if they weren't there, as if they were the ghosts rather than him. It was hard to tell if he was breathing, any movement of his ribcage smothered under the heavy overcoat and woollen scarf, and only the very observant managed to catch him blinking, an act that felt tiny yet monumental somehow. To be frozen on the spot in the street felt like a sad way to go, but it was a story that had been told many times before. To stand motionless, defenceless, powerless, yet still be present, still blinking, felt like something else, something deeper.

"Doesn't this one do anything?" asked Takara, peevishly. "It's not very entertaining, is it?"

The Grey Clown turned to glare at Takara.

"Where do you think you are? At the travelling fair? Here to cast your jaded eye over the sideshows and performing freaks?"

"You tell me," said Takara. "It's your cabaret, chum."

She ran her eyes over the scene in disapproval.

"Enlighten us, what is it supposed to be doing?"

"It's not an it. It's a he," said The Grey Clown. "An actual person and an actual life."

"But is it really? If it was an actual person with an actual life, then it would be living it. Doing something. Fighting back. Not just standing there, giving in to the inevitable."

"The inevitable?"

"Yes. It's always the same with ghosts. The inevitable tragic end. But actual people with actual lives don't wait for tragedy to overcome them. They find a way to escape their certain fate. They bluff and blag and they wrong-foot adversity, and if that doesn't work then they fluke their way out of whatever pickle they've got themselves into, or at least try their very best to."

"And you're an expert on reality, now, are you, Takara?"

Sam butted in before Takara could reply.

"What does it say on the front of that newspaper?"

The group leaned forward to peer at the fading headline.

"SHOPPERS SHUN HIGH STREET AFTER THEATRE DEATH," said Jonno, helpfully reading aloud in capital letters.

For a moment, there was a faint flicker in the market trader's eyes, as if someone was walking over his grave.

Pat marched forward and snatched up the paper.

"Following the recent tragedy at the local theatre, shoppers say they are now unwilling to visit nearby shops and hostelries," she declaimed, her voice ringing with authority. "Mary Price, 22, of Westwood Grove, spoke for many when she told our reporter: 'This place be cursed! I seen the hellfire and damnation in the cracked paving stones, I smelt the stench of sulphur from the pits below, I stared into the glowing red eyes of the devil himself! It was him, I tell you. I saw him! On that very night, when that poor girl lost her life. I saw him with his lies and his conjuries and his terrible deeds. I was there! And now he's made this place his playground. He's sown the seeds of destruction into the streets and the alleyways. He's laid down his poison like a trap! And he's waiting - waiting for us to take the bait. Well, I won't fall for it, you hear? I'm staying away and so should you. It's a curse! The devil himself!'"

"Oh dear," said Gerald. "That does sound concerning."

"Poppycock!" retorted Pat. "The ravings of a demented wretch. Nothing more, nothing less."

"Does it say anything else?" asked Sam. "Anything about what happened at the theatre?"

"Let's see," said Pat, turning back to the newspaper with the gravity required for such an endeavour. "Right…what do we have here…as reported in previous issues…fallout from the awful event…shocked onlookers comforted by the police, fire brigade and a passing priest…ah, right here we are."

She cleared her throat and then began.

"On the night of November the 12th, 1886, a great tragedy took place during a performance by the renowned and much-admired magician, The Mighty Malphas. A disturbance in the balcony during his world-famous knife-throwing trick caused the magician to lose his balance during the final knife throw. The knife, which on so many previous occasions had simply beheaded the flower held aloft by the magician's assistant, pierced the poor girl's heart, killing her instantly."

"Oh no," said Sam.

"The Mighty Malphas was later remanded in custody. He has pleaded not guilty to the murder of Marianne Kingsley, 28, and has entered a plea of death by misadventure. His case will be seen in the High Court in the new year."

Takara looked delighted.

"How fabulous!" she said, beaming with pleasure. "Bravo, my dear Grey Clown, bravo! I take off my hat to you, cry hurrah and huzzah, and raise my cane to the skies."

"Whatever are you going on about?" demanded Pat.

"Don't you see? It's a triptych. Oh, I love triptychs. Three is most definitely a magic number. And better still, it's a triptych puzzle. A work of art!"

"Takara, please," said Sam, mindful of Pat's soaring blood pressure.

"Look, it's simple. The girl from the factory suffered her terrible fate because she went to visit a dead relation, right? And the name on the gravestone was Marianne Kingsley. And the chap frozen rigid in front of his failing market stall has lost his livelihood because of the tragic death of one Marianne Kingsley. And the other ghost, that we've yet to visit, was, if my memory serves me well, a forlorn looking fellow with a *silver dagger* – did you get that? - on the table before him. Who I am quite happy to wager the contents of Jonno's lunchbox will turn out to be the Grand Mephisto."

"The Mighty Malphas."

"Yes, him too. So all we have to do now to solve the puzzle and save the day and free these pitiful unresolved souls from their endless torment, and hopefully go on our way with a cloakroom ticket and a pat on the back from our clown friend here, is to visit the third guy and see what he has to say for himself. Oh, it's all too perfect."

The Grey Clown stood looking at Takara, its face stern and stoney, shaking its head. "You never learn, do you?" it said. "You really are incredible."

"Why, thank you, my dear sir!" grinned Takara. "On we go then. Onwards to the scene of the crime!"

37

The Grey Clown placed the snow globe on the final table.

Their surroundings once again melted away, to be replaced by a neat and elegant theatre.

This was a classier affair than the space constructed by the actors of the early 70s. There were no preening delusions of high status – no grand arch or gold gilt or secret spyholes for those in the know. This wasn't trying to be something it wasn't and getting it horribly wrong. It was a simple space that knew its purpose. It was browns and deep reds and years of craft and appreciation for that craft. It was dust and history and the lingering echo of a story well told.

The man from the table now stood centre stage, his attire matching the setting perfectly. The sharply cut black suit of a showman, the dark red bow tie of a magician, the dark red carnation of a poet, the jet black hair of a romantic hero - a swordsman perhaps or a smuggler. A silver dagger gleamed in his hand, catching the spotlight and sending shards of anticipation flickering around the room. And his skin was rich flesh and blood rather than washed out grey. Alive and well, for now. Here was a man who was used to being centre of attention, poised and ready in his natural habitat.

Stage right – to the right of the performer, to the left for the audience, where your eyes go for the beginning of a story – a young woman stood before a black wooden board. The board was adorned with scatterings of small stars, some arranged as known constellations, others mapping out hitherto unseen galaxies, often geometric spirals ruled by the golden ratio. Scores of pockmarks dotted between the dancing stars, tiny craters left by the silver daggers after every performance. The pockmarks told a story of their own, of safe options and near misses and gasps and shrieks of amazement. They were the applause that never died away.

To begin with, they'd talked about using a celebrated knife trick. He'd palm the dagger as he appeared to throw it and a hidden stagehand would push another through the back of the board – all done so quickly that no one would ever spot the illusion. But as they practiced the trick, they couldn't shake the feeling that they were lying to the audience. Yes, the rest of the act was full of misdirection and sleight of hand, masterful arts that told their own truth, but this was the finale – it didn't feel right somehow. The time for deception had passed. The audience had to believe that tragedy was only a hair's breadth away, even if the last thing they really wanted to witness was genuine tragedy. They'd paid for the thrill of the possibility, for the excitement of the biggest gamble of all.

So they worked on the knife throw for real. No stagehand, no safety net. A series of silver daggers thrown to silhouette the glamorous assistant, and the final, dramatic throw to close the show in style. And on the opening night, the stunt went by without a hitch. Marianne held a purple flower in her left hand, gazing at it wistfully, as if considering the departing gift from a failed love, and the final knife sliced through the air and through the flower, narrowly missing her tender frame. Cue applause, delight, relief, satisfaction. And they'd shared an emotional embrace afterwards, because the thrill of the brush with death had made them both feel more alive than ever.

Sam, Takara, Pat, Gerald, Jonno and The Grey Clown were seated at the centre on the front of the balcony, the perfect vantage point, as if the entire scene had been set up for their viewing pleasure, which, of course, it had. Sam scanned the audience on the balcony, looking for potential troublemakers. The newspaper report had stated that a disturbance in the balcony had distracted The Mighty Malphas at a crucial moment, so one of these people was going to be responsible. But which one? The crowd was a blur of fashionably turned out humanity – the men in dark suits and single-breasted waistcoats, the women in full skirted-dresses and patterned shawls – all murmuring with appreciation as the tricks and illusions were presented for their delectation. No one stood out quite yet.

Takara shifted restlessly in her seat

"Is there popcorn?" she enquired of no one in particular. "Bring me popcorn."

The Grey Clown bristled but kept silent.

"We're about 50 years too early," said Jonno, with evident pleasure. "We could have picked up some whelks from a street trader if we'd have been allowed to roam the cobbles before coming here. But it appears there was no time to waste. You'll just have to chew your nails."

The Mighty Malphas strode to the lip of the stage and took a black velvet blindfold from his inside jacket pocket. He held it above his head with both hands and displayed it to the crowd, turning left and right so that everyone in the theatre could inspect it properly. Then he walked calmly over to Marianne and tied the blindfold across her eyes, whispering in her ear as he did so.

Sam kept scanning the audience. Who was it going to be?

As the first of the daggers slammed into the wooden board around Marianne, Takara became more restless, rocking slightly in her seat.

Who was it going to be?

"I thought we were going to get a nice private view," hissed Takara, her eyes darting around her. "I didn't realise there would be so many of *them*."

"These aren't ghosts," said The Grey Clown. "They're echoes."

"They're a menace."

Then Sam spotted them. One man, two women, over on the right-hand side of the balcony, right above stage left.

The women were laughing, their bare shoulders rocking with

mirth. Their dresses were slightly different to those around them – off the shoulder, more gathered at the waist, paired with gloves that stretched to their elbows and jewellery that rattled from their necks and wrists without ever giving the impression of great worth.

The man was in a tailored black suit and wore white gloves, the white gloves of an entertainer. Even though he was close to the front row of the balcony, he was standing up, presumably blocking the view of the poor unfortunates seated further back. He had turned towards his companions and seemed to be in the midst of his own private performance, to an audience of two. He reached behind the ear of his first companion and pulled out a boiled egg to shrieks of delight. He produced a battered bouquet of flowers, clearly hidden beneath his suit jacket, and held them aloft as if they were the product of a great magical triumph. He piled a handful of silver coins on his elbow and then brought his hand down in a sudden snatch, catching almost half of them. He smirked and he sparkled and basked in the attention of his friends, ignoring everyone else and everything else around them.

He reminded Sam of somebody.

The third, fourth and fifth silver daggers slammed into the board, to appreciative gasps and murmurs from the audience.

The man in the black suit and white gloves produced a top hat and a silver cane.

The Grey Clown, Takara, Pat, Gerald and Jonno all followed Sam's gaze and watched as the man in the black suit and white gloves made comically grandiose gestures with the top hat and cane, to the amusement of his companions.

Takara had stopped shifting in her seat now. She sat stock still, frozen in the moment.

The Mighty Malphas drew out the final silver dagger.

The man in the black suit and white gloves paused for a second.

There was something familiar about the way he held himself.

Something familiar about his melodramatic gestures, his mischievous demeanour, the way he presented himself to the world, 20% gracious, 80% smug.

Something familiar about the hint of a flourish in his hair.

Sam looked at the man and then looked back at Takara and then looked at the man again.

"It's you, isn't it?"

Takara didn't say a word.

"I don't know how it's done or what it means, but that man over there – that echo of someone who lived over a hundred years ago – is actually, impossibly, unbelievably you, isn't it?"

"It can't be," said Takara. "I had a moustache."

"What?"

"Stiffly waxed."

The man threw the top hat into the air.

"Or was that a few years later?"

The man deftly caught the upturned top hat on the top of the cane and let it balance there, a brief moment of calm and control.

The Mighty Malphas drew back his hand.

Marianne held the flower to the left of her body, a foot above the third dagger, impaled safely in the wooden board.

There was no stagehand ready with a false dagger.

They'd decided they didn't need one.

And then everything happened at once.

The man with the black suit and the white gloves flicked his wrist and the top hat span into the air again. The Mighty Malphas tensed himself for the final throw. The second female companion howled with laughter and flailed her arm into the first female companion. The first female companion spat out her drink and kicked out her leg involuntarily. Marianne gazed into the comforting void of the blindfold and smiled. The man in the black suit and the white gloves howled with laughter too and then suddenly lost his balance when the first companion kicked his chair. The second female companion howled even louder. The top hat gave way to gravity and crashed from the balcony onto the stage. The Mighty Malphas jumped with surprise, but the throw had already begun.

The dagger flashed through the air, spinning chaotically towards Marianne and the big finale.

There was a scream.

And then it was over.

Sam, Takara, Pat, Gerald and Jonno sat in their seats, staring at the stage in shocked silence. There was no eruption of noise, no sudden bedlam. The scene had frozen once the deed had been done and hints of phosphorescent green began to lick at the boundaries of their field of vision, eager to reclaim this dark episode and file it away in the void where it belonged.

The Grey Clown glared at Takara.

"You'd forgotten, hadn't you? How could you possibly have forgotten this?"

Takara shook her head slowly, her gaze empty.

"I don't know."

"When your friend read out the newspaper article, didn't that ring a bell or two for you? Remind you of something?"

"No, I…" Takara faltered. "I got up to so much back then. There were so many of…" She trailed off again. "I don't know."

"And you were looking forward to this," sneered The Grey Clown. "You thought it would be *fun*."

"Yeah."

"Well, the triptych is now complete. I await your answer."

The theatre fizzled out of existence, leaving them back in the bar, the three members of The Unresolved seated at the three individual tables, a study in grey.

"Well," said Pat, eager as ever to crack on. "Any suggestions? Anyone got the faintest idea?"

"Takara knows," said Jonno.

Takara chewed her lip and inched back towards the safety of the shadows.

"We all know," said Sam.

The Grey Clown looked at Sam expectantly.

"Well, it's her, isn't it?" said Sam. "It's Takara. I don't know what question you're asking, but the answer is Takara. She was the starting pistol. She knocked over the first domino. She was the opening word of a story that connected The Mighty Malphas, Marianne, the woman who saw the devil at the theatre, the death of the market and the shops and the local livelihoods, the man chilled to the bone before his stall, the woman in the graveyard, the foreman and bosses and the workers on the factory floor, and the bomb that came to finish everything. I don't know what you could be asking that ties all of that together, but the answer is Takara. It's her fault and her responsibility."

The Grey Clown nodded.

"Thank you. Just what we wanted to hear."

The three members of The Unresolved started to grow translucent, their greyness giving way to thin air.

The universe breathed a sigh of relief.

The Grey Clown produced a purple and yellow raffle ticket and handed it to Sam.

Sam turned the raffle ticket over in his hand and thought about what he'd just witnessed. The Mighty Malphas whispering in Marianne's ear. Marianne's tender smile seconds before the dagger hit.

He walked over to the cloakroom, and there it was on the counter, with a matching purple and yellow raffle ticket attached to it – the black velvet blindfold.

Sam picked it up without ceremony and walked back over to The Grey Clown. It didn't seem necessary to show the blindfold to the others. What was he going to say? That they'd done it? That they'd won? If it was a victory, he didn't feel like celebrating.

The Grey Clown looked at Sam with something approaching sympathy.

"There's nothing you could have done. It was always going to end this way."

It nodded over to the back of the room, to the door with the staircase leading upwards.

"Thank you for your visit."

It smiled its icy rictus smile.

"Please don't come again."

38

They emerged from a cobwebbed fire door at the back of the theatre into a rough patch of greenery behind the church, a lofty Anglican structure that presided over the area with a simple, solid grandeur. The church had been built half a century or so before the cemetery and had a plain and rather modest air, like a reserved older cousin lurking in the shadow of a flashy relative. Its graveyard and catacombs were unassuming, municipal affairs. No dramatic statues or wild mausoleums here.

The church and the cemetery were separated by the high street, which looped around the church, marooning it in a lazy spiral of slow-moving traffic and absent-minded, unobservant pedestrians. Oddly for a church, it was built facing north south, rather than the usual east west, which meant that when the worshippers knelt before the altar they were facing the pagan gods of Scandinavia rather than any warmer Biblical climes. In his more idle moments, Sam liked to think that explained a lot about his locale.

The companions picked their way around the side of the church to the front of the building, where a triangular garden provided a refuge for a regular smattering of dreamers, thinkers and street drinkers. It was a modest but serene space, an unexpected moment of respite from the hustle and bustle – and, once a month, it hosted a community ran food fair where the great and the good could buy artisan treats and hand-painted cupcakes for the price of a weekly shop.

They were in luck. It was that time.

In the early afternoon sun, Sam felt himself blinking at normality, as if it was in some way not to be trusted. He couldn't remember pausing to rest or succumbing to sleep since he had left his house in what he struggled to remember as twilight, but time had passed and the moonlight of the cemetery and the shifting scenes in the theatre bar now seemed like a fading dream.

He tilted his face to the sky and let the warmth of the sun burn away the memories for a second.

Beside him, Takara surveyed the food fair with a glassy, distracted gaze, as if her mind was still somewhere deep underground. Time may have been flowing on, but she wasn't ready yet, not quite there. She went through the motions of scanning from stall to stall, but nothing registered on her face…until something at the far end of the market caused a tiny ripple of life to spread across her features. Her eyes started to uncloud and the faint beginnings of a smile teased the edge of her lips.

"Back to work we go," she murmured.

The food stalls hogged the edge of the triangular garden, leaving the central patch of greenery bare. Multi-coloured bunting bedecked with exotic symbols fluttered in the light afternoon breeze, and ornate heraldic banners hung behind each stall, advertising their wares with a tribal flourish. In another age, this kind of rich artistry would have represented unions and workers collectives on long marches for fair pay and time off in lieu, but now it had been co-opted by commerce, albeit a strain of commerce ran by the people themselves.

All human life was there, in much the same way that all inhuman life had been at the nocturnal boot fair.

And every imaginable foodstuff was waiting patiently.

Quiches, pastries and flans. Tajines, souvlakis and thick farmhouse stews. Burritos, fajitas and piping hot queso flameado. Honey roasted chicken. Honey roasted turkey. Honey roasted parsnips. Things that should never have seen honey or an oven, but were honey roasted anyway. Stuffed peppers, disembowelled aubergines, dislocated avocados.

Brownies, biscuits and cakes fashioned from reveries and fairy tales. Rice and peas, rice and beans, rice and chicken. The very best patties. Seasonal ingredients. Ethical spices. Locally sourced titbits. Artisanal lattices and handwrought bonnes bouches. Cupcakes, cupcakes, cupcakes, cupcakes.

Poised at the apex of the market, like a patriarch seated at the head of long oak table, was the pie stall.

The food stall of dreams.

In the realm of food, the pie is the king.

No, that's not quite right.

In the realm of food, the pie is the emperor.

And the realm of food is the realm of everything.

Takara paused at the pie stall and tipped her head, as if paying her respects.

"Look at these things," she said to Sam. "Aren't they spectacular?"

There was a pork pie the size of a baby's head. It looked like a squat medieval castle made out of pastry, built to withstand months of bloody siege warfare. It could have been used to shatter a shop window during a smash and grab or lobbed as a hostile missile during an inner city disturbance. It was gruff, majestic, the end of the world as you knew it, thousands of calories in their purest form.

There were steak and kidney pies that looked like they could feed an army on the march or sustain a capacity home crowd over an entire season – thick and rich and emanating warmth and vitality, as if they came with their own internal energy source.

There were puff pastry pies designed to dissolve upon the slightest contact, so light and effortlessly fragile that their meltdown seemed like a form of destiny.

There were filo pies, homity pies, curry and Cumberland pies, pot pies and pumpkin pies, mushroom and tofu pies, chicken pies, mince pies, walnut pies and Woolton pies, and golden brown spinach and feta pies with names that could decimate Scrabble tournaments.

And there was a banoffee pie, the empress of the pies.

It was a dense, gooey vision of heaven, a spiral of cream and gloop that felt like it was beckoning you over, tempting you to bathe in its giddy delights. If a miniature Cleopatra had been seen basking in the centre of this most banoffee of banoffee pies, no one would have complained or raised an eyebrow. This was a substance to revive the skin and the soul, to purge the grime of reality once and for all.

"We stand each side of a barrier," whispered Takara in awe. "You in a world of change and decay. I in banoffee."

As Takara gazed wistfully at the stall, The Duke's words floated through Sam's mind.

"If you add another Important Thing, or two, or, more dangerously, five or six Unimportant Things to her head, the initial Important Things simply fall out, never to be considered again."

Jonno wandered over to the cupcake stall, a look of distaste on his face.

"Huh! Cupcakes!" he sneered. "The foot soldiers of gentrification."

"Now then Jonno," said Pat. "They're not to my taste, but there's no need to be rude. Nothing wrong with foot soldiers."

Gerald nodded and reached into his pocket for his wallet.

Jonno's sneer deepened as he cast his eye over the wares on offer.

The choice was simple. You could have a yellow one, a pink one, a yellow and pink one, a pink and yellow one, or you could go home and make yourself a nice jam sandwich instead.

"These things make me sick," Jonno spat. "Everything that's wrong with the world in a single, horrifically priced, mouthful."

"Come on, be serious," said Pat. "They're just cakes."

"Never! They're the self-satisfied declaration that I'm Alright Jack And Don't You Forget It. They're tweeness weaponised and tasked to destroy everything that stands in its way. They're privilege as a virus, sugar as a battering ram, the acne of capitalism raging over the dying body of a fair society."

No one said anything to this. How could they?

Gerald opened his wallet with intent.

"Is everyone OK with a pink one?" he asked. "There doesn't seem to be much choice."

Takara nodded solemnly.

"I hear what you're saying, I really do," she said. "And I will admit that I've felt the same myself. Definitely. Deeply, passionately. I mean, how can you be on the side of the righteous when the price tag makes your eyes bleed? I get it. It just doesn't add up."

Sam knew Takara well enough now to know that there was a "but" fast approaching.

"But…well…is selling overpriced nibbles to people who can afford overpriced nibbles really a sign of the world being overcome by a terrible evil? Or are we just seeing fools being parted from their cash in exactly the same way they've always been throughout the ages? Huh? OK, yes, the poor original inhabitants of this fine borough can't afford to splash crazy money on fluorescent pastries - but would they have anyway? I honestly think I've met far more morally bankrupt individuals than mere cupcake sellers."

Takara glanced over to the far side of the market.

"Talking of which…"

By the entrance of the market, like a silver-tongued spiv trying to entice passers-by into a den of vice, was the cider tent.

It sold only one brand of cider – Knucklehead - which was brewed locally by an anarchist collective.

Knucklehead was insanely popular – strong enough to blind a horse, the colour of molasses blended with unleaded petrol, and served exclusively in five-litre plastic jerry cans.

The local dignitaries would talk up the culinary diversity and social vibrancy of the food fair, but everyone knew that without Knucklehead it would be nothing. If cupcakes really were the foot soldiers of gentrification, then Knucklehead was la resistance, unwashed and unbeaten, lobbing flaming Molotovs in the hot sun.

Striding towards the cider tent with a visible sense of purpose were the Big Heavy and the Heavy Heavy. The Heavy Heavy was carrying a black leather kit bag, the kind usually favoured by boxers, and the Big Heavy was flexing his hands as he walked, like he was warming up for something.

"Answer me this, then, Jonno," said Takara, nodding over towards the Big Heavy and the Heavy Heavy. "Would you rather be on the side of the people-powered community – the pie makers and the cider drinkers and, yes, the cupcake bakers, all modern day revolutionaries, stealing from the affluent foodies to give to the needy local denizens, many of whom could be mistaken for the stall holders themselves. Or do you stand with these hoodlums, dumb brutes who want to destroy everything they don't personally profit from?"

Someone had once told the Heavy Heavy that the best way to get money from a mark was to lean on them, and he'd taken that at face value ever since.

He stood over one of the anarchists working at the cider stall and pivoted the bulky upper half of his body forward.

"What are you doing?" spluttered the anarchist, as he became enveloped by a sudden mass of gangster flesh. He had a scrum of thirsty customers to attend to and this was really not helping.

"It's collection day," growled the Heavy Heavy.

The problem with leaning on anarchists is that you could never be sure who you were leaning on. If no one was particularly in charge, then who was going to pay out?

The anarchist shrugged. "Nothing to do with me, mate."

For a credo that abhors the system, it was a good system.

Takara turned to Sam with a familiar grin.

"Time for some more fun."

39

Takara rooted around in her trouser pockets for a moment and then came to a standstill, her features struck by a puzzled frown.

Whatever she was looking for wasn't where she thought it would be.

Then slowly, and with some trepidation, she held open her jacket, as if she were in the final, crucial stages of cracking a safe or defusing a bomb.

Sam was once again struck by the lining.

It was deep and fluid, endless and ancient, symbiotic and amniotic, an emotion in slow motion.

And all hand stitched.

Takara reached into the void and pulled out a matchbox, very similar to the one that the Heavy Heavy had produced in the front room of the Costa several thousand years ago. Takara flicked it open with her left hand and a cockroach crawled out on the ground before them, just like before. If Sam didn't know better, he'd have said that Takara had somehow reached back through time and grabbed the very same matchbox and the very same cockroach that he'd seen in the Costa. But that would be madness. No one could do that.

Takara closed the matchbox with her thumb and forefinger and then flicked it open again, and another cockroach crawled out onto the ground before them. It scurried over to its companion and stood there, looking as confused as it's possible for a cockroach to be.

Takara held out her hand, like a surgeon motioning for a scalpel.

"Rain stick…I mean, sonic enlarger."

Sam looked as confused as the cockroach.

"Oh yes, sorry," said Takara. "I forgot you're not that guy yet. Don't worry, I'll have it here somewhere."

She reached into the lining again and out it came, the DB11, state of the art, top of the range.

The runes glowed, the fire traced, you know the drill by now, and the cockroaches, once again the size of woodland boar, sped off towards the Big Heavy and the Heavy Heavy.

"Fly my pretties, fly!" cried Takara, never one to let slip a moment of melodrama.

"She never said that, you know, the Wicked Witch," butted in Jonno. "It's not in the film. Not even in the director's cut. No one has any idea where that phrase comes from."

"Oh, do shut up, Jonno."

The cockroaches were almost upon their prey when the Heavy Heavy opened the leather boxer's bag. And there it was, the DB10, recently outmoded, sliding down the charts, but still a serviceable bit of kit.

"Damn," said Takara. "They've been shopping."

The Heavy Heavy waved the DB10 inexpertly towards the approaching giant cockroaches, rather like someone trying to ward off an avalanche by waving a sausage at it. Nevertheless, the runes glowed, the fire did its thing, and the leading cockroach zapped back to its natural, matchbox-sized state – a sudden and clearly unexpected turn of affairs that spooked the second, still giant-sized cockroach, which bolted in panic in the opposite direction.

The Heavy Heavy allowed himself a look of smug satisfaction, until he realised that the giant cockroach was heading full tilt for the pie stall.

The resulting carnage was almost like a work of art. In a better, kinder, more sophisticated world, future generations would have studied an embroidered tapestry of the mayhem caused by an unnatural beast crashing at full speed into the food fair's most beloved offerings.

There was filo everywhere.

Steak and kidney pies arced through the air like hand grenades.

The injuries caused by the pot pies and the walnut pies are still talked about to this day.

Decimated puff pastry rained down like the ash from a volcanic eruption.

And the gargantuan pork pie – thick and solid and forbidding – rolled off the stall and sped towards the Big Heavy and the Heavy Heavy, gathering pace at an alarming rate.

Takara was beside herself.

If you've ever wondered what it must be like to be a single pin facing the devastation of an oncoming bowling ball, then wonder no longer.

The Big Heavy and the Heavy Heavy did try their very best to get out of the way of the now-hurtling pork pie, but they were large units with a low centre of gravity who weren't used to sudden agility, and there was a certain inevitability to the collision between pie and hoodlum that was impossible to escape.

And as the cockroach squealed and the filo flew and the Heavies screamed in terror and the monstrous pork pie began to glow red with unstoppable momentum, a spark of electricity leapt from the metal poles of the market stalls to the iron railings encasing the triangular garden, from the street lights to the traffic lights, from the wind chimes to the cake stands, from the flagpoles to the weather vane at the top of the church, from the wrought iron gates of the cemetery to the brass key plates on the disused public toilet.

Sam had seen this before.

The endless, opaque everything that flowed from corner to corner and point to point and joined up every dot in every dimension throbbed once again in technicolour - but this time as if a battery was being recharged in a single burst.

And the exotic symbols on the bunting glowed in recognition.

The humungous pork pie was just about to strike the Big Heavy and the Heavy Heavy, presumably to send them spiralling away at matching 45-degree angles, when time crashed to a halt.

"I know this is what you do, but must it really be so infuriating?"

The Inspector glared at Takara, whose face was caught in a mask of sheer glee, eyes wide, eyebrows mid-dance, cheeks flushed and ready for more.

The Inspector snapped her fingers with impatience.

Takara jerked back into life.

Reality remained on pause, the bedlam halted temporarily.

Takara took a moment to survey the scene, her face still aglow with the excitement of it all.

"Oh, come on," she said, gesturing at the chaos stuck in perfect freeze frame. "Doesn't it all bring a tear to your eye? You have to admit this tableau has a certain beauty to it."

"Absolutely not," huffed The Inspector.

Takara smirked the smirkiest of smirks.

"I don't believe you for an instant," she said. "Look, who was that guy we went on that pub crawl with? You remember. There was a bunch of them. Painters and artists and ne'er-do-wells and the like. And there was that one chap who wouldn't give up. When everyone else was ready to drop, he was insistent on one more drink. Or two. Or several. And when we all thought that perhaps we were venturing too far into the seedy part of town, he wanted to go further, press on, keep on drinking in the debauchery. It was like he was getting high on every sight, sound, smell and experience. You remember. He did some sketches or something of it all afterwards."

"Do you mean William?"

"That's the fella! He had a thing for you, you know."

"He did not."

"Well, he would have loved this. And there was a time when you would have loved it too."

The Inspector walked over to the pork pie and tapped it with a cane. A black cane with a bright red handle, the same shade as her shock of spiky hair. A ripple of electricity, looking suspiciously similar to the electricity that had ricocheted around the food fair, ran through her red earrings, and the pie fizzled out of existence.

"You're wrong, Takara," The Inspector said, turning to look at her. "I never loved it. I didn't even enjoy it. If you'd spent any time thinking about anything other than yourself, then you'd know that. I only went because..." She paused for a moment, suddenly derailed by her memories. "...well, because...just in case..."

"Just in case what?"

"Just in case something happened."

"Lots of things happened, Satomi."

"Yes, but...to you."

Takara grinned.

"You were looking out for me? Oh, how sweet!"

"Yes, well that's what I do, isn't it? And that's what I'm doing now. Again. Looking out for you and clearing up your mess. Your stupid, thoughtless, unnecessary mess."

"It's not unnecessary, you know that."

"Yes, but it is stupid. Deeply, deeply stupid. And I don't see why we have to carry on with this nonsense. There must be another way."

"Well, you know who you need to speak to about that, don't you?"

The Inspector's glare intensified.

"Damn you, Takara."

Takara curtsied, her face part bashful, part proud, part triumphant.

The Inspector walked over to the Big Heavy and the Heavy Heavy, stopped to adjust something on her black and red cane, and then tapped them both once on the forehead. A look of blissful amnesia spread across their features.

"Well, I have had enough," said The Inspector, slowly and purposefully. "And you know what? I think I will speak to him. And he's not happy with you at the moment, so that probably wasn't the cleverest of suggestions."

The Inspector clicked her fingers and a team of similarly clad agents swooped in to restore order and put everything back in its place.

When it was done, The Inspector nodded in approval.

"I'm off to file what I hope will be my very last report on your mischief. I suggest you take the time to do something useful as well."

"Like what?"

"Give me my dress back, Takara."

Another click of the fingers and The Inspector was gone.

40

The food fair sprang back into life, a picture postcard vision of a lovely afternoon out.

The stalls were intact and thriving. The customers were tucking into everything and more with a carefree gusto. The Knucklehead was flowing, the anarchists were singing, the bunting was flapping in the cool breeze. And the Big Heavy and Heavy Heavy were wandering among it all, a beatific look splashed across their faces, still caught in the hypnotic spell of The Inspector's black and red cane.

"Wait, what? The Inspector is Satomi?" spluttered Sam.

"Yes, of course. Didn't you work that bit out?"

"God, no wonder she hates you so much."

"She doesn't hate me. She adores me. Everyone adores me. And I adore her. She really does mean the world to me."

"Well, you have a funny way of showing it."

Pat cleared her throat.

"I hate to interrupt this touching exchange, but something strange seems to be happening to our two hefty friends here."

It was true.

The gruesome twosome were still wandering around the market with a look of glazed contentment on their faces, staring at the cupcakes and cocktails with a freshly lobotomised blankness, but their heads had begun to roll around alarmingly on their necks, like their tendons and ligaments had suddenly lost their usual tension.

Jonno had once attended a pottery evening class when he was a younger man, and in a moment of boredom had placed a fishbowl slightly off centre on one of the potter's wheels.

That had been a happy time. He watched the lolling heads of the Big Heavy and the Heavy Heavy with a nostalgic glow.

Takara sprang forward and placed a guiding hand on the two heavies' backs, steering them gently out of the triangular garden, across the road, and into the cemetery, pointing them towards the rose garden and the distant necropolis. They staggered off with a wobbly purpose, as Takara darted back to her companions.

"She acts like she knows it all, but Satomi really does need to sort her tech out," Takara said, with a brief roll of her eyes. "That should keep those two clowns occupied for a while, but even so we ought to get a move on."

"To where?" said Sam.

"Well, what's next on the list?"

Pat stepped forward. This was her department.

"Right then, let's take a look," she said, flipping open her pocketbook. "We still need the following. Four small golden goblets decorated with an engraving of a slumbering lion. Heaven knows where we'll find those."

"Charity shop?" suggested Sam.

"Yes, because someone's going to conveniently donate four very specific goblets to their local thrift store, aren't they?" said Jonno.

"Well, they have to be somewhere. Where do you suggest?"

Jonno shrugged.

"God knows. If I cared, I'd say the Pound Tardis, but I assume our dear friend here would have informed us if they had any in stock."

Everyone looked at Takara.

Takara looked somewhere between fuddled and befuddled.

"Maybe? I don't know what we have. I'm not sure anyone does. We just reach for whatever it is whenever someone asks for it and it's usually magically there. I don't really question it."

"Would Balfour know?" asked Sam.

"Probably. Why don't we ask him next time we swing by?"

Pat looked back down at her pocketbook.

"A hero's headdress," she continued.

"Oooh, that's a good one," said Gerald. "Very evocative."

Sam looked like he was having a good idea, K spice be damned.

"Hey, didn't the heavies mention somewhere called The Emporium? I can't imagine you plump for a name like that unless you specialise in the weird and wonderful. Antiques, valuables, rare memorabilia, that sort of thing. Could we try there?"

Takara pursed her lips.

"I don't know if that's a good idea."

"Oh really?" said Pat.

"Maybe we've got some at the shop. Let's ask Balfour about that too."

"Nonsense," said Pat. "The Pound Tardis is well known for carrying bits and bobs and minor league whatnots. We won't find a hero's headdress there. We'll go to The Emporium."

Takara nodded silently.

"What else?" said Pat. "A pocketful of posies."

Sam produced the bunch of purple flowers.

"Will these do?"

Takara smiled and nodded appreciatively.

"Very good," she said with affection. "You really have come a long way, haven't you?"

Pat tutted and rustled her notebook.

"So that just leaves an emerald key, The Book Of The Dead, and two hundred pounds in polished two pound coins."

"Two hundred pounds in polished two pound coins?" said Sam. "Who's going to have that?"

Everyone looked at Takara. Takara shrugged.

"Someone who likes money," deadpanned Jonno.

"Someone who really likes money," said Sam.

Takara nodded once more.

"And I can think of someone who fits the bill perfectly," she said, glancing over towards the cemetery.

"Right then," said Pat. "We have the makings of a plan. Off to The Emporium we go."

Takara sighed. "OK then. This way."

She led them across the triangular gardens towards the post office and the old library.

The old library was built around the same time as the fire station and shared some of its gothic grandeur. The entrance was flanked by four grand pillars while the first floor balcony boasted seven tapered columns bearing the busts of seven hallowed thinkers – Homer, Chaucer, Milton, Shakespeare, Dickens, Socrates and Sir Walter Scott. When he was a child, Sam had been told that these were the actual seven pillars of wisdom and part of him still believed that to this day.

The post office was mentioned in the Guinness Book Of Records, under "Longest Argument Ever To Have Taken Place In A Municipal Building". It was where dreams went to die.

They had just passed the souvlaki stall when Takara raised her hand, stopping the party dead in their tracks.

"Look," she said, her voice dropping to a whisper.

Seated in deck chairs by the iron railings at the edge of the triangular gardens were the four members of the black and white team. Three of them were tucking into generous slices of banoffee pie, while the other was busy with a small bag of something.

Also seated in deck chairs, twenty yards to their left but facing pointedly in the opposite direction, were the four members of the blue and red team. They each had a plastic pint glass of Knucklehead, drawn from the five-litre plastic jerry can that was placed between them, and had the look of a group of dedicated hard grafters enjoying a well-earned rest.

Beside the black and white team lay the green bottomless bag.

Beside the blue and red team lay – what else? – a blue and red bag.

"Looks like our rivals are taking the weight off for a minute," whispered Takara.

"Mmm, that banoffee pie looks good," murmured Gerald.

"You've just had a bellyful of cupcakes. How can you think of banoffee right now?" said Pat.

"Once I start, I just can't stop," sighed Gerald. "I think I'm a sugar addict."

"Those bags look full, don't they? I wonder what they've got?" said Sam.

"My thoughts exactly," nodded Takara.

Everyone looked at everyone else.

"Is there anything in the rules that says you have to find the items yourself?" said Takara, almost as if she were thinking out loud. "Would it be acceptable to, um, how can I put this, *liberate* an item or two from another team?"

"By liberate, you mean steal?" said Pat.

"Well, kind of. More redistribute."

"Redistribute?" said Pat.

"Yes, like communists," said Takara. "Or Robin Hood. Or better still, a communist Robin Hood. Which I suppose is what he was, wasn't it? All that taking from the rich and giving to the poor was just one step away from seizing the means of production and declaring everyone equal pigs on an equal farm."

"I'm not sure that's what communism is," said Sam, looking at Takara and wondering, not for the first time, what actually goes on inside her head.

"Anyway, is there anything in the rules that says we can't nab stuff from the other teams?" asked Takara.

"Well, technically no..." began Pat.

"Great, let's do it."

Takara's plan was simple.

She would go and engage the team in conversation, dazzling and distracting them with her usual wit and good humour (her words), while someone else – Sam was quickly voted into this role – would sneak up and grab whatever they could from the bottomless bag.

Then they'd have all the items, win the competition, save the day, and everyone could go home, or at least have a nice slice of banoffee pie to celebrate.

"You like saving the day, don't you?" said Pat.

"It's the best," beamed Takara.

Everyone took up their positions. Pat, Gerald, Jonno and Sam lurking behind a nearby vegan bratwurst stall, Sam ready to creep forward, and Takara in her natural, preferred place in the world – in plain sight, the centre of attention, the undisputed star of the show.

The team were discussing their food choices.

"This dessert, although semantically inaccurate, is pleasing to the taste," observed Number Two.

"Semantically inaccurate? How so?" inquired Number Three.

"It is categorised as a pie, even though it does not utilise pastry," replied Number Two. "You will observe that the base is crushed biscuit."

"Also it does not have a pastry lid," added Number One, helpfully. "It is surely closer, in terms of construction and constituent parts, to a flan?"

"A flan? I disagree strongly with that assessment," said Number Three, shovelling in another mouthful of banoffee.

There was a pause and then Numbers One to Three turned to look at Number Four, who was busy with their bag of something.

"Why did you not select the agreeable confection, Number Four?" asked Number Three.

"Flame-grilled sizzling steak Wotsits," Number Four said, tucking in enthusiastically. "What a time to be alive!"

The remaining Numbers shared a quizzical look, as if encountering an unexpected syntax error.

Takara saw her chance and stepped into the team's field of view.

"Afternoon gents!" she exclaimed, ratcheting up her charisma to a sudden maximum. "How goes the search?"

The team members observed her with a shared emotional blankness.

"We are on our break," said Number Two.

"Twenty minutes," said Number One. "We currently have seven minutes, 24 seconds remaining."

"Very nice, I'm sure," said Takara, nodding encouragingly. "Always good to kick back when you've had a fruitful morning of treasure hunting, am I right?"

"We are not required to discuss our undertakings during our break," said Number Three, stonily.

Number Four popped a steady stream of flame-grilled sizzling steak Wotsits into their mouth, as they regarded Takara with a cold detachment.

Takara wasn't used to working with such a tough crowd.

"Well, er, yes," she said, losing her confidence for a millisecond, before glancing at the blue and red team and finding inspiration. "You know, I would have thought that canny game players like yourselves would have seized upon this chance when the other lot" – at which point she looked meaningfully at the blue and red team – "were momentarily distracted to crack on and get this thing won once and for all."

"They are also on their break," said Number Two. "I believe they are concurrently scheduled."

"All activity is temporarily discontinued during our break," said Number Three.

"Six minutes, 14 seconds remaining," said Number One, with a look of blankness that somehow also said, very clearly, "leave us alone".

As soon as Sam saw that Takara had successfully caught the attention of the black and white team, he began advancing towards the bag on his belly, like a commando crawling under barbed wire during basic training. If any of the team had turned their heads even slightly, they would have caught sight of him immediately, a human slug huffing and puffing its way forwards. As it was, Pat, Gerald and Jonno cast an interested eye over the proceedings, wondering if Sam could possibly be any more conspicuous.

Once Sam reached the bag, he opened it gingerly and peered inside. The pocketful of posies, the velvet blindfold (plus raffle ticket), the unspecified amount of grave dust (approx a handful), the key (at once both hypnotically kaleidoscopic and profoundly colourless), and the bogus music box were still all present and correct, but joining them were four small golden goblets. Sam couldn't make out if they were decorated with an engraving of a lion, slumbering or otherwise, but he assumed that they passed muster. The black and white team had clearly earned their banoffee slices.

Without thinking, Sam reached forward and grabbed the key. It belonged to Takara, Balfour and Harrington after all, so he was simply reclaiming misplaced property.

He reached out again for the golden goblets but something made him stop.

He looked up at the four members of the black and white team, who were reclining on their deck chairs and staring balefully at Takara as she began the second stage of her distraction campaign.

She called it the waterfall of words.

It was one of the wonders of the modern world.

It was a cascade of ideas and images, an all-enveloping, all-encompassing, seemingly never-ending torrent of thoughts and notions and stories and side-stories that went beyond mere conversation and reached the realms of the metaphysical.

It was poetry in freefall, information reaching terminal velocity, it was the sum of human knowledge in cloudburst form. It was the sound of the sea, the call of a distant siren, it was a split second after the big bang, with the needle jumping towards the red. It was overwhelming and illuminating and unforgiving and impossible. It was nouns and verbs and adverbs and adjectives, oh so many adjectives, raining down like crystal spires, endless and infinite, over and over and over and over, like numbers going on forever.

It was everything and nothing, the germ of an idea and the end of recorded time, it was everything you never knew you didn't know about all there ever was.

It was the waterfall of words and the black and white team were powerless to resist.

Sam glanced at the blue and red team, cheerfully enjoying their pints of Knucklehead, totally unaware of what was unfolding behind them, and then back at the black and white team, sitting targets in an unfair firefight, and he realised that it wasn't right, that he just couldn't do it.

He stood up and shook his head while his compadres glared at him in consternation.

He walked over to Takara and handed her the key.

"I believe this belongs to you," he said.

The black and white team looked as alarmed as it's possible to look when your faces are an emotionless blank.

Number Four reached down and grabbed the bottomless bag in what could have been interpreted as a moment of panic.

Takara glowered at Sam and then held the key up accusingly.

"OK then, guys. I think you have some explaining to do. Where did you steal this from, huh?"

Number Two held Takara's gaze impassively.

"We did not steal it."

"Yeah, I'm sure," huffed Takara.

"We were given it."

"Given it? Who by?"

"The man at the boot fair."

Takara looked like someone had walked over her grave.

"This man, what did he look like?"

"I no longer retain that information," said Number Two, with a steady confidence that would have been the envy of any passing politician.

"Small man? Big overcoat? Air of menace? That kind of thing."

Number Two took a moment to consider.

"No, he was a large man. One of a set of two."

Takara breathed a sigh of relief.

"Phew, OK. Well, we know who that is."

"And where did you get the golden goblets?" asked Sam.

Number Two snorted with laughter and said, "why would we ever possibly tell you that" at exactly the same time that Number Four said, "the tall shop with the preoccupied staff".

Takara's eyes widened.

"Oh, wonderful," she said. "The book shop. I should have known."

The blue and red team stood up, drained their pint glasses, and began to make their way out of the triangular garden.

Number One consulted their watch and nodded to Number Two.

As one, the black and white team rose to their feet.

Number Two handed Takara a plate of unfinished banoffee pie, a faint look of resentment flickering across their face.

"Break time is now over."

For a moment, Takara almost felt guilty.

"Book shop?" asked Sam. "What book shop?"

What kind of person could half finish a slice of banoffee pie, Takara wondered.

Could that person even be a person?

"Takara? I said, what book shop? I've never seen a book shop on the high street."

Takara tore her gaze away from the unfinished banoffee and looked up at Sam.

"That's because the people who work there don't want you to see it," she said. "They've got better things to do with their time than sell people books."

Both teams had now gone – the blue and red team heading off towards the Pound Tardis, and the black and white team marching over to the old library.

"Some of the brightest minds of our generation work in that bookshop," continued Takara. "Artists. Poets.

Musicians. Historians. Philosophers. All engaged in vital endeavours that require their full attention. Having to deal with customers as well simply wouldn't be fair on them."

"You have a very fluid understanding of the meaning of fair, don't you?" said Sam.

"Look, it'll all make sense when you see it," said Takara.

"Well, that would be a first," said Pat, brandishing her walking stick. "I'm looking forward to it."

"Excuse me, boss."

Takara looked at Balfour – for it was he – with astonishment.

Dressed in his long brown shop coat, with his flat cap pulled down as far as it could go and his horn-rimmed glasses glinting disconcertingly in the afternoon sunlight, Balfour looked like a glitch in the system, like a CGI element that was glaringly out of place.

"Balfour! You're out of the shop!"

"Yes boss. I had to shut the shop up and come and find you."

"You've shut up the shop!?! You of all people? I don't think I've ever known such a thing."

"I know, boss. But I had no choice."

"What is it, Balfour?" asked Sam.

"It's Mr K. He's gone missing."

41

The exact location of Mr K's restaurant lingered tentatively in the collective memory like a folk tale or an urban myth.

There definitely had been an actual restaurant at one point, everyone was sure of that. It had been a much-loved and widely recommended fixture of the local area, and everyone but everyone had passed through its doors at some stage, that much was beyond question.

Precisely where it had been located, however, was the matter of passionate debate. Some people swore blind that it had been a few doors along from the local pub – they related misty-eyed tales of stumbling in after an evening's convivialities in the same way that ravaged travellers emerged from the Sahara babbling about a life-saving oasis. Others were insistent that it had been opposite the site which now housed the B&Q but which back in the mists of time had been a striking art deco cinema. They remembered stories, passed down from generation to generation, of a celebrated eatery on this very spot, popular with the cinema goers of the time, and were certain that Mr K had wanted to continue the tradition, for personal reasons unknown.

Similarly, no one could remember when Mr K's disappeared from the high street, or how.

It had been a fact of the high street for an age now that as soon as anyone turned their back for even the slightest moment, a shop would suddenly disappear and be instantly replaced by another. If you were lucky, its wares would still be available online. If you weren't, you spent the rest of your days questioning your memory, wondering if the place had ever really existed at all.

Mr K's was different. There was no shop. There was no website. There was no printed menu. There was just a phone number.

If you knew what you wanted, then you knew who to call.

And everyone wanted Mr K's spice.

Takara nudged open the front door of the Costa, led everyone through to the back room and the industrial fridge, and eventually they were all back in the octagonal room, gazing at the floor.

The purple circle was pulsing.

"Balfour, go back to the shop, if you could please," said Takara, looking at the pulsing purple circle with a frown. "If everything goes haywire, then I'm going to need you and Harrington in position."

"OK boss," said Balfour. He stepped onto the brown circle and promptly disappeared.

Takara looked up at her remaining companions and took a deep breath.

"Alright then everyone. Link hands please."

She reached out for Sam's hand.

"I hope everyone's ready. Brace yourselves."

She stepped onto the purple circle, and their surroundings melted away, this time to be replaced by an antechamber set in an underground cave.

There was a row of dark mahogany office desks that looked suspiciously similar to the one in the back room of the Costa, and a group of industrious people either sitting at the desks or flitting between them, conspicuously busy with the business of the day.

Two features, however, dominated the room.

First was a large black telephone set on a table by itself. It was sturdy and old-fashioned, with a rotary dial on the front, and looked like it was made for important communications only.

Second was a vast circular metal door set into the cave wall at the back of the room. It had an imposing, brooding presence – like something you'd find in a bank vault or a military bunker – that made Sam wonder whether it was there to stop people from getting in or something else from getting out.

Standing in front of everything, at the very fore of the foreground, was a small, neat man, dressed in dark suit trousers and a purple tunic, done up right to the neck.

He bowed his head slightly, with slow ceremony.

"Takara," he said gravely. "Thank you for getting here so quickly."

"I came as soon as I heard, Mr K," said Takara, with a similar solemnity.

Pat coughed.

"I'm sorry, as always, to interrupt, but didn't Balfour say that Mr K had gone missing?"

"He has," said Mr K, mournfully.

"This is the Blessed Mr K," explained Takara. "I believe you are the third?"

"It is my honour and my duty," the Blessed Mr K intoned.

"The Mr K that's gone missing is the original."

"And the best," said the Blessed Mr K.

"Quite so," said Takara.

"He is the originator of the spice and the father of us all," the Blessed Mr K continued. "He is the visionary and saviour, the preserver and the protector. We are all," he turned and motioned towards the workers at the mahogany desks, "his children."

The large black telephone on the stand-alone table gave off a loud, authoritative ring.

A worker rushed over to answer it.

"Hello, Mr K's. Can I help you please?"

Silence.

"I'm very sorry to say that all orders are currently suspended," the worker told the telephone. "We hope that we will be able to resume normality, or as close as we can get to normality, very soon."

More silence.

"I'm afraid so sir. We are currently facing unexpected supply issues. We apologise for any disruption."

The telephone was returned to its cradle.

"What happened, Mr K?"

"I think it would be easier if I showed you," replied the Blessed Mr K, and nodded towards one of the workers.

"Oh god," said Jonno. "We're going through the big door, aren't we?"

A group of workers came forward with purple rubber gloves and black and purple face masks. The masks were decorated with the same livery that had adorned the courier's food box, with the roots from the strident K extending from chin to cheek and ear to ear. A worker fitted it on Sam's face and then adjusted a series of straps, making sure it was snug and close, like a membrane.

"Please do not, under any circumstances, for your own safety, take off your masks once you are inside the kitchen," said the Blessed Mr K.

Takara looked at Sam and raised her eyebrows.

"Open the airlock," commanded the Blessed Mr K.

A worker stepped forward and began to turn a large circular handle to the right of the vast circular door.

Slowly and with a great feeling of ceremony, the circular door swung open.

The Blessed Mr K nodded to Takara and led the way into the airlock.

"Please be assured that an instant death, albeit a highly pleasurable one, lies beyond the airlock for all those without the correct facial protection," said the Blessed Mr K. "Should your masks become breached at any time, you may wish to say your prayers without further delay."

The circular door shut behind them with a resounding clang.

"Isn't this marvellous?" beamed Takara. "I do love a sense of impending doom."

The Blessed Mr K nodded again and another worker began to open the second door at the far end of the airlock.

The door swung open to reveal another underground cave, roughly four times the size of the antechamber with the black telephone.

A mist of purple and black particles hung in the air, with golden sparks arcing between the particles like static electricity. The mist was lighter than the billowing fog that had accompanied the courier, but it felt more permanent, a significant part of the ecosystem. This mist wasn't going anywhere any time soon. This was its home.

In the midst of the mist lay the kitchen – or rather the kitchens.

Arranged in rows that stretched the full length and width of the cave were a staggering array of individual cooking stations, each with its own oven, sink, fridge and worktop. The row closest to the airlock was occupied, with chefs in black uniforms and purple aprons busy chopping and seasoning and simmering to the point of perfection, but the rows behind them were dark and silent, stretching off into the gloom like unmarked crosses at a war cemetery.

The Blessed Mr K surveyed the scene and sighed.

"Usually this would be a sight to behold," he said. "The greatest kitchen in the world creating the finest food ever to be savoured. We use individual cooking stations because we believe that cooking should be personal and distinctive, created as part of an intimate one-to-one conversation between chef and diner. That taste that makes your head spin and your synapses shiver isn't just the K Spice working its mysterious magic. It's the sense that each dish is a sacred covenant, a love letter penned in secret by your greatest admirer."

"Mr K! You're making me tingle," said Takara, with a blush.

"But now that conversation has fallen silent. The kitchens have all but been abandoned. The miracle workers you see before you are using up the very last of the K Spice, cooking the final meals of the day, perhaps the final meals of all time."

A chef walked up to greet the Blessed Mr K. She was wearing the same black uniform and purple apron as the others and, like them, wasn't wearing a face mask. Her dark eyes had gold sparks floating in the iris while the whites of her eyes were tinged purple. She bowed her head towards the Blessed Mr K in respect.

"Karisha," said the Blessed Mr K in return. "How are we getting on?"

"We're down to the last few grams," said Karisha, mournfully. "After this, there's nothing more we can do."

"You've checked the reserves?"

"These are the reserves, my lord. The tallies are all depleted."

"How can this have happened?"

"We don't know."

The Blessed Mr K frowned.

"But then we aren't allowed to know," added Karisha.

The Blessed Mr K's frown deepened.

"I'm sure you've heard many scurrilous tales about Mr K and the outrageous lengths he's taken to protect the secrets of the K Spice," said the Blessed Mr K to Takara and her companions. 'Well, most of them, you'll be unsurprised to learn, aren't true. His tongue is still intact. There has been no hypnosis. But one thing is accurate. He does indeed summon the spice in a locked room."

"The Master's Chamber," said Karisha, in awed tones.

"No one save Mr K has ever been allowed inside the Master's Chamber," said the Blessed Mr K.

"But Mr K has gone missing," said Takara. "And you said you had something you wanted to show us."

"I did."

"He also said that if we didn't wear our masks we'd pop our clogs in here," chipped in Pat. "But she isn't wearing one," she went on, gesturing towards Karisha. "And they aren't wearing one either." Another gesture towards the cooks. "I thought this place was meant to be certain sudden death?"

The Blessed Mr K turned his attention to Pat, her yellow hiking jacket, and her walking stick cum totem pole. His face was that of a seasoned restaurateur dealing with a difficult late-night client.

"The servants of the spice have no need of a mask, because they have grown up with the spice, they live alongside the spice, they welcome the spice as their guide and constant companion," the Blessed Mr K explained. "To them, it signifies not the end, but the beginning. A joyous, gracious beginning."

"So they experience that amazing feeling we got from the spice all the time?" asked Sam.

"Oh no," said the Blessed Mr K. "When you grow up with the spice, you transcend that state of bliss. You become immune to it, if you like. And that places them in the perfect position to cook and craft with the spice. They gain their pleasure from the pleasure of others."

"And if they don't have the spice?" asked Sam.

The Blessed Mr K glanced at Takara.

"Your young friend is perceptive," he said, before turning his attention back to Sam. "Let us say that the servants' relationship with the spice is a little unconventional. They can live without it, but it would be like removing colour or taste or smell from the world. Like suddenly switching your surroundings from three dimensions to two. They are immune but they are in thrall. It's all they've ever known."

The purple and black mist pulsed expectantly and a flurry of golden arcs sparked from particle to particle in a sudden frenzy.

This mist, the lifeblood of the tunnels, was excited.

"We best sort out your supply issues, then," said Takara.

The sparks crackled in agreement.

42

The Blessed Mr K led the companions through the cooking stations to a wooden door at the back of the cave.

It was thick and nondescript, a solid slab of oak that looked like it had been there for centuries and the cave had formed around it.

There were no markings or signs on the door, but it exuded a firm air of: "do not enter".

"Endless praise to the master, the originator, the most-exalted and never-bettered, the treasure chest and the mountain top, the undisputed and very best," said the Blessed Mr K. solemnly.

He reached for the door handle and pulled it down, pushing the door forwards.

"It's just open?" said Jonno, incredulously. "Your sacred Master's Chamber and the door's unlocked?"

"No one would dare enter the Master's Chamber so there is no need for it to be secured," replied the Blessed Mr K. "We will be the first to cross this threshold. No one has ever ventured here, other than the Master himself."

The room was small and dark, lit only by a collection of candles that gave the impression that they would never burn out. The flames were constant and attuned, flickering at the same time and with the same intensity.

Along the left-hand wall were three filing cabinets and a tall pot plant.

An expansive mahogany desk, clearly from the same stock as the others, lay against the front wall. Above the desk was a large whiteboard.

Along the right-hand wall was a complex and convoluted spice rack, full of twists and turns that seemed to defy perspective. Taken as a whole, it was difficult to focus on, a confusing blur of right angles and ingredients.

"Don't even try to look at it," said the Blessed Mr K.

On the whiteboard was a list of the usual spices that you'd expect to find in something like paneer pasanda – cumin and cardamom, jaiphal and javritri, turmeric and red chilli powder – but at the centre of the board was a large K written in the same elemental livery as the one on the courier's food box.

At the end of each branch of the K was the name of a spice.

"Behold," said the Blessed Mr K, in hushed awe.

Karisha pressed her palms to her chest and nodded her head.

"The secret of perfection."

At the end of the first upright branch was written Raja Mirchi.

Ghost chilli.

At one time the hottest chilli on the planet. 170 times hotter than Tabasco sauce. So hot that it was once used by the Indian Army in hand grenades for crowd control.

At the end of the second upright branch was written Kalpasi.

Black stone flower.

An earthy, aromatic spice that also serves as a pain reliever. Reaching up from the depths of the earth, the black stone flower comforts and heals.

At the end of the first downwards branch was written Jaiur.

Sichuan pepper.

Made from the dried berries of the prickly ash tree, jaiur has a lemon flavour which numbs the mouth in the manner of a mild electric current.

At the end of the second downwards branch was written Ossame.

Grains of paradise.

A peppery spice used in folk medicine and voodoo rituals, employed to conjure good fortune in the face of despair. Also placed in bedrooms to induce luck of a more carnal nature.

Karisha frowned.

"This can't be everything," she said. "These spices wouldn't create the K Spice. They're all pulling in opposite directions."

"What's that?" said Sam, pointing at the board.

Sure enough, at the point on the K where the four branches converged, was the name of another spice - Chari Phool.

Star anise.

Antiviral, antibacterial, antifungal, with the taste of liquorice. Illicium verum in Latin. True seduction.

Only there was something about the lettering of chari phool. It wasn't solid black like the other spices. At its centre was light. And every minute or so that light would expand and increase in intensity until it reached the point of explosion. Like watching a volcanic eruption in miniature. Or the birth of a flame.

"There's your magic ingredient," said Sam. "It looks like an exploding star."

"A supernova," said Takara.

Karisha was animated now.

"Yes, yes, that's it. I'm sure I heard the Master mention supernova anise once. I thought I must have been imagining things."

"Would that do it?" asked Takara. "Combine everything together to make the K spice?"

"I've no idea," said Karisha. "I've never cooked with it before. But star anise heals and beguiles. If a star can manage that, what could a supernova achieve?"

"Phoo-wee. I think we all know the answer to that!" grinned Takara.

Sam turned to look at the spice rack.

He scanned his eyes over the shelves and columns and tiny alcoves holding the jars of spice, but every time he tried to study a particular spot, his focus span off at an unexpected angle. He tried his best to concentrate, gritting his teeth and hoping that the ciliary muscles in his eyes would follow suit, but all to no avail.

He stepped back, his head spinning.

"It's like trying to read an eye chart with the letters jumping around all over the place," he gasped. "I just can't get a grip on it."

"Here, let me."

Karisha stood before the spice rack like a devotee facing a holy shrine.

People often say that they feel humbled when they've done well at something, but they're almost always lying. Success doesn't humble you. It invigorates you, emboldens you, makes you feel like you can achieve the unachievable, usually because you've just managed to pull off the near unachievable without setting off any alarms.

Only two things truly humble a person.

Failure.

And the sudden, mind-blowing, life-changing, irrevocable knowledge that who you are and what you believe and what you strive for means absolutely nothing when faced with the infinite wonder and complexity of whatever it is you want to call this open-ended, ever-expanding impossibility that we're all currently floating around in.

Karisha beheld the spice rack with a look of true humility.

She scanned the contents calmly and as she did so, the golden sparks floating in her irises flickered with quiet joy – like a system recognising a password, like an outcome responding to a possibility. Her eyes were the eyes of someone having a good idea that would stay with them for life. The look of a key being turned and a lock clicking open.

"Wonderful," she said, quietly. "Just wonderful."

"What can you see?" asked Sam.

"Everything," Karisha said, breathlessly.

Jonno drew in his breath.

"I think he meant about the spices," he said.

"Oh yes, of course, sorry."

The sparks were still dancing in her eyes. How could she talk about stock levels at a time like this?

The Blessed Mr K placed a supportive hand on Karisha's shoulder.

"It's all there, everything we need, everything we've ever wanted." Karisha started to sob quietly. The emotion was too much for her.

"Everything?" said Jonno.

"Yes! Yes!" smiled Karisha.

"Even the supernova anise?"

Karisha turned to the spice rack again, her features awash with happiness. She looked lovingly over every alcove, every jar.

Her face froze.

Eventually she found the words.

"I didn't notice because there isn't a space for it," Karisha said, still quietly, but now with a sense of disbelief. "All the shelves and alcoves are full of jars and every jar is at least two third full. It's all there. Everything I've ever cooked with and everything I've ever thought about."

"But you've never cooked with supernova anise before," said Takara.

"Not knowingly."

"Which is why you didn't think about it."

"I suppose not," said Karisha with an air of confusion.

"Then you need to think about it now. Take a moment to prepare and then focus your mind on supernova anise. And then look for it on the spice rack."

To everyone except for Karisha (and possibly the Blessed Mr K, who didn't become the Blessed Mr K by giving away his secrets when he didn't need to), the spice rack remained an impenetrable blur of angles and perspectives, a choppy sea full of razor blades. All they could do was observe the glory of the spice rack reflected on Karisha's face, watch the warm glow of a miracle pass across her followed by a single dark cloud.

"I can see it," Karisha said, as the cloud settled on her brow. "I can see the jar."

"Yes?"

"It's empty. Not a grain, not a trace. Just empty."

"I think we've found our supply issue," said Takara.

Pat started to rummage briskly through the papers on the mahogany desk.

"It seems pretty obvious to me," she said, mid-rummage. "He ran out of spice, so he would have ordered more. Find the order slip, you'll find the man."

Everyone set about the task with gusto. Pat went through the papers on the desk. Takara, Sam and Gerald searched through the filing cabinets, pulling out paper files and rifling through the forms and slips and miscellaneous items within. Jonno watched them with the air of a man who was happy to let everyone get on with it while he enjoyed a moment of rest. The Blessed Mr K carried out his version of very much the same thing. And Karisha gazed at the spice rack with a kind of post-coital melancholy, letting out sighs that managed to be ecstatic and heartbroken at the same time.

Pat threw the papers back down on the desk with disgust.

"Got anything?" she asked the room in general.

"Nope," said Takara.

"Nothing here," said Sam.

"No luck here either," said Gerald.

"Sadly no," said Jonno, polishing off the remains of his sandwich.

"How about you?" asked Pat, rounding on the Blessed Mr K. "You must know how the ordering system works."

"I have never been permitted inside the Master's Chamber before," the Blessed Mr K said, with a beatific simplicity. "You know as much as I do about its inner workings."

"Me?" snorted Pat. "Don't be ridiculous. I haven't the first idea how things might work in this madhouse. I mean, nothing makes sense here, does it? He might have well kept the order book in the pot plant."

Everyone turned to look at the pot plant.

Everyone stepped towards the pot plant.

Everyone rummaged through the pot plant, access allowing.

Pat was right. There was nothing in the pot plant.

But behind the pot plant, they found a safe door. A small safe door. The kind of safe you'd put the petty cash in.

"Combination?" Pat asked the Blessed Mr K, the word bordering on a command.

"As before, I have never been…"

"Yes, yes, OK, we get the picture," said Pat, cutting him off. "Go on then, Gerald. Work your magic."

Gerald was halfway through taking a crowbar out of his backpack when Sam stepped forward and pulled at the safe handle. The door swung freely open.

"Stands to reason," Sam said, with a grin. "No need to lock the safe if you don't lock the front door."

Pat looked like something had gone down the wrong way.

"I am humbled," she said, with a grimace.

She was lying, even though in this case, it was true.

Takara reached into the safe and took out a red petty cash box, a small silver framed photo of a red haired woman wearing a white ballgown, and a dark red oblong book, roughly five inches high by eight inches across.

Sam gazed at the framed photograph.

"Who is she?"

"That my young friend is Eleanor Lockhart," said Takara. "Star of silver screen. Breaker of hearts. Consort of the rich and powerful. Daredevil and pioneer. She scaled Everest before she was 21. She won an Oscar on her 24th birthday. In a single day, she invented an attachment for the Swiss Army Knife and wrote a jitterbug tune that was popular in most of the Benelux countries and at least one American state. She was a pin-up and an inveterate liar. She was a true star and, at one point, my own personal hero."

"Why would Mr K have a framed photo of her?"

"Maybe he has good taste?"

"She seems too good to be true."

"Of course, that's what I like the best about her," said Takara.

"You're as big a liar as she is," snorted Jonno.

"That's 'you're as big a liar as she is, *sir*', to you, sweetheart," smiled Takara. "And don't you forget it."

Pat took the dark red oblong book from Takara and started to leaf through it.

"This is it!" she exclaimed. "The order book. Now, let's see…what's today's date?"

Much murmuring and shaking of heads.

"Nobody knows? Really? OK, well, how about the day?"

More of the same.

"Anyone? No? Hmm, well that's going to make this slightly trickier than I'd envisaged, but anyway. Here, look, the last entry is a rendezvous. Meet RG on Sunday at the vegetable market, 1.15pm re bulk order of SA."

"That's impossible," said the Blessed Mr K. "The master never leaves the tunnels. Not any under circumstance. It's simply too perilous for him to do so. There are countless entities who either seek to do him hard or wish to acquire the knowledge that he and only he is party to. Most of the suppliers deal with my colleague the Estimable Mr K. The select few that deal with the master himself come to the master."

"How do they get into the tunnels?" asked Sam.

"The master has given the Estimable Mr K a key. And when occasion dictates, he will pass that key onto a supplier."

"Oh dear," said Takara. "It doesn't happen, by any chance, to look like this?" And with that she produced the key that they'd confiscated from the black and white team.

"The master's key!" exclaimed the Blessed Mr K, his eyes wide.

"My key actually," said Takara, "but I do vaguely recall lending one of my keys to your dear gaffer. How can you tell it's the same one?"

"I sense the spice upon it," said the Blessed Mr K.

Karisha nodded solemnly in agreement.

"Ah right," said Takara, pursing her lips. "Well, if Mohammed doesn't have a key to get underground to meet the mountain, then the mountain will have to…hang on, I'll start this again…"

"So that's it, then," said Sam. "Mr K left the tunnels and his enemies saw their chance and pounced."

The Blessed Mr K looked like he was about to cry.

"Not during the market," said Takara. "Never. Our dear friend The Inspector and her crack team of party poopers would never allow it. Something else will have happened, I bet you. He'll just be languishing in a cage somewhere or something."

"Or stuck in an obsidian cube," said Pat, pointedly.

"Ah, no, I got Harrington to double lock the thing until this has all blown over. Can't be making the same mistake twice. Look, I reckon if we go and see the lovely and never at all unreasonable Inspector, she'll be able to clear this up in no time."

The Blessed Mr K grasped Karisha's hand and nodded, still on the edge of breaking down.

"We cannot risk following the master," said Karisha, holding onto the Blessed Mr K. "We will remain here."

"Sounds like a plan," said Jonno, taking out his lunch box.

"Not you, Jonno," barked Pat. "Come on, jump to it. I've got a particular job in mind and it's got your name written all over it."

Takara looked at Jonno and grinned, enjoying his discomfort as much as Jonno had enjoyed hers.

"Just one more thing before we go," she said. "Sam, my dear boy, can you do me a favour? Take a look in that cash box, will you?"

Sam opened the lid of the red petty cash box.

His face reflected the glow of two hundred freshly polished two pound coins.

"Splendid," said Takara, picking up the silver framed photograph of Eleanor Lockhart.

She gazed at her idol adoringly for a second and then planted a single kiss on her lips.

"With you on our side, dear Eleanor, how can we possibly lose?"

43

The door to the public toilets opened very slowly, as if whoever was pushing it forwards was worried that they might damage the outside world somehow. A few cautious seconds passed and then Takara's head emerged into the mercifully unharmed outside world and scanned the surroundings, all done at a suitably clandestine pace.

The coast was clear.

In fact, the coast was unusually, even worryingly, clear.

The side street that housed the public toilets lay between the northerly wall of the cemetery and the southerly wall of the Tesco, and looked directly across to the triangular gardens of the church. By rights, the companions should have had a clear view of the dregs of the food fair – the last few dawdling customers casting a mostly disinterested eye over the remaining mushroom vol-au-vents and chocolate rice crispy cakes; the stallholders packing up their wares with the tired efficiency of people who've had quite enough of this for now, thank you very much; the drinkers and the street poets and local visionaries stumbling after invisible will-o-wisps of inspiration in their usual headlong fashion – but there was no one to be seen.

How long had they been in the tunnels?

It had felt like no time at all, not even an hour.

But the above ground of now bore little relation to the above ground of before.

And it didn't just feel clear.

It felt abandoned.

"It's OK," whispered Takara back to the others before

realising that there was no one to overhear. "Everyone seems to have gone."

Sam, Pat and Gerald tiptoed out into the daylight, with a grumbling, harrumphing Jonno bringing up the rear. Strapped to his back was one of the outsized rectangular boxes that had last been spotted on the cycle courier and he appeared to be entirely undelighted by the prospect. The branches of the capital K on the box stretched and retracted as before, like an ancient oak tree performing its morning calisthenics, and every time they moved Jonno gave the shudder of a man being massaged by a sheet of sandpaper.

"Find some supernova anise, they said. Fill up the box with it, they said," he muttered disgruntledly under his breath. "Don't worry about the itching, they said. You'll get used to it, they said. Or you better do, they said. Because it gets a whole load worse once you put something inside the box, they said. No, the others can't take turns carrying it, they said. This is a job for you and you only, they said."

There was something about Jonno carrying the box that reminded Sam of the minotaur.

Takara led the party across the high street to the triangular gardens. There was nothing there – no litter, no scraps of ripped bunting, no dirty paper plates, no discarded jerry cans of Knucklehead, no festering piles of something unsavoury. The only sign that anyone – or anything – had recently been in the vicinity was a charred patch of grass in the middle of the garden. Like someone had been careless with a supermarket barbecue. Or a pocket flame thrower.

Gerald surveyed the scorched grass with satisfaction.

"Kleinflammenwerfer," he said, wistfully. "One of the most beautiful words in existence."

They continued through the garden to the steps up to the entrance of the church. Six grand columns, not too dissimilar to the ones at the Grand Temple in the necropolis, rose to form a lofty alcove, the ceiling a good sixty feet above them.

Five uniform doors lined the front wall, each the same width and painted the same dark red as the doors at the fire station, and halfway up the wall, dominating the alcove like a sentinel, was a large wooden cross, also painted dark red.

Pat went to open one of the red doors, but found Takara's restraining hand on her arm.

"No," said Takara. "Whatever's passed through here wouldn't have gone into the church. It wouldn't have dared."

Pat locked gaze with Takara for a second and then turned the door handle.

The inside of the church was light and airy with two rows of columns reaching up to the heavens. The ceiling was unnervingly high, so high you had to pull your head back until you cricked your neck to look at it, and even then there was only so much you could take in before your muscles screamed in protest. It was unreasonable and unnecessary, the ceiling of a deity who wanted you to suffer as you cast your eyes up towards him, who wanted you to always remember your place.

The windows were bright and plain, letting in lots of sunlight. If they had once contained stained glass, perhaps depicting pious saints or dutiful worshipers and definitely no daggers dripping in blood or churches on fire, then that stained glass was long gone.

This was a straightforward, no-nonsense house of love.

A house of tough love.

Rows of simple red chairs, the kind you'd find in a doctor's waiting room or a small community centre, led up to a thin wooden podium adorned with a cross.

Behind the podium was a vast blank white wall stretching upwards, so plain and unadorned it was almost oppressive. Here was the backdrop for the sermon of the day and the backdrop wasn't impressed by your frivolity. The backdrop wanted to crack on.

Takara shuddered.

"What's the matter?" asked Sam. "You're not worried about ghosts in here, are you?"

"It's not that," said Takara, a slight flush coming to her cheeks. "It's just churches. The last time I was inside one of these places things didn't turn out so well."

"You mean with Satomi? I thought everything went exactly as you'd planned?"

"Oh, it did. That's the problem."

Directly behind the podium was a small raised platform.

There was something lying on the platform but they weren't near enough to make out what it was. A bulky shadow.

"I can remember everything about that day. The rage I felt going into the church. The elation I felt wearing the dress. I was sick with anger, practically blinded by it, trapped even, but then there was something about the setting, the feeling of the dress on my body, the hurt and confusion and pain on everyone's faces, the shock and power of my words, the clamour, the screaming...oh I never felt so alive."

"And now?"

"Now...it's a little more complicated."

As they drew closer to the bulky shadow, five more shadows appeared from the margins.

These were dark humanoid figures, clad in ragged garments coloured varying shades of green, the interlocking shapes and splurges creating a confusing, distracting backdrop. Their faces were smothered in grime and discontent, their arms swathed in black ink and tribal exaltations. Gold glinted at their earlobes or between their nostrils, their footwear was torn and in some cases covered in what must have been ancient runes, and their heads were swaddled in black wool or the thick fabric of that most fearsome of garb – the hoodie.

"Thank goodness for that," said Takara, with a sigh of relief. "Hi fellas. Great to see you."

The anarchists nodded a silent greeting.

"What's that on your back, Jonno?" called one. "I thought you said being a traveller wasn't for you."

There was laughter, but it was grim laughter.

Laughter under difficult circumstances.

"Who's that?" asked Sam, nodding towards the bulky shadow. It was a body, slumped and lifeless.

"We found him at the farmer's market," said the anarchist that the Heavy Heavy had been leaning on earlier. "At the far end. Away from the high street. Where all the interesting stalls are."

It was a simple idea really. Once a month, four different fairs or markets would happen at the same time, bringing a flood of people and custom to the area.

There was the food fair in the triangular garden in front of the church, stuffed full of culinary treats to gladden the soul and harden the arteries. There was the farmers market, held in the side street between the Tesco and the cemetery, where earlier Takara and her pals had sneaked out of the disused public toilet. There was the artisans market, held in the next side street along, where local craftsfolk offered everything from art and jewellery to clothing and ceramics. And there was The Braderie, held in the little park behind the Old Library, which featured a random assortment of stuff that didn't fit into any of the other markets – junk and collectables, bric-a-brac and antiques, precious rarities and rubbish from the attic, stuff and nonsense. Like a boot fair, but at ten times the price.

The farmers market mostly offered your usual fruit and veg, fresh from the soil and ready for the pot, but at the far end of the street, the stalls became slightly more unusual.

No one in their right mind would try to eat the stuff offered here.

The pickle stall, where the onions and the eggs were joined by murky jars containing indistinct objects that looked like they should really be in a medical laboratory – was that an eyeball, was that a spleen, was that…no, best not think about that one.

The honey stall, ran by operatives in white hazmat suits, who handled the produce with tongs and a sense of trepidation.

The cactus and carnivorous plants stall, where the items for sale had clearly taken bites out of each other.

The spice stall, surrounded by a golden haze.

"Who is he?" asked Sam.

"We don't know," said the anarchist.

He rolled the body onto its back to reveal an old man with a young face. He could have been 75. He could have been 25. He could have been both. He was neat and trim and had the healthy sheen of someone who'd looked after themselves, but there was no escaping the grey hair and the wrinkle lines around his eyes.

His eyes were open.

Wide, open, unblinking, staring into the beyond, like the figures sitting at the tables in the theatre bar. But while their eyes had a grey sheen to them, glazed over in stasis, this man's eyes were purple, the purple of the K Spice.

"Do you know him?" Sam asked Takara.

"I do," she said, her eyes locked on the man's, drawn by the purple. "It's Rex, from the spice stall."

The purple of the man's eyes swirled, like fluid in a lava lamp.

"I don't know if that's his real name, but that's what everyone calls him. Rex. A royal name for true royalty. The king of condiments, the sultan of sensation, the nawab of nutrition. If you want your taste buds to dance with glee under a cloudless, moonlit sky, then Rex is your man."

"Mr K had an appointment with RG. R for Rex!" said Sam. "But what happened to him?"

Takara knelt down and started rummaging through Rex's pockets.

"Hey!" protested Sam. "You couldn't do it with The Unresolved and you still can't do that here. This is definitely a violation of personal space!"

Takara ignored him and carried on going through Rex's pockets.

"It's wrong! Stop it!"

The anarchists looked on with interest, like medical students observing an appendectomy.

These notions of right and wrong. How fascinating.

"A-ha, here we go!" said Takara.

She got to her feet and held something up for everyone to see.

It was a snow globe.

Inside was a tiny street scene. A clutch of market stalls. A handful of ravenous pot plants. A body lying on the paving slabs.

"This will answer a few questions for us," Takara said, grinning.

"On with the show."

44

The plan, like all good plans, started with an act of deception.

The large black telephone gave off its loud, authoritative ring. The Blessed Mr K calmly picked up the receiver.

"Mr K's. How can I help you?"

A muffled voice at the other end of the line answered in a panic.

"Oh yes, hello. Thank heavens you're there. I really need your help. It's an emergency."

"No need to be alarmed, sir. We'll do everything in our power to assist."

"Yes, yes, thank you," said the voice, slightly breathless with anxiety. "It's my brother's wedding day, you see. And there's been a problem with the food we've ordered for the reception."

"An order placed with us, sir?"

"No, no, erm…" The voice tailed off in shame. "It was with The Hanging Stone."

"Oh dear, sir. We were all very sorry to hear about poor Mr Barnaby. I'm sure with time and patience, and perhaps a little therapy, he'll be back stirring the pot with his usual alacrity. It must have all been a terrible fright for him."

"Yes, well we didn't read about it in the papers and even if we had I'm not sure I'd know what a Palmetto Bug is," continued the voice. "So we had no idea that The Hanging Stone was out of action."

"The perils of being a single point of failure, sir."

"Listen, the reception is soon, like very soon, almost imminent, and we need a big batch of your highest quality dish as soon as you can make it."

"Our highest quality dish, sir? That would be the Sawai Bahadur. I must warn you that it's not an inexpensive choice."

"Don't worry about the cost. It's my brother's wedding day. Money's no object! All we're worried about is how quickly you can get the stuff cooked up."

"In no time at all, sir. This is Mr K's. Our chefs are always on standby. How many people do you need to cater for?"

"250."

Now it was the Blessed Mr K's turn to sound panicked.

"I'm not sure we have enough of a particular ingredient to make 250 Sawai Bahadur dishes, sir. I will have to check with my superior."

The voice was incandescent.

"Do whatever you have to do! We need this food right away!"

"Funny, isn't it?"

"What?"

"We couldn't hear the voice on the other end of the line at all when we were in the room with the black telephone," said Sam. "But now we can hear everything. Clear as crystal."

"That's because…look, just watch…"

Mr K put on his special spice rack glasses and then turned to face his supplies.

"We have just enough," he said to the Blessed Mr K, who was standing at the doorway with a worried look on his face.

"Hey, I thought he said he'd never been in that room," said Pat. "What did he call it? The Master's Chamber or some such nonsense. I knew he was spinning us a tale!"

"Well, he's not technically in the room, he's …"

"Oh, do shut up, Gerald!"

"Good news, sir," said the Blessed Mr K. "We have the ingredients we need to complete your order. If you could just supply us with an address and our cycle couriers will bring it to you presently."

"No, no, there's no time to waste on cycle couriers," barked the voice in response. "Give us your address and we'll come round and pick it up with our van."

"I'm afraid we don't have a physical address any more, sir. At least not one that makes any sense. Perhaps we could arrange a rendezvous?"

"OK then. Where?"

"Do you know the disused toilet by the side of Tesco?"

The door to the public toilet opened and a man stepped out who looked like the missing evolutionary link between Mr K and the Blessed Mr K. He wore a dark suit and a dark shirt with a purple tie. At his wrists, purple cufflinks glistened in the way that only purple cufflinks can.

"The Estimable Mr K, I assume," said Takara.

Standing before a big black van, conspicuous in its lack of markings, were three figures. One hefty man. A second heftier man. And a third man who stayed in the considerable shadows of his companions.

"Oh no! It's the Big Heavy and the Heavy Heavy!" cried Sam. "It's a trap. We have to warn them!"

"There's nothing we can do," said Takara. "This has already happened, remember?"

The Big Heavy opened the back of the black van and offered what was supposed to be a welcoming smile to the Estimable Mr K.

"Here, let us help you with everything," he said, his face an unsettling mix of leer and grimace.

A couple of workmen, dressed in the same uniform as the cycle courier, started carrying bags of culinary paradise over to the black van, and the Heavies made a big show of helping out, taking bags out of the hands of professionals who were doing a perfectly decent job on their own, putting things down in what was obviously the wrong place, offering constant and unneeded words of encouragement and commentary, and doing everything they could to get in the way and turn a simple transfer of goods into a disorganised kerfuffle.

The third man, meanwhile, used the cover of the shadows, that seemed to wrap around his features like a familiar cloak, and the distraction caused by the theatrically hapless Heavies, to sneak his way to the back of the Estimable Mr K.

He paused for a moment and the air around him throbbed with concentration. The shadows receded a little and the beginning of the man's features started to come into sharp relief. His face was still obscured but there was a sense of the man - of nobility and pride, of pain and disgust, of the grimmest of grim determination.

His hand slid into the Estimable Mr K's pocket like it wasn't there, like there was no flesh and blood to cause any disturbance, and it emerged holding a key.

The Heavy Heavy slammed shut the door of the van and bared his teeth with a jollity that somehow felt threatening.

"Mmm, I can't wait to tuck into this delicious feast you've prepared for us," said the Big Heavy, as the third man retreated into the shadows. "I have to say, it smells…"

"Divine?" said the Estimable Mr K.

"Precisely."

"Hello? Rex? Ah, my dear fellow. You're keeping well, I trust?"

Mr K stood at his desk in his chamber, a hint of tension rippling across his features. In his hand was the receiver of a big red telephone, identical in design to the big black telephone, but coloured a vivid emergency red, the red of warning lights and fire stations.

"My, that does sound delightful," Mr K continued. "I'm so sorry to have to hurry you onto business, but I'm afraid we're completely out of your most precious spice. Yes, the supernova. You wouldn't happen to have any in stock, would you?"

Mr K listened intently.

"This is weird," said Sam. "How come we could hear the voice of the person ordering the food for the wedding, but we can't hear Rex?"

"It's a different telephone?" suggested Takara. "Maybe the red one is a secure line."

"But it's not consistent," said Sam. "We can't hear, then we can hear, then we can't hear again. It all just feels so...selective."

"Like the snow globe is choosing what to show us."

"Yes. I don't like it."

Mr K smiled, the tension ebbing from his features a little.

"That's excellent news, thank you so much. Could you meet me later today in the octagonal room? 4pm perhaps? Splendid. Oh, and you'll need the password, of course."

Mr K turned to the Blessed Mr K and the Estimable Mr K, who were both standing at the door.

"Do we know what this month's password is for the octagonal room?"

"It's still xylophones," said the Blessed Mr K. "They haven't changed it in ages."

"Hey!" cried Takara. "That's our secret password! No one's meant to know that!"

Mr K nodded and shook his head with disbelief.

"Still xylophones, it seems. Yes, I know. You can say that again. Right then, I'll see you at four. The Estimable Mr K will be along shortly with the key."

Number Two considered the object with their customary mixture of blankness and confusion.

"What is your evaluation of this mechanism?" they asked Number Four, who was regarding the object with a similar measure of bewilderment. "I assume this falls within your local culture remit?"

"Er, yes, of course," replied Number Four.

Number Four picked up the object and made a show of giving it a thorough examination.

"In my considered opinion," began Number Four, in the manner of someone who wasn't entirely sure what was about to come out of their mouth next, "this is either a portable trap or a torture device of some sort."

Number Two nodded with approval and looked over to the boot fair stall holder, an overweight man in a string vest who was beginning to wonder if his life was really going exactly as he'd planned.

"What is this?" demanded Number Two, proffering the object.

"Egg slicer, mate. Three for a pound."

Takara looked at Sam and smiled conspiratorially.

Number Two turned to admonish Number Four only to find that they'd been replaced by a large man in a black suit. Thinking that they must have made a positioning error, they turned in the other direction, only to find another even larger man, who looked like he was doing his best not to break into a pivot.

"Three for a pound," said the Big Heavy. "Now that is a bargain."

Number Two had nothing in their database that could serve as a worthy response.

"But do you know what's even more of a bargain?" asked the Big Heavy with a glower. "Something for nothing. After the evening I've had, I shouldn't be feeling so generous. But it looks to me like it's your lucky night, and maybe if it's your lucky night, then it can be my lucky night as well. Do you know what I mean?"

Number Two most definitely did not.

"We can see what you're doing and we like what we see," continued the Big Heavy. "And we just want to help out. Consider this a pat on the back from a secret admirer."

And the Big Heavy pressed the key into Number Two's hand.

"Now you ain't seen me, alright?"

Number Two stared back at him with empty, mournful eyes.

"Rex? There's a problem. The Estimable Mr K has lost the key. Yes, yes, it is impossible, I agree, but here we are. Ah, that's very kind of you, and I suppose it would be fitting for the Estimable Mr K to clean up this mess himself, but you've always dealt with me direct and there's a good reason for that. There's nothing else for it. I'll have to come to you."

There were the muffled sounds of protest from the Estimable Mr K.

"It's the food fair this weekend, isn't it? Look, no one will notice me among the crowds. It'll all be perfectly safe."

The third man spoke out of the shadows to the Big Heavy and the Heavy Heavy, his presence little more than a disturbance in an indistinct patch of black and dark greys.

"Now is everyone clear on what you need to do and when?"

"Yes boss," said the Heavies.

"And have you synchronised your watches?"

"No boss," replied the Heavies. "But it'll be OK. We don't need the watches."

"Are you sure?"

"Totally. We know what we're doing."

The snow globe started to shake, as if it were being engulfed by an approaching earthquake.

Everything else in the church remained perfectly still.

Takara reached out instinctively and grasped Sam's hand.

The snow globe reached what felt like maximum velocity.

And then it shattered.

For an instant, before the images suddenly disappeared, everything happened at once.

Mr K emerged from the public toilet and quickly joined the anonymity of the crowd, making his way towards the farmer's market. It was a busy one today. Lots of curious, hungry people.

The Heavy Heavy picked up his black leather kitbag, and he and the Big Heavy started making their way towards the Knucklehead Stall.

Rex stood at his spice stall, wearing a deep mauve backpack. He jiggled around nervously, as if conscious of a precious burden.

The Inspector closed the gate of the cage and looked at its inhabitants with satisfaction.

Sam tilted his face to the sky and let the warmth of the sun burn away the memories.

The third man took a small bottle of ointment and dabbed a few drops into a handkerchief. Beside him, three more henchmen cast generous shadows.

Takara took the matchbox out of her pocket.

Mr K shook Rex's hand with evident pleasure.

The first cockroach blinked out of existence.

The pork pie gathered speed.

A spark of electricity leapt from the wind chimes to the cake stands.

The third man came up behind Mr K and pressed the handkerchief to his face.

The Inspector snapped her fingers with impatience.

A henchman held a struggling Rex, while the third man opened the mauve backpack. He took out a spice jar brimming with golden, fluorescent grains.

"Looks like a good batch," the third man said to Rex.

Rex nodded silently, his gaze fixed fearfully on the spice jar.

The third man licked his finger and dipped it into the jar.

"Try it for me," he said, pressing his finger to Rex's lips.

The Inspector tapped the Big Heavy and the Heavy Heavy on the forehead with her black and red cane.

Rex's eyes glazed over with a purple sheen.

The henchmen loaded Mr K's inert body into the back of the black van. An alarmed chatter began to spread among the onlookers.

The Inspector clicked her fingers.

The images, overlapping and increasingly out of focus, started to fade and then slipped out of view.

"Oh dear," said Takara. "It looks like we've been had."

45

There was a pause – a single heartbeat of shocked silence – and then the door to the church startled rattling, like a tempest had suddenly blown up outside and someone was desperately trying to get in.

Then the windows followed suit, the frames shaking with a fevered urgency, those big clear panes of glass letting in so much bright light they practically became opaque.

The flames of the ceremonial candles dotted throughout the church began to tremble.

Like they knew something.

Jonno motioned to Rex.

"What are we going to do about him?"

"We don't need to do anything," said Takara. "The spice may have knocked him out, but like everyone who works with the stuff professionally, he'll have developed an immunity. Not as effective as Mr K's chefs perhaps, but it's keeping him safe for now. After all, what's the number one rule of being a good salesman?"

"Don't get high on your own supply," said Jonno.

"Precisely. He'll be fine."

"OK, then, but what are we going to do about that?" Sam pointed nervously at the rattling door.

"I'm afraid we're going to have to go and face whatever's on the other side of it," said Takara. "We need to find The Duke and The Inspector. And fast."

"The Duke?" Sam spluttered.

"Yes. Out of the frying pan into the sea of molten lava, as the old saying goes."

Takara opened the church door as tentatively as she'd opened the door to the public toilet. When reality was as fragile as this, the last thing you wanted to do was break it.

Sam had expected to be assaulted by a howling gale, but all was calm and quiet. A few lone figures scurried across the high street, shoulders hunched, body language taut in the face of imminent peril, but there was nothing obvious to run away from.

And still the door rattled.

"Something's not right here," said Takara, frowning.

Then they all felt it. The atmosphere thickened suddenly, like a humidity, like it was filling up with something, filling up with possibility. And the air got thicker and thicker, and fuller and fuller, until they could feel it on their skin, that sense that the world around them was just about to burst.

And then, with a flash, it started.

The spark of electricity, ricocheting like a pinball, pinging from point to point, gathering energy as it went, barrelling with glee, playing out a symphony, every point of contact a passage in the most exhilarating composition the world has ever imagined - from the metal poles of the market stalls to the iron railings encasing the triangular garden, from the street lights to the traffic lights, from the wind chimes to the cake stands, from the flagpoles to the weather vane at the top of the church, from the wrought iron gates of the cemetery to the brass key plates on the disused public toilet.

"No, no, no," said Takara. "This shouldn't be happening now. I haven't done anything."

And the spark, rather than completing the circuit and then fizzing out into the infinity of the sky like it did last time, lingered on the brass key plates, as if it was itching for a lap of honour.

Pulsing, juddering, vibrating, like it was about to lose control.

"No, this isn't right," said Takara, starting to shake along with the spark. "This shouldn't be happening, and it shouldn't be…"

It lost control.

Whatever the word is for a spark of pure chaos completing one more circuit than it's supposed to, place it here.

Use at least one Z.

Preferably three or four.

"Oh my god, if this carries on going then…"

Off it went again.

Takara grabbed Sam's hand and ran.

"We need to get out of here! Now!"

They ran across the triangular garden, over to the Old Library and into the side street beside the post office, Takara and Sam leading, Pat and Gerald and Jonno hard on their heels.

The side street looped around the back of the Old Library emerging back onto the high street by the estate agents.

Not an evil estate agents. Not the Death Star of all morals. Not the black hole of all decency and humanity. Not the end of all hope and the destruction of the world as we knew it.

Just a regular local estate agent. Nice guy, trying to do the right thing in a world where the right thing is impossible.

A world where the right thing can only lead to the wrong thing.

The side street, though, was different. Away from the demands of the high street, a handful of unusual ventures were trying their best.

There was the clock museum.

Such a beautiful, perfect notion.

A gathering of timepieces to tell the oldest story there is.

A story of elegance and design, a story of memory and loss, a story of times past and time passing, a swish of the pendulum, a whirr of unseen clockwork.

Walking among the grandfather clocks and the mantel clocks, moving from the wall clocks to the cuckoo clocks, drifting by the lantern clocks and the skeleton clocks, was like attending a party hosted by time itself.

Admittance by appointment only.

Wouldn't it be great to say there was a mug museum too? With its spiky warmth and echoes in the walls.

Alas, there wasn't a mug museum. The clock museum had got there first.

There was Helene, the sound sculptor. If you needed someone to create a flutter of tumbling noise for a music festival installation or a wash of disorienting fuzz for an art piece in, say, Stockholm airport – best experienced during an enforced stopover during an unseasonal snow storm (true story) – then Helene could help.

There was the puppet hospital.

The Living Living Room – an ever changing, endlessly replenished living room where everything in sight was for sale, including the till, the counter, the window sills, the curtains, the front door, and (if the price was right), the shop assistant themselves.

Staff turnover was high.

The harp factory.

The palace of Turkish delight (actually very popular)

The carpet sanctuary.

And then there was The Emporium.

46

Takara pounded her fist against a thick wooden door, windowless but with a thin strip of metal placed at eye level.

The outside of The Emporium was equally as unwelcoming. Most of the façade was a blank brick wall, painted the shade of dreary grey popular in correctional institutions during the 1970s, and the few windows around head height were painted black, both the frames and the panes themselves. Gaps where the black paint had flaked and peeled away over the years gave only the slightest hint of the treasures that lay within – a glimpse of fabric, a shimmer of pearl.

The only indication that this was, in fact, a shop, open and welcome to the general public, was a large crimson and gold sign which read, in elaborate Victorian fairground lettering: "THE EMPORIUM".

The metal strip slid open abruptly and two eyes peered suspiciously out at them. Two eyes set in a thick black stripe, with hints of white face paint at the edges of the black stripe.

"Oh, it's you," hissed the acid tones of The Inspector. "What are you doing here?"

"Let us in," said a panicked-sounding Takara. "Something weird is happening out here and it's definitely nothing to do with me."

The door flew open and The Inspector leant out to take a proper look. In the distance, the spark of electricity could be seen completing yet another circuit.

The air began to thicken again, the particles throbbing.

"What have you done this time?" said The Inspector.

"Nothing, I told you. It wasn't me. I didn't do anything."

"Get in. All of you."

Sam found himself in an alleyway running along the side of the building. It was a scruffy and neglected alleyway, littered with random scraps of rubbish – crisp packets, crushed beer cans, unpaid council tax bills – and splattered in an impressive variety of animal droppings, from bird to fox and beyond.

Set halfway along the side of the building was the real front door of The Emporium. Mostly glass and festooned with a warming display of fairy lights, it looked jarringly out of place in the scruffy alleyway. In the centre of the door was a large, brightly coloured sign that read: "OPEN".

"It's a shame we can't have the front door facing the street," sighed The Inspector. "But it would attract all sorts of attention. And that really wouldn't do."

She pushed open the front door and led them inside, as a bell jangled brightly.

For a moment, Sam wondered if he was back in the tunnels.

It wasn't that The Emporium had the same impossible infinite dimensions as Takara's cave – that would require a rearrangement of laws and truths that simply isn't imaginable above ground – and it wasn't that it was as densely packed with goods as the Pound Tardis – no one can stack shelves quite like Balfour and Harrington – but it all felt recognisable somehow, as if this was the mother ship, the prime influence, where it all began.

As far as the eye could see, there was something interesting.

Something unusual. An oddity. A curio.

And it was all jumbled together with no rhyme or reason, as if each item had been placed in the nearest spot to hand and that had been the end of it.

There was clothing everywhere.

Jackets and blouses and cravats and cloaks and ponchos and petticoats and hats and boots and full costumes of every type from every era, from prehistoric to the far future.

If you were a thwarted heir trying to wrest your birthright from an evil relation or a disgraced detective seeking to clear your name by uncovering an establishment scandal or a double agent perfecting the ultimate act of betrayal or a crazed overlord on the path to galactic domination, then there was an outfit here for you, often with a full range of props and accessories to match.

Oh, the accessories!

There were wigs and masks and crucifixes and feather boas, tiaras and cufflinks and monocles and earrings shaped like lightning bolts. There were firearms and paintings, stuffed animals and robots, musical instruments and statues, magic lamps and treasure chests, broomsticks and switchblades, stone tablets and chessboards, spell books and cigarette holders, crystal balls and golden tickets, and what looked uncannily liked a full size time machine.

And all of it seemed strangely familiar.

Sam walked along the costume rack, his mind fizzing with déjà vu.

A voluminous red dress, layers of ruffled chiffon, grosgrain ribbon and tulle petticoats. A classic American cop outfit, dating from, roughly, January 15, 1981 to May 12, 1987. A black leather catsuit, unforgiving and ready for action. A white suit, white shirt, white bow tie and white Stetson hat, perfect for a slippery bad guy.

Sam picked up a patterned tie and turned it over in his hand, examining the diagonal stripes that ran its length – some thick red, some thin orange, some strings of ornate box shapes in white and red, some strings of ornate box shapes in red and orange.

It made him think of…not his childhood, but young adulthood.

It made him think of claustrophobia and panic.

It made him think of a hot day stuck inside.

"I feel like I've seen this tie before," he mused out loud.

"I'm sure you have," smiled The Inspector, a hint of pride showing in her otherwise dramatic features. "Depending on your taste, you'll have seen many of these items before."

Sam furrowed his brow.

"I know it, but I can't quite place it."

The Inspector laughed softly, affectionately almost.

"It's from a classic heist gone wrong movie, a true story told by the finest storytellers."

Sam's eyes widened, an image forming in his mind.

"You know those early sequences in the film where the main character's on the phone, his eyes sparkling with fear and uncertainly and excitement and vulnerability? He's in way over his head and he doesn't know what to do and it's all so intoxicatingly magnetic. *He* is all so intoxicatingly magnetic."

"Yes, yes."

"This is the tie he was wearing."

"It can't be."

"Oh it can, and it is," said The Duke, walking towards them from the back of the shop. "In fact, everything you see around you is either from a film or a TV show or a play or a moment in history. We collect them and occasionally sell them to suitable new owners."

The Duke wore the same dark suit as before, and had the same neat, precise air, but this time there was no feeling that he was merely passing through, heading on to the next destination. This was where he was meant to be. Surrounded by culture in his rightful place and home.

Sam picked up a necklace, a golden pendant inlaid with one large red stone and three smaller stones, fashioned as teardrops.

"Beautiful, isn't it?" said The Duke. "I always thought my dear Satomi would have looked good wearing this, but as you can see she has chosen her own sartorial path."

The Inspector's eyes flashed.

"Well, who could compete with darling Kim Novak?" she said. "I could only ever have been a disappointment."

"And this?" asked Sam, picking up a crystal phial of clear liquid.

"A most precious item," said The Duke.

"Yes," nodded The Inspector. "Do you remember the scene in Vivre Sa Vie, where Anna Karina sits, alone and unloved, in the cinema, crying? Well, that's…"

Pat exhaled loudly. She'd seen more than enough.

"Well, this is all very tasteful, I'm sure," she said, pursing her lips as she surveyed the items closest to her with disdain. "And no doubt it would turn the head of a particular type of sophisticate, but I have to say it all looks like random junk to me. I mean, which Oscar winner is this trinket supposed to be from?" she continued, picking up a sword with a green gemstone inlaid at the tip of its handle.

"Hawk The Slayer," said The Inspector. "1980 but the world really wasn't ready."

"I've never heard of it."

"Really? I'm so surprised," said The Inspector. "Don't worry – you wouldn't like it."

The Duke smiled and clasped his hands together in a way that clearly signalled that all conversation had now finished.

He turned to look at Takara.

"I assume that your presence means that you have come to return my book."

"Ah, well, er, no, not quite," said Takara, shifting uneasily. "I was just on my way to attend to exactly that when something else came up."

"It did?"

"I'm afraid she's telling the truth for once," said The Inspector. "I saw it with my own eyes. The electrical spark is doing the rounds as usual…"

"Excellent," said The Duke, nodding towards Takara. "I'm pleased to hear you haven't neglected all of your duties."

"But the problem is that it's not stopping," continued The Inspector. "It's going around and around and around and around. And it's growing stronger as it does so."

"Oh dear," said The Duke. "Whatever have you done now, Takara?"

"Nothing! I told you. It's nothing to do with me."

Sam placed the phial of Anna Karina's tears back on the counter.

"Why do you assume it has something to do with Takara?" he asked. "It started up while we were in the tunnels with the Blessed Mr K. Takara didn't do anything. She was with us the whole time."

The Duke looked at Sam with the same expression he'd used in the cemetery. Part displeasure, part pity.

"Let me ask you a question, Sam," he said. "What would you say are Takara's strongest qualities? Not necessarily her best qualities, but the ones that define her, for good or for bad."

Sam frowned for a moment, thinking.

"Well, she's confident," he said, tentatively. "She's fearless, I suppose. She's, erm, unpredictable? Which is, well, can be, not all of the time, but can be, um, entertaining? She's certainly interesting to be with. I've never met anyone like her before."

Takara blushed and bowed slightly towards Sam.

"She's selfish, self-obsessed, vain, thoughtless, impulsive, erratic, and has such a minute attention span that she's actually a danger to others," chipped in Jonno.

Takara's blush deepened.

"Quite so," nodded The Duke approvingly. "We're all so proud of her. And all so proud of her unique talent for chaos."

"Proud?" said Sam, disbelievingly.

"Of course! Everywhere she goes, something disastrous happens. Everything she touches falls apart. There isn't a situation or a conversation or a relationship that can't be made so much worse by her intervention. And she never does it how you'd expect. So you can never plan or mitigate for her involvement. She's truly unstoppable."

"Ain't that the truth," muttered The Inspector, bitterly.

"So what do you do when one of your nearest and dearest has such a mercurial, capricious talent?" asked The Duke. "You put it to good use. You use her chaotic energy to power something wonderful."

"The spark of electricity!"

"Yes!"

The Duke's dark eyes glittered.

"Have you ever wondered how it all works? How all of the impossible things that you've experienced could be made possible?"

"Never," said Sam. "I don't dare."

"Quite right too," nodded The Duke. "Some things are better left unsaid. But rest assured it wasn't always this way. When I discovered the tunnels…"

A loud snort came from Takara.

"Discovered?" she said, her voice dripping with disdain. "You mean like an intrepid explorer? Machete in hand, chopping your way through the unchartered forest?"

"Well, perhaps discovered is going a bit too far," said The Duke. "When we first ventured into the tunnels…"

He paused to see if there was to be any further protest.

"…they were dark and dormant. An abandoned network of fading memories. A relic of magnificent times gone by. There were hints of the glory that had once flourished within – the artistry of the stained glass window in the octagonal room alone told a thousand stories – but alas it was a place that had forgotten how to be itself."

The Duke looked at Takara and smiled.

"So when my darling asked if she could use a cave we found in the tunnels to house her own nascent collection of precious things – for who could fail to be inspired by what you see around you in The Emporium – I thought nothing of it. In fact, it seemed like it was possibly for the best. She had already proved to be a handful over quite a number of incidents, and so a deserted underground cavern really felt like the best place for her, and for everyone."

"But we had no idea what the tunnels were then. We had no idea that they ran on and fed from chaos. And so we had no idea that letting Takara's chaotic spirit loose in the tunnels was like plugging them into the mains."

Takara smiled.

"How is the impossible made possible?" asked The Duke. "Because, fundamentally and crucially, there is chaos at the heart of everything. Chaos in the birth of a good idea. Chaos in a moment of passion and a leap of faith. Chaos in destruction and inspiration. Chaos in a supernova and a lightning strike. Chaos in the point of connection where the whole becomes so much greater than the individual parts. Where everything and everyone is finally plugged in."

The lightning bolt broach on The Inspector's lapel sparkled.

"And so we weren't just plugging the tunnels into the mains."

"You were plugging them into chaos," said Sam.

The Duke nodded.

"The ultimate power source."

The green gemstone at the head of the sword began to glow.

Sam thought of all of the inexplicable things he'd encountered. The nocturnal boot fair. The K Spice. The Grey Ghost. The sonic reducer. The gargantuan pork pie. The Pound Tardis. The black and white team.

Takara's moustache. Takara herself.

And he thought of his life before. And how empty it had seemed.

"So this is the trade-off we have made," said The Duke. "In order to benefit from the chaos of the tunnels, we must feed it chaos, keep it plugged in. And so we give Takara free rein, invite her to be herself, with everything that entails. And we stand back and watch with satisfaction at the pandemonium that follows in her wake. What a delight it is. Her greatest asset. Her one true talent"

Takara raised her eyebrow but said nothing.

"Of course, that's not to say that we don't get involved when we have to," The Duke continued. "To make sure everything doesn't get entirely out of hand, my darling Satomi is here to be The Inspector. To monitor the chaos. And keep everyone in check."

"And what a splendid job she's done," said Takara.

The Inspector blushed, glaring at Takara.

Sam considered everything The Duke had said and then thought back to the church door, rattling in the thickening air.

"Something's gone wrong," he said.

"I'm afraid so," The Duke said. "Usually Takara unleashes enough chaos to make the spark do a single loop of the charge points, and that's enough to keep the tunnels topped up. But either Takara did something while you were in the tunnels to upset the system or something has happened to the tunnels themselves, and now it seems we're stuck in an endless charge loop. Which is not the best of news."

"What happens if the tunnels keep charging?" asked Gerald, his practical mind intrigued by the possibilities.

"We don't know. But I can only imagine it'll involve some sort of explosion."

47

All eyes turned to Takara.

"Look, I've told you so many times now. I didn't do anything."

"Yes you did."

"You stole my dress."

"You mislaid my book."

"You lost your balance."

A metal box on the shop counter started to make a harsh mechanical noise. A sharp and guttural noise, as if it was trying to expel an unwanted object.

"What is that?" asked Jonno.

"It's a telegraph," said The Inspector. "Quite a famous one actually. You know the bit in For A Few Dollars More where The Man With No Name sends the bogus telegram to the El Paso sheriff? The one that gets him and his men out of the way while The Man and his buddies blast a hole in the wall of the bank and steal the safe that holds 'almost a million dollars'? Almost a million! Well this is it. The one and the same."

"I thought it was the telegraph from Three Amigos," said Takara.

"No, we swapped that for the sword."

The telegraph continued clanking and rattling and eventually a strip of paper started to emerge from a slot in its side. The Duke leant forward and lifted the strip towards his face, allowing it to carry on feeding out of the machine while he read.

"WE HAVE MR K STOP WE CONTROL SPICE STOP WE RULE THE SCHOOL STOP"

"How charming," said Takara. "It's like being harangued by a cocky juvenile."

"WE WILL DESTROY TUNNELS STOP"

"I think the tunnels are way ahead of you there, pal," said Pat.

"UNLESS STOP"

"Unless stop? Or unless. Stop," frowned The Inspector. "This bit doesn't make any sense."

"I think they're being dramatic," said Sam.

"YOU GIVE US THE BOOK OF THE DEAD STOP"

"Oh, for god's sake."

"Bloody hell."

"Come on, enough is enough. We know you've got the book so stop messing around and hand it over."

"OR TAKARA STOP"

The machine ground to a halt.

The Duke leant forward to read the final few words.

"M STOP"

There was a silence. The Duke exhaled stoically.

"Well, at least we know who we're up against now," he said.

"We've always known it was him," snapped Takara. "Him and his two thugs."

"Oh really?" said Pat, sounding distinctly unamused.

"Yes! I told you. In the Pound Tardis, if you remember! When we realised they had one of our keys! My god, does no one listen to a word I say?"

Sam coughed lightly.

"Erm, Pat and Gerald weren't in the Pound Tardis with us then," he said gingerly. "I think they were still in...you know where."

Pat glowered at Takara.

"I wasn't there either, if that helps," chipped in Jonno, never one to leave a simmering pot unstirred.

The Inspector looked at The Duke.

"You know, I sometimes wonder if Jonno isn't somehow part of the way Takara creates all of her chaos," she said. "He definitely has own talent for rubbing salt into a wound."

"Yes, I agree," replied The Duke. "They certainly make a good team."

"Shut up! You too, Jonno!"

Jonno shut up, his work done.

Sam shook his head.

"OK, then, I'll ask, as usual. Who or what is M?"

The Duke fixed his eyes on Sam.

"He runs the B&Q."

A bell tolled in the depths of hell.

The B&Q sat in the centre of the high street – an unwelcome intruder from the crass world of big business. Around it lay an elegant curve of Edwardian buildings, still tall and proud despite years of neglect and accumulated grime, but the B&Q was from another time and another headspace. It didn't care about style or grace. It made no effort to blend in with the architecture of the past. It was a squat brick box with a huge orange store sign that looked like every other squat brick box with a huge orange store sign in the country.

The B&Q would have been an affront in any location, but here it felt especially sore, as it was an ugly reminder of what had been lost.

The Regent Cinema opened in exactly the same spot at the start of 1933. From the outside, it looked like a fortress, a grand citadel of culture built to withstand the philistine hordes, while inside, a large foyer with chandeliers, ceiling to floor mirrors and a sweeping staircase led to a cavernous, almost cathedral like, performance space. You didn't just passively watch a movie in a room like this, especially not in the 1930s. Stepping into The Regent was more like going to church and communing with a higher power, the vast space and faraway ceiling giving a sense of the infinite and the omnipotent.

Fittingly, the opening night film was King Kong. A royal picture for a royal occasion. A glimpse of the unknown in a temple of wonders.

Here was another world. Where the mayor of the borough cut the ribbon and a brass band played a rousing rendition of the national anthem. Where the hubbub and disorder of the high street was replaced by a succession of marvels – an opening cartoon, a newsreel, a supporting feature called The Vanishing Lady, such images and sensations to bathe the mind in awe.

And then the lights dimmed. And the gong sounded. And the heroine screamed. And the trees parted. And the magical dots of black and white, monochrome that somehow sang in technicolour, the blacks so perfectly black, the whites almost a magnetic silver, picked out the first sighting of the beast.

And the cinema roared in terror.

All that was gone.

The Duke picked up an oval amulet, one of many items he had from the greatest monster movie of all time.

"He is not, by all accounts, a particularly nice man. Or a particularly good boss. He treats his employees and customers and the very notion of running a B&Q with contempt. In fact, I would go so far to say that he treats the notion of the high street itself with contempt."

Jonno shrugged.

"All bosses are like that. Vive la revolution!"

The Duke regarded Jonno with a dry amusement.

"That's as maybe," he said, "but with M it all somehow feels personal."

"Like a resentment," said The Inspector.

"Like revenge," nodded The Duke.

"But if he hates the high street so much, why does he want to control it?" said Sam. "And why does he want to destroy the tunnels?"

"And why does he want the book?" said Gerald.

All eyes turned, once again, to Takara.

Takara exhaled.

"Look, I don't have the book. I'm sorry. I don't know what happened to it. I wish I did have it, so I could give it back to you, so you could hand it over to M, and we could restore both Mr K and the high street to their rightful state and save the tunnels at the same time. But I don't. So I guess we'll just have to give him me."

Pat nodded with approval.

"That works for me."

The Duke and The Inspector also nodded, slowly, with a touch of reluctance.

"I suppose we have no choice," said The Duke.

"Off to B&Q we go, then," said Pat.

"No."

Sam's voice was clear and adamant.

"No, we can't," he said. "Not yet."

"Why in the heavens not?" said Pat.

"Because it's not time. Because we haven't found all of the items."

"What?" said Pat. "You're still thinking about the treasure hunt? I hardly think that matters right now."

"It's all that matters."

"Sam, I know you're trying to be nice, but the hunt really doesn't matter," said Takara. "It's just something we do to keep ourselves amused."

Sam looked at Takara.

"We?"

"OK, alright. If you want to be nit-picky about it, then I suppose it's mostly yours truly," said Takara, with a faint shrug. "The guy you met, the one you said was my brother. Remember him? Supercilious, smug, unhelpfully verbose and frustratingly vague, more like an avatar than a normal human being. Well, that was me. I thought you would have guessed from the cut of his jib, which I have to say was cut impeccably well."

"But he was a man..." Sam started to say before trailing off.

"Oh yes. And what a man. Pleased with himself, his own importance, and the fact he got to stand on a little box to deliver his speech. I do love those gender switch costumes, as you know, and if the costume comes with a barbed comment on the male psyche then all the better. Say so myself, but one of my stronger performances."

Sam looked dazed.

"But why?"

"Why do I bother? Well, it's fun, of course, and I do like to see people struggle, and being in a position where you know where everything's hidden but no one knows that you know gives you such a warm glowy feeling that's hard to quantify. Plus it creates chaos, and as we've heard chaos is what keeps the cogs turning down there. And if I set the rules, act as the chief villain, and oversee everything as a kind of counterspy, then the potential for chaos really is limitless."

"So you do know where The Book Of The Dead is then."

Takara flinched.

"Ah, well…"

She struggled for words like a castaway grasping for driftwood.

"I, erm, well, it's hard to, um, I mean, look…it's hard to explain." She took a deep breath to buy herself some time. "I know where all the items should be."

"Really."

"All I can think is there's been a hilarious mix up with the planning and someone's going to have a story about this that we're all going to laugh ourselves silly about later on."

Sam's features hardened.

"So that's it then. Everyone's been playing this game as if it were real and you've been playing knowing that it isn't with the twist being that you didn't realise that it's real after all."

"Well, when you put it like that…"

"And that's why we need to complete the hunt. Because you've lost control of the chaos."

There was a silence.

"Which means the tunnels are capable of anything."

Pat shook her head in despair.

The Duke and The Inspector regarded Sam with interest, turning over what he'd just said in their minds.

Jonno glanced at Takara, trying not to be noticed.

Gerald thought about cupcakes.

And Takara looked like she'd just caught a whiff of the K spice.

"I hate to say it, but I think you might be right," she said. "The previous games have been fun and it's always enjoyable seeing people blundering into traps and falling over tripwires, but this one's been different. I've never encountered anything like The Grey Clown before. I mean, that was quite, well, difficult, and emotional."

"Like someone, or something, is trying to make a point," said Sam.

Pat shook her head once more.

"Oh, for goodness sake," she said. "Let's do it your way then, if we really must."

"We must."

"So what's next on your list?" asked The Inspector.

"It's why we came here," said Sam. "We need a hero's headdress."

48

As soon as Sam mentioned the hero's headdress, a spark lit in The Duke's eyes, part interest, part excitement, part engagement, like someone had finally flicked the switch on his back marked "ON".

This is what he was here for.

Unsurprisingly, there were a variety of choices.

Like there are a variety of elements in the periodic table.

Or a variety of words for snow.

The Inspector stepped behind the counter, keeping watch in case there were any more unscheduled visitors, while The Duke led them to the back of the shop.

Past the mannequins and electric chairs.

Past the skeletons and golden spears.

Past the boulders, stacked in ascending order of size.

Past the throne to end all thrones.

The Duke gestured to an open doorway, beyond which were an infinity of overflowing shelves and a ladder on castors.

"The Hat Room," said The Duke, with a dramatic flourish and a wink to Takara, who was keeping well back. "What is your heart's desire?"

Sam didn't know where to begin.

"I don't know," he said, suddenly paralysed by choice. "The exact wording was a hero's headdress."

"Ah, but a hero to whom?" asked The Duke. "We all have different people we admire."

"A hero to everyone, I suppose."

The Duke chuckled softly.

"Batman? Superman? Hercules?"

"Who do you like?" Sam asked The Duke.

Takara rolled her eyes, seemingly for both herself and Satomi, who would have done the same, had she not wisely elected to stay at the front of the shop.

"Oh, I'm drawn to the light, dear boy," said The Duke. "My heroes are luminous, magnetic."

"Like Pacino."

"Yes, but only in Dog Day Afternoon. I'm very particular."

"Well, do you have any of their hats?" asked Pat, briskly. "These luminous heroes of yours."

"Of course."

The Duke walked beside the shelving, running his hand lightly over the hat boxes. There was an affection to his touch, like a caress.

He stopped at a box labelled FDA012. He gently opened the lid and slowly took out a fedora, holding it as if it might crumble into dust were it handled too roughly.

"Oh, I know this one!" said Gerald, with delight. "It's Indiana Jones, isn't it?"

"No, no," smiled The Duke. "That's FDA003. I don't think you could believably call Dr Jones luminous. There are many famous fedoras in film, but this one belongs to The Man Who Fell To Earth."

They stared at the hat in silent reverie.

It felt like they'd risk huge offence if they did anything else and no one wanted to offend The Duke. Not even Pat.

The Duke placed the hat back in the box and moved on, his fingers still trailing as he went.

"But I can't show you that one without showing you this..."

He paused at a box labelled HDR002.

The Duke held up a white headdress topped by four thick golden bands.

This time there was no need to feign the reverie.

Sometimes you can feel the history of a room when you walk into it, feel the weight of past events, hear the echoes of what once was. If you're lucky you can sense the ghosts walking right through you.

This headdress had seen history. It had led the charge into battle. It had witnessed the world passing from one era to another.

"Startling, isn't it?" said The Duke. "The headdress worn by Peter O'Toole in Lawrence Of Arabia. The most luminous performance of all time."

Sam looked at The Duke holding the headdress and suddenly felt the import of the moment. He was never going to experience this again.

"What's in HDR001?" Sam asked.

The Duke smiled at Sam, a smile of recognition.

"Lawrence's original headdress. Slightly less photogenic, but the real thing."

"Can we see it?"

"I'm afraid not. There are too many spirits locked up in that box. It would be unwise to release them."

Sam gazed at the headdress in the Duke's hands, his mind a blur of echoes and visions.

A hazy orange sky and a dark horizon.

An expanse of desert rising like a tidal wave.

Dazzling sunlight dancing before distant apparitions.

The deepest, purest eyes looking upwards with a quiet purpose.

Takara coughed.

"I'm sure everyone's having a lovely time and I am sorry to spoil the party, but is this it? Men from a very particular time in history – a golden age, I'm sure – having feelings in a way that only men from that particular time can, it appears. Is that all that's on offer? Luminous man after luminous man after luminous man. Aren't there any, you know, luminous women?"

The Duke smiled, placing the headdress back in its box.

"Forgive me, darling. You're quite right," he said, as Takara's gaze hardened. "The tunnels don't want my hero. They want yours. And I have just the thing."

49

Takara, Sam, Pat, Gerald and Jonno made their way cautiously through the deserted high street.

Much to his displeasure, Jonno still had the large rectangular box strapped to his back. He'd tried his best to leave it at The Emporium, arguing that they'd all seen the jar of supernova anise being taken by the third man – who he supposed was the dreaded M – and so there was no longer any point in lugging the box around with them, as they weren't likely to find the jar just lying around somewhere, were they?

But it had been to no avail.

Jonno wasn't sure exactly what they were taking out, but they were definitely taking it out on him.

Directly in front of Jonno, Sam carried a large white hat box.

He had accepted the task with good grace.

This was an honour rather than a burden.

They passed by the supermarket where Sam's journey had started, all that time ago, and reached a crossroads and a set of traffic lights.

Just across the road from the supermarket there was a bank and a chip shop, the former boarded up, with the cash points blocked off, and the latter still open for business, the welcoming glow of deep-fried batter and hand-cut chips spilling out onto the pavement.

The area was once famous for hosting the most robbed bank in the country. The branch opened in the dying days of the 19th century and survived two world wars, the moon landing, and countless political and sporting disappointments, but seven robberies over eleven years at the start of the 21st century brought its story to a close.

This wasn't that bank. That was further up the high street.

The shutters on the Pound Tardis were pulled down tight. Normally at this time the shop would be open, dispensing vital supplies in moments of crisis, but Balfour had been a man of his word.

They pressed on silently, passing the fishmongers and the charity shop, the butchers and the supermarket, the kebab house and the phone shop, the sweet shop and the Portuguese cafe.

Eventually, they reached the Greggs, the last shop before the B&Q.

It was open, of course it was open.

What kind of calamity could close the gates to heaven?

Gerald peered inside wistfully. There was no one there. No customers waiting patiently at the counter. No workers in branded hats and aprons scurrying from oven to till and back again.

There were just the sausage rolls.

Beckoning.

Takara placed a tender hand on Gerald's shoulder.

"Be strong, my friend," she whispered in his ear. "Now is not the time. We need to focus on the ordeal ahead."

Just past the Greggs was a small side street that led to the car park behind the B&Q. Not too long ago, it had also led to the Dead Ball Snooker Club, a shady late night establishment tucked into the building behind the Greggs, the insalubrious yin to its wholesome yang. The club had started innocently enough, the well kept tables and reasonable bar prices attracting players from the outer reaches of the borough, but a slow decline in its latter years saw the tables pushed to the wall and the club used for rowdier nocturnal activities.

Takara was a fan of rowdy nocturnal activities, but even she knew where to draw the line. She glanced at the boarded up club entrance at the far end of the side street and shook her head silently.

Finally, it was upon them.

Usually buildings of import leave something behind. There is a presence, even in absence – the energy of times gone by, the ghost of what once had been.

But here there was nothing.

No lingering echo of the sturdy magnificence of The Regent or the roar of the crowd on the opening night. No vibrations or reverberations. Just an emptiness that felt horribly permanent.

The squat brick box of the B&Q sat there, like a forgotten place holder in a story that had been abandoned long ago. A bright orange sign spanned the length of the building, a dash of colour that felt territorial rather than welcoming. Was it a finishing line or a starting line or a do not cross line, the kind you'd see erected around a serious incident? And was that lurid shade of orange meant to attract innocent passers-by or to give a desperate last ditch warning?

Here comes a candle to light you to bed.

(Aisle 4, General Household)

Here comes a chopper to chop off your head.

(Aisle 7, Kitchen)

Outside the B&Q were two sets of temporary metal shelves. Most B&Qs offset the unrelenting drudgery of DIY – the endless racks of grout powder, floor trim, underlay, mould resistant paint, brackets, wall plugs, white laminate scotia, wood preservative, gripper rods, toilets seats and self-levelling screed – by having a half-hearted attempt at a garden centre out the back. Never mind that sinking feeling of your soul imploding as you compare a needless variety of acrylic worktops, the logic ran – at least afterwards you'll be able to lift your spirits with a water feature and a pot plant.

But this B&Q didn't have any space for a garden centre. There was a car park and a boarded up snooker club out the back. So every day a hapless lunk had to drag the metal shelves to just outside the front door and stack them with a random assortment of greenery, and then make sure the shelves remained intact throughout the day.

Takara had been clear about their plan of attack. Their best chance of getting past the B&Q alive was to stick to the opposite pavement and hope to blend in with the nondescript camouflage of the shops on that side of the street – an estate agent, a betting shop, and a cupcake shop that had opened in a blaze of optimism after a food festival one month and whose owners now wept tears of remorse on a daily basis.

As they inched slowly forwards, a figure came out to tend to the shelves.

A familiar figure.

Shoulders hunched, head bowed, its arms and legs and torso still black with dirt, the filthy backpack replaced by a grubby apron and an orange name tag, the short lengths of chain on its ankles and wrists rattling as it began to straighten the pot plants and double check that the plants and the price tags matched up.

"The minotaur," whispered Sam, in awe.

"So this is where it was off to," muttered Jonno. "No wonder it sounded depressed."

Once again, if the minotaur heard them, it didn't show any sign of caring, but then once again, it appeared to have weightier matters on its mind.

"Plant duty again. Me. Reduced to the lowliest of the low and made to feel grateful for it," the minotaur grimaced, as it got to work. "They could have given me something worthwhile or interesting or maybe just slightly boring, but no. Have I not suffered enough, I ask myself every morning, and once again I am faced with the grim reply: no, you have not suffered enough. You have not even begun to suffer."

Someone had moved the polka begonia in front of the price tag for the golden pothos. Wearily the minotaur moved everything back to its rightful place.

"Devil's ivy, they call this," it said, peering balefully at the golden pothos, a fairly nondescript houseplant that didn't look remotely demonic. "So called because it's almost impossible to kill. You can stick it in a darkened room and it'll still stay green, still keep growing and going on. They say it's a friend of the darkness, but is that any kind of friendship? Sounds like a life sentence to me. And I should know one of those when I see one."

Someone had bought a Chinese money plant. They always did. The minotaur took a replacement from its basket and placed it on the shelf.

"Look at this place," it said, taking a moment to gaze up and down the high street. "I would call it a dump but that's doing a disservice to dumps. A grave disservice. Ask anyone about the dump and they'll tell you that dumps are fun. The destruction, the catharsis. Even the rainiest day at the dump is a day to cherish. But there's no fun here, is there? Fun died here a long time ago."

Someone had dropped a till receipt. A paint brush set, two rollers, a bottle of white spirit, and four tins of mould resistant paint. Always with the mould resistant paint. The minotaur bent down slowly to pick it up.

"Remember what this high street used to be like. When this was the cinema. When this was the centre of the world. We had everything. Two art stationer shops, book shops, haberdashery shops, three quality shoe shops, Tesco, Boots, a ballet school behind the Co-Op, two record shops, two toy shops, a big department store where the Superdrug is now, a huge restaurant and deli where we now have a loan shark, two boutiques, a tropical fish shop, five banks, a fabulous community hall, a beautiful library. All gone now."

"I'm sure the Tesco is still there," said Sam, still whispering.

"Tescos are like cockroaches," said Gerald, gnomically.

There was an expectant pause, but he had nothing further to add.

The minotaur groaned, its mighty frame and blackened horns shaking.

"I used to be someone back then," it moaned. "Now I'm just something."

And with that it looked up and met Jonno's gaze head on.

The minotaur looked at Jonno and Jonno looked at the minotaur.

They saw each other and they recognised each other.

Jonno felt the weight of the oversized box on his back, and the pointlessness of that weight.

"We're all trapped," said the minotaur. "Trapped in the maze."

And it turned back to tend the shelves.

Takara saw her chance and took it.

"Come on, let's go," she said, chivvying everyone along. "I'm not exactly sure what just happened, but we need to get out of here and get out of here now. If we have anything to discuss, we can discuss it later."

"What did just happen, Jonno?" asked Pat, as they moved onwards.

"I said later," said Takara.

Jonno shook his head.

"I don't know. I really don't know."

Beyond the B&Q lay the outer reaches of the high street, the final few shops before the big crossroads.

Beyond the crossroads was a mishmash of local shops and cafes (and the former most robbed bank, now – inevitably – an estate agent), as if someone had gone through a list of what should have been on a high street and added everything that had been forgotten.

But that small stretch between the B&Q and the crossroads felt different. Like a no man's land, like an aftershock, the few establishments foolish enough or uncaring enough to stand shoulder to shoulder with the mouth of hell.

Sorry, I mean the B&Q.

First came the pub. Not a proper pub, but something that used to be worthwhile – a hardware store perhaps or a post office – turned into a place where you could sit on a tea chest and drink ale from a tin mug and kid yourself it was culture.

Then there was the general store. In theory, supposedly like the Pound Tardis, but in practice as far from the bijou perfection of the Pound Tardis as it's possible to get.

It was called All Kinds Of Everything, like it was mocking itself, and it was three times the size of the Pound Tardis, and contained at best a tenth of the stock, most of it utterly useless. You could wander its aisles for days without finding anything you needed, or anything anyone needed. It was defiantly, wholeheartedly, unfit for purpose. If you had to choose a shop that was obviously acting as a front – say for a drugs cartel or a secret book shop – then this is the place you would have chosen.

Finally, there was the opticians.

And above the opticians was the tower.

50

Looking at it now, Sam was surprised to notice how much the tower above the opticians resembled the watchtower of the fire station. Both had a jagged, brutal feel – serious red brick structures born of the Industrial Revolution, built for soot-splattered days and turbulent nights. But while the fire station tower rose proudly into the sky like a totem, a symbol of the dark power of the building and what lay within, the tower above the opticians somehow managed to lurk in the background, slipping out of focus whenever you turned your attention to it. "Move along, nothing to worry about here," it whispered slyly to your subconscious. "This has been here for as long as you can remember. No need to give it any further thought."

The opticians looked the way it always looked. The shelves in the front window were mostly empty – a handful of outmoded glasses frames, several seasons past their best, gave the impression of an enterprise that had lost the will to live a long time ago – and the brightly lit interior was also empty. There were no visible staff members and no visible customers and there was no visible reason to venture inside.

"Are you sure this is the place?" asked Pat.

"Oh yes," said Takara, cheerfully. "I told you they didn't want to be disturbed, didn't I?"

Takara pushed open the door to the opticians and stepped inside.

There was a moment where reality stiffened, like it was experiencing a sudden shock.

The clear air became hazy, while reality tried to decide what to do, and then the hazy air became clear again.

And before them, joyfully occupying the space where the drab opticians should have been, was a bookshop.

Or rather, a shop with some books in it.

A lot of books.

There are some shops that look like they've been meticulously planned. An interior mapped out and then stock added accordingly. No cramped spaces, no surplus or excess. But then there are other shops that look like they've grown organically from a single item, like bacteria multiplying and spreading over every available surface, a fervid culture with a life and a direction of its own.

There were shelves everywhere, there were books everywhere. There were wide spaces and impossible spaces. There were sudden turns and dead ends. There were random jumbles and doomed, long abandoned attempts at order. There was chaos and there was life.

It felt like there should have been a roadmap handed out at the door, but a roadmap that constantly redrew itself, ever in flux.

Behind the main desk sat a tall woman with even taller hair.

She wore dark blue overalls and her hair spiralled a good eight inches above her forehead, a rising tower of curls and confidence. Sticking out of her hair were a random assortment of metal objects – springs and hairpins and allen keys and the like – and broken bits of clockwork were sprinkled on her shoulders like dandruff.

She stared intently at a small object that she was holding in her left hand and gave no indication of having noticed that she was no longer alone in the shop.

"Books are on the shelves," she said, addressing the middle distance without taking her eyes off whatever was nestling in her hand. "Categories are at the top of each shelf. Fiction and poetry on the ground floor, all the other stuff upstairs. The cafe's between floor two and floor three. Don't go to the top floor unless you really really mean to go to the top floor. Have a rummage and try not to make too much noise."

In her hand was what looked like a tiny Ferris wheel, perhaps two inches tall, placed on a miniscule metal plinth. A panel was open in the side of the plinth and the woman was tinkering inside with a very fine silver tool.

Her brow furrowed intently – half concentration, half consternation.

"Do carry on, won't you?" she said, as she moved the tool micrometre by micrometre. "Can't you see I'm busy?"

Sam leant forward to try and get a better look.

"What are you doing?" he asked.

"What does it look like I'm doing?" huffed the woman. "I'm trying to fix this Ferris wheel. Which I'd be able to get on with if someone wasn't standing in my light."

"Oh, sorry," said Sam, jumping back a step.

Pat, as ever, wasn't impressed.

"Is this what passes for customer service in this day and age?" she demanded, her walking stick vibrating with indignation. "Look at you, wrapped up in some sort of personal project and not giving a fig about anything else. I mean, I assume you work here, but perhaps you don't? I can't see any evidence to support the claim that you do."

"Rota's on the wall," said the woman, with the briefest of head gestures, the springs and micro screwdrivers and snippets of magnetic coil in her hair jangling as she did so.

As one, the companions turned to regard a large yellowing sheet of metal stapled to the wall, which had fridge magnets with names on them placed in the varying sections.

As detailed by the rota, there were six main duties in the shop.

1. TALKING TO CUSTOMERS
2. IGNORING CUSTOMERS
3. READING BOOKS
4. MAINTAINING ORDER AND BALANCE
5. SERVING TEA AND/OR CAKE
6. IMPORTANT RESEARCH

There was a fridge magnet with a name in each section, apart from 4 – MAINTAINING ORDER AND BALANCE – which was empty.

"My name is Katia," said the woman, "and as you can see from the rota, my name is in section 1 – TALKING TO CUSTOMERS – which is why, despite the huge personal inconvenience, I am talking to you now."

"There doesn't seem to be a section on the rota marked HELPING CUSTOMERS," said Sam.

Katia pursed her lips.

"No one took a job here to help people," she said. "We come here because we're all engaged in significant and essential work – projects that have taken over our lives – and yet there is nobody in the world who's willing to pay us for that work. Is it our fault that society has broken down to such an extent that there is no funding for our life-changing endeavours? Thank the stars, then, for this heaven-sent bookshop, which employs without any expectation. Other than to do your very best work, no matter how unbearable the distraction."

"Nice work if you can get it," nodded Jonno.

"Very nice. But before you get any ideas, all the positions are full."

"But there's no one working in section 4," protested Sam.

"Not today there isn't," said Katia with a tone which suggested that today was much like any other day.

Pat still wasn't satisfied.

"This is a disgrace," she fumed, her walking stick now approaching critical.

"Listen, you're looking for a book, right?" said Katia.

"How did you know that?" said Sam.

"We get a lot of your type in here," replied Katia. "Look, all the sections are all very clearly marked. Have a sift through and maybe you'll find what you're after. Feel free to take anything that looks like it might be right. All I ask is that you keep it down. And please, most of all, make sure you don't disturb the haiku."

The ground floor was divided into five separate areas – three for fiction, two for poetry.

The first was labelled "Fiction – Believable".

This area took up the majority of the shop floor and was crammed with bestsellers, old and new, and books that had managed, by timely accident or canny design, to make some sort of fleeting contact with the Human Condition. Or at least what the Human Condition was deemed to be upon date of publication.

The area was further subdivided into topics. Where lesser book shops might have arranged their wares by author surname in alphabetical order, this store grouped everything together by various themes, themes which appeared to change month by month.

This month the "Fiction – Believable" section offered the following:

Anguish
Upheaval
Betrayal
Mistaken Identity
Trains

The second area was labelled "Fiction – Unbelievable, But You Don't Really Mind".

Most of the really good stuff was here.

Again there were various subsections, but unlike the "Fiction – Believable" section, these subsections were set in stone - month in month out, year in year out, the rules of engagement set forever more. They were:

Robots
Time Travel
Sorcery
Happiness
Wells

"Wells?" said Sam, with disbelief. "Who writes books about wells?"

Takara ran her finger along the spines of what seemed to be a series of beautifully designed books, all with a different well at the base of the spine. She slid out Book 17 from the shelf and ran her eyes over the cover, which featured a garland of white skull-shaped flowers wrapped around a black and red well.

"The Missing," she said, quoting the title. Her eyes moved upwards to the critic's quote above the title. "'Breathtaking', it says here."

The third area was labelled "Fiction – You Must Be Joking".

There were no subsections to this area. The main heading was damnation enough.

On the wall between the two main shelving units in the "Fiction – Unbelievable, But You Don't Really Mind" area, was a frayed poster covered in inky thumb marks, that looked like it had hung there for the best part of half a century. In lettering so plain and unadorned it somehow felt ornate, the poster read:

"I have lent this book to many writers and more readers, and all of them thought it good and original, a book different from any other. They could see there were things wrong with it - a novel is a prose narrative of some length that has something wrong with it - but they felt that, somehow, the things didn't matter." – Randall Jarrell, 1965

Takara smirked and glanced over at Pat.

If there was a rug to be pulled or a button to be pressed, Takara could never resist.

"The things they put on posters these days, eh Pat?"

Pat regarded the poster coolly.

"1965, hardly the present day," she shrugged, dismissively. "And really who cares what anyone thinks about fiction, believable or not. I like my books to be factual and precise. Fiction is for the birds."

Takara frowned. This really was most disappointing.

At the desk, Katia let out a low chuckle.

"Hear hear," she said, still peering intently at the Ferris wheel. "Fiction *is* for the birds. For flying high on an upcurrent of hot air. My favourite way to travel."

"It's all nonsense," snorted Pat.

"Of course it is," replied Katia. "And unsound nonsense too, as the poster quite rightly says. No one wants perfection, do they? In things perhaps, like this beautiful object I'm doing my level best to fix, but not in stories and certainly not in people. We're all flawed, one way or another. Some more than most. But the flaws let the magic in and send ripples of electricity coursing in the most unexpected directions. They make everything come alive."

"Still nonsense," said Pat. "Like all art really."

"Oh yes. The best art is imperfect too," nodded Katia. "Sometimes I think the most beautiful exhibits in a gallery aren't the paintings on the walls, but the people standing in front of them."

Sam turned towards the far corner of the shop.

"Does that apply to the poetry as well?"

"Definitely not," said Katia, with a small frown. "Poetry is far more treacherous."

There were two area for the poetry – poetry and haiku.

The first contained everything that wasn't haiku, thrown together in such a haphazard way that it could only have been done by someone in a terrible hurry.

Was there an accidental poetry to the way the varying themes had been jumbled together?

No, it was a flustered mess, there for the unravelling.

The second consisted of a tall thin shelving unit, divided into tiny compartments, each containing three shelves.

The first shelf carried five books.
The second shelf carried seven books.
The third shelf carried five books.

It was as perfect a display as could be.

Beside the haiku shelf was a simple sign:

"Do not remove any haiku without replacing it first."

Everyone stared at the sign.

There was a silence, broken only by the tinkering of Katia at the front desk.

Eventually, someone had to say something.

"But that's impossible," said Sam, confidently speaking for them all.

Katia nodded as she worked.

"Quite so. The haiku cannot be disturbed. It would shatter the beauty," Katia said, sighing. "Our folly is that we achieved perfection. But has it really done any of us any good?"

Gerald stepped forward.

He had spent his time in the shadows of the book shop, but now his moment had come.

"Did you mention something about a cafe?"

51

At the top of the stairs to the first floor were two fibre glass figures that looked like they had once gathered dust in The Emporium.

The first was a man in his mid-fifties with white hair and a neat white beard. He was wearing a crumpled cream suit and light brown brogues, with an open necked white shirt under the suit. He had a weary, faraway look in his fibre glass eyes, as if he had seen too much for too long, and had chosen eternal suspension in plastic over having to endure any more.

The second was a dog, caught mid bark.

Both of the figures were slightly translucent, their features picked out in fibre glass so thin it let the light pass through them.

Takara patted the fibre glass dog on the head.

"There's a good boy," she said affectionately.

The dog, still mid bark, glared balefully.

"Always nice to be among friends," said Takara, with a smirk, and headed off to explore the first floor.

As with the ground floor, the areas were clearly divided by category. The overall theme seemed to be science, with many of the categories beginning with P – pathology, pharmacology, phrenology, paradoxology, pyrgology, pharology, pseudology, phlebotomy, philematology, palaeontology, psychology and countless more in a similar vein.

In the far corner, roughly corresponding to the haiku section on the floor below, was a shelf marked, in rather excitable script, Science Of The Month.

This month's science was Emetology.

Feeling a tinge of idle curiosity, Takara took a book from the Science Of The Month shelf and surveyed the cover.

She hurriedly put it back on the shelf.

"Another breathtaking tome?" enquired Pat with a grin, whose knowledge of science was clearly more comprehensive than Takara's.

"You could say that," shuddered Takara.

At the back of the first floor, again roughly corresponding to the floor below, was a desk.

Sat at this desk was a wiry man in a chunky red woollen jumper that hung from his frame like an afterthought. Crumbs and various food stains littered the red wool and there were ragged holes, one just below the neckline and another on the right hand wrist, that looked like they were the result of hours of absentminded chewing.

The desk was littered with pencils, sketch pads and battered, leather-bound tomes that looked well studied to the point of disintegration. The man was bent over a drawing board, what was left of his thin, black hair spiralling in unruly directions, untempered by comb or worries about personal appearance. Pushed up over his hair, keeping it all in place like a hair band, was a pair of black ray bans, a surprising sight considering the man had the pallor of someone who hadn't seen sunshine, or even daylight, for quite some time.

Again, the man gave no indication that he was aware of any company, his focus entirely on his work. As he made precise and considered marks on the paper before him, Pat picked up one of the leather-bound books on the desk.

"The Forest Of Lost Children," she said, reading the title aloud. "Sounds like a cheery affair. Any good?"

The man nodded towards the wall above the desk where another large yellowing sheet of metal bore a familiar grouping of fridge magnets with names on them.

In section 2 - IGNORING CUSTOMERS – was a fridge magnet labelled Simon.

"Oh, I see," said Pat. "Another of humanity's gifts to customer service."

Simon frowned, moving his pencil very, very slowly.

"Well, you have to admit he's good at what he does," said Takara with a grin. "I don't think I've ever been ignored so wholeheartedly. Hats off to you, Simon."

Pat picked up another book.

"The Pine Cone Bride," she read aloud. "Continuing the rustic theme, I see."

Sam walked behind Simon to take a look at his drawing while Gerard started inspecting the pencils with a connoisseur's air. Simon's frown deepened. The ignoring had usually made its point by now.

"He's not happy," said Takara, with interest. "He's making out like he's ignoring us, but I can tell we're getting to him. I wonder what it would take to break him?" Takara looked over to Gerald. "Hey, Gerald, how many of those pencils do you think you could snap in one go?"

Simon gritted his teeth.

"Aw, leave him alone," said Sam. "He can't help it, can he?"

"Whyever not?" asked Pat with a huff.

"His name's in section 2," said Sam simply. "The rota has spoken."

Takara nodded with appreciation.

"Very true. All hail the rota." She turned back to the desk. "It's OK Simon, you don't have to worry about ignoring us. We're not customers. We're bounty hunters."

Simon exhaled with frustration.

"Will you *please* leave me alone?" he scowled. "Can't you see I'm busy?"

Takara took a moment to savour the look on Pat's face before replying.

"We're all busy, Simon," she said. "Some of us have got golden goblets to find, don't you know? Which I dare say is a touch more important than whatever doodle you're troubling yourself with."

"It's actually pretty good." Sam stood behind Simon, taking in his work. "What is it, Simon?"

Simon put down his pencil, admitting defeat.

"It's a scene from a story," he said. He glanced at Pat. "The Forest Of Lost Children."

"I don't know that one," said Takara. "What is it? Cornish?"

"Swedish actually. Swedish folklore."

Pat was overcome by a "well that explains everything" look.

"Swedish folklore!" she exclaimed, her voice brimming with italics. "How niche."

Simon bit his lip, his features hardening.

"Excellent," said Takara, nodding her head. "Niche is big business these days. Limited edition, luxury item. Only make a handful and charge a fortune for them. Change the shade of blue on the cover and print up another run that's even more limited edition for an even higher price. Charge what you want really. Draw what you want too."

"More nonsense," said Pat.

"Not at all," said Takara. "The point isn't the worth of the creation but the scarcity of the object. People pay through whatever orifice you specify just to get their hands on an artefact that hardly anyone else has. That rosy glow that comes from knowing you own something everyone else doesn't? That's true art, that is."

"I'm only making one copy," said Simon.

"Genius!" clapped Takara. "Imagine the bidding war."

"And it's not for sale."

"What??"

"I'm making it because it has to be made."

"My god."

Sam was still studying the drawing.

In the middle of a thick forest of spruce trees lay a clearing.

A familiar looking clearing.

Soon there would be a fire, with flames dancing up to the heavens, but for now there were just footprints in the dust.

In the foreground, a woman in a long turquoise dress stood staring out of the drawing, staring out at the viewer, staring at Sam. Her long red hair cascaded onto her shoulders and downwards, while silver bangles jangled from her wrists, as much as bangles can jangle in a line drawing. At her ankles, a detail you could easily miss if you weren't paying close attention, a tail snaked out from underneath the turquoise dress. A vivid red tail to match her vivid red hair.

"Who is she?" asked Sam, with wonder.

"She's the mother of the forest," said Simon. "The mother of the lost children."

Unusually for her, Pat seemed spooked.

"Come on, we've seen enough," she said, marching over to the stairs. "Where did you say the cafe was?"

Simon nodded upwards.

52

The second floor covered the arts.

If it took your hand and danced between the raindrops or held its breath and jumped into a pit of knives or stretched its arms out wide and tried to commune with a higher power or snapped its fingers and froze time for a single, perfect second, then there was a book about it here, usually with an out of focus black and white photo on the cover.

There was no desk, and no one sitting at it, because there was no need for guidance on this floor, only exploration.

Also they couldn't afford to put a till in on every floor, so anyone who actually wanted to pay for something had to head downstairs and hope for the best.

In the centre of the second floor sat a circle of six green chairs and lounging in one of chairs, and looking very comfortable indeed, was a woman with long, straight hair the colour of straw.

She was engrossed in a book, barely blinking.

The rota suggested that this – Section 3: READING BOOKS – was Jo.

Helpfully, Jo was sporting a flower-shaped name tag which confirmed this suspicion. The name tag was green and yellow – the same shade of green as the chairs and the same shade of yellow as Jo's hair – and it nestled neatly and satisfyingly against her jumper, which was also a matching shade of straw yellow.

"Look, it's Jo," said Takara, consulting the sheet of metal on the wall and then glancing back at the woman in the chair. "The prophesy has come true. The rota has spoken once more."

“And she’s reading,” chipped in Jonno, sardonically.

“As it was written, so it shall be,” nodded Takara, solemnly.

Pat started to step forward to engage Jo in what Pat thought passed as conversation, but Sam grabbed her arm and stopped her in her tracks.

“Don’t,” he whispered. “She looks so happy and so perfect somehow. It would be a shame to disturb her.”

Sam was right.

Jo looked like she was finally and effortlessly at one with the universe, a round peg in a round hole.

The cover of the book featured a large black and white drawing of a woman. She was naked and standing on one leg, her hair billowing to the viewer’s left, and standing on her forehead were a tiny eagle and a small, bearded, naked man holding a lightning bolt that was almost as tall as he was. At her feet were hundreds of tiny, seated figures, arranged in a semi-circle, and dramatic, cumulonimbus clouds surrounded her like acolytes, selfless devotees for a larger-than-life goddess. To her right, the sun peeked timidly from behind her billowing hair, while in her left hand she grasped a crescent moon.

Jo turned a page, her eyes locked on the words in front of her.

“I suppose you have a point,” said Pat, reluctantly. “She’d probably be as much help as the others anyway.”

“We don’t need her help,” said Gerald. “We know where we’re going.”

As Katia had promised, the cafe was lodged, slightly impossibly, between the second and third floor.

Viewed from below, all you could see was the staircase stretching upwards. And viewed from above, all you could see was the staircase stretching back down again. But halfway up/down the staircase was a door.

A door that should have opened into thin air.

Gerald opened the door eagerly.

The cafe was cosier than you'd expect for a room that occupied an impossible halfway house between what seemed real and what really couldn't be.

You'd think if you were going to make your home in an unlikely crack between dimensions then you'd spread out and make use of all of the boundless, unimaginable space. Indulge and luxuriate and leave the explanations for another time. But this was a cramped and homely affair, with a seating plan that barely made it into double figures, as if the cafe thought that by making itself as inconspicuous as possible it might somehow escape being noticed by the cold light of day.

It was a crazy plan, but it seemed to be working.

Sitting at one of the tables was the blue and red team. Their pints of Knucklehead long dispensed with, they were now busying themselves with slices of gypsy tart.

Ah, gypsy tart.

If banoffee pie is the empress of pies, then gypsy tart is its renegade half sister, wild-hearted and a danger to public health. Made from evaporated milk, muscovado sugar and the blood red mist of a blissful glucose overdose, gypsy tart – when baked properly – should leave its victim in a state somewhere between a stroke and a coma. It was first made on the Isle of Sheppey, a desolate island off the north coast of Kent, and it was the forbidden fruit in the Garden Of England – fatal but irresistible.

"Oh sweet temptation," said Takara, speaking not just for herself, but for the nation as a whole. "One day my tombstone will read: 'Here lies Takara. She liked gypsy tart just a bit too much'."

Gerald marched up to the cafe counter where a woman was busy packing various snacks into white cardboard boxes. At his approach, she glanced up for a moment, but instead of surveying this new customer, she looked straight past Gerald to where Jonno was standing, the large rectangular delivery box still strapped to his back.

"Ah, finally!" she said, throwing her hands up in, if not a fit, then at least a flurry, of pique. "What time do you call this? It's ten minutes to and you were told to get here for twenty past! I've been packing solidly for what feels like several lifetimes now, and as you can see the boxes have been piling up and up and up. You better crack on with it and quick smart."

She paused to consider a startled looking Jonno.

"Hang on, you're not the usual guy. What happened to the usual guy?"

This, suggested the rota on the wall behind her – Section 5: SERVING TEA AND/OR CAKE - was Belinda.

Her attire was practical but fashionable – dark blue dungarees, white t-shirt with long sleeves, red neck scarf – and her hair had the faintest hint of a quiff. Her sleeves were rolled up in a manner that suggested that they were always rolled up – ready for action, whatever the action might be – which made Sam wonder why she bothered having sleeves at all.

Sam quickly decided to keep that particular question to himself.

"Come on, not usual guy! Explain yourself."

Jonno met Belinda's gaze with world-weary disapproval. Which was the way he met most people's gaze, but Belinda wasn't to know that.

"I am not your, or anyone else's, delivery boy, thank you very much," he said. "I'm only here because…"

Everyone looked at Jonno with interest.

"Yes, why are you here?" said Pat.

"Because he," replied Jonno, nodding towards Gerald, "can't stop stuffing his fat face and someone has to stage an intervention before the worst happens."

"He has to buy new trousers?" asked Sam.

"Worse than that. Much worse."

Belinda turned to face Sam, at which point she caught sight of the white hat box.

"Oh my dear god," she said in amazement. "Don't tell me The Duke has gobbled his way through the Black Forest already. That was meant to last the week. At least. Does he think I'm made of gateau?"

Belinda clearly had a lot on her plate, both metaphorically and un-metaphorically.

"No, no, don't worry," said Sam, reassuringly. "It's a hat box, not a cake box. It's got, you know, a hat in it."

"I've heard it all now!" exclaimed Belinda, and turned decisively back to her packing.

Belinda was surrounded by what looked like the remnants of the food festival. Pies and cakes and baklavas and all manner of quiches, not to mention a suspiciously high number of vegan bratwurst.

Before her, Belinda had a long list of names, all written in red capital letters, and she appeared to be packing up a box for each name. As everyone looked on with varying degrees of curiosity, she turfed half a dozen vol-au-vents, a jumbo samosa, and a handful of meringues into a white cardboard box and folded it shut with satisfaction.

On the top of the box was inscribed, in distinctive purple lettering: With Compliments Of The K Foundation.

Sam looked confused.

"The K Foundation? Weren't they caught up in some sort of scandal? Something to do with a Scottish island?"

"Different K Foundation," said Belinda, not looking up.

"There was a film, wasn't there? I can't remember all the details now."

"Totally not the same K Foundation. Trust me."

"Yes," said Takara, stepping out into the light. "This is a rather more close knit operation."

Belinda broke into a broad smile.

"Takara!" she beamed. "Oh, that explains everything. You should have said that these clowns...sorry I mean fine, upstanding people, were with you. I might have treated them with a bit more courtesy."

Sam gazed at Belinda's smile with wonder.

This was the first time he'd seen anyone be pleased to see Takara. Up until now she'd been greeted with annoyance, irritation, frustration, exasperation and outright hostility. It was actually quite disconcerting seeing someone acting as if she was something other than a problem they really could do without.

"All going well, I trust," said Takara, with a nod.

"Yes, yes," said Belinda. "You know how it is after the food festival. Lots to do!"

"Well, I hate to add to your burden, but my friend here is in dire need of a slice of your finest – and by which I mean your most toxic – gypsy tart."

Gerald did look like it was something of an emergency.

Belinda handed over a gratifyingly gooey wedge of gypsy tart.

"On the house," she said, with a grin.

"You're too kind," said Takara. "Everything OK with the key?"

"Actually, I wanted to talk to you about that," replied Belinda.

Sam's head was still spinning.

All throughout their time together, Sam had wondered whether he could truly trust Takara, and every time he came close to a conclusion something happened to make him start wondering all over again.

Was she really lending a helping hand or was she actually helping herself? And what was she helping herself to?

Takara's words came floating back through Sam's mind.

"The keys are our little contribution to the high street. They give certain, select individuals, representatives of businesses that we feel contribute positively to the community, access to the tunnels. Which they are then free to use as they see fit."

As they see fit.

What were they using the tunnels for?

Takara looked concerned. "What seems to be the matter?"

Belinda blushed slightly.

"It's nothing really. It's just the key."

Takara stared at her.

"I was making some spanakopita for the food festival," Belinda continued. "You know the stuff – crumbly and flaky and gooey and crispy all at the same time, like a fairy waltzing across your tastebuds."

"Yes, I thought I noticed some on the pie stall."

"Well, I started with the pan of spinach and it was perfect – rich and sodden and mixed with eggs and feta and some of that cheese we brought back from the expedition…"

"Oh, wonderful."

"And it had got to a point where it looked like lava. Thick green lava, bubbling with cholesterol."

"The best kind of lava."

"And it really was bubbling. Pockets of air bursting again and again through the gooey surface. It was making quite a racket."

"I can almost smell it."

"So I was thinking about the batch for the food festival and thinking about the batch for the tunnels and I suddenly got a scare – like, oh my soul, where's the key gone? I don't know. I guess we'd all heard about Mr K misplacing his key and I just had a worry – what if I've done the same? So I patted my dungaree pocket and there it was, I could feel it. And I don't why I did it, but I just took it out to take a look at it. You know, just to check that it was really there…"

"Oh dear."

"And I had it in my hand and I was looking at it and those keys really are quite hard to see at a certain angle. I know that's one of the design features, but it can be quite inconvenient at times. Just a thought for the future. Anyway, I turned it round in my hand to get a better look and it just slipped between my fingers."

"Into the pan of spinach lava, I presume?"

"Yes," said Belinda, mournfully. "The spinach was piping hot, I really couldn't reach in and get it out without doing myself some damage. So I just left it in there."

"To marinate."

"I'm afraid so. Eventually the spinach was cooked and I drained the pot and retrieved the key. And when I got it back, it looked like this..."

Belinda held up a gleaming emerald key.

A grin slowly rippled across Takara's face.

"Oh, I see what's happened here," she said, reaching for the key. "Actually, Harrington did tell me that there was a very slim chance of this happening. Something to do with the alignment of the inconsistent polychromatics, I think it was. Or was it the semi-osmotic kaleidoscopics? One of the two. Or maybe a combination? I don't know. I do find it hard to listen to this kind of stuff. Anyway, not to worry, no harm done, and, look, here's a replacement."

Belinda took receipt of a regular opaque key with a sigh of relief.

"Thank you so much," she said, with gratitude. "I was beginning to wonder if I should be worried."

"No, no, not at all," said Takara. "I suppose there is the question of what affect the marinating magic key would have had on the spinach, and I guess you could ask questions about what eating anything made with said spinach could do to your nervous system, internal organs and spiritual wellbeing, but hey. Not much we can do about it now. If you see anyone acting suspiciously just send them my way."

Takara paused for a minute to allow the full irony of that last statement to hang pertinently in the air between them, like an unspoken threat or a shared regret.

"OK, well, thank you," said Belinda, eventually. "Be sure to let me know if there's anything I can do in return."

"Well, there is one thing," said Takara, slipping the emerald key into her inside jacket pocket. "Do you have any idea where we might pick up some golden goblets?"

53

The sign at the bottom of the stairs leading up to the third, final and very top floor, read simply: "Are you sure?"

When Takara had mentioned the golden goblets a haunted look had come over Belinda's face – the look of someone remembering something they'd hoped they had forgotten.

Takara looked at the sign and grinned.

"If there's one thing I like better than a blunt, unwelcoming sign, it's a snooty, passive aggressive one," she said. "Always puts a spring in my step. The only way they could have topped this was if it had read: 'Are you really sure?' With the emphasis on the really of course."

Halfway up the stairs was another sign.

"Are you really sure?"

"Oh perfect!"

At the top of the stairs, and thus at the top of the book shop itself, was a circular room, about two-thirds of the size of the other floors. Save for a sash window which looked out onto the high street and an alcove which housed a selection of framed posters and the yellowing metal sheet of the rota, the walls were taken up entirely with shelves, and those shelves were crammed with books. And not just any old books - there were no trusty paperback companions, well-thumbed travel guides or sprightly domestic manuals here - but big, bulky, ominous tomes that look liked they'd existed since the dawn of time, or least since the dawn of the printing press.

You could feel the knowledge thrumming in these walls, sense the weight of the accumulated wisdom. This was not a room where you'd let a relaxing hour slip gently by. It was a room of purpose, and a room fit for that purpose.

The rota was clear.

Section 6: IMPORTANT RESEARCH

And there was only one name fit for the job – Peter.

A huge desk took up at least a quarter of the floor space and sitting at that desk was a man who looked like he hadn't left the room for quite some time.

He was a formidable presence, as bulky as the books he consulted for his vital work, and he had the air of someone who (a) really shouldn't be disturbed, (b) didn't have any experience of being disturbed, and (c) wasn't sure how they'd react if anyone was to give it a try.

"Oh dear," whispered Sam.

"What is it?" whispered back Takara.

"Important research. How will we ever be able to interrupt that?"

Takara shook her head in silence.

The desk was covered with all of the expected accoutrements of important research. A selection of the ominous tomes, taken momentarily from the shelves. An ink pot and a large ink blotter. A quill, an ink pen, a biro, and a variety of crayons. A solar powered calculator, which looked like it had never been switched on. A pocket atlas and a 1972 London A-Z. And a brass picture frame, positioned so that only Peter could see the loved one within.

On the bookshelf directly behind Peter's desk, four golden trophies were lined up in what was unmistakably pride of place.

The first was an Oscar. A golden knight grasping a gleaming longsword standing on a reel of celluloid. A design classic for the highest accolade.

The second was a golden mask, one eye solid, one eye hollow. A BAFTA, putting its best face forward with inscrutable style.

The third was a golden pillar with a globe perched on the top. You could hazard a decent guess even if you'd never seen one of these before. You could also do a fair amount of damage with one if the urge arose. Professor Plum, in the conservatory, with the Golden Globe.

The fourth was a new one on them all. A curving golden stem rose to a bulbous head surrounded by a broad golden disc. It looked like both a religious icon celebrating the space race and one of those collars that prevent dogs from scratching their own eyes out.

"What is that?" whispered Sam.

Takara shook her head once more.

"It is the most significant, and the most worthwhile, trophy of them all. The others merely award excellence. Trinkets in comparison."

Peter's voice had a rich, soothing quality, infused with class, taste and the quiet privilege of having all the time in the world. It felt like a whiskey that had been distilled for at least two hundred years, in a barrel made of the oldest and rarest oak in existence.

It felt like the silence in the drawing room of a mansion that isn't open to the general public, and even then is only frequented by the highest echelons of nobility.

It felt like a library where no one ever needed to be shushed.

"Any old film can win an Oscar," Peter continued. "But only the finest endeavours will be rewarded with laurels such as these."

Instinctively, they all took a step towards the desk.

"Consider the posters we have on display. Have any of those won something as commonplace as an Oscar, do you think?"

As Sam started to scan the posters, a warming feeling began to envelop him, like a comforting hug, like a gentle wash of radiation.

They weren't interrupting the important research.

They were surrendering to it.

And the posters were there to welcome them, the names of the films a whispered siren's call.

The Crystal Casket. The Haunted Castle. The Hypnotist's Revenge. The Four Troublesome Heads. The Vanishing Lady. The Infernal Cauldron. The Cave Of The Demons. The Magic Lantern. The Clockmaker's Dream. The Artist And The Mannequin.

"Wonderful, aren't they?" said Peter, his voice a rich mix of indulgence and devotion. "One man's vision, his life's work. You could live inside the worlds created by these posters. Walk around them, feel the dust in the air. I feel like I do that every day. And those titles are just magnificent. The perfect titles for stories that really need nothing else. I mean, look at them – the titles themselves tell the entire story. Everything else is just admin."

Peter was right. There was an uncanny depth to the artworks, a sense that they went back much further than they should. On the face of it, they were simple oil paintings, mostly monochromatic with the occasional splash of colour, the atmospheric light and shade of classic noir, but somehow they appealed to all five senses. You could smell the bubbling cauldron, hear the screams emanating from the cave and castle, taste the bitter tang of revenge.

"Which story would you live inside?" Peter asked Sam, with an offhand charm that almost felt like a threat.

"Don't answer that, Sam," chipped in Takara. "It's not worth the risk."

Peter smiled a broad smile of satisfaction, as if he'd received the reaction he was hoping for.

Sam scanned the posters, wondering why they felt like they'd always been waiting for him.

"What are you researching?" he asked Peter. "The life story of the director?"

Peter laughed, soft and low, the contented laugh of patriarchy.

"Gosh no! I know his life better than I know my own. Better than he knew it. His childhood in central Europe – we think Liechtenstein, but no one is completely sure – the son of a hypnotist. Their move to Paris at the turn of the century, cultural refugees hoping for a better life. His refusal to follow in his father's footsteps and the rift that caused between them. The move to London and his work as an illusionist. The knowledge that this was his purpose. That here was his path. The return to Paris. The stage show that broke boundaries and invented universes. The move to film, capturing the stage show for all eternity. The triumph. The betrayal. The sorry end."

"What was his name?"

Peter shook his head.

"There is a level of brilliance where names become irrelevant."

Pat snorted.

"You don't know, do you?"

Peter smiled that patriarchal smile once again.

"The everyday stars have two names. Two neat names to be lit up in lights on the front of the theatre. The pretentious everyday stars have three names, although some," Peter said, looking at Sam, "don't have that option. The true stars have just one name. There is no one else. No mistake, no competition. But this man was the next level up. He had no name. Just a single letter. As you can see from the posters."

Sam ran his eyes over the poster for The Artist And The Mannequin.

Two figures, painted in white against a dark blue and black background. The artist in front of an easel, lost in his work, his face bathed in rapture. The mannequin of a woman standing before him, a look of disdain on her face. A splash of red in the space between them. Was that spilt paint or spilt blood? And that sound...was that the sound of the mannequin breathing?

In the corner of the poster was a single letter.

Takara instinctively glanced back towards the staircase. She didn't remember there being a door to the room they were standing in and she really didn't remember anyone closing said door, but there it was.

"So what are you researching then?" asked Sam. "How the films were made?"

"In a way."

Takara glanced at the door again.

There was a door just like it in the background of the poster.

"Look," Takara said, with the first hints of a gathering urgency. "We can see you're busy and we don't want to disturb you any more than we have, so why don't we move on to the purpose of our visit. We've come…"

"I know why you're here," said Peter.

"And I know why you're here," he continued, looking at Sam.

"Oh, this is getting spooky," drawled Jonno. "What is it you always say, Takara? What fun!"

"What are you researching?" repeated Sam.

Peter paused, the consummate scholar of melodrama.

Jonno pulled up a nearby chair.

"There's one film in particular," Peter said, eventually. "The Vanishing Lady."

"Ah," said Sam, nodding. "You want to know how he did it."

"Oh no, not at all. I know exactly how he did it."

Peter gazed at the poster. A woman, her features blurred, succumbing to the darkness.

"I want to know why."

54

An excited chatter filled The Regent as the crowd waited for the supporting feature. They'd already seen so much – the opening ceremony, the brass band playing God Save The King, the cartoon and the newsreel – that it almost felt unreal that there should be more to come.

Before long, the excitement would turn to anticipation which would turn to trepidation and then to real fear, as King Kong stepped out of their nightmares into the reality of the silver screen, but that still lay ahead. There was another feature first – a short film, that no one had heard of.

Or, at least, almost no one.

"It's a common error to confuse The Vanishing Lady with The Lady Vanishes," said Peter, settling into his natural role of lecturer, sage and raconteur. "The latter, as I'm sure you know, is a piece of fluff directed by a two-bit journeyman that modern audiences struggle to remember."

From the comfort of his armchair, Jonno shook his head slowly in disbelief.

"Whereas the former is a groundbreaking piece of cinema history conjured by a true visionary," continued Peter. "With a running time of almost four minutes…"

"What??" spluttered Pat.

Jonno buried his face in his palm.

"Do not mistake quantity for quality," said Peter. "Or breadth for depth. It only takes a moment to unzip reality and to change the way the world works and the rules on which it depends. Once the line has been crossed, the line has been crossed."

Pat turned to the door.

"I've heard enough. Come on, let's go."

"No one," said Peter, "is going anywhere."

And the door, closed firmly before them, appeared to agree.

"What this film contains is the realisation that all doesn't necessarily need to be as it appears," continued Peter once more. "And that is a potent idea. And a potentially dangerous one. An idea that, deployed artfully, with malicious intent, could do a great deal of damage indeed."

Suddenly everyone was listening.

"If only you could see for yourselves."

At which everyone – bar Peter, of course – turned to look at Takara.

Takara looked back.

"What?"

"Come on Takara, out with it," said Pat.

"I haven't the faintest idea what you could mean."

Sam smiled.

"If you can find one in Rex's pocket, maybe there's one in your own?"

Takara slid her hand into her right-hand jacket pocket with faux reluctance and drew out a snow globe with faux astonishment.

"Oh, what a surprise," she said, placing the snow globe on Peter's desk. "However did that get there?"

The lights dimmed in The Regent and the supporting feature flickered into life.

An oak panelled drawing room in what looked like a country mansion. The room was empty except for a wooden chair centre stage and a drape thrown over something bulky stage right - to the right of the performer, to the left for the audience, where once again the start of the story lay waiting. It was difficult to work out exactly what that bulky something could be. A bookshelf perhaps? Or a cage? Directly behind the chair, a window opened to the sight of a fulsome rowan tree, its berries subsumed in the hazy black and white of the cinematography, while the oak panels bore intricate carvings, full of twists and curlicues.

A door opened stage left and for a moment everything wobbled.

Like scenery in a theatre.

A man stepped through the door and presented himself to the audience. He was dressed, as before, in a sharply cut showman's suit, topped by a dark red bow tie and dark red carnation, but his slicked back jet black hair was now flecked with spots of silver. And his skin, once rosy flesh and blood, now seemed undercut with a wash of grey. He drew his shoulders back, still the consummate performer, but something was absent. The process had begun.

Almost everyone drew in a sharp intake of breath.

"It's him," whispered Sam. "The Mighty Malphas".

Takara stared at the stage, her face devoid of emotion.

Peter smiled. He knew what was coming.

The Mighty Malphas bowed an introduction and then took a white square of cloth from his inside jacket pocket and held it up for the onlookers to examine, turning left and right so that everyone could inspect it properly, just as he had with the blindfold. It didn't matter that the audience was in the cinema, the other side of the fourth wall, rather than in the room with him. He had his routine and he was sticking with it.

He placed the square of cloth on the floor in front of the wooden chair and then moved the chair on top of it.

The scene was set.

The door opened a second time but less dramatically so the wobble wasn't as noticeable.

This time a woman stepped through the door. She walked calmly to the space in front of the chair and cast her gaze downwards, her hands clasped before her. Unlike The Mighty Malphas who had thrown his arms open to the audience, ready to catch their adulation, she remained cold, passive, ready for the inevitable.

In her left hand, she held a purple flower.

"No, it can't be!" exclaimed Sam, his voice cracking.

Takara's pursed lips twitched.

"Is something the matter?" said Peter, his voice rich with self-satisfaction.

"What year was this movie filmed?" asked Pat.

"Just before the turn of the century - 1896. But it remained in the vaults for years, unseen until this day."

"But that's impossible," said Sam. "We were there in 1886. We saw her die."

As soon as he said the words out loud, Sam realised how preposterous they sounded. But there were no other words that would do. They had been there. They knew what they'd seen.

The woman with the purple flower took a step backwards and lowered herself carefully into the chair.

The Mighty Malphas bowed to the audience once more and then whipped the drape from the bulky something with a dramatic flourish, revealing a black wooden monolith.

Sam felt a puzzled chill pass through his body. What were they trying to do?

The Mighty Malphas carefully laid the drape over the woman with the purple flower until she was completely covered.

A rustle of anticipation ran through the crowd at The Regent.

And in the middle of the stalls, one figure sat bolt upright, taut with attention.

Then Sam spotted the mistake.

The drape hadn't covered all of the woman's body. At the very bottom, a few inches above the white cotton cloth, there was a glimpse of the hem of her dress.

The Mighty Malphas drew himself upwards, as if he was about to spring into action, and then a split second before he whipped the drape from the woman, the hem of the dress blinked out of existence. The drape billowed upwards, caught in the dramatic updraft of the big reveal, and The Regent screamed as one as the empty chair lay before them, the woman nowhere to be seen.

"Well, it's pretty obvious how he did that," said Pat. "A simple edit. About as close to magic as you can get with a pair of scissors and a roll of masking tape. Which isn't very close at all."

"Ah, but this was 1933 remember," said Peter. "This was an unknown film and the general public still wasn't used to cinema trickery. To them, what they saw with their own eyes had to be the truth, even if the truth was plainly impossible. You can imagine how they responded when they followed this up with King Kong. I believe they were still carrying out bodies a few hours after the film had finished."

"If it looks right, it is right," said Sam.

"Precisely," nodded Peter. "And that act of collective faith is exactly what transforms this into an instance of pure magic, at least to a scholar like myself. But what I find truly wonderful about what we're watching is that The Vanishing Lady is the very first film to contain an edit of this kind. The hoi polloi at The Regent didn't know it but they were witnessing a historical document. M really was a visionary and a pioneer."

"But you're not interested in how they did it," said Sam.

"No," smiled Peter.

The trick wasn't over. The Mighty Malphas waved the drape over the empty chair, like a mystic summoning a demon, the film jumped slightly as the next edit was made, and the woman with the purple flower reappeared. Only this time a silver dagger was plunged into her chest.

The crowd screamed once more.

And the figure centre stalls stared at the screen. And the woman with the purple flower with the silver dagger plunged into her chest stared back at him, her expression one of tender surprise, of trust melting.

Then for the big finale. The Mighty Malphas covered the woman with the drape once more, this time making sure to cover every inch of her dress, made some suitably mysterious hand movements, always mindful that a good performance should contain a dash of melodrama, and then whipped the drape away, the scene hardly flickering as the editor warmed to the technique.

And there she was, Marianne Kingsley, the purple flower still in her hand, the dagger removed from her chest, revived and restored.

Sam frowned.

"It's not her."

"What?" said Peter.

"Marianne Kingsley. His assistant. The woman we saw die in 1886. She looks like her and she's dressed like her, but it's not quite her. I can see it now."

The crowd cheered as The Mighty Malphas and the woman who wasn't Marianne took a bow.

The light of the flickering screen bathed The Regent in a triumphant, spectral glow.

The Mighty Malphas smiled with relief.

The audience got to their feet, applauding the ending they'd been hoping for.

And the light of the screen picked out the figure in the centre stalls.

The sharply cut showman's suit. The dark grey bow tie and deep grey carnation. The slicked back hair, now entirely silver. The ghost of Christmas Present watching the ghost of Christmas Past.

"The Vanishing Lady ran at The Regent for two and a half weeks and he came in for every performance," said Peter. "Sat in exactly the same place, at the very middle of the stalls, and acted in exactly the same way, frozen with attention. And at the end of the applause he allowed himself a small smile and then left the theatre, to return at precisely the same time the following night. The maestro watching the maestro. Over and over."

"And you want to know why," said Sam.

"I'd give anything," said Peter.

"He wasn't watching himself," said Takara. "He was watching her."

Everyone turned to Takara.

"Hoping to improve the performance, you mean?" asked Peter.

"No. He was watching her come back to life."

"But he knew it was an illusion. He'd set it up himself after all."

"As Sam said, if it looks right, it is right. And if everyone else believes it's the truth, then maybe you'll believe it's the truth as well, caught up in that collective faith you mentioned."

"But he kept coming back."

"Because he kept being transformed by their belief. If you allow it to be, that kind of truth can be addictive."

Sam looked over at the posters and felt a tinge of sympathy. The titles that occupied the middle ground between the seen and unseen, the here and the just-here. The Haunted Castle. The Clockmaker's Dream. The Crystal Casket. And he felt that comforting pull once more as he contemplated the poster for The Artist And The Mannequin. The look of devotion on the artist's face. The splash of red in the space between them.

Takara got to her feet.

"I think I know why we're here."

55

With a grimace which communicated an uncomfortable mix of reluctance and displeasure, Peter handed over the four small golden goblets decorated with an engraving of a slumbering lion.

"You did say you'd give anything," Jonno reminded him with a smirk.

"And now you know," added Takara.

"I only have your word for it that this Kingsley woman actually existed," huffed Peter, clearly a man unused to not having the upper hand. "You might have made the whole distinctly questionable story up on the spot."

"Oh, she was for real, alright."

Takara turned to Gerald. Lovely, helpful Gerald.

"Gerald," she said, seeing him with freshly appreciative eyes. "I wonder if you could possibly do me a favour? Do us all a favour really. We don't have a great deal of time, so I'm going to skip the usual flattery and convoluted appeals on behalf of the greater good, and head straight to the action, by which I mean temptation, enticement and flat out bribery."

"Go on," said Gerald, cautiously.

"In exchange for one of Belinda's finest – and I mean very finest – lemon meringue pies – and I really don't think it's an exaggeration to say that your taste buds really haven't danced between shooting stars until you've experienced a slice of that heavenly confection dissolving on your tongue – would you be willing to go and get his nibs and herself and bring them to the B&Q?"

Gerald looked blank.

"The Duke and The Inspector."

"Oh, er, right," said Gerald. "Yes, I suppose so."

"Wonderful!"

"Payment in advance."

"I'd expect nothing less," nodded Takara, with approval. "Tell Belinda I sent you. She'll see you right."

Takara then pivoted to Jonno. Stupid, annoying Jonno.

She smiled, softening for a moment.

"You've always been here, haven't you? Even when I wished you weren't. Here with a barbed comment or here with an unhelpful observation or here with a shrug and an eye-roll and just the most obvious delight when everything goes wrong. My tormentor and my reflection. I cheer when I see the back of you, but then it's not the same when you're not here."

Jonno sneer-smiled his usual sneer-smile at Takara, but somehow that felt softer too.

"Same old Takara," he said. "For a moment there, I almost thought you were going serious on me."

"That's what you want, isn't it, my little one man Stockholm Syndrome," said Takara with a sudden spark. "Well, no dice, I'm afraid. And I'm pleased to say that you hanging around like the very worst smell isn't going to be all for nothing. You're about to become extremely useful."

Peter was staring at the hat box, still in Sam's hands.

"Can I see it?"

Peter's voice, still rich and luxurious, now carried a twinge of quiet urgency.

Takara took in the scene – the shelves overflowing with ancient wisdom, the posters opening a doorway to another world, the desk dotted with pertinent bits and vital bobs, the electricity sparking with increasing vigour outside the sash window, the brass picture frame twinkling in reflection – and nodded at Sam.

Sam opened the hat box with a ceremony that felt surprisingly tender.

In the box was a leather flying helmet with oversize goggles pushed up onto the brim. The goggles were pitch black and shaped like an exploding star while the leather of the helmet was dotted with a litany of blemishes – the defiant graze of a near-miss bullet, the scorch of an almost-fatal explosion, the remnants of shattered glass and stubbed out cigarettes and spat out liquor shots, and a row of miniature mission marks paying tribute to long-forgotten foes.

And there on the right-hand side of the helmet, neatly positioned at eye-level, were two initials, engraved in silver – EL.

Peter took a sharp intake of breath.

"Oh my," he said, his face bathed in awe. "Isn't it magnificent? Wasn't she magnificent?"

Takara picked up the brass picture frame and gazed with admiration at the photograph of Eleanor Lockhart.

"She really was," nodded Takara. "A hero's headdress fit for a true hero."

Sam closed the hat box before Pat could begin determining the veracity of the marks and blemishes.

"What's your connection with Eleanor, Peter?" he asked.

"She was my spiritual godmother," Peter replied. "Or rather my spiritual great great godmother. I have no family connection to her, of course, as no one's entirely sure who she really was or if any of her exploits actually took place, but I have felt a strong bond with her ever since I came of age. She's my light and my inspiration."

"Even though she was probably a fake and a liar?" said Sam.

"Of course. Mythology trumps reality every time."

Sam took another look at the photograph.

The flash of red hair. The flowing white ballgown. Perfectly posed, brilliantly contrived.

"Who is this then?" he asked.

"I've no idea," smiled Takara. "But to me she looks like revolution."

Takara turned to Peter and gave a small respectful nod. Peter returned the gesture.

"Keep up the important research, my friend," said Takara. "We will return once we have answers. Or better still, more questions."

They worked their way back down the bookshop, sweeping past the employees who were all lost in a haze of preoccupation. Belinda was standing over a vat of simmering spinach lava with the opaque key in her hand, a quizzical look on her face. Jo hadn't moved from the green chair, but now the book lay on her lap, closed for a moment with a scarlet bookmark keeping her place. She stared into the middle distance, past the crescent moon and the cumulonimbus clouds, and seemed at one with the moment, refreshed and rejuvenated. Simon was at his desk, hunched over a drawing, chewing at the neckline of his red jumper as he made his way through the Forest Of Lost Children, one pen stroke at a time. The fibre glass man and the fibre glass dog kept their positions, synthetic sentinels at the top of the stairs. And Katia sat with the fully restored Ferris wheel in her hand, staring at her handiwork, with the expression of someone who was wondering how this had been completed, as if the work had been done by another person entirely.

A bell jangled as they stepped through the door onto the pavement outside, and, in their wake, as the door sprang back to a close, reality folded in on itself, replacing the book shop with the opticians.

Everything, including the rota, was gone.

The spark of electricity pinballed from telegraph pole to telegraph pole and back again, as if it was losing patience.

The high street was all but deserted, with even the doors of Greggs shuttered against the oncoming storm.

The only figure visible was standing exactly where they'd left him, in front of the temporary shelves outside the B&Q.

"Tradescantia nanouk – seven. Cycas revoluta – four. Monstera deliciosa – thirteen," the minotaur said, surveying the stock and making the appropriate marks on the sheet on its clipboard. It took a moment to glance up at the sparks rattling from pillar to post. "I count them all out and then I count them all back in again. Only three stolen today – a good day. Not sure there's really much point doing the stock take from the look of things, but ho hum. If the world is going to end today, then at least the shelves will have been in order."

Takara stepped forward tentatively, slowly making her way into the minotaur's field of vision.

"Which plant is your favourite?" she asked.

The minotaur looked at Takara with dismay.

"So this is to be the final torment," it said, mournfully. "I, once the pole star, of royal birth, born into a life of fable and destiny, with the promise of a match struck in darkness, reduced to servitude and defeat, charged to rearrange the shelves that no one really cares about, chained to irrelevance, forced daily to come face to face with my shortcomings, am now asked which plant is my favourite?"

"Yes. Is there one?"

The minotaur picked up a bushy fern-like plant potted in a white bucket.

"Ficus benjamanica exotica," it said. "The weeping fig."

Jonno nodded.

"Good choice."

The minotaur regarded Jonno with another look of recognition, its deep brown eyes almost tinged with pity, before turning back coolly to Takara.

"You've come to ask me to do something," it said. "I can tell. People like you always say something of little consequence before moving onto their true intention. It is all so petty and so tiresome. But you also know that I would never do anything for someone like you. Which is why you've brought him. Your dog on a chain. Your minotaur."

"Hey, hang on…" Jonno's protest quickly faded away.

Takara turned to Jonno and placed her hand on his forearm.

"It's the last piece of the puzzle. We'll never get out of here without it," she said to him. "We can't do this without you, Jonno." She smiled at him softly. "We need you."

Jonno pursed his lips and then sagged, with a resignation that the minotaur knew all too well.

"She wants you to get the Blessed Mr K," he said.

"He needs to be there," nodded Takara. "But we can't spare the time to get him ourselves."

Right on cue, the shelves rattled as the electric spark did another frantic round.

"Look at this place, it's about to explode."

The minotaur turned the proposition over in its head.

"You're going in to see him? The boss?"

"We are."

"And you're going to end this once and for all?"

"We're going to try."

"And I'll finally be free?"

"I hope we'll all be."

The minotaur looked at Jonno again, taking in the heavy burden of the spice box on his back.

"If I take the staff lift, I can get to the Blessed Mr K quickly. They won't even see us come in."

Takara bowed her head slightly.

"Thank you."

The minotaur frowned, unsure how to process these unfamiliar words.

"You'll need to go through to the kitchen department," it said. "Right at the very back. They're holding the other Mr K there."

56

The electric front door of the B&Q swung open with a sullen, almost reluctant judder, as if the only reason it was opening was because it was programmed to do so and had it been given any significant say in the matter, no one would be getting into the store, not now, not ever.

The opening stretches of what was optimistically marketed as a "quality retail experience" appeared to be designed along similarly petulant lines.

Directly inside the door were several stacks of orange buckets, presumably to be used as a quirky alternative to regular shopping baskets, but they'd been piled so high that it was impossible to grab hold of one. The result was an unwelcoming landmass of orange plastic, which when viewed from deeper inside the premises resembled both a thought-provoking sculpture of a synthetic iceberg and one of those mountains in the American Midwest that had an uncanny knack for attracting extra-terrestrial visitors.

Once past the buckets, shoppers were confronted by a display marked, with brutal efficiency, "Pest Destruction". Here insect and rodent annihilation was promised in a gleeful variety of ways. There were mouse traps and rat traps that sounded like they'd been designed by a team of serial killers – the Rat Reaper Death Box, in particular, had a disquieting air of job satisfaction. There were flea bombs, which seemed like an overreaction. There was ant killer, wasp killer, bed bug killer, cockroach killer and dust mite killer with brand names which ranged from deranged (Nope) to pathological (Xterminate). There were sprays and powders and chemicals, all promising differing levels of engagement – ultra power, scorched earth, end of days. And for the insects, mercy was in short supply. If the natural insect killer bomb didn't get you, then the total insect killer surely would.

How to escape? The buckets blocked the right-hand path, the wall of Insect Armageddon barred the way ahead, the only possible option was to the left…straight into the jaws of the paint station, the Mount Doom of the DIY superstore.

Have you a particular shade of green you think would give your living room the lift it so sorely needs? Perhaps you've brought in a watercolour that has given wings to your inspiration, hopeful it could be used as a reference?

Ha! You fools!

As the natural insect killer bomb is my witness, there is nothing for you here.

In theory, this should have been a joyful spot, where a paint alchemist used an unwritten lore passed from generation to generation to create the perfect hue to match even the most dreamlike vision, mixing various shades of paint with the spark and panache of a true magician.

But the paint chart at the paint station revealed the grim reality.

Where you might have expected a selection of pastels with fragrant, meadow-like names, blocks of sludge accompanied descriptions that were either a horrible joke or harbingers of imminent demise.

Deadly Nightshade. Gathering Storm. Rain Of Fire. Golden Hemlock. Heaven's End. Tainted Dawn. Judgement Day.

The back of the paint station was secured with a line of yellow and black tape, which read "Police Line, Do Not Cross".

This was also either a horrible joke or left over from a recent incident.

Sam took in the ill-tempered surroundings of the B&Q and frowned.

"Doesn't something feel a little off to you about all this?"

Takara thought about all of superstores and hypermarkets, shopping centres and retail villages, factory outlets and business parks that she'd ever been to in her life, especially the ones that had poisoned the once-thriving high streets of the towns nearby.

"Not really, no."

Takara ducked under the "Police Line, Do Not Cross" tape and ventured further into the store.

Here lay the deeply prosaic, barely beating heart of the B&Q. The place that enabled the endless cycle of repair and retreat, repair and retreat, that kept the houses in the area in a constant state of not-quite-finishedness. Dynasties may rise and fall, empires might burn bright before falling into the sea, legends could find glory only to collapse in disgrace, and there would still be two and a half inch paint brushes and tubes of ready mixed plaster to tackle the same old snag list in the same old crumbling backstreet semi again and again and again and again.

If hell is other people, then purgatory is their DIY to-do-list.

As they headed towards the back of the store, Takara started to notice things that made her wonder if Sam might actually have a point.

The spirit levels filled with a red viscous liquid rather than the usual workmanlike yellow.

The sledgehammers and baseball bats that had unsettling chunks of white material embedded in them.

The bedside lamps that crackled like tiny Van De Graaff generators.

The doormats which read: "All Flesh Is Grass".

Maybe something was a little off.

Finally, they reached the back of the store and the kitchen department.

It is a truth universally acknowledged that the kitchen island is the most demonic invention in the history of humanity.

In the kitchen island you will find all seven of the deadly sins – pride, greed, lust, envy, gluttony, wrath and sloth.

Kitchen island owners may be reading this with disbelief but deep down they will recognise it as the truth.

In the centre – where else? – of the kitchen department, there was a kitchen island display.

Behold the tools of oppression – the carving knife racks, the deep drawers, the butcher's block, the high stools, the breakfast bar. Was it any accident that these echoed the implements used throughout history to keep the peasant classes in their place, on their knees in the mud in front of their lords and masters? The tyranny of the carving knife. The greed of the deep drawers. The brutality of the butcher's block. The vanity of the high stools. The triumphalism of the breakfast bar.

Takara thought back to her comrades on the high street and in the tunnels.

She felt a warm glow of solidarity as she pictured the different ways they'd found to upend the system – the anarchists brewing cider that seethed with defiance, the cupcake bakers redistributing wealth with dangerous levels of icing sugar, the curry makers sparking a revolution of thought with the most riotous of spices, and the booksellers trading servitude for dreams of a better land.

She looked at the kitchen island display and she saw a battle line, drawn between commerce and community.

Who could see it any other way?

And there, standing squarely on that battle line, one hand resting with cold propriety on the kitchen island display, was her nemesis, ready and waiting.

57

He was dressed differently this time.

The dark red bow tie and the dark red carnation were gone, and the white shirt along with them. They'd been replaced by a black cashmere jumper, the neck slightly higher than the norm but not so high that it covered his flesh and blood. The sharp black showman's suit remained, but the pairing of the jumper with the suit gave the impression of a someone who'd given up playing to the crowd a long time ago.

The slicked back hair was now entirely white. The silver of the cinema had given way to the stark finality of teeth and bones, of dying stars and the bright light beckoning you to infinity.

The only splash of colour was provided by an orange B&Q name tag on his lapel, which bore a single letter – M.

He smiled the cold, dead smile of the abyss.

The smile that seemed to be reserved for greeting one person and one person only.

"Finally," he said, fixing an unblinking gaze upon Takara.

Sam shivered.

"The Mighty Malphas," he said, a nervous chill in his voice.

"Of course," replied M. "Who else did you expect?"

Sam thought back to the single letter on the cinema posters and the ticker tape juddering out of the telegraph and nodded.

Pat stepped forward, walking stick to the fore.

"Well, we've kept our side of the bargain," she said. "Here's Takara, as requested. But it doesn't look to me like you've kept yours."

A flicker of amusement danced across M's features, the kind of amusement that the powerful usually display in the face of the impotent.

"My side?"

"Yes," said Pat. "If this is to be a hostage exchange, where's your hostage?"

M looked around the kitchen island display and then the wider kitchen department with mock surprise.

"Oh yes, the little man!" he said, as if suddenly remembering a minor detail. "I knew we'd kept him for something. You're quite right. I'll have him fetched without delay."

M clapped his hands together three times in a way that looked uncomfortably familiar.

"Gentleman! Bring out our houseguest please."

A back door opened and the Big Heavy and the Heavy Heavy lumbered into view. They were wearing their black suits, as before, but in line with the uniform policy of their employer, they were sporting orange B&Q name tags – one labelled BH and the other labelled HH.

M ran a tight ship and he didn't care who knew about it.

The Big Heavy came first, leading a drained looking Mr K. Poor Mr K was unused to human contact at the best of times and thoroughly unsuited to life above ground, so this unsavoury experience had clearly taken quite a toll. He looked like he needed a good sit down and a nice cup of tea as a matter of urgency.

Behind them came the Heavy Heavy, wheeling a large black wooden board on castors. He brought it to the right of M and then knelt down to flick a series of brakes to fix it in position. He gave the board a test wobble, to which it responded with admirable indifference, and then stood back, satisfied.

The board looked unchanged since that fateful night at the theatre. The stars still picked out the same geometric patterns of galaxies and constellations, even though the stars in the night sky had blinked out of existence the moment Marianne breathed her last – or at least they would have done if the rules of physics were as bold as the rules of poetry. The pockmarks, once the endless applause of audiences gone by, now felt like unheeded warnings of the most terrible kind, each strike a voice in the darkness that had been ignored.

M gave a motion with his hand and the Big Heavy marched Mr K into position in front of the wooden board.

"Now," said M, taking a silver dagger from his inside jacket pocket. "You are faced with something of a dilemma, Mr K. I am not so uncivilised that I would consider tying you to the board like some sort of beast so your choice is this. If you move from your current position in front of the board, I will definitely kill you. But," – and with this, M threw the silver dagger towards Takara, who caught it in one swift action – "if you don't move when Takara throws that dagger at you, there's a very good chance you'll be killed as well. Damned if you do, damned if you don't, as all the best greeting cards say. Look at it this way – at least you'll have more of a chance than my dear Marianne did on that awful night, which was no chance at all."

"What makes you think I'm going throw this dagger at anyone?" asked Takara, the blade flashing in her hand.

"Because if you don't, I will be extremely upset."

An electronic ding sounded towards the back of the store and the doors to the staff lift slid open.

A gasp went up as the Blessed Mr K took stock of the situation.

The minotaur looked on with a sigh.

Another day of disappointment.

"Splendid," said M, his sense of presence inflating with the growing audience. "We have company. Welcome, do come in. Although I must admit I was expecting a rather larger guest list than this."

The front doors shuddered unenthusiastically open and a few moments later Gerald ducked under the "Police Line, Do Not Cross" tape, with The Duke and The Inspector not far behind.

"Oh perfect," beamed M. "So glad you could make it. I did ask the Grey Clown to join us as well, but unfortunately he sends his apologies. Something to do with a deep distaste for materialising in the corporeal world, if I remember rightly. I'm sure he's terribly disappointed to miss this particular get-together, but it really can't be helped."

The Duke looked distinctly unimpressed.

"What the devil is going on here?"

M's smile dipped, the grim stare he'd used to greet Takara back in its place.

Sam felt a pang of relief. This seemed more natural somehow.

"Well, if it isn't my least favourite nobleman, The Duke," said M, the word Duke delivered with an undercurrent of venom. "And his darling daughter too. What are you calling yourself again these days? The Inspector, isn't it? How hilarious."

"This from a man who chose to describe himself as mighty," spat back Satomi. "Not the move of an inadequate at all."

"I was simply following theatrical tradition."

"Huh! I know overcompensation when I see it."

Sam crept over to Takara.

"Daughter?" he whispered, incredulously.

"Not now."

M walked over to Mr K and then turned to bow to his audience.

"As we're all finally assembled, may the festivities begin," he said with his best showman's projection. "I've gathered you here for an evening of nostalgia. A historical re-enactment. Or an historical re-enactment, if you want to be pernickety about it. A chance for some to relive what you'd think was an unforgettable occasion," – at which point he turned to stare pointedly at Takara – "while for those who weren't able to attend on the night," – and now he turned to stare at The Duke and The Inspector – "an opportunity to experience it all for the very first time."

"Picture the scene. A theatre, an audience, a fateful disturbance. But I'm getting ahead of myself, rushing forward to the terrible finale. Picture the scene again, but focus if you will on just two people. The performer and the assistant - colleagues, lovers, and creative equals. He is young and dashing, she is young and beautiful. They are both young and full of hope. And full of ideas. They want to astonish and entertain, but they also want their audience to question what they've just seen. Are these people really who they seem? And has what happened really just happened? Can any of this be trusted?"

"So they started with a knife trick. A masterclass in misdirection and sleight of hand. But as they worked on the trick they realised that the best way to deceive their audience was to confound them with the truth. The crowd would come expecting chicanery and would leave in a haze of ecstatic confusion. How did they make that look so real? And the magic would lie in the lingering sense of doubt. If it looked real, did it mean it was real? Had they just witnessed the impossible?"

Pat laughed and shook her head.

"It was just a knife trick."

"Oh yes, it was just a knife trick," said M, his eyes flashing. "We understood that. Our first tentative marks on the page, the theatre stage our sketch pad. But it was the concept that mattered. If we felt that we could use reality to create a deception that felt like a reality then we knew that we could pull off what would come next. Because we had plans. Big plans. We'd heard whispers of something new happening in Paris – a new art form, a new language – and we were convinced that this is what we needed to realise our vision. We were young and naïve and we believed we could alter reality and the perception of reality, and we knew that this new necromancy was our doorway in."

"So it was decided. We would move to Paris and learn the dark arts of the motion picture. And we would be married, we would embark on this adventure as man and wife. The date was set, the dress was chosen. Our future was a glittering path that lay ahead. All we had to do first was perfect the knife trick."

The room fell silent.

"The invites to the performance were sent," continued M, his voice softer now. "Some guests attended, albeit with the lowest of expectations. Other guests didn't deem the venture worthy of their time. The hoi polloi made up the numbers. And fate played out in the most fatal way possible."

"So you accept the accident was fate then," said Takara. "A cruel trick played by the universe. Nothing more, nothing less."

"Of course it wasn't fate!" roared M. "Our fate had already been written, you could see it in the stars. The trick would be a success. The move to Paris would be a triumph. And our wedding day would be the happiest day that anyone had ever experienced ever in the history of mankind. That was our fate! And that's what you stole from me. Because that's what happens when you don't take fate seriously. When you don't pay full attention or you don't even turn up or you somehow feel the spotlight is on you when it really isn't. Fate turns sour. Fate becomes poisoned."

"That's not how it happened," said Takara.

"That's exactly how it happened," said M. "You wouldn't admit the truth then and you still won't admit the truth now. Which is why we're going to relive that night one more time."

M motioned to a spot on the ground facing the wooden board.

"Here is your mark, Takara," he said. "Precisely four yards and two inches. The same distance I stood from Marianne on that night. We're going to re-enact the throw, but with two important changes. First, you and I are going to trade positions. You will throw the knife, while I will provide the distraction. Second, on the night we dispensed with a hidden stagehand to push a knife through the back of the board – we were doing it all for real, after all. But this time, my friend the Big Heavy will stand behind the board with a knife of his own. And if you refuse to throw, then he will do the job for you."

The Big Heavy moved into position.

M picked up a saucepan and a metal ladle from the nearest kitchen island.

"Is everybody ready?" ask M. "Then act…"

"No, hang on," interrupted Sam.

M shook his head in consternation, as if he was trying to locate a troublesome mosquito.

"Why are you doing this?" Sam asked. "You've said your piece. Your point's been made. What's the use of putting everyone through this needless re-enactment? I mean, it's not going to bring her back, is it?"

M fixed his gaze on Sam, the pesky mosquito pinpointed.

"Because Takara has to learn. A lesson that she's steadfastly refused to learn over her entire existence. That actions have consequences. And those consequences have to be paid for."

Takara shrugged.

"Sounds a bit far-fetched to me."

Sam gave up. He knew there was no coming back from that one.

"Go on, then. Carry on."

M scowled a stony told-you-so at Sam.

"You're too kind."

And then everything happened at once.

M held the saucepan and the metal ladle aloft, striking an action pose like an athlete awaiting a starting pistol. Takara tensed herself for the imminent throw, the silver dagger a portentous weight in her hand. The Blessed Mr K started to mumble something indistinct to himself over and over, his soft whisper heavy with trepidation. The minotaur let out a low groan of despair – it knew how this was going to end. Mr K gazed into the disquieting void that lay between himself and Takara and steeled himself for the inevitable. The Big Heavy pressed his blade against the back of the wooden board – one swift thrust forward and the deed would be done. The Heavy Heavy wondered why he was never given any of the fun jobs. M shot a meaningful look at Takara, accompanied by a sharp nod. Takara drew back her hand. Pat looked at Takara. Jonno looked at Takara. Gerald thought about cupcakes. Takara brought her hand forward in a flash. M rattled the metal ladle around the inside of the saucepan, making a sudden abrasive clatter. Takara jumped with surprise, even though she'd been waiting for that moment. The dagger left her hand and flashed through the air, spinning chaotically towards Mr K and the big finale.

There was a scream.

And then everything stopped.

58

The silver dagger hung frozen in midair, a millimetre away from the centre of Mr K's forehead.

If Takara's plan was to attempt a close shave, then her aim had been way off.

A bead of sweat that had started to run from Mr K's temple to his chin was caught in perfect freeze frame, as were the assembled onlookers.

The Inspector walked calmly over to Mr K and plucked the dagger from midair, sliding it into her jacket pocket for safety. She paused for a moment to consider the scene and then walked over to the Heavy Heavy and repeated the process with his dagger. She then walked over to M and commandeered the metal ladle and the saucepan. She glanced around the store, considering her options, before placing them back in their original position on the nearby kitchen island. It wasn't perfect, but it would have to do.

She then snapped her fingers and everyone sprang back to life.

Or at least some people sprang back to life.

Time was still frozen. This official intervention wasn't over quite yet.

And it was interesting to see who had remained stuck and who had become unstuck.

Mr K, the Blessed Mr K, Pat, Gerald, Jonno, the minotaur, the Big Heavy and the Heavy Heavy were still frozen in time. Whereas Sam, Takara, M and The Duke joined The Inspector back in the unreal world.

"I think that's quite enough of that, don't you?" said The Inspector, with the finality of authority.

M stared at her, his eyes devoid of surprise or contrition.

And then he began to clap. Long, slow, mocking handclaps. Claps that throbbed with derision, like strychnine dripping onto black ice.

"Well done," M said. "Very good. Your party trick. So great to see it in action."

"Laugh all you like, but someone has to have some responsibility around here," said The Inspector.

"Oh really?" said M. "Responsibility, she says. But does she only mean the responsibility of thwarting wrongdoing? Or does she also include the responsibility of keeping appointments?"

"You're not still going on about this, are you?" said The Inspector. "As we've told you so many times over the years, we were busy."

"Doing?"

"Other things."

"The world doesn't revolve around you, you know," said The Duke, sternly.

"No, it doesn't!" said M. "The world keeps on turning! For everyone! There isn't a single person on this dismal planet that can stop it from turning – apart from HER!", and with this M shot out an accusatory finger at The Inspector, straight and unwavering, a guilty verdict made flesh.

"She can click her fingers and everything stops! What a talent. And if only she had had the decency to accept the invitation and to witness her sister's usual infuriating stupidity, then she could have clicked her fingers that night and my Marianne would be with us here today."

"In an urn," said The Inspector. "She'd be long dead by now."

"Yes, but she would have lived. We would have had our life together. We would have revolutionised cinema together. It would have been The Vanishing Lady supported by King Kong, not the other way around! And we'd have found a way to keep her with us. Found a way to transform her from one of those people," – at which M swept a dismissive hand towards Pat, Gerald and the rest of their frozen compadres – "into one of us!"

Sam wondered what he had possibly done to qualify as one of "us".

"It's not as simple as that," said The Inspector, quietly.

"There is no them and us, surely you understand that. No chosen few," nodded The Duke. "We thrive in the tunnels because we surrender to chaos and the essence of chaos is that it is random. It leaps before it looks, it lashes out in the darkness, it points a finger without thinking. Why have you been able to chase the ghost of a broken heart across time where others have been stuck in the here and now? It's certainly not because of some special quality that you possess. Chaos doesn't pick people out, like a student choosing people for the football team. It lights the fuse and closes it eyes, feeding on the pleasure of smashing everything up and starting again."

"And anyway," The Duke continued, his voice growing more tender. "If there really is an us, as you put it, can you really say that you're truly one of us any longer? Since that awful night, you've been stuck between the two – half alive, half spirit, half there, half here."

"Yes," nodded M. "Because I haven't let go."

"You really haven't," said The Inspector.

"I've stayed like this so I can reach across the divide," said M. "So I can bridge the gap between us and them, resolved and unresolved, dead and alive. So I can transform her. And bring her back."

"No one can bring anyone back," said The Duke.

"They can. It's just that no one's ever tried."

M's features hardened, his patience worn thin, his frame now taut and ready.

"Snap your fingers, Satomi."

"It won't make any difference."

"Snap your fingers."

Satomi snapped her fingers and everything sprang back into action.

The bead of sweat completed its journey to Mr K's chin. The Heavy Heavy slammed his empty hand into the wooden board with a yelp of pain. The Blessed Mr K continued his mumble only to suddenly stop short. And Mr K – completely overcome with shock at not having met a bloody demise – swiftly lost consciousness and crumpled to the ground.

The Big Heavy was despatched to furnishings and before long returned with a Colenso dark blue linen affect relaxer chair, which Mr K gratefully sank into.

"Now if we're all ready," said M, once Mr K was settled. "Onto the main event."

He turned to look at Takara.

"It's time."

Takara looked blank.

"For what?"

"The book, Takara."

"Which book?"

M's eyes blazed with fire and scalding steam sprayed pure venom from his ears and nostrils, the surrounding air particles pulsating with rage.

OK, his eyes narrowed a little bit.

"Oh, you mean The Book Of The Dead?" said Takara, with as much absent-minded charm as she thought she could chance. "I don't believe I have it with me. Awfully sorry about that."

"I think you do," said M. "Empty your pockets."

Takara make a great show of emptying her jacket pockets, inside and out, producing a dizzying selection of pocket watches, several embroidered handkerchiefs, four sets of keys – one of which she stared with utter amazement for a good 30 seconds – a ball of twine, some cupcakes, an allen key, a bottle opener, some pocket change in at least seven different currencies, a box of matches, and a French pack of playing cards, with the familiar picture cards replaced by royal werewolves in varying stages of transformation – V (the Jack, the first hint of lupine whiskers), D (the Queen, fangs and pointed ears), and R (the King, the full anthropomorphic monty, howling at the fullest of full moons).

"And now the bag."

Takara shifted uncomfortably and tried to look confused.

"The blue bag," prompted M. "The one on your back."

Takara took off the bag and slowly began to unpack.

"This may take some time," she said. "This is a bottomless bag, you know."

In fact, it took no time at all – it appeared that if something had randomly taken Takara's fancy then she'd stuffed it into her jacket pocket and reserved the bag for the important stuff.

Out it all came.

Four small golden goblets decorated with an engraving of a slumbering lion; a black velvet blindfold; the music box that played the pertinent tune; a handful of grave dust; the red fountain pen; two hundred pounds in polished two pound coins; a pocketful of posies, and the emerald key.

"Hang on a second," said Jonno. "If you could fit all that stuff in your bag, how come I'm lugging this spice box around?"

"Sorry dear heart," grinned Takara. "We needed to win the sympathy of our friend the minotaur here. You can hand it over now."

She took possession of the box and added it to the pile of loot.

Finally, she brought out a silver picture frame bearing a photograph of the beloved Eleanor Lockhart.

"Is that mine?" asked a startled Mr K.

"Or Peter's?" said Sam.

Takara gazed at the photograph lovingly. On first glance it looked to be the same photo – the same flash of red hair, the same white ballgown – but in this one she was wearing the flying helmet.

"No, this one's mine. Mine all mine."

M tutted impatiently.

"Come on, Takara. I think you'll find there's one more thing in the bag."

Takara smiled and winked at Sam.

Then she reached into the bag and rummaged around in the void for what seemed like a little too long, like she was drawing out the tension, milking her moment in the spotlight.

Which, of course, she was.

Then, her eyes widening with mock surprise, she appeared to grasp hold of something and she brought it out slowly into the light - a black tome bearing an intricate tangle of golden runes and a large, totemic skull picked out in squares of silver leaf.

The Book Of The Dead.

"You had it with you all along!" exclaimed Sam.

"Of course," said Takara. "I keep everything with me at all times."

M's eyes blazed, for real this time.

"At last."

Jonno peered at the book with mild disbelief.

"Is this thing supposed to have come from ancient Egypt? I was expecting something more in the reeds and papyrus line. You know, forged in the desert, sealed with the terror of the infinite, maybe with some hieroglyphs on the cover. This looks like it comes from The Duke's props cupboard."

"Well, it's not a first edition, admittedly," said Takara, "and I think there have been some revisions – I must say, I rather like the nifty skull on the cover – but this is still a genuine, one hundred percent certified, couldn't possibly be anything else, Book Of The Dead."

"I hope for your sake it is," said M, ominously.

"Me too."

Everyone turned to look at M.

"What now?" said Sam.

M took a moment to smooth down his jacket and straighten his name tag, making sure he was ready for the ultimate performance.

"Now, as I'm sure many of you know," he began, "The Book Of The Dead is a guide to negotiating the afterlife, a manual for surviving the perilous journey to paradise. It contains spells and incantations to aid you on your quest and to protect you from the most terrifying fate imaginable – the second death. As the ancient scriptures say – to die once is an inconvenience, albeit an inescapable one. To die twice is the last gasp and the final full stop, when death really catches up with you."

"Chief among those incantations is the Opening Of The Mouth ritual. This is to allow the deceased to function in the hereafter – to speak, to breathe, to eat and drink and live again. To be reborn. So you may elude the second death and take your place in the promised land."

M gestured to Takara.

"Open the book. Find me the ritual."

Takara opened The Book Of The Dead and started to flick through the pages.

"Right then, what do we have here," she said. "Protection from animals. A spell for being transformed into a falcon of gold. A spell for being transformed into a lotus. A spell for using the ferryboats in the Underworld. A spell for sailing in the Great Barque Of Ra and sailing over the circle of fire. Wow, neat. I like that one. A spell for leaving yesterday and coming into today. A spell for not doing any work in the realm of the dead. Oh great. They really have thought of everything, haven't they? Lots of spells about snakes. A hymn to the sun god. And here we go...for preparation for the final judgement, the Weighing Of The Heart, the journey's first step – the Opening Of The Mouth. Oh...damn."

"What is it?" said Sam.

"It says here you have to conduct the ritual in the presence of the dead body."

"No!" said M.

"Or – hang on, hang on – in the presence of a significant item from the person's life."

Everyone looked at M.

M looked mildly panicked.

"Well, we have the wooden board you used for the knife trick," said Pat. "I assume that has to rank as a significant item, no? What's more significant than the final curtain?"

"Nothing, I suppose," said M, sounding less than convinced.

"It won't work." Jonno was born sounding unconvinced so this was his moment. On a sliding scale of Maybe to I'm Not Sure, he was placed firmly at No Chance At All. "If you were an anguished spirit doomed to purgatory by the injustice of a traumatic and extremely bloody event, would you respond to an incantation featuring the instrument of your demise? It's like trying to resurrect Marie Antoinette using a guillotine. Not exactly enticing."

"I don't suppose the dagger would work?" said The Inspector, reaching towards her jacket pocket.

Jonno snorted. "What do you think?"

"I think it's worth a try." M surprised everyone with this. "I think it's worth trying anything." He gestured to Takara. "Read the spell."

Annoyingly, Jonno was right.

Neither the wooden board or the silver dagger carried the right amount of significance.

Pat found this all extremely unsatisfactory. If there's one thing she couldn't bear – be it in people, machinery or hoodoos, hexes and conjurations – it was inefficiency.

"We obviously need an item associated with a happier time," she said. "Perhaps a gift – a love token perhaps. Some jewellery or, er, a nice hat." Pat was clearly out of her depth here. "Can you think of anything?"

M shook his head. "We were too poor for frivolities. All of our happy times were in our daydreams – our plans and hopes for the future."

"Like your wedding," said Sam.

"Yes."

"You said you'd chosen the dress."

"She had."

"What did it look like?"

The faintest of lights shone for a brief millisecond in M's eyes.

"Oh, it was spectacular," he said. "It was like a thunderstorm in heaven. Like a firework display of the purest white. An avalanche of lace and embroidery that felt like the dawn of time and the end of everything. A starburst, a supernova, a vision of deadly perfection. A dress that could rule the world. Fit for a queen. For an empress."

"Like a Christmas tree made out of lightning?"

"Yes exactly!"

A strange expression had passed across The Inspector's face.

"That's my dress!" she said.

The Duke glared at Takara.

"My dress," repeated The Inspector weakly. "For my wedding."

M snapped out of his reverie.

"What? Do you still have it?"

"No," replied The Inspector, her voice trailing off. "It was stolen."

"By her," said The Duke, his glare intensifying.

Takara attempted her usual "who me?" sheepish smile, but quickly abandoned it as a pointless endeavour.

"Now look," she started, with the air of someone who was looking forward to finding out what she was about to say. "Stolen is a strong word. I merely borrowed the dress. Like The Book Of The Dead. A loan, let's say. I was always going to return it."

"I suggest that now would be a good time to do just that," said The Duke.

"Ah yes, now I can see why you'd think that, I really do. And I would really love to hand it over right this instant. But as you can see from all the flotsam and jetsam I've turfed out of my jacket and the bottomless bag, unfortunately I don't have the dress with me at the moment."

"Yes you do," said Sam.

Takara looked startled. "What?"

"You said you keep everything with you at all times."

Takara bit her lip.

"Oh Sam. Pure lovely Sam. Nothing gets past you, eh?"

"Takara," said The Duke, both as a warning and a threat.

"Oh well, it's been a good run," said Takara, smiling wistfully. "The times we've had together. The very best of times. It was my wedding dress too, you know. Such a shame it wasn't my wedding as well. I suppose the time has come to return it to its rightful owner."

She knelt down and picked up the framed photograph of Eleanor Lockhart.

"My darling Eleanor. A true hero. Only the queen of deception could be trusted with a secret like this."

Takara reached into the photograph and gently pinched the white ballgown, pulling it carefully through the silver frame into the real world. Like a magician drawing an endless stream of scarves from a top hat, she slowly teased the dress into existence, every last inch of fabric, every brilliant aspect and tiny detail.

It was a wonder.

"Now that should do the trick," nodded Jonno, approvingly.

M's face shone.

"Begin."

59

This time something happened.

As soon as Takara read the final word of the incantation – itself a tongue-twisting assault course of tricky diphthongs and words she had to blindly throw herself at and hope for the best – The Book Of The Dead shut with a dramatic thud and the golden runes on the front cover began to pulse, as if a current was being fed through them. Then the squares of silver leaf lit up one by one, running from left to right and back again, like a progress bar on a loading screen, until the skull was fully illuminated.

The wedding dress glowed with anticipation.

The air particles in the centre of the room started to vibrate and tiny patches of reality turned first opaque and then sepia. Unlike the skull which lit up in a precise order, these patches appeared randomly - one here, one there, one just behind the other – to create an approximation of a figure, half colour blindness test, half impressionist painting.

Before long, there was a sense of a woman, the sepia patches picking out her hair, her dress, her eyes, but she was incomplete, not fully rendered, gaps of thin air creating the impression of someone who was half here and half nowhere.

"Marianne!" cried M, rushing forwards.

His embrace slipped through the gaps.

There was nothing there for him to catch hold of.

"Stand back!"

Although the image was partially formed, the voice was stern and strong. A voice laced with decades of disappointment and disapproval. A voice that had been waiting impatiently in the shadows for its chance to be heard.

"But my love," protested M. "Why do you appear to us like this? We performed the ritual. We called you to join us."

"You did no such thing!" said Marianne, the sepia patches of her eyes gaining contrast. "The Opening Of The Mouth isn't a summoning spell. It merely allows those that have passed over – in this case myself – the ability to communicate. Usually with others on the other side, but it seems something has drawn me to this spot."

"You heard my call!"

"I've been hearing your call for decades."

"What?"

"I've been watching you and listening to you for a lifetime. More than that."

The blood drained from M's face.

"I've seen everything," said Marianne. "Every photograph you kept of me, every sentimental possession, even every memory you cherished and preserved of the time we spent together – it all provided a window. A way for the departed to watch over those left behind. And I've been watching. And waiting. And watching some more. I suppose I should feel grateful that you kept these windows open for me, and I did feel gratitude for a while. But it wasn't long before the gratitude ran dry."

"But the films!"

"Oh god, the films!" groaned Marianne, spots of thin air congealing into sepia only for other patches of sepia to fade away. "They showed promise to begin with. I was always going to enjoy The Infernal Cauldron and The Cave Of The Demons and I don't think you messed up my ideas too badly – although I do have a few notes, when you have a moment – and The Four Troublesome Heads was inspired, I'll give you that. But the woe-is-me latter period – give me strength! The piteous artist, tortured by loneliness and injustice. The self-regarding auteur, endlessly training his camera on the anguish that had long since ceased to be of interest to anyone else. The bleeding heart that kept on bleeding."

"It was all for you!"

"I know! That's what makes it even worse. No wonder you got left behind, while the theatres thrilled to the slapstick cops and the wild west, the train robbers and the fantastic beasts. I know you were trying to capture magic – I still believe that you believe that – but you can't capture magic with your hands tied behind your back."

Takara chuckled.

"Be careful what you wish for, eh?" she smirked at M.

"Don't you start!" hissed Marianne, her eyes burning into Takara. "You're almost as bad as he is. Look at you with your pathological mischief and your carefree narcissism, the merry prankster doing everything she can to try and disguise the guilt that eats away at her every waking moment. Not just the guilt of my death, but at the death of everything – of the high street and community and the world before all of this," at which she gestured furiously at the surroundings of the B&Q, "all of which started the night you thoughtlessly decided to mess around on a theatre balcony."

"What rot! All of that isn't my fault."

"Of course it isn't! But you think it is – that's why you're running your little operation with the tunnels and the keys and all that – because you're trying to make amends. Because you think it's all about you!"

There was a silence, the kind of silence that felt like it could go on for quite some time.

Marianne looked at her wedding dress and smiled.

"It could have all been so different," she said, looking back towards M. "All of this time spent calling out to me. All of these films reaching into the darkness. Trying to bring me back. I know you felt you were trying to do the right thing, but whatever made you think that I wanted to come back. Or that it should be me that has to come back."

"Every ghost wants a second chance," said M.

"But I'm not a ghost. And I'm not a member of the Unresolved either. I am Resolved. And I am ready to depart."

"But I don't want you to go. I don't want to lose you again."

"Then you only have one choice," said Marianne. "And it was the choice that you always had, if only you thought to realise it. If you want us to be together then it isn't me who should be coming back to you. It's you who should be joining me."

Marianne reached out a sepia hand, half there, half not there.

"But I can't," said M. "I don't know how."

"You just have to admit what you've yet to admit. Resolve what is still unresolved."

"But admit what?"

"That's it's not your fault."

"I know it's not my fault."

"It's not anyone's fault," said Marianne.

"But..."

"It's not Takara's fault for fooling around on the balcony. And it's not Satomi's fault for not being there to stop time. And it's not even your fault for throwing the dagger."

"But the dagger killed you."

"And I wanted you to throw it."

Marianne brushed M's fingertips with hers.

"Cross the barrier. Join me."

M reached forward and clasped Marianne's hand.

This time there was something to hold onto.

He pulled her close.

And as they embraced, his body flowed into the empty spaces, his flesh and blood merging with the sepia, his unresolved spirit finally returning home.

The endless, opaque everything that flowed from corner to corner and point to point and joined up every dot in every dimension throbbed one more time in technicolour.

And then they were gone.

"Oh dear."

Takara looked spooked.

"Oh dear," she said again. "This isn't good. This isn't good at all."

Everyone looked at Takara.

"What is it?" asked Sam.

"Listen, you know all the stuff we said about how the tunnels run on chaos and it's my job to create the chaos? Well, that isn't entirely accurate. It isn't that the tunnels feed off the chaos – they're actually trying to wipe it out. The energy surges through the tunnels and reality is at its most fluid when the tunnels are tidying up, putting everything back in its right place. That's why the electrical pulses have been heading for overload. Mr K's not where he should be. Mr K's business isn't doing what it's meant to be doing. Add that to The Book Of The Dead being missing in action and Satomi's wedding dress being unaccounted for – two measures I'd put in place just to keep the chaos ticking over at a low level - and it was all getting much too much. Now add the departure of M, and the sudden job vacancy at the B&Q, and I think we might be heading for meltdown. Like imminently. Extremely so."

As if to prove her point, the vertiginous pile of orange buckets at the front of the store started to clatter to the ground.

"We haven't got much time," Takara yelled.

She turned to Mr K and the Blessed Mr K.

"Gentlemen, thank you for your patience. It's been a pleasure, as always. We really do need to catch up and have a good old laugh about this all very soon, but right now could you please make your way back to your quarters as quickly as possible."

"Here," said the minotaur, handing over a jar. "I found this in the boss's office. I've been keeping it with the seed packets."

Mr K's eyes widened. His sense of smell was second to none.

"Supernova anise!"

"The staff lift is right behind you," said Takara. "The Blessed Mr K knows the way."

She turned to The Duke and The Inspector.

She looked at The Duke and bowed her head slightly.

"I know I've asked for your forgiveness for a thousand times and I know that I don't always deserve that forgiveness, but I hope this time you can find a space in your heart for some mercy."

She placed The Book Of The Dead in The Duke's hands.

"Your book returned, as promised."

The Duke smiled.

"I'm starting to wonder if you don't have a system after all."

"I do! He's called Harrington. You really must meet. Next time!"

Then Takara turned to The Inspector.

She gave the dress – the beautiful, impossible dress, still like a Christmas tree made out of lightning, still a spectacular dream – back to her sister.

"I'm sorry. I really did think it was for the best."

Satomi hugged the dress and gazed at Takara.

There was still some work to do with this relationship.

Next, Takara turned to Pat, Gerald and Jonno.

"I suppose this is it, then," she said solemnly. "The end of the line. The end of the treasure hunts."

"What?"

Pat's face was a thundery mixture of shock and deep disapproval.

"Well, you're not going to take part now you know I'm behind it all, are you?"

Takara faltered a bit in the face of Pat's increasingly hostile frown.

"Are you?"

"I don't see why not," replied Pat, briskly. "We've always thought the treasure hunt was the most shoddily constructed, incompetently run and unprofessionally adjudicated clown show we've ever experienced – infuriating, illogical and utterly inconsistent – so the fact that you're actually the mastermind behind the whole sorry affair is actually something of a comfort."

"Yes," said Gerald. "The next time I have any kind of crisis of confidence about anything to do with the hunt, I will be able to console myself with the words – it's not you, it's Takara."

Pat, Gerald and Jonno nodded in unison.

"Although may I say, I enjoyed some of the extracurricular touches on this one – the banoffee pie, in particular, was excellent."

Takara gave the smallest of curtsies.

"How about you, Jonno?" she said. "Will you still be gracing us with your unsolicited presence?"

"Someone has to keep an eye on you, don't they? I mean, here you are wrapping everything up and yet as far as I can see, the tunnels still seem to be incredibly upset about something."

Jonno was right.

The orange buckets were still raining down in an avalanche of hard plastic. The traps on the Pest Destruction shelves were snapping into action and leaping into the void, a fatal deluge of Rat Reaper Death Boxes and natural insect killer bombs, while the powders and chemicals were exploding in a haze of brightly stained, cold-hearted destruction. The pots of paint in the paint station were bursting open in a frenzy, as if their moment had finally come, as if their names - Deadly Nightshade, Gathering Storm, Rain Of Fire, Golden Hemlock, Heaven's End, Tainted Dawn, Judgement Day - had been looking forward to this moment all along. Carving knives were flying in every direction imaginable, while the kitchen islands seemed even smugger than usual, if such a thing were possible. If this was to be the end of the world, then it was an end of the world that they clearly approved of.

Outside the B&Q, the electric spark was still doing its frantic rounds, only now with a momentum that felt like this was it, that it had finally reached the point of detonation.

The high street was ablaze with energy, rattling from the shop shutters to the traffic lights, from the iron railings to the street lights, from the Pound Tardis to the Costa to the Greggs to the book shop, sparking off the cemetery gates and weather vane at the top of the church to the side street with the clock museum, the harp factory and The Emporium, bolts of electricity raging in pure blue-white light like the Spectral Staircase in a fury.

Takara pulled out the pocket watch with tiny hourglasses instead of numbers and stared at it intensely.

Mr K and his companions had left a few minutes before, The Duke and The Inspector not long after them.

"We just need to hold our nerve," Takara said, her eyes still locked on the pocket watch. "It won't be long before they're back in position and the tunnels will settle back down. Mr K and The Book Of The Dead and the wedding dress are a powerful combination."

The electric spark didn't seem to have received the memo.

"But what about M?" said Sam.

"What?"

"Who's going to run the B&Q now?"

Takara smiled, as if she'd just remembered a pleasant dream.

"Oh yes, thank you for reminding me."

She turned to the minotaur and placed a conspiratorial hand on its back, beaming her most charming smile, Takara at her very, very best.

"Now then, my friend. Can I interest you in a new job?"

60

It had been another busy morning at the Pound Tardis.

The morning stocktake had taken ages, as usual. They'd been running low on pizza cutters, set squares and orange and yellow tennis balls tethered for no discernible reason by short lengths of orange and yellow rope to other orange and yellow tennis balls, so Sam had had to nip down to the Impossible, Endless Cave Of Precious Things and get Harrington to sign out some extras, which took forever, as always.

Harrington and his one finger typing.

Then there'd been a big debate about whether to update the window display. Balfour wanted everything to stay as it was – he argued that the consistent look of the current window display was an important part of maintaining the shop's identity on the evolving high street and that it was vital to honour place and tradition in uncertain times. He also knew who would be given the job of enacting the update and he really could do without the aggravation. Takara thought that since the high street had changed so much since the minotaur had taken over running the B&Q that they really couldn't afford to be left behind, not with such a dynamic new force in retail setting trends and generally calling the shots. Sam wasn't really sure what either of them were talking about, but he quite liked the idea of shaking things up a bit. Nothing like a fresh start to put a spring in your step.

Sam looked at a box on the shop counter, which was at once all the colours and no colours at all. The key box.

"Are we still going to be handing out these?" he asked.

"I don't see why not," said Takara. "Just because the minotaur is all touchy-feely, reaching out into the community, man of the people, even though he's not even a man, which everyone seems to be conveniently ignoring, that doesn't mean he hasn't got sales targets or that head office isn't going to be piling on the pressure when the feelgood honeymoon finally comes to a close. Big business is still out there and they've got deep pockets and dirty tricks on their side, so we need every advantage we can get."

"It's just that the anarchists were in yesterday. They said they were thinking about a new project."

"How exciting!" said Takara, clapping her hands. "Yes, give them an extra key if they need one. I mean, everything's back in its right place now, more or less, and the tunnels have calmed down again, give or take, so it's perfectly safe to start going back down there, I imagine."

"You imagine?"

"Well, who can really know for sure?"

Sam looked at Takara, thinking he still had a lot to learn.

"When was the last time you were in the tunnels?" he asked.

"Me? Only yesterday. You know the octagonal room with the stained glass windows? The one with the dots of light on the floor? Do you remember how I said that I hadn't worked out where all of the lights go to yet? Well, the anarchists aren't the only ones who've been having ideas. I've got a little theory on the boil about the yellow dot."

Sam picked up the key box and opened the lid.

"Takara, can I ask you something?"

"Of course."

"Does it matter that we didn't finish the treasure hunt?"

"What do you mean? Of course we finished it. We found all the items and saved the day. Or stood by and watched appreciatively while the day saved itself. Which is pretty much the same thing."

"But we didn't carry out the final instruction."

"Final instruction? I don't remember that."

"I remember distinctly," said Sam. "The man running the treasure hunt – who was actually you, if I've been following this all correctly - said 'Once you have all the items, turn to page 422 of The Book Of The Dead, where you will find a map showing you the location of The Door. You will then proceed to The Door and unlock it with the emerald key. The first team to collect all of items and unlock The Door will be declared the winners'."

"He did?"

"Yes, you did."

"Oh! How interesting! Well, I'm sure it doesn't really matter. The point of the treasure hunt wasn't to find the items, was it? It was to reunite M and Marianne, the star-crossed lovers torn asunder by time and tragedy. What a story! What a production! The melodrama that everyone's talking about. Theatreland's newest sensation."

"And we did that so that's all that counts."

Takara smiled suddenly.

"Which reminds me! Oh my gosh, I almost completely forgot. I've been meaning to give you this."

She handed Sam a folded piece of paper.

Sam opened it and found himself looking at a work chit for the supermarket bakery.

Takara smiled again.

She took the chit out of Sam's hand and ripped it in two.

"Excellent. Thank you very much," she said. "As long as you aren't going to make a habit of this kind of behaviour then I'm willing to overlook it this time. Let's say no more about it."

Takara took her glasses from her inside jacket pocket and tapped them on the side.

Her fashionably cut blue suit changed into a slightly less well cut blue suit and a clipboard appeared magically in her hand.

Takara shook her head in consternation.

"Oops! Butterfingers!"

She quickly tapped her glasses again.

Her ill-fitting blue suit was replaced by a sharply cut white suit and white trilby, with a matching white cravat and white silk handkerchief.

"Oh, for goodness sake. What is up with this thing today?"

She tapped her glasses again and returned to her initial attire. Fashionably cut suit, perfectly polished brogues, a stylish wave to her hair. Cool, classic Takara.

"Oh well. Why try to improve perfection, eh?"

Takara looked at Sam, dressed in the same brown overcoat as Balfour and Harrington, and felt a sense of calm.

"Right then," she said with a grin, the makings of a sparkle in her eye, her hand jangling something in her pocket. "Would you mind keeping an eye on the shop for me for a little bit? I've got something I need to go and take care of."

The Quiz

Hello and welcome to the end of the book. Well done for getting this far. I hope you enjoyed the show, but as the cast gather on the stage for the first of many curtain calls, we have some questions for you.

Have you been paying attention? Let's find out.

The following will test your powers of observation, your powers of guesswork, and your knowledge of the stuff that I like. If you've been reading the same books, watching the same movies and TV shows, and listening to the same bands as I have for the past god-knows-how-many-years, then this will be a doddle.

Once you have all your answers, head to our website www.thetunnelsbook.co.uk, where you will find instructions on how to submit your answers. The first person to get all the questions right wins a prize. A real prize. A really big prize.

Good luck!

1. What book was Jo reading?
2. Who were the two fibre glass figures on the first floor of the book shop?
3. Who sold Takara the Temporary Contemporary table?
4. Who are Harrington and Balfour named after?
5. The items on the costume rack in The Emporium appeared in which TV shows and movie?
6. Which movie is the tie from? (This one's easy, the answer's in the book!)
7. Which movie is the necklace from?
8. Which is the best line in Hawk The Slayer?
9. Which book did Sam read as a young man?
10. The middle names that Sam didn't have are a hat tip to a literary character, a song, an author, and another literary character. Name them.
11. Talking of hat tips, there are a couple of references to an Edwardian writer who is a great favourite of mine. Who is he and what were the references?
12. Which famous detectives attended the boot fair?
13. King Kong wasn't really the opening night movie at The Regent. I made that bit up. But it was the opening night movie at another cinema in 1933. Which one?
14. What was the fourth award in Peter's office?
15. What song was playing in my head when I wrote the Pound Tardis word poem?
16. What does the K in Mr K stand for?
17. Who designed the sculpture park in Oslo?
18. Who was William?

Thank you

I had lots of help with this book from many talented friends. Thanks to Billy Reeves for the incredible painting on the cover, and to Sarah Christie for working her design magic. Thanks to Angus Batey for being the first person to read and like the book – that meant a huge amount. Thanks to Adrienne Cullum for editing and stress-testing the book to its limits. It became ten times stronger in the furnace of her critical eye. Thanks to Julian Sedgwick for the kind words of encouragement and for lending a sympathetic ear. Thanks to Martin Millar for being a literary (and publishing) inspiration. I strongly advise reading one of his books next. Supercute Futures is particularly good, but they're all a delight really.

I'd also like to thank Elvis Costello, as I was really inspired by his brilliant quote about Olivia Rodrigo.

"That's how rock'n'roll works. You take the broken pieces of another thrill and make a brand new toy."

If you enjoyed this book, please consider buying a copy for a friend. Maybe it's their birthday soon? Blimey, is it Christmastime already? Or perhaps you could give them a copy completely out of the blue to (a) show them how much you love them and (b) show them what a wonderful person you are.

Wow, you're amazing. I can see that now.